Set on You

Set on You

AMY LEA

BERKLEY ROMANCE
New York

BERKLEY ROMANCE
Published by Berkley
An imprint of Penguin Random House LLC
penguinrandomhouse.com

Copyright © 2022 by Amy Lea
Excerpt from *Exes and O's* copyright © 2022 by Amy Lea
Penguin Random House supports copyright. Copyright fuels creativity,
encourages diverse voices, promotes free speech, and creates a vibrant culture.
Thank you for buying an authorized edition of this book and for complying with
copyright laws by not reproducing, scanning, or distributing any part of it in any
form without permission. You are supporting writers and allowing Penguin
Random House to continue to publish books for every reader.

BERKLEY and the BERKLEY and B colophon are registered trademarks of
Penguin Random House LLC.

Library of Congress Cataloging-in-Publication Data

Names: Lea, Amy, author.
Title: Set on you / Amy Lea.
Description: First edition. | New York: Jove, 2022.
Identifiers: LCCN 2021039424 (print) | LCCN 2021039425 (ebook) |
ISBN 9780593336571 (trade paperback) | ISBN 9780593336588 (ebook)
Subjects: LCGFT: Romance fiction. | Novels.
Classification: LCC PR9199.4.L425 S48 2022 (print) |
LCC PR9199.4.L425 (ebook) | DDC 813/.6—dc23
LC record available at https://lccn.loc.gov/2021039424
LC ebook record available at https://lccn.loc.gov/2021039425

First Edition: May 2022

Printed in the United States of America
6th Printing

Book design by Daniel Brount

To everyone who rarely sees themselves represented in books and movies.
To everyone who doesn't conform to mainstream beauty standards.
You are worthy of an epic love story. We all are.

author's note

Dear reader,

I can't thank you enough for choosing my debut romantic comedy, *Set on You*, as your next read. While this book is written in a light, humorous, and sarcastic style, I would be remiss if I did not provide content warnings for my readers regarding the serious issues it explores: fatphobia, cyberbullying, and references to racism, fitness/diet culture, and cancer.

Crystal's journey as a curvy, biracial Chinese woman is one single, fictional experience, filtered through my own worldview as a Chinese Canadian who grew up in a predominantly white community.

I cannot underscore enough how important it is to depict heroines of all marginalizations who practice self-love and body positivity, particularly in romance. Similarly, Crystal isn't a heroine who needs to learn to love and respect herself, because she already does. That being said, this book explores the nuance—the "in-between"—that self-love is not a tangible thing you achieve and hold on to forever. Loving oneself all day, every day is an individual journey, with vastly different outcomes for everyone.

In *Set on You*, I tried to avoid depictions of the unhealthy side of fitness culture. Crystal is an advocate of working out and lifting weights as one of *many* means to living a healthy and balanced lifestyle and does not count calories or keep track of her weight. However, the very theme of fitness and gym culture may be triggering to some readers.

As you read in the dedication, this book is my love letter to anyone who, like myself, doesn't often see themselves represented in mainstream media. In an industry that is starved for representation, I do not take this responsibility lightly and have consulted beta and sensitivity readers while writing this book. That being said, I am not perfect and I emphasize that the fictional experiences portrayed are not intended to be prescriptive, or representative of a single community or marginalization.

With love,
Amy

Set on You

chapter one

THE GYM IS supposed to be my safe place. The place I de-stress, reenergize, and ponder random wonders and mysteries, like: how was I delusional enough to think I could rock a middle hair part circa 2011?

That's why I'm equal parts horrified and appalled that my Tinder rebound, Joe, has sprung onto the treadmill to my right.

I brace myself for an awkward, clunky greeting, but thankfully, his attention appears fixed on the treadmill's touch pad. As he presses the dial to increase his speed, I catch a whiff of eau de wet dog. He not-so-subtly glances in my direction before averting his eyes.

Sure, Tinder Joe was kind enough to order me an Uber after our lackluster quarter-night stand two weeks ago. But it's highly coincidental we'd end up at the same gym, in all of Boston. I wonder if he's stalked me. Maybe I blew his mind in bed? So much so he went FBI on my ass, located my gym, and staged a casual run-in? Given my social media presence, it isn't out of the realm of possibility.

At every opportunity, Dad warns me of the dangers of posting my whereabouts on Instagram, lest I be kidnapped and sold into sex slavery, *Taken* style. Except Dad is no Liam Neeson. He doesn't have "special skills," aside from his legendary sesame chicken recipe. And so long as the Excalibur Fitness Center continues to sponsor my membership in exchange for promotion on my Instagram, I'm willing to risk it.

Tinder Joe and I lock eyes once again as I catch my breath post–sprint interval. Our shared gaze lasts two seconds longer than comfortable and I can't help but notice how his perfectly coifed boy-band hair remains suspiciously intact with each giraffe-like stride. Whether he stalked me here or not, my first instinct is to flee the scene.

So I do.

I take refuge in the Gym Bro Zone, aka the strength-training area.

As a gym regular, I exchange respectful nods with the other patrons as I enter. A familiar crowd of 'roid-pumping frat boys loiters near the bench presses while simultaneously chugging whey protein shakes like they're on the brink of dehydration. Today, they're donning those cringey neon tank tops that hang too low under their armpits. To their credit, they're nothing if not devoted to their daily routines. And after catching a glimpse of my sweaty, tomato-faced self in the wall-to-wall mirror under harsh fluorescent lighting, I'm not in any position to judge.

A guy man-splaying on the bench press grunts excessively, chucking a set of dumbbells to the floor with a loud *thud*. Normally this would grind my gears, but I'm too busy bounding toward a majestic sight to care. My treasured squat rack is free. Praise be.

The window squat rack is one of exactly two racks in this facility. It boasts a scenic view of a grungy nightclub across the street, a long-rumored front for a murderous motorcycle gang. The natural light is optimal for filming my workouts, especially compared to the alternative—the rack cloaked in shadow next to the men's changing room, which permanently reeks of Axe body spray.

The window rack is close enough to the industrial-size fan to let me savor a stiff breeze mid-sweat, but not close enough that I'll succumb to wind-induced hypothermia. It's also in the prime position for gawking at the television, which, for unknown reasons, is cruelly locked to the Food Network. I worship this squat rack the way Mother Gothel regards Rapunzel's magic hair. It gives me life. Vigor. Four sets of squats and I'll be high on endorphins for at least a day, fantasizing about the strength of my thighs crushing the souls of a thousand men.

Giddy at the very thought, I stake my claim on the rack, setting my phone and headphones on the floor before heading for the water fountain. The man with a goatee, who rocks knee-length cargo shorts and an actual Sony Walkman from the nineties, approaches at the same time. He graciously waves me ahead of him.

I flash him an appreciative smile. "Thanks."

My back is turned for all of three seconds while I take a sip. Freshly hydrated and eager to crush some squats, I spin around to find an exceptionally broad-shouldered figure stretching directly in front of my window rack.

I've never seen this man before and I'm certain I'd remember the shit out of him if I had. He's tall, well over six feet, with a muscular build that liberally fills out his unassuming gray T-shirt and athletic shorts. One look at his enormous biceps and it's clear he knows his way around a gym. A black ball cap with an unrecognizable logo shadows his face. From the side, his nose has a slight bump, as if it's been broken before.

I shimmy in beside him to pick up my phone, purposely lingering for a few extended beats to transmit the message that this rack is OCCUPIED. He doesn't get the memo. Instead, he proceeds to clasp his massive hands around the barbell, brows knit with intense concentration.

Either he's fully ignoring me, or he genuinely hasn't noticed my presence. The faint beat of his music is audible through his earbuds. I can't identify the song, but it sounds hard-core, like a heavy-metal lifting tune.

I clear my throat.

No reaction.

"Excuse me," I call out, inching closer.

When his gaze meets mine, I jolt, instinctively taking half a step back. His eyes are a striking forest green, like an expanse of dense pine trees dusting untouched misty mountain terrain in the wilderness. Not that I'd know from personal experience. My exposure to the rugged wild is limited to the Discovery Channel.

I'm nearly hypnotized by the intensity of his eyes, until he barks a "Yeah?" before reluctantly removing his right earbud. His voice is deep, gruff, and short, like he can't be bothered with me. He momentarily lifts his ball cap, revealing wavy, dirty-blond locks that curl at the nape of his neck. It reminds me of the scraggly hairstyles worn by hockey players, the kind you just want to run your fingers through. And he does just that. My throat dries instantly when he smooths his thick mane with one hand before dropping his ball cap back over the top.

Deliberately ignoring the dip in the base of my stomach, I nod toward my headphones hastily strewn at the base of the rack. "I was here first."

Expression frosty, he arches a strong brow, regarding me with contempt, as gym bros tend to do when women dare to touch what they deem as *their* equipment. "Didn't see your stuff."

Undeterred by his brush-off, I take a confident step forward, laying my rightful claim. When we're nearly chest to chest, he towers over me like a behemoth, which is more intimidating than I anticipated. I expect him to back off, to see the error of his ways, to realize he's being a prick, but he doesn't even flinch.

Swallowing the lump in my throat, I find my voice again. "I'll only be a few minutes, max. We could even switch in and out?"

He sidesteps. For a second, I think he's leaving. I'm about to thank him for his grace and humanity . . . until he dares to load one side of the barbell with a forty-five-pound plate, biceps straining against the fabric of his T-shirt.

"Seriously?" I stare at him, hands on hips, gaze settling on his soft, full lips, which contrast with the harsh line of his stubbled jaw.

"Look, I need to get to work in half an hour. Can't you just use the other rack? It's free." As he ruthlessly balances the rack with another plate, he barely spares me a passing glance, as if I'm nothing more than a pesky housefly.

I pride myself on being an accommodating person. I wave other cars ahead of me at four-way stops, even if I have the right-of-way. I always insist others exit elevators in front of me, as my parents taught me. If he had just been polite, half-decent, even the slightest bit apologetic, I probably would have let him have it. But he isn't any of the above, and I'm shook.

"No," I say, out of principle.

His jaw tightens as he rests his forearms on the bar. The way he leans into it, stance wide and hulking, is purely a territorial move. He gives me one last, indignant shrug. "Well, I'm not moving."

We're locked in a stare-off with nothing but the faint sound of Katy Perry singing about being "a plastic bag drifting through the wind" over the gym sound system and a man grunting on the leg press a couple feet away to quell the silence. My eyes are dry and itchy from my refusal to blink, and the intensity of his stare offers no sign of fatigue.

When Katy Perry fades out, replaced by an Excalibur Fitness promotional ad, I let out a half sigh, half growl. This guy isn't worth my energy. I retrieve my headphones from the floor and stomp to the less desirable rack, but not before shooting him one last evil eye.

11:05 A.M.—INSTAGRAM POST: "ASSHOLES WHO THINK THEY OWN THE GYM" BY **CURVYFITNESSCRYSTAL**:

Real talk: This morning, an arrogant dickhead with nicer hair than me callously stole my squat rack. Who does this? And if you're guilty of this crime, WHO HURT Y'ALL?

I don't know him personally (and I don't want to), but he struck me as the kind of person who loathes puppies and joy in general. You know the type. Anyway, I ended up channeling all my anger into my workout while blasting my current jam, "Fitness" by Lizzo (trust, this song is fire).

Final thoughts: Most people at the gym aren't assholes. I promise. 99% are super helpful and respectful, even the steroid frat boys! And if you do encounter that unfortunate 1%, just steer clear. Never give them power over you or your fitness journey.

Thanks for listening to my TED Talk,

Crystal

Comment by **xokyla33**: YAS girl! You're sooo right. You do you!! ♡

Comment by **_jillianmcleod_**: I just don't feel comfortable working out at the gym for this reason. Would rather work out at home. ♡

Comment by **APB_rockss**: U promote embracing your curves/size but all u do is work out and live at the gym? Hypocrite much?? ♡

Reply by **CurvyFitnessCrystal**: @APB_rockss Actually I spend one hour in the gym working out each day. Devoting time every day for yourself, whether it's at the gym, taking a walk, or in a bubble bath is hugely beneficial for all aspects of ♡

your life, including mental health. Also, you can both love your body and go to the gym. They aren't mutually exclusive.

• • •

AFTER YESTERDAY'S INCOHERENT Instagram rant, I took a much-needed soul-searching bubble bath. My response to the person who called me a hypocrite unintentionally sparked a fierce debate of epic proportions between my loyal followers and my haters. I try not to pay the trolls an iota of attention, but after Squat Rack Thief and two glasses of merlot, I was feeling a tinge combative. And it's been building for months.

For seven years, I've striven to shatter harmful, fatphobic stereotypes in the fitness industry. I've built an Instagram following of two hundred thousand based on my message of self-love, regardless of size. The drama over me being "too big" to be a personal trainer yet "not big enough" to represent the curvy community is typical in the abyss of the comments section. There's no in-between.

The crass body-shaming and occasional racist slurs have become more commonplace with the growth of my following. For the sake of maintaining a positive message, I've ignored the hateful comments. The fact is, I love my curves. Most of the time. I'm only human. Occasionally, the trolls manage to penetrate my armor. When this happens, I allow myself a short grace period to wallow. And then I treat them to a proverbial middle finger in the form of a thirst trap (a full-length body shot, for good measure).

But last night, sometime before my rainbow glitter bath bomb dissolved entirely, it occurred to me that my followers are probably equally, if not more, hurt by the comments. If I want to stay authentic and true to my body-positive platform, maybe it's time to start speaking out.

Today's workout is the perfect time to ruminate over my strategy.

But to my displeasure, Squat Rack Thief is back again, for the second day in a row. He's stretching in the Gym Bro Zone. Must he have such magnificent quads?

He narrows his gaze in my direction as I shimmy through the turnstiles. Instantly, his expression goes from neutral to a deep scowl, as if my mere presence has derailed his entire day.

I eye him sideways before shifting my faux attention to the generic motivational quotes plastered on the wall in an aggressively bold font: *If it doesn't challenge you, it won't change you.*

Evading him for the duration of my workout is harder than I expected. Wherever I go, he's looming in my peripherals, taking up precious space with his gloriously muscled body.

When I woke up this morning, it crossed my mind that he could be an Excalibur Fitness newbie who hasn't grasped the concept of gym etiquette. I fully intended to give him the benefit of the doubt. Maybe he was simply having a bad day. Maybe he spent the entire night staring into the vast distance, roiling with regret. Lord knows I've had my fair share of rage-workouts.

All of these possibilities lose legitimacy when he conspires to out-pedal me on the neighboring assault bike. When I catch him eyeing my screen, I channel my inner Charlie's Angel and full-throttle it.

At the twenty-calorie mark, we both stop, panting, hunched over the handles. My "no-makeup" makeup has probably melted entirely, and I'm seeing spots. But my exertion was worth it—I beat him by a whole 0.02 miles. He practically seethes when he reads my screen. Evidently unable to cope with my victory, he pouts, promptly hightailing it to the machines.

Not half an hour later, it's officially game over when I witness him saunter away from the leg press without bothering to wipe down the seat. The darkest places in hell are reserved for those who don't clean the machines after use.

Compelled to speak up on behalf of all hygiene-policy-abiding gym patrons, I set my dumbbells down and march forth.

He's in the zone as he does a round of effortless pull-ups. I stand, mouth agape, unintentionally mesmerized by the taut, corded muscles in his arms flexing with each movement.

He gives me a Chris Evans vibe, but with slightly longer, luscious locks. I don't know if it's the glint in his hooded eyes or the dimples, but he has a boyish look to him that makes him appear faintly approachable when he isn't scowling at me.

When he catches me gawking at him like a crazed fangirl thirsting for a selfie, he pauses, dangling from the bar. "How's the view from down there?"

I'm about to say *godlike*, both because it's entirely true and because it's my default to compliment people. I do it for a living. But the last thing this guy needs is a confidence boost.

I consciously make a flat line with my mouth, channeling Mom's severe expression when she's supremely disappointed in my life choices. I hold out a paper towel, generously pre-sprayed with disinfectant, for his convenience, of course. "Are you forgetting something?"

He blinks. "Not that I'm aware of."

"You forgot to clean the leg press."

He releases the bar, sticking a smooth landing as he eyes the paper towel pinched between my fingers like it's been dipped in sulfuric acid. "Keeping track of my workout or something?"

"No," I say, a little too defensively. "But you need to wash the machines when you're done with them. It's a rule here. People don't want to touch your dried sweat." I inwardly cringe. I might as well have an I'd-like-to-speak-with-a-manager angled bob. But I can't back down now. In fact, I double down, pointing to the sign on the wall to our right that reads *Please wipe down machines after use.*

He doesn't even glance at the sign. Instead, he appraises me, arms folded over his broad chest. "I'm not done with the machine. Are you unfamiliar with supersets? You know, when you cycle through multiple exercises back-to-back—"

"I know what a superset is!" I snap. Heat rockets from my lower belly to my cheeks when I realize I've unjustly called him out. This is mortifying. I silently will myself to disappear into an obscure, nonexistent sinkhole. Maybe this is cosmic retribution for not minding my own business.

He flashes me a knowing smirk and struts back for another set.

As if this painful interaction never happened, I slink away into obscurity to film my back workout tutorial on the cable machine. It's a prime opportunity to promote my sponsored sweat-resistant activewear.

I'm midway through filming a shot of ten cable rows when Squat Rack Thief materializes out of thin air. He chooses to park his massive body directly in front of the camera, of all places, blocking the shot. In my silent fury, I lose all focus, with zero recollection of whether I'm on the first rep or the tenth.

He leans lazily against the machine, wearing a smug grin that I'm beginning to think is his natural resting face.

"Yes?" I ask through clenched teeth, irritated at the prospect of re-filming the entire segment.

He produces a paper towel from behind his back, swishing it in front of my face. "Here. So you don't forget to wipe down the seat."

His sarcastic tone combined with his sneer tells me he isn't doing this out of the goodness of his heart. This is a hostile act of aggression, cementing our rivalry.

Before I can formulate a cutting response, he drops the paper towel into my lap and waltzes toward the changing room.

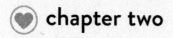 **chapter two**

SQUAT RACK THIEF has graced Excalibur Fitness with his cocksure presence for the third day in a row. I've officially designated him my gym nemesis.

I've been here for less than half an hour and I'm already fantasizing about "accidentally" spritzing him with a bottle of chemical disinfectant.

It all started with an unfortunate encounter at the entrance. He silently held the door open for me and another patron, as if he'd suddenly transformed into some chivalrous gentleman. I frowned at him, cautiously following while trying not to admire his finely muscled ass for longer than a hot second.

Turns out, my skepticism of his chivalry was well-founded. Apparently, he's limited to one act of kindness per day (or so I thought), because not fifteen minutes later, he cut in front of me at the water fountain, where he proceeded to take his sweet time filling his monstrosity of a water bottle. To the brim.

After unapologetically stealing my place in line, he rushed off to the bench press like a vaguely sexier version of Superman to assist Patty, an elderly gym regular who never misses an opportunity to complain to everyone in her general vicinity about the gym's various failings (the "frigid" temperature, the "thug" music, and the lack of "ambience"). When Squat Rack Thief flashed her a semi-authentic, angelic smile after saving her from being crushed flat by the barbell, I had to steady myself. Does this man have an alter ego?

I shift my focus from his egotistical yet highly confusing self to Mel, my new in-person client. We're swapping Instagram horror stories during a quick break after a biceps and triceps circuit.

"There was this guy who DM'd me dick pics every day for months after I posted a bikini picture." She twists her mouth, gagging at the memory as she shows me the photo on her phone.

I lean in, feigning curiosity, pretending I haven't already creeped her entire account back to 2012. The shot is perfectly framed. She's smize-ing into the distance, lush barrel-curled hair draped over one shoulder, legs dangling in what appears to be some posh, exclusive rooftop pool for beautiful people only. She's rocking a vibrant Barbie-pink bikini.

Mel is one of a handful of fashion, beauty, and lifestyle Instagram influencers who isn't a size zero. All her photos are perfectly curated against the backdrop of her all-white, ultramodern apartment, featuring fresh florals, pastel accents, and weekly high tea brunches. She had been reticent about joining the gym for years due to a high-heel-induced knee injury, but she requested a muscle-building plan after discovering we both lived in Boston.

We hit it off right away. We're both twenty-seven. We're both Chinese, although she's adopted and I'm half Irish. We're both staunch proponents of the body-positivity movement. And we also share an unapologetic obsession with reality television, particularly anything related to *Real Housewives*.

"Okay, damn. You're serving some serious looks here. Not that it's an invitation for dick pics." I pause, eyeing the bonkers number of Likes on the photo.

She wipes a single drop of sweat from her forehead with her perfectly polished acrylic nail before continuing her story. "It was the weirdest one I've ever seen. It was bent. Like . . . super off-kilter to the side. Like a hook."

"A *hook*?" I clarify through a startled yelp.

"Like an umbrella hook, Crystal. No exaggeration. Do you think penises can break?"

I'm about to tell her I haven't the faintest idea, followed by a rant about how dick pics are never attractive, hook-shaped or otherwise, when Squat Rack Thief parks himself on the bench beside us.

His mouth is curled upward in amusement, which is shocking, because I was unaware those channeling the spirit of Darth Vader were capable of joy. I wonder how much of our penis conversation he's heard.

After Paper Towel Gate yesterday, I vowed not to stress over this punch-worthy, smug stranger. But it's more challenging than expected when he's sitting so close, filling my nose with his enthralling, freshly laundered scent, drawing my attention to how marvelous he looks in his maroon hoodie and ball cap.

I wonder if Squat Rack Thief is the type to send unsolicited dick pics. Once that completely unfounded thought registers, I will it away to the desolate, dust-caked corners of my mind. Why am I thinking about his penis?

You know what they say about large feet . . .

As he takes a long swig from his water bottle, our eyes lock in mutual loathing. It feels more like a challenge, lingering before I blink it away. *Crystal, be zen. Channel your inner peace.*

I refocus on Mel, who gives him a curious once-over.

"Anyway," I say, clearing my throat to defuse the tension, "we're doing sled pushes next."

She grimaces. The last time I assigned sled pushes, she dry-heaved and sweat off her eyelash extensions.

I cheer her along one length of the aisle as she huffs, puffs, and mutters curse words with each labored stride. I wait for her to begin the second length back, but she hesitates.

"Looks like I don't have to finish my rounds after all." She gestures joyously toward Squat Rack Thief, who is casually lunging with dumbbells directly in the middle of the pathway. *Mel's* pathway. Who does this guy think he is?

My mouth is open wide, like an infomercial mom who's astonished the detergent removed the stubborn tomato sauce stain on her white blouse. "Sorry. One minute," I mumble.

Arms crossed, I storm toward him, blocking his attempt to lunge around me. "Did you not see us just now? We were here." I manically gesture to Mel, who is observing with keen interest, resting on the sled.

Without a word, he continues around me, as if I'm a mere blip, a pothole in the road to avoid. I'm on the brink of calling him a pompous prick, but I bite my tongue and walk away, for the sake of maintaining the illusion of professionalism in front of my client.

"What's his deal?" Mel asks as I begrudgingly turn the sled horizontally, toward a less ideal aisle.

"He's just been pissing me off." I flash him the stink eye, though he doesn't notice. He's mid-lunge, smug face red from exertion, definitely *not* lamenting the weight of his transgressions against me like a decent human.

Mel lifts her perfectly shaped brows. "He checked you out earlier. Like full-on head to toe, while we were talking about dicks."

"He was probably plotting to assassinate me."

"Or he was undressing you with his eyes."

Had someone suggested this to me years ago, I would have immediately expressed my doubt. But now, after years of working on myself and my confidence, I don't doubt it.

Despite always being into sports, I never had the body of an athlete. I inherited Mom's genes. Big frame, muscular, with thick thighs, boobs, and no shortage of booty—the opposite of my older sister and Dad's side of the family, all of whom are slim and petite. For me, a low body fat percentage isn't in the cards genetically. Accepting that fact and getting to this place has taken some time. I now focus exclusively on de-stigmatizing and demystifying the gym for people who may not have felt they belonged. I prioritize the goal of confidence. Not calorie deficits, and definitely *not* the number on the scale.

"Mel, just three more laps," I instruct like a hard-ass, changing the subject entirely. "Finish strong before girls' night."

Tonight's glorious plan to re-watch a rom-com on Netflix with my sister, Tara, is just what I need after all this gym and Instagram drama.

Squat Rack Thief lingers in my peripheral vision as I follow Mel down the aisle. He rests against a machine, catching his breath. When I turn to meet his gaze, he flashes me a shit-eating grin.

• • •

I FULLY INTENDED to be a mature adult. I really did.

But after mulling over the aisle thievery in the five minutes since Mel left the gym, all I could picture was Squat Rack Thief's smart-ass expression. The same one he'd worn as he cut in front of me at the water fountain, and when he brandished the paper towel in my face.

I've been a pushover a lot of my life. Back in grade school, I let the other kids get first pick of my own Barbies (I ended up with Ken doll ninety-five percent of the time). I was relegated to the least favorite Spice Girl (Posh Spice) for themed birthday parties. I always let the procrastinators copy my homework two seconds before class in high school. And worse, I lacked the agency to speak up or demand otherwise.

When I discovered the gym and the fitness community in college, I vowed that would change. Here in the gym, I'm not a doormat. I'm strong and capable. I refuse to let people walk all over me, especially this infuriating, far-too-sexy stranger.

So when Squat Rack Thief forgets his phone on the mat when he moves on to the bench press, I feel little moral obligation to return it immediately. There's a high chance I'll stew into the late hours, besieged with guilt and regret over this. But then I remind myself: He was asking for it. It was only a matter of time before I snapped. He deserves to sweat a little.

I imagine myself running off with his phone into the sunset in a baller getaway car, laughing manically as I floor the gas. But then I remember I'm not a petty criminal. I have morals. Which is exactly why I temporarily stash his phone among the shelf overflowing with jump ropes, random accessories, and cable attachments, purely to ensure it's safe from being crushed under someone's running shoe.

Pleased with my good deed, I fasten my own phone onto my tripod and begin to film my latest lower abdominal routine, which involves sitting twists, flutter kicks, and enough leg raises to put Jillian Michaels out of commission.

I'm halfway through the workout when a large figure appears over me.

It's him.

He kneels on the mat, lips tight, vibrant green eyes firing laser beams at me. From this angle, I have a close-up view of the thick swoop of his eyelashes. They're unfairly long and lush for the male species.

He's so close, his fresh laundry scent mixed with testosterone overrides my senses. The smell of sweat usually isn't appealing, but on him, it's marginally addicting. I refrain from purposely inhaling it like a drug addict.

"What did you do with my phone?" he asks calmly as my legs drop to the mat. He's ruined my video. Again.

A doe-eyed, beauty-pageant-worthy expression overcomes me.

I even toss in an innocent, slow blink for dramatic effect. "I don't know what you're talking about." I shift onto my knees to face him, ready for a confrontation.

He doesn't fall for my theatrics. "I know you took it. I left it here five minutes ago."

"People tend to steal things in this gym. Like squat racks, for instance. How do you know it wasn't some other random who stole it?"

"Because." His eyes roam my face, hunting for any sign of weakness, like a take-no-shit homicide detective. "You're smiling. You're breathing hard. And you're avoiding eye contact."

No matter how justified, deceit has never been a strength of mine, even if I didn't actually steal it. To keep my hands occupied, I reach back to tighten my messy bun. "Look, Nancy Drew, I'm trying to film an ab tutorial here. Do you mind?"

I'm about to cave and point him toward the shelf where his phone is stashed, but I'm momentarily distracted by his gaze flickering toward *my* phone, which is still recording. With one smooth movement, he plucks it from the tripod and drops it into the pocket of his shorts.

I lurch forward, but it's too late. My phone's gone, deep into the faraway depths of his nether regions. "Hey! What the hell?"

His lips curl into a satisfied smile. "I'm not giving it back until you tell me what you did with my phone."

I don't let his mesmerizing smile knock me off course. This is war. I won't be compromised. "I need my phone."

"So do I," he says smoothly.

"What, for Tinder?" I'm being a complete and total hypocrite right now. In fact, Tinder Joe is on the treadmill again as we speak.

He scoffs. "No, actually. For important stuff."

"Well I use mine for *important stuff* too. I'm a fitstagrammer." I have no idea what possessed me to reveal my profession. He could use this against me. Or worse, mock me. I expect him to snort in derision or look me up and down, unable to comprehend how someone like me is qualified to give fitness advice.

But he doesn't. His gaze is unwavering. "I need my phone for work too."

I'm tempted to ask him what he does. I imagine it's something physical. Perhaps he's a lumberjack. Or a Captain America stunt double. Or maybe a pouty underwear model plastered in black and white on a billboard in Times Square. But then again, he isn't pretty enough to be a model. Maybe he's some sort of semipro hockey player, given his wavy hair flow.

Based on my not-so-subtle observation (or glaring), I've deduced he may not be one of those fist-bumping frat bros in a neon bro-tank. I'd place him a bit older, maybe late twenties, early thirties.

"Do you really need it for work?" I challenge him, taking his irritated expression as a personal life achievement.

He nods curtly.

"Is it life or death?"

Surprisingly, he actually says "Yes" with little effort. Now I'm dying to know what he does. But I'll never ask.

"Prove it."

"How?"

"Stop stealing things from me. Workout machines, floor space, my place in line at the water fountain." I wave a vague hand around the gym.

He scoffs. "Has it ever occurred to you that I might need the equipment or the space too? This isn't *your* gym." We hold mutual stares for a couple breaths before he finally relents. "Okay, I'll give your phone back. *If* you give me mine. At the same time."

I nod, standing to unearth his device from the shelf a couple feet away. "For the record, I was going to give it back before you left."

His eyes widen upon seeing his phone. I suppose he's just thankful I haven't flushed it down the toilet, which, to be fair, crossed my mind.

I dangle his phone at chest level, snapping it back before he has a chance to swipe it from my death grip. "On the count of three?"

He dips his chin.

One.

Two.

Three.

He swiftly reclaims his phone from my fingers while simultaneously holding mine out of reach.

Traitor. He would be the type to break the sanctity of a pact. The man has zero morals.

I growl. "Seriously? We had a deal."

His lips curl into a closed-mouth grin. "Tell me your name."

"I don't reveal my true name to strangers at the gym."

When he steps forward, closing the gap between us, my ears pound as the blood rushes to my head.

He holds my phone low, graciously permitting me a quick visual of the screen. It's still on the record video setting, which is interrupted by a flurry of Instagram notifications. He grins like a Cheshire cat when my username pops up. "Crystal."

When he says my name in that deep, smooth, sultry voice, my knees weaken. I nearly dissolve into the floor.

Despite being five foot eight, inches above being considered short, any frantic attempt I make at reclaiming my phone is a complete failure. With his arm outstretched, he holds it many feet out of reach.

I groan. "Okay, you know my name is Crystal. Happy? Now give it back." I can see the screen enough to recognize that a Tinder message has just popped up.

His eyes light up as he reads it aloud. "Zayn wants to know if you're up for Netflix and chill . . ." He pauses, squinting at the screen, as if confirming the words. "*Chillaxing*."

"Do not respond!" I lunge for my phone again, but he snaps it farther back.

I'm desperate to preserve what little dignity and control I have left. It's not like I know Zayn. He's a random Tinder match whom I swiped right on for the sole reason that he resembled Dev Patel in his photos (swoon). But given his use of the word *chillaxing*, he's probably an automatic *No*.

Squat Rack Thief looks like a Marvel villain on the brink of annihilating Earth and all its inhabitants. "I'm gonna ask him to define 'Netflix and chill-*axing*.'"

It occurs to me that he revels in my desperation, like the sicko he is. In fact, it probably encourages him, gives him some sort of high. So I switch my tactic. "Go right ahead. I dare you." My tone is unwavering. It channels confidence, even though the absolute last thing I want is a vengeful stranger sending embarrassing messages on my behalf.

Unfortunately, my challenge backfires. He types the message

and triumphantly hits *Send*, tilting my phone to prove he sent the message.

"I assume you're pretty familiar with the Netflix-and-chill routine?" I say.

"You think so, huh?"

"Yup."

He shakes his head. "Nah. And I'd come up with a better pickup line than that."

I half-scoff. "Hit me with your best shot."

He smiles and strokes his defined jaw, pretending to be pensive. "Well, GIF wars always work. Or maybe I'd use a classic joke."

"A classic joke? Like what?"

He leans his elbow on the machine beside us. "Okay . . . Are you ready to be wowed?"

I give him a deadpan look.

He softens his entire face, his demeanor transitioning from Squat Rack Thief to fake-charming-man-with-mesmerizing-smile before my eyes. His teeth are brilliantly white, although one is marginally crooked in the front, which makes him slightly more human. His ears also stick out a smidge, but it just adds to his faux charm. "Are you a bank loan? Because you have my interest."

My expression is one of stone, so as to not give him an ounce of satisfaction. The joke is lame. But the way he says it so earnestly, it's borderline adorable. The moment that thought registers, I mentally smack myself.

He goes for it again. "Are you my appendix? This feeling in my stomach makes me want to take you out."

My abdominals ache from suppressing my laugh. This is an ab

workout all on its own. "Okay, these are next-level horrible. I hope you haven't actually used these on a real, live woman."

He feigns offense, holding his palm to his chest. "Those were my best ones." Taking one last glance at my screen, he dangles my phone at chest level. "Zayn responded . . . with a wink face," he says flatly, handing my phone back.

With ninja speed, I snatch it before he changes his mind and holds it hostage forever.

"What's your name?" The words tumble out of my mouth before I even register what I'm saying. Why do I care to know his legal name? Squat Rack Thief suits him just fine.

I hold my breath, awaiting his answer.

Amused, he opens his mouth, but no words come out. Instead, he just strides away.

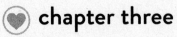 **chapter three**

"THANKS FOR LETTING me crash tonight," Mel says gratefully, bundled on the living room floor next to me in a bougie silk Ted Baker pajama set that probably cost more than my couch.

Tara dive-bombs us on the air mattress, clad in her homemade iron-on *Team Peter Kavinsky* T-shirt. "Okay, put on *To All the Boys.* My body is primed and ready." She tosses a full-size canister of Pringles at us.

"Really, Tara? *Plain?*" I take this as a personal affront. This is why I don't let my sister choose the snacks.

She scowls at me, reclaiming the Pringles, holding them snugly to her chest, as if protecting them from harsh words. "Original flavor is the best, thank you very much."

"Sure, if you like the taste of salty cardboard," I say.

Tara scoffs. "Coming from the girl who thinks pretzels are remotely in the same league as chips." She turns to Mel, her French braid whipping me in the cheek in the process. "She's one of those *pretzel* people," she whispers conspiratorially, eyeing me as if I'm a rare race of mole people rumored to dwell in the sewers.

Mel nods gravely, like she understands.

I give Tara a swift kick in the shin. "I refuse to abide by such slander."

Tara pretends to yelp in pain for all of two seconds before launching into a long-winded tale about the latest rando she supposedly "fell in love with." She met this one in the elevator of the hospital where she works. Allegedly, he had soul mate potential. She knows this because he gave her a Werther's Original and told her he liked her floral-print nursing scrubs before getting off at his floor.

"A butterscotch candy? Are you sure he wasn't a toothless senior citizen?" Mel asks.

"No, he was no older than thirty," she chirps back defensively.

"Jesus, I'm shocked you didn't get roofied," I lament.

Our girls' night turned into a slumber party after Mel's nineteen-year-old brother insisted on hosting a raging keg party at her apartment. I quiver at the thought of college students staining her crisp white couch, a staple in most of her Instagram photos.

Unlike Mel's place, my apartment isn't white and modern. It's a converted firehouse, clad with exposed redbrick walls and vibrant, boldly patterned furniture, predominantly refurbished by Mom and me. Repainting and reupholstering antique pieces became an obsession of ours during the summer before I graduated from college. To this day, I still scour yard sales, flea markets, and home décor stores, hunting for items I definitely don't need.

The best thing about my apartment is the literal firepole, extending from the open loft that doubles as Tara's room down to the spacious living area. With my coffee table pushed against the television stand, we've managed to cram an entire queen-size air mattress in here.

We're barely paying attention to the movie, despite our love for Lara Jean and Peter Kavinsky. Instead, we're highly distracted by food, wine, and conversation. I wasn't sure how Mel would gel with my sister, given her up-front, boss bitch personality and Tara's tenderhearted, sensitive nature. But they seem to be getting along like a house on fire. Things start off with group brainstorming for my self-love campaign, but after a few glasses of wine and random *aww*-ing at Peter's dopey adorableness, the conversation shifts.

"Did you have any more interactions with Squat Rack Thief after I left today?" Mel asks. She pulls her thick hair into a perfectly sleek high ponytail. I envy girls like her who can put their hair back so effortlessly, without a million baby hairs sticking up on end. When I attempt it, I resemble a juvenile orangutan with bedhead, unless I hairspray my flyaways down.

Tara groans. "Is she still complaining about this guy?" I'd told her about the initial squat rack thievery, and she called me "petty," which is ironic. She's the girl who spitefully planned her now-canceled wedding for August, the month her former mother-in-law-to-be was planning a trip to Iceland.

"They have this sexual tension thing going on," Mel explains.

"Not true." I wrangle two broken Pringles from the can.

Mel rolls her eyes dismissively. "You guys full-out stare at each other from across the gym."

"*Hate-stare.* And I'm ignoring him from here on out."

"Oh, come on. He seems like a really nice guy. He's always

holding doors for people. The other day I saw him help that man who looks like Dr. Phil with his deadlift form."

I sigh, reaching to tuck the protruding tag into the back of Tara's T-shirt. "Okay, but why should he get a gold star for being a half-decent person? My standards aren't *that* low."

Tara pulls her braid over her bony shoulder and examines her split ends. "I need to see a picture of this guy before I can make any judgments."

If only I didn't have a mental picture of him and his smug smirk permanently etched into my memory. "You're out of luck. I don't even know his name." I conveniently omit the fact that I did ask him, and he walked away from me. Truthfully, it stung a bit, like the dull ache of a tiny papercut you desperately refrain from whining about every time you wash your hands.

Mel sits upright to sip her wine. "He's hot. Like, really hot. Super tall. Muscles for days. Lifts heavy, which means he has a lot of endurance . . ." she adds, suggestively waggling her brows.

Tara nods appreciatively while painting her toenails a hideous plum color. "Why aren't you hopping on his bandwagon?"

"This so-called *sexual tension* is a myth. We're nemeses, if anything."

Tara clasps her chest, nearly dripping nail polish on my carpet. "Seth and I didn't like each other at first either," she starts, her expression darkening as she turns to Mel to explain. "Seth was my fiancé. We met at the hospital. I proposed to him . . . but we called off the wedding a couple months ago."

Her ex-fiancé is the reason she's been occupying my loft/den. Seven months before their elaborate one-hundred-fifty-person wedding at the Sheraton, Seth broke things off out of nowhere.

Tara showed up at my door at two in the morning in her pajamas with only a suitcase full of books, in desperate need of junk food and a place to stay. One night swiftly turned into two months, with no sign of her leaving.

Given her fragile state, which involved sobbing and listening to Taylor Swift on repeat, I've been reluctant to suggest she move out. Only in the past few weeks has she resumed wearing actual pants and filling in her eyebrows. Mom and I suspect she'll be back on the dating scene soon. Tara *loves* love, preferring Valentine's Day to Christmas.

"Any plans to start dating again soon? Even just casually?" I ask.

Tara shivers as she crunches another Pringle. "I don't do casual. If I don't even know a dude's middle name, I'm not about to touch their penis."

Mel cringes. "The dating world is terrifying. I've seen the specimens on the market."

"I'd rather pluck my pubes out one by one than resort to online dating. Tinder looks like a barren wasteland," Tara adds, eyeing me to confirm. "You've been Neil-free for what, a few months now?"

My stomach clenches at the mere mention of Neil's name. "Yup."

Mel shifts onto her stomach, propping her chin up with her hands. "What happened with this Neil guy?"

"He's my ex." I shoot Tara a warning glance. The last thing I want to do is muddy our night with talk of Neil. He never fails to dull my mood.

"He's like the Justin Bieber to her Selena Gomez," Tara tells Mel, as if that explains the entire dynamic between Neil and me.

"Except he's a greasy failed musician who thinks he's God's gift to womankind. Crystal's his chronic second choice when things go south with his ex."

I shrug when Mel looks at me. Tara's depiction is fully accurate. Neil and I met at a Halloween party. I'd been coerced by a college friend to go out at the last minute. I didn't have a costume, so I haphazardly grabbed a random flower crown, threw on some iridescent makeup, and went as a Snapchat filter. Neil was a monk. I asked him if he was celibate, and he slapped the wall, wheezing with laughter, before sinking a beer pong point. That probably should have been my first clue.

Even though he'd just gotten out of a relationship, he seemed entirely into me. He laughed at everything I said and mimicked my mannerisms. He flirted shamelessly, touching my arm and squeezing my waist.

"You're so different than my ex," he'd said, chugging back the remainder of his red Solo cup. I found out later his ex, Cammie, was a literal model. A taller version of Daenerys from *Game of Thrones* with her silver-blond hair and slender figure. The opposite of me. Half Asian and curvy.

I blushed. "I don't know how to take that."

He smiled, tugging a strand of my hair, leaning closer to me. "It's a good thing. Trust me."

And I did. I ate up all his words, reassuring me that I was special. That we had some sort of unparalleled connection. We dated casually for almost a year despite my whole family hating him after he showed up wasted at Dad's birthday party and decided it was the appropriate occasion to debate controversial world issues. After that, I no longer brought him around my family or friends for fear he would offend someone. He never bothered to introduce me to his people either. It was like we existed in our own little bubble, just the two of us holed up in my apartment for days on end. Then, without warning, he dumped me to go back to Cammie.

"I'm over him now," I reassure Mel and Tara, even though the words come out stiff and robotic. Truthfully, I still miss him sometimes. And the hurt triples every time he pops back into my life like a bad zit, asking for relationship advice.

Mel shifts onto her knees to face me. "Well, if you're over Neil, maybe you should hook up with someone who looks like Squat Rack Thief."

"Agreed." Tara fans herself for unknown reasons, since she has no clue what he looks like.

I stifle a laugh. "I'm not trying to be the thirst police here, but it's not going to happen. No more random hookups for me."

Immediately after Neil broke up with me, hookups filled the void. They were fun and empowering. I may have gotten what I wanted physically. But in the light of morning, the reality of waking up beside a drooling rando who doesn't even own a bed frame and a fitted sheet is all too bleak, followed by that gnawing feeling. That fleeting tease of affection, being connected with someone, anyone, for a brief time. Remembering how good it feels. How wonderful it is to be touched, embraced. And then just gray. Bleak. Nothingness. Overwhelming loneliness.

And so, for the past two weeks since Tinder Joe, I've sworn off random hookups in favor of waiting for something real.

Despite Mel and Tara's hopes, this war between me and my gym nemesis has to cease. There will be no fireworks and random hookups, especially not with him. In fact, there will be nothing but two enemies going their separate ways.

10:00 A.M.—INSTAGRAM POST: "SIZE POSITIVE CAMPAIGN" BY **CURVYFITNESSCRYSTAL**:

Take out your scales and tape measures and throw them in the trash! You won't be needing them.

You might be thinking: Crystal, sit down. Pour a glass of wine. Why are you asking me to throw out my $200 fancy-schmancy scale?

Okay, I got a little dramatic. What I mean to say is, stop relying on your scales and tape measures to make you feel good about yourself. Today is the official launch of my spring/summer campaign, SIZE POSITIVE. It's my challenge to track your fitness progress based on HOW YOU FEEL, without the constraint of numbers that studies show actually cause anxiety and discourage people.

As most of you know, I struggled with my weight for years. In the gym changing room in middle school, I started to recognize that all the other girls were tiny compared to me. I loved gym class, but I grew self-conscious of changing in front of everyone else, so I'd go into the bathroom stalls. To hide. One day, my gym teacher told me I couldn't change in the stall anymore, and I went home and cried.

If I could talk to my 12-year-old self, I'd tell her she's worth so much more than just the number on the scale. I'd tell her to practice eating until she's full, not stuffed. To eat what makes her feel good, not just because she's sad or bored. To go out for lunch with friends and just have fun instead of worrying about how many calories one Subway sandwich is.

A massive part of fitness is mental health. If you're unhappy, stressed, and constantly being hard on yourself, your body will reject progress. And you certainly won't be as inspired to keep pushing forward when it's tough.

That's why I'm challenging you to join the Size Positive campaign by ignoring the haters and the numbers, and living your best life. Your size means nothing if you aren't happy. Who's with me?

Comment by **trainerrachel_1990**: I love this!! So joining in. ♡
Screw the scales.

Comment by **BradRcerrr**: So u think its ok for ppl to be obese ♡
as long as they're "happy"? LOL

Comment by **_jillianmcleod_**: Can relate. I hated getting ♡
changed in the locker room too.

Comment by **Pilatesgirl1016**: Thanks for sharing your story ♡
and this amazing campaign! So inspirational. I agree, I feel so

much better when I'm not weighing myself. Haven't done it in years. I just focus on my progress at the gym.

Comment by **Kelsey_Bilson**: How do I track my progress without ♡ dieting or weighing myself? Isn't it calories in, calories out?

Reply by **CurvyFitnessCrystal**: **@Kelsey_Bilson** I'm not saying ♡ to stop tracking these things outright if it's working for you. But if it's starting to upset you or stress you out, stop for a few weeks and just listen and respect your body.

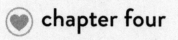 **chapter four**

EVERY YEAR ON Easter Sunday, the following things happen like clockwork:

Mom's side of the family, the McCarthys, congregates at Grandma Flo's bungalow. We watch *Willy Wonka and the Chocolate Factory*, the original version, squished on the stiff floral couch while indulging in a week's worth of Mini Eggs.

Tara entertains the family with her uncanny (and eerily accurate) impression of Veruca Salt singing, "I want the world. I want the whole world. I want to lock it all up in my pocket. It's my bar of chocolate. Give it to me *now!*" while I plug my ears.

Mom's "third child," a dreadful five-pound Chihuahua named Hillary (yes, Mom named her after Hillary Clinton), incessantly whines at all the male family members for attention. And when she doesn't get it, she lashes out by peeing on Grandma's Persian rug.

By dinnertime, everyone is already too sick of each other to bother with polite conversation. Dad chokes down Grandma's dry turkey, while Mom stomps his foot under the table when his happy-go-lucky façade begins to wear thin. Then, Mom and Uncle Bill toss passive-aggressive comments back and forth over who does more for Grandma Flo.

This year is different.

Grandma Flo didn't invite us for dinner. Instead, she and her two childhood girlfriends took an impromptu road trip to the Plainridge Park Casino, which is entirely out of character. She doesn't even approve of bingo or scratch tickets. Tara is convinced she's going through an elderly life crisis.

Since no one was aware of Grandma's wild casino plans until two days ago, we're having a low-key hot pot dinner at my parents' place in the suburbs.

Dad is pleased about the food because he gets to dodge Grandma's turkey until Thanksgiving. His side of the family owns a popular Chinese restaurant, so he's impossibly picky about food quality.

"Do you have at least six months' salary in your emergency fund?" Dad asks me, patting the corner of his mouth with one of the carefully halved takeout napkins he has a habit of hoarding.

I groan. "Dad, seriously. Stop worrying. I'm not spending frivolously. My gym membership and all my clothes are sponsored. I have a huge check coming in the mail from Nike. And I have more than enough money saved and invested for the future, just in case."

Since the beef broth started simmering, Dad has been on a well-intentioned rant about how I need to reevaluate my career options, given my current income is "temporary." He constantly badgers me about getting a "real job" for the sake of "long-term financial security." Even after the success of his commercial cleaning business, he still pinches pennies, to the extreme. Tara and I even signed him up to be on TLC's *Extreme Cheapskates.* When the producers called him and asked him to be on the show, he declined and refused to speak to us for five days.

"I don't mean to cut you down. Your fitness account is a great hobby. But I'm your father. It's my job to worry about you." He casts a grim glance at me as I mix my dipping sauce.

He never hides his disappointment that I didn't follow the plan of joining corporate America after getting my business degree at Northeastern like a good Chinese girl. But by my third year, I was already making significantly more than a typical entrance salary through endorsements and paid posts alone. It seemed ridiculous to settle for less money, being stuck in a bland cubicle from nine to five, and taking orders from a disgruntled baby boomer who doesn't know my name.

Mom would usually echo Dad's grievances, but tonight, she's visibly shook over Grandma Flo. "I just find it bizarre," she says out of nowhere, clumsily dipping her beef into the soy sauce. After almost thirty years of marriage to Dad, she has yet to master the art of chopsticks. Dexterity isn't her thing.

"Maybe she wanted to have a relaxed Easter this year, since Bill and Shannon are with the kids in Europe," Dad suggests.

"But a casino? On a religious weekend? She's a devout Catholic." Mom shakes her head, clutching a trembling Hillary in her arms. The rest of us detest having Hillary at the table like a human, but Mom refuses to relent, taking it as a personal attack when we complain. In fact, she spends half her time talking to her instead of us.

I nod, swallowing a mushroom while avoiding Hillary's beady little black eyes. "You're right. Something doesn't add up."

Tara struggles to extract a fish ball from the hot pot. "Give Grandma a break. The holidays have been tough on her since Grandpa."

I'd never really thought about it like that. Grandpa's death three years ago has been rough on everyone, particularly Grandma. "Maybe. But I thought she loved hosting."

"She does," Tara agrees. "If she didn't want to stick around to host this year, there must be a reason."

A mental image of a grieving Grandma Flo makes my heart ache. "What if I try to call her right now? See how she's doing?" I suggest.

Mom leans in, cradling Hillary, practically digging her elbow into mine. "Yeah. Let's check in on her."

Dad lets out an extended sigh before taking a gulp of his water.

Before Tara or Dad can protest, I've already hit *Call* and set it to speakerphone. It trills five times before she picks up.

"Hello?" Her shrill voice shatters my eardrum.

Cringing, I hold the phone farther away from my ear. "Hi, Grandma. It's Crystal."

"Oh, Crystal. Hi." Awkward silence. It's quiet wherever she is. There aren't any of the dings and chimes you'd expect to hear in a casino. "Listen, I got your text on Facebook about my appointment next week and I meant to put a thumbs-up, but I hit the poop button instead. You know how I am with those darn touch screens. Good thing you didn't inherit my wide McCarthy thumbs. I hope you weren't too offended, dear." Tara and I look at each other and try not to crack up. These emoji blunders are commonplace for Grandma Flo. Last month, she inserted five Laugh-Crying Face emojis on a *Rest in Peace* Facebook eulogy post for her recently deceased friend. She'd mistaken it for a sad face. "Happy Easter, by the way," she adds.

"No worries. I figured the poop emoji was a mistake. And happy Easter to you too. I was just calling to see how your girls' trip is going. Any big casino winnings?"

"Casino?" She pauses for a moment, as if I've just inquired about life on Mars. I meet my family's suspicious gazes as she bumbles on. "Oh, right. Yes. The casino. It's good. No winnings, though," she says with shaky laughter.

"What games have you played?" Mom pipes in. She sets Hillary down, which results in more incessant whining. "Patience! Don't be rude," she fury-whispers to her, as if Hillary is a human child.

There's another pause from Grandma. "Uh, bridge."

"Bridge? At a casino?" Mom's nostrils flare.

"Oh, sugar. I meant blackjack."

Silence lingers as Dad stands to dump more broth into the hot pot. Grandma has never set foot in a casino in her entire life. She's clearly lying. But why?

I contemplate going full detective mode, picturing Squat Rack Thief's penetrating glare when I hid his phone. But I blink myself back, suddenly feeling guilty. If Grandma feels the need to come up with an elaborate lie to get some space this Easter, who am I to be bothered?

"Well, um, I'm glad you're having fun." I decide to let her off the hook, given that Mom is leaning halfway across the dining table, ready to launch into an interrogation. "We miss you."

"I miss you guys too. Your dad must be pleased he doesn't have to eat my turkey this year," Grandma says knowingly.

Dad's eyes grow wide. "Did you tell her?" he whispers to Mom, who shakes her head in unconvincing denial.

"Well, I'd better get going. Love you, dear!" Grandma says, before the line cuts.

I blink slowly, stirring my dipping sauce as I digest the bizarre conversation. "What was that all about?"

Mom flattens her lips, hoisting Hillary back onto her lap. "She was definitely not at the casino."

• • •

FOLLOWING THE STRANGE call with Grandma Flo last night, as well as some nasty comments on the launch of my Size Positive campaign, I distract myself at the gym. It's empty, as expected on Easter weekend. Even the staff are off, making the facility accessible solely via swipe pass. Apparently, gym bros also take Easter off to celebrate, because it's only me and two other women killing it in the Gym Bro Zone.

This positive female energy is diluted the moment Squat Rack Thief stomps through the turnstiles, emitting enough testosterone to fill the entire facility. He's wearing his normal ball cap, track pants, and a dark green hoodie, which brings out the mossy hues in his eyes. We make reluctant eye contact as he stalks past me, prowling his way to the changing room.

Despite glowering at each other several times during our respective workouts, we keep our distance. He's doing a leg day. I'm focusing on biceps and shoulders.

This strange, silent truce is actually tolerable. Maybe now we can return to being complete strangers, despite the fact that he knows my name, profession, and Instagram handle, all of which are easily exploitable pieces of information.

Speaking of Instagram, I need to check my emails. I'm waiting for Maxine, a particularly needy client, to confirm our virtual check-in this afternoon. But when I come up for air from my downward dog position to grab my phone, it isn't on the mat where I left it. To ensure I'm not delusional, I retrace my steps, scanning the floor around all the machines I used today. But it's nowhere in sight.

Unless my phone disappeared into thin air, there's only one other explanation. I zero in on Squat Rack Thief, who's currently occupied on the inner and outer thigh machine. Seemingly, our truce is null and void.

Tired and grouchy, I march in front of him, hand on hip. "Alright, I'm done with this game. Just give me back my phone."

He stares at me, mid-set. "You'd have to be sick and deranged to steal someone's phone at the gym."

"I didn't take your phone. I simply stored it for safekeeping."

"I didn't take your phone either, *Crystal*." He smiles ever so slightly, drunk with power when he says my name.

"You did," I shoot back. "I had it with me the entire time. Except when I was stretching. I left it on the mat."

He grimaces as he completes his last rep. Letting the tension go on the machine, he leans forward, breathing hard. "Someone else must have taken it, then, because I didn't."

"I don't believe you."

"Well, believe it. I don't have it." He opens his palms to proclaim his fake innocence. "Although I kind of wish I did. Imagine all the Tindering I could do on your behalf." He's overcome with glee at the very thought.

Ignoring him, I nod toward his lower half, which looks far too appealing in those low-hanging Under Armour shorts. "Empty your pockets," I demand.

He gets up from the machine, shoving his hands in his pockets, extracting his own phone. "See?"

I don't know what's come over me, but I reach out to pat both of his pockets myself, like an overzealous TSA agent at the airport. His pockets are light and empty, except for the jingle of his keys. No sign of my phone.

"Did you just frisk me?" His deep, rumbling laughter makes my insides coil in a way it shouldn't.

I scoff, quickly losing interest. My phone is definitely not in his pockets. If he didn't take it, who the heck did?

I dart away to conduct one last thorough inspection of the gym. I rack my brain for possible explanations. Did one of the ladies lifting steal it? Both of them were completely unassuming. Normal. Middle-aged. Mom-energy. Matching low-maintenance hairstyles. One was even wearing a tennis visor. Certainly not the type who would conspire to steal a dented iPhone 10 with a tacky bedazzled case from a clearance bin in Chinatown. But then again, anyone can be a klepto.

The chilling possibilities linger up until Squat Rack Thief slinks past me, snickering as I'm bent over like an idiot, peering into the dirt-filled crevices of the shoulder press.

I whip around, following him like a dog to a bone. "You hid it somewhere, didn't you?"

He spins on his heel, walking backward past the treadmills at a snail's pace. "Believe me, if I wanted to mess with you, I could think of much better ways to get under your skin." The wicked way he says *get under your skin*, so deep and velvety smooth, nearly knocks the wind out of my chest. But only momentarily.

I let out a literal growl as he ducks into the men's changing room, out of sight.

A waft of Axe body spray assaults my senses when I come to an abrupt halt in the doorway. I take a quick scan around. There are no other men in the gym right now except for Squat Rack Thief. And I *need* my phone. My client is waiting for me. I can't be a no-show. I pride myself on being reliable, on time, and always there for my clients. My entire brand and reputation rest on this.

Screw it.

chapter five

E NTERING THE MEN'S changing room is foreign. The layout
is identical to the women's changing room—rows of lockers
in the front, showers and toilets in the back. But it's like I've
stepped into Narnia, or a beast's lair. The simple fact that I'm not
supposed to be in here sends a pang of nervous energy trickling
down my spine as I creep past the first row of lockers.

On the brink of aborting this entire mission, I spot Squat Rack
Thief in the second row. He's rifling around in his locker, his bare
back to me. I take a moment to admire the hard ridges of muscle
over muscle that make up his torso. He has one of those tapered
shapes. Broad shoulders and narrow waist.

I'm not supposed to see this. My palms aren't supposed to get
clammy. My ears aren't supposed to burn. My body isn't supposed
to be tingly south of my belly button. I've officially become a Peep-
ing Tom, a creeper, a voyeur. I squeeze my eyes shut. I really ought

to turn around and get out of Dodge. If I leave now, I can forget I ever saw this. But I can allow myself one more look, right? Just one.

I bet he's one of those guys with the damn V. The outline that goes straight down to the . . .

Shit. He is. Life is cruel. What did I do to deserve this harsh fate?

He's fully facing me now and I have no idea where to cast my eyes. His prominent six-pack? The dusting of light brown hair on his chest? His V? His hulking shoulder muscles? His gorgeous eyes, wide with surprise when he sees me standing there like the stalker I am? His body is a work of art. It belongs in a Parisian museum, protected by velvet rope and an armored guard.

He appraises me, lips curving into a half smile. He's both amused and understandably confused. "Crystal. How can I be of assistance to you?"

I widen my stance, recalling the real reason I'm here, which does *not* involve hungrily admiring Squat Rack Thief's body in any way, shape, or form. And I'm definitely *not* going to fantasize about it later.

"I know you took my phone. Stop messing with me and give it back now."

He lets out a half laugh, as if I'm certifiably insane. And maybe I am. But my entire life is on that phone. Photos. Pre-edited business content. Videos. My clients' workout plans. The worst part: I ran out of iCloud storage months ago and was too lazy to buy more. If I lose this phone, I lose it all.

"You sure you're not a little confused and exhausted from all those shoulder presses?" he asks, unable to squash his patronizing amusement.

"I don't get exhausted. Ever. I appreciate the concern, though," I add, voice sweeter than Grandma Flo's sugar pie.

"Oh, I could exhaust you." His eyes blaze, and I nearly choke at the innuendo (whether he intended it or not). "In fact, I think you're already at the end of your rope with me right now."

"Not even close."

"It really doesn't take much to get you all riled up." His gravelly voice almost distracts me as he inches in front of his open locker.

My eyes dart behind him. It isn't a coincidence that he shifted his body in front of his locker like a bodyguard stationed outside a nightclub. He's holding my phone hostage in there. I'm convinced.

Like a panther focused on its prey, I storm toward him.

We're face-to-face, chests heaving, connected in yet another face-off. But this time, his chest is bare, and I'm losing the battle to resist ogling him with each passing second.

To distract myself, I search his face far and wide for something to critique. Anything at all. And I come up empty. I hadn't noticed until now that his pupils are surrounded by soft rings of gold.

The severity of his expression tempers with a slight brow raise. I take it as a sign of weakness. It's my time to pounce.

I gaze left to fake him out before making a break for his locker. As I stick my hand in, he blocks me with his shoulder. I attempt to push him backward with my forearms, but his body is like a sturdy tree. One of those majestic three-thousand-year-old trees in Yosemite. He doesn't even budge.

He watches me, mouth twisted in amusement as I step back in a huff. "You're not getting in my locker," he says, as if it's just pure fact, as simple as one plus one equals two. He extends his arm to the side, palm against the locker, blocking me from any future attempt. But I don't give up that easily.

Fully aware of his strength, I make one last go of it.

He stops me as I lunge toward him, placing his hands square on my shoulders. He turns me swiftly yet gently against the lockers. "Keep trying all you want. I can do this all day."

The coolness of the metal against my back offsets the warmth of my skin. I desperately try to ignore how he smoothly circles his right thumb over my shoulder. His hooded eyes hold my entire body captive, despite the fact that his grip isn't all that tight. He's not holding me here against my will. I could probably leave at any time. In fact, I probably should. But I don't, and I don't know why.

I don't dare blink. Blinking is for the weak. We only break eye contact when his gaze flickers to my lips. I glance at his too. They're not too thin and not too thick. In fact, they're perfect. My inner cavewoman desperately wants to feel them against mine. And that's when I question my sanity. If there was an appropriate female equivalent to "thinking with your dick," my mug shot would be right alongside. The real Crystal, a woman of logic and all things practical, would never be attracted to this infuriating asshole.

Unexpectedly, his lips brush against mine, stealing my air. Heat flushes through me like a violent tsunami, ready to obliterate everything in its wake. All of my internal organs clench. My muscles seize. My eyes close. My toes curl.

Am I even still alive? Did he really just kiss me?

I'm frozen in place and time. I can't physically move.

His kiss is featherlight, testing, as if he's unsure if he should continue. He tastes familiar somehow, minty and fresh, bringing me alive slowly but surely. His hands loosen on my shoulders, as if confident I won't pull away from him. His right hand drifts up the nape of my neck and into my hair.

I panic, because my hair is a tangled, sweaty rat's nest. But as I feel the pads of his fingers stroking up and down the back of my skull, I'm lost in this moment. I want to savor it forever. I tilt my chin upward to deepen the kiss, which he takes greedily. There's a tremor in his hand as the pad of his thumb skates over my cheekbone. No one has ever touched my face like this, as if treasuring every curve and line.

It's only now that I realize my arms are hanging like dead noodles. I snake my hands up his hard stomach, over the ridges of his shoulders. His muscles clench under my palms. I'm practically on my tiptoes when I lock my fingers behind his neck, pulling us completely flush. He lets out a tiny sigh of relief into my mouth.

His lips open and close against mine in a slow rhythm. I moan into him, and he pulls back for half a second. There's a stormy change in his eyes as they darken to an electric mossy hue, my new favorite color. The air shifts around us, as if we're in the eye of a chaotic twister.

It's desperate, needy, wild. I pull him down, closer to me until I can feel him, hard against my stomach.

Our kisses devolve into a frantic flurry of hair pulling, teeth clinking, and lip biting. The further his tongue goes, the deeper I slip into a haze, a daydream that I never want to wake from. Every time his lips dare to leave mine for a split second, I pull him back to me, harder, closing the gap between us, wanting more and more.

Who am I and how did I end up making out with a stranger in the men's locker room? I really ought to tear myself away and run.

But the feeling of his lips on mine is like an explosion of euphoria. Of everything I want and need. The perfect taste. The perfect sensation. The perfect pressure. The perfect everything.

His hand dips around my bottom, hooking underneath my right thigh, lifting it around his waist. A low groan escapes his mouth, vibrating into mine as my hips roll against his, sending a blinding jolt to the forgotten corners of my body. His lips dart hungrily to the side of my mouth, down my jaw, and over my neck as he hoists me off the ground completely. He backs me up against the locker again, my legs hooked around his waist.

I've never been picked up by a man before. To call this "exhilarating" is the understatement of the century.

"Fuck," he whispers in my ear as I rock against him, one hand linked around his neck, the other gripping his hair. He's looking *at* me, not through me. In all my hookups, I don't think I've ever held eye contact for longer than two seconds before looking away. In fact, I don't even remember linking eyes with Neil.

Squat Rack Thief's expression is the perfect mixture of pleasure, adoration, and sincerity. I didn't know he was humanly capable of this. I revel in it. I lose myself in it.

I'm about to spontaneously combust from the pressure alone when the changing room door squeaks open.

His head jolts back in the direction of the door. His muscles clench and seize underneath me, holding me in place for a breath. All I want to do is capture this moment and freeze it in time. Our eyes are still locked as he sets me down more gently than I'd expect, flashing me a *Shit, we're busted* look.

A stout, balding man barely covered by an impossibly tiny towel strolls around the corner, whistling. Red-faced from the sauna, he stops dead in his tracks when he catches sight of me, chest heaving, lips swollen, caged against a locker. I only see the man's stunned reaction for a fraction of a second, because Squat Rack Thief shifts, as if protecting me from sight.

I blink, the silence yanking me back to reality. Cheeks burning like the fiery flames of hell, I inch past Squat Rack Thief and scramble out of the changing room without looking back.

On my way to take shelter in the women's changing room, I nearly bulldoze one of the gym ladies from earlier. The one with the visor.

"Excuse me, hun. Is this your phone?" She holds my white iPhone in her extended hand. "Accidentally took it from the mat area, thinking it was mine. I left my phone in the car today. Guess it's just habit."

Instead of being ecstatic to be reunited with my beloved phone, all I can think is, *Crap*.

I was dead wrong.

Squat Rack Thief is innocent.

"Oh, uh, thank you for returning it," I manage through my fog. I can barely look this lady in the eye without blushing.

With my phone safely in my possession, I spend at least half an hour in the changing room, hunched over on the bench in a daze. I can't leave. The risk of crossing paths with Squat Rack Thief on the way out is too great. He probably thinks I'm a total loon, falsely accusing him of stealing my phone and climbing him like a ladder in the changing room.

Despite my best efforts, even after I'm showered and dressed, my heart rate stubbornly refuses to settle to a resting BPM.

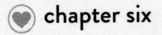 **chapter six**

ENTER THE GYM, ball cap hanging low over my eyes in a poor attempt at going incognito, or as invisible as possible in hot-pink Lululemon leggings. My gym bag snags on the turnstiles. I tug it twice before pulling it free.

When the combination lock in my bag makes a loud, echoing *clunk* against the stainless-steel turnstile, Claire, the redheaded girl behind the front counter, holds her hand over her mouth. She does a piss-poor job of not laughing in my face.

So much for stealth mode.

I take a cautious scan around as I head for the changing room, fully expecting to meet Squat Rack Thief's inevitable taunting look from one of the machines I'm planning to use. All the regulars are here. The veiny gym bros. The hard-core female body-builder flexing up a storm in the mirror, admiring her impressive, award-winning, competition-ready figure. Yet Squat Rack Thief is nowhere to be found.

Head down, I busily film my planned segments for the day. But every time a tall, muscular dude enters the gym, my stomach free-falls and I do a double take. I'm on guard, just waiting for him to show. But he doesn't.

Truth be told, I'm relieved. How am I supposed to face him again after yesterday? It was undoubtedly the hottest moment of my life, and my clothes stayed on the entire time. In fact, I'd go as far as saying it was better than sex. I'd be lying if I said I hadn't thought about it. All day and night.

Unfortunately, there's a ninety-nine-percent chance he thinks I concocted the phone thievery as an excuse to attack him in the changing room. Not only does that make me look like a desperate, sex-crazed lunatic, but I can't help but ponder what would have happened if that bald man hadn't walked in and interrupted us. Would we have gone any further? Probably, given we were dry humping against the lockers, my legs hoisted around his waist like a pretzel. And worse, I catch myself wishing we had, which goes against my vow to take a break from random hookups.

While we didn't actually have sex, no faceless Tinder random has ever made me feel . . . *that* before. No less a nemesis who refuses to tell me his name.

I chastise myself for my lingering thoughts of him as I exit the gym, thighs already burning from my workout. I must resist thinking about that man, no matter how many abs he has, or how deep his V line is.

By the time I'm half a block away from home, my mind has

spiraled into hypotheticals. What if he's avoiding me? He must be. Either that, or he's come down with a sudden illness, or he perished in a freak accident. Avoidance is the most logical explanation, though. It's no coincidence he's suddenly changed his schedule after days of coming to the gym at the exact same time. Obviously he doesn't want to face me.

Maybe he can't stomach the awkwardness, similar to how I long to disappear into dust and nothingness when I see Tinder Joe, who, by the way, still acts like I don't exist.

I attempt to push Squat Rack Thief out of my mind as I check the mail in the lobby and head up to my apartment, flyers, bills, and a massive package of sponsored protein bars in hand.

The moment I open the front door, I'm unexpectedly greeted by a bright-eyed, newly permed Grandma Flo wielding a batter-covered whisk. She's wearing Tara's flour-covered apron, which reads *GET SOME*.

Before I can even ask why Grandma Flo is in my apartment, the whisk is halfway down my throat, choking me. "Do you taste the butter?" she demands, luminous hazel eyes boring into mine like an operative interrogating their latest captive under seizure-inducing fluorescent lights.

When I gag dramatically, she takes mercy and removes the whisk. "Uh, yeah. I taste the butter. Why?" I ask, catching a glimpse of Tara snickering on the couch among a pile of books.

Tara followed me on the Instagram train. She's a bookstagrammer, someone who reads 483,398 books a year and posts reviews. With thousands of followers, she receives stacks of free books in the mail from publishers who want her to advertise and review upcoming releases. Reminding her to keep her books in her room instead of littering my living room with them has become my second job. Tara makes some money from her bookstagram, but certainly not enough to warrant it being a full-time job, which is the only thing that saves her from Mom and Dad's disapproval. She has a "proper" job as a registered nurse in the neonatal ward at the children's hospital.

Satisfied with my response, Grandma Flo swivels back to my kitchen, still talking. "At the church potluck, Janine asked Ethel if my shortbread was *store-bought*. The gumption!"

Janine Fitzgerald is Grandma Flo's church nemesis. As the story goes, their rivalry began over a coveted church pew and went downhill after a particularly dramatic Bible study. I only half-listen as Grandma goes on a long-winded rant about how Janine likes to hold her hands in the air during sermons, purposely to block her view.

I plop onto the couch beside Tara. "How long has she been here?" I ask, voice low.

"Two hours. She said she had some business in the city. She walked in on me while I was naked. Didn't even bother to knock."

"Why were you naked in my apartment?" I fury-whisper. "And aren't you supposed to be doing a shift at the hospital?" I kick off my running shoes and toss the unopened mail on the coffee table.

She shakes her head, promptly ignoring my first question. "Yeah. I got sent home early."

The look on her face tells me there's a story here, so I remain silent, just waiting.

"I was the unfortunate victim of pea-green explosive diarrhea."

I cover my mouth, stifling a bubble of laughter as I open my laptop to begin my workout plan for a virtual client in Arkansas. "That's the best thing I've heard all day."

"It was so potent. You would have fainted," she says, expression grave.

"Anyway, why is Grandma here?" I ask.

Tara opens her mouth, itching to spill the tea, but stops when Grandma Flo emerges from the kitchen, plate of cookies in hand. She sets them in front of Tara, who she feels is "much too thin" and at risk of "withering away" at any given moment.

After settling into the chair, she fusses with one of my tiny succulents on the side table. Apparently unsatisfied with its state, she carelessly dumps the remainder of Tara's tea over the top. RIP succulent. Grandma Flo has never had a green thumb.

"As you know, I canceled Easter this year," Grandma Flo starts slowly, choosing her words carefully. She delays, picking at a loose thread in the stitching of my chair.

I half-close my laptop to give her my full attention. "Were you actually at the casino?"

She shakes her head. "No. I was . . . *with* someone."

"With someone?" Tara and I ask simultaneously.

She flashes us her ring hand, unveiling what looks like a ruby, flanked by an elegant yellow-gold band. "I'm engaged." She holds her breath, as if bracing for our reaction.

While Tara launches to her feet and shrieks in delight, practically crushing Grandma with a hug, I sink into the couch, only narrowly saving my laptop before it topples to the floor. My mind refuses to compute her words. "*Engaged?*" What fresh hell?

The only man I can picture Grandma Flo with is Grandpa. Though he passed away of bone cancer three years ago, I never imagined she would date again. I think about how they used to sit side by side in matching La-Z-Boys watching *Wheel of Fortune* and *Jeopardy!* every single night. Or how their wild nights out consisted of attending a Tuesday sermon, then heading home at eight to devour a bag of Chex Mix while gossiping about their fellow churchgoers.

"I didn't even know you were dating." The words sound foreign coming out of my mouth as I turn to Tara. "Did you know?"

"No," Tara says. "Isn't it funny, though? Grandma has a more active dating life than us." She stares at the space on her finger where her massive princess-cut diamond used to sit. I'm half convinced one of the worst parts of her breakup was giving up the ring.

"Who are you marrying?" I ask, turning my attention back to the matter at hand.

"Martin Ritchie," Grandma says, smiling like a lovesick baby deer.

Tara cuts in. "Oh! We know him. The guy that lives down the street from you, right?"

Grandma nods with pride. "The very one."

"That guy? Really? The one with the mustache who you and Grandpa used to play bocce ball with?" I conjure up a blurry image of his thick, eighties-porn-star mustache in my mind. He was always in a striped polo shirt, from what I can remember.

Grandma Flo goes on a ramble about how active Martin is. Something about boating and tennis. Her eyes go misty and sentimental as she details their weekend getaway on Cape Cod. The seafood. Her seasickness. His unwavering support. The romantic sunset proposal. I barely absorb a word. I don't know how to process this information. It isn't that I'm upset she canceled our family Easter tradition. It's the fact that she's essentially been leading a double life.

"Wow. I mean, I'm shocked. But I'm happy for you," I force out, along with a sweet granddaughter-esque smile. "When is the wedding?"

She shrugs. "We haven't gotten that far. A summer wedding would be nice, though it's such short notice. We'd be hard pressed to find any available venues—"

A wheezy gasp comes out of Tara's throat, startling me. She looks like she's just come up with a cure for a life-threatening disease. "Oh my God. I still have my wedding venue. The Sheraton. And most of my vendors."

Grandma blinks. "You didn't cancel them?"

"Not yet. They're holding my deposits and I thought . . . maybe there was hope Seth would change his mind." She pauses, chin trembling. "But he won't. So you can have it all if you want. Then all that money and planning won't go to waste."

The furrow deepens between Grandma Flo's thin brows as she considers this bizarre proposition.

I grip the edges of my laptop, studying Tara's unreadable face. "And you'd be okay with this?" I honestly don't know how I'd feel witnessing someone else walk down the aisle at my venue, on my date, with my décor and music, knowing it was supposed to be me.

"I am, actually." Tara looks genuine. By the way she's lowered her shoulders, I think she might even be a little relieved. "You know Dad would be all for it. It would be *responsible and economical*." She mimics Dad's voice.

Grandma Flo smiles in agreement. "You know, I think I might

take you up on that. I'd have to discuss it with Marty first, but I'm sure he will love the idea."

As she and Tara embrace in a sentimental moment, I try to envision what Grandma is going to wear. Will she go for a traditional bridal gown? A ball gown? Some sort of elegant pantsuit? The whole thing is bizarre and near impossible to imagine, as I've only ever seen her wear her signature Grandma outfits. The ones adorned with nature patterns on the front. A pair of loons. A maple leaf. A fox. Certainly not a wedding dress.

"Oh, that reminds me," Grandma Flo says, clasping her hands together. "Do you have plans tomorrow night?"

"I don't think so." I rest my head against the back of the couch and stare at the ceiling, silently willing life to return to a simpler time when Grandma Flo wasn't taking over Tara's wedding. Better yet, when I wasn't climbing my nameless nemesis in the gym after vowing off random hookups. I need a strong drink.

"Good. I'd like you to meet Martin's family. We made a reservation at Mamma Maria's."

I let out a prolonged sigh at the thought of spending my night socializing with strangers. Tara covers up my less-than-enthusiastic response by fawning over the ring, interspersed with detailed wedding talk. I throw in the odd nod and squeal so as to appear semi-thrilled while still in shock. Grandma eventually packs up the rest of her cookies (for Martin) and leaves, but not before expressing disapproval of my leggings, pointing out my severe camel toe.

"Crystal." Tara tosses the sequin throw pillow at me the moment the door closes. "Don't you dare go all *Meet the Fockers* on Martin. He's a sweet old man."

I toss the pillow back. It bounces off her knee and onto the floor. "What makes you think I'll go Robert De Niro on him? I don't own a lie detector test."

"Yet." She pauses. "And because that's just what you do. You go into mama-bear mode. On everyone."

I pull back, brows knit. "No. I don't."

She gives me a pointed look, as if this is something she's been meaning to bring up. "You've hated every guy I ever dated. Did you know Seth was terrified of you? You didn't even speak a word to him until probably six months into our relationship. And that was just to ask him to borrow his veggie spiralizer."

I stare at her. I never did give the spiralizer back. Probably because zucchini pasta has become a staple in my diet, and also because I just knew Seth was going to suck. But maybe Tara has a point. The last thing I want to do is upset Grandma Flo if she's found a second chance at happiness.

"I'll be nice. I promise."

chapter seven

MARTIN NO LONGER has a mustache. I've spent the past half hour staring at the bare skin of his upper lip, as well as the sizable mole on his neck. There's a hair poking out of the center that I'm resisting the urge to pluck.

He's been droning on and on about his many family members as they enter the private room in the restaurant. He spares no detail with the backstories, like how his great-niece got straight A's in every course in her latest college semester at Duke despite dealing with asbestos in her dorm room.

I know he's just being friendly, trying to acquaint our families. But finding out the breadth of his eldest daughter's latest shingles flare-up isn't exactly ideal conversation prior to eating a four-course Italian dinner.

"Crystal, can you come here for a second?" Mom interrupts. She tugs at my elbow, gifting Martin a massively fake smile. I've inherited her inability to temper her facial expressions, particularly when she is displeased.

"Yeah?" I whisper, leaning in.

Mom's nervous gaze flutters around the candlelit room, taking in the awkwardness that is our two families, standing divided on either side of the table.

Mom's side of the family, the McCarthys, are a formal bunch. We're a small group, with Mom only having her brother and his two kids. We're not overly boisterous, like the Chens, Dad's side of the family.

Everyone is trying to remain calm and collected while feeling hella uncomfortable at the sight that is Grandma Flo draping her entire body over Martin on the chaise lounge, posing harder than Tyra Banks for photos. Martin hasn't stopped showering her with cringeworthy affection all evening.

Martin's family appears to be your standard white, down-to-earth, Midwestern, American-born-and-bred crowd. He has three kids, plus their grown children, and a bunch of siblings, all enthusiastically talking about their cottages and the upcoming fishing season. They're also taking advantage of the open bar, cheerfully slapping each other on the back and shouting many decibels too loud for this room.

"Just wanted to save you from the shingles conversation." Mom winks, pushing her bangs from her eyes. After one conversation, it's clear Martin is an oversharer. The opposite of Grandpa's perpetually crusty, reserved nature.

"How are you feeling about it all?" I ask her sympathetically. She, of anyone, probably took this news the hardest. She was really close to Grandpa. Tara claimed Mom was fine, but I don't trust her, given her paranoia I'll channel Robert De Niro and ruin the entire dinner.

Mom fiddles with her champagne flute, forcing another grin.

"Fine. Why wouldn't I be? If Grandma is happy, so am I." Apparently Tara wasn't exaggerating.

She has a point. Grandma looks so full of life, dressed in a classy gold lace dress and matching shawl. Her short gray hair is neatly styled into old-school waves. She is still tucked under Martin's arm, mid–Julia Roberts laugh, as he gazes at her like she's the light of his life.

"You look gorgeous tonight." Mom takes in my navy cocktail dress. "It's been a while since I've seen you out of your Lulus." As much as she'd deny it, I know her comment is a slight against my career choice.

"You know I can't wear anything but Align leggings for the rest of my life," I say, deciding this isn't the time or the place to get into it. And besides, these leggings are everything. Lululemon credits me for converting hundreds of women to the glorious, life-changing comfort that is their Align legging. "No Hillary tonight?"

Mom lets out a sorrowful sigh and I immediately regret bringing it up. "The restaurant wouldn't allow it without proper paperwork to prove she's a service dog."

I level a hard stare at her. "Mom, Hillary is not a service dog. You have to stop telling people that."

Mom clutches her chest, appalled that I *went there*. "She's like a therapy dog to me."

"We talked about this. It's a real certification, you know. Some people need them for legitimate health reasons. Not just because they're obsessed with their dog and can't leave them alone without having a meltdown."

Mom apparently disagrees, rolling her eyes in defiance. She chugs the rest of her champagne like it's water as Grandma Flo announces it's finally time to sit down for dinner.

She made name cards for everyone, as she always does for family dinners. They sit among the brightly colored ranunculus floral arrangements, artfully prepared by Tara and Mom earlier today.

Unfortunately, the families are purposely intermixed, one of us between two or three of them, to help us get to know each other. An introvert's worst nightmare.

I have the luxury of sitting smack-dab in between Martin himself and a place card that reads *Scott* in flowing calligraphy. Of all the Ritchie family members I was introduced to tonight, I don't recall meeting anyone named Scott. As the waiters begin to serve the salad, I notice every seat at the table is filled, except for Scott's.

Martin leans in to me, crunching his Caesar salad. A bit of crouton flies out of his mouth, landing dangerously close to my wrist, and I immediately set it onto my lap under the protection of the tablecloth. "You'll be beside my grandson, Scotty." He gives me a glowing smile, as if I've hit the jackpot as far as seating arrangements are concerned. Joy.

I'm momentarily distracted by Dad throwing Martin's son an animated high-five across the table. Dad is one of those people who can walk into a room full of strangers and exit fifteen minutes later with new, lifelong best friends. He's a quintessential extrovert, the first to arrive at a social gathering and always the last to leave.

"Looks like Scotty is running a bit late," I say, eyeing the empty chair beside me.

A green-eyed woman with a stylish bob, whom Martin introduced as Patricia, his daughter-in-law, shifts forward diagonally across from me. "He told me he was coming right after his shift," she says, glancing at her watch. By the way her nose is wrinkled with annoyance, I'm assuming that's his mother.

"He's a firefighter, my grandson," Martin informs me proudly. "Followed in the family footsteps."

I scan Martin, trying to imagine him as a firefighter forty years ago, to no avail. "You must be proud of him."

Grandma Flo pipes up from Martin's other side. "Oh, Tara, speaking of Scotty. Wait till you see him. The man is a looker."

Both Tara and I shift uncomfortably in our seats. Since Tara's failed engagement, Grandma Flo has been obsessed with playing matchmaker for her.

It isn't that I want my grandmother setting me up with random dudes. But out of principle, I once asked why she hasn't tried to set *me* up. She waved it off, calling me one of those "independent types." She then followed it up by admiring my *face*, going on about how I'm a perfect mix of my parents, and how rare it is that I'd have my mom's hazel-gold eyes. Complimenting my "facial beauty" is typical when people try to compensate, falsely assuming I'm in need of a confidence boost where my body is concerned.

For Tara's sake, I attempt to shift the focus away from her singleness. "If Scott is such a looker, why is he single?" I toss in a grin to ensure everyone knows I'm joking.

"He's not." Martin nods back toward Patricia. "He's dating that professional figure skater. Diana. Isn't he, Patricia?"

Patricia nods. "They've been together about six months now. Though she's on tour doing Disney on Ice," she adds, distractedly glancing at her watch once again. "I don't want you guys to have to wait for him. He's probably still at work, as usual."

Martin shrugs. "Duty calls."

My annoyance with this tardy Scott character only grows upon confirmation that he's the sole reason no one except Martin has touched their salad yet. It's already seven thirty. I ate light in anticipation of a massive meal tonight, by seven at the latest. I wondered why they were delaying cocktails and appetizers.

Martin sets his hand over the back of Grandma's chair before pressing a kiss on her temple. "Scotty won't mind if we get started. I'll go ahead and start my speech." He tosses his cloth napkin onto the table in front of him, standing with his full glass of red wine. Everyone shifts their attention to him.

"Before we eat, I'd be remiss if I didn't thank my family and Flo's family for coming this evening, and Tara for giving us an entire wedding," he adds with a wink, highlighting Tara's misfortune for the fifth time tonight. Everyone giggles uncomfortably while Tara white-knuckles her salad fork.

"I don't know if everyone knows this, but Flo and I attended the same elementary school. We were classmates, all the way until the eighth grade. She was by far the prettiest girl in class, with her little pigtails," he says affectionately. "When I was—"

Martin's speech is rudely interrupted when the door to our private room busts open.

The Ritchies erupt with enthusiasm, shouting, "Scotty!"

My eyes settle on the hulking figure taking up nearly the entire width of the doorway. The forest-green eyes. The Chris Evans face.

No freakin' way.

It's Squat Rack Thief.

Squat Rack Thief is *Scott*.

I don't know if I've ever wished myself to disappear into oblivion more than I do right now.

chapter eight

THE UNIVERSE IS officially conspiring against me. I must have done some seriously messed-up shit in a past life.

Scott, better known as Squat Rack Thief, is borderline unrecognizable in non-gym wear, without the ball cap casting a grim shadow over his face. His wavy hair is damp and pushed back, as if he's fresh from a shower. Under the warm candlelight, the deep jewel-tone hues of his eyes pop like emeralds. He's wearing a sport coat over a pale blue button-down shirt and beige pants, all of which fit with unfair precision.

When he spots me next to his grandpa, he stumbles backward a step, gripping the doorframe. Clearly, this is as shocking to him as it is to me. In fact, I half-expect him to turn around and sprint out of the restaurant.

Seeing him here is jarring, given the last time we were in each other's presence, every square inch of our sweaty bodies was pressed together.

My stomach clenches as Martin cheerfully bellows, "Scotty! My boy!" from his standing position.

My mind races as I come to the full realization that the man who gave me the best kiss of my life was not single. He was taken. The sincerity in his eyes when he looked at me was a massive lie. Nothing but a farce. An Academy Award–winning performance.

And worse, I feel awful for Diana, his figure skater girlfriend. I'm all too familiar with the betrayal, heartbreak, anger, and feeling of unworthiness that accompany being cheated on. Looking back, I have reason to suspect a few weeks' overlap between myself and Neil's ex, Cammie, before he officially went back to her. The last thing I'd ever want to do is to be *that* person to another woman. Not that the onus of blame should rest on the third party. But I don't want any part in the narrative at all.

Scott tears his deceitful eyes from me, giving his grandfather a warm, genuine smile. He rounds the table toward us to pull Martin into a loving hug. "So sorry I'm late. Had a fire call at the end of my shift."

"What happened?" Martin asks.

"Some kids started a kitchen fire. Their parents weren't even home. If the neighbor hadn't called 911, it woulda been bad. They were all shaken up. Really young too. The crew and I stuck around to make sure they were okay," he humble-brags.

A mildly audible snort escapes me. My brain cannot reconcile the image of morally corrupt Squat Rack Thief comforting small, trembling children. He has to be exaggerating. In fact, I'd bet money he was at home, lazing around in low-cut boxers. He probably lost track of time diligently organizing his various protein powders, or worshipping his own reflection in the mirror.

Martin forgivingly waves him off. "Atta boy. Always knew you'd make me proud."

Scott nods in faux-hero solidarity and then turns, embracing Grandma Flo with the biceps I've only recently discovered are used to save people's lives from fires . . . and to lift me against lockers. "Flo, you look stunning," he tells her, the corners of his eyes crinkling ever so slightly.

Not only is it irritating that Scott is flashing her a wholesome, charming smile, but it rankles that he's already well acquainted with *my* grandma.

I feel like I'm in the twilight zone. This reminds me of the time my high school friend Kelsey started dating our English teacher when we went away to college. Aside from how inappropriate and creepy it was, him showing up at our dorm room parties felt wildly bizarre. Like two very separate worlds that should never, ever collide.

Scott meets my eyes again. His Adam's apple bobs when he registers the open seat, *his* seat, directly beside mine.

Before he sits, Martin introduces us. "Scotty, this is one of Flo's beautiful granddaughters, Crystal Chen."

I want to slap away Scott's smug expression as he holds his hand out. "Scott Ritchie. Nice to meet you, *Crystal*," he says, as if we've never met. As if we didn't get hot and heavy in the gym changing room forty-eight hours ago.

He doesn't bother to hide his amusement. If he feels the slightest bit guilty for cheating on his figure skater girlfriend with me, there is zero evidence to support it. And it's infuriating.

I want to call him out on his infidelity, right here, right now.

Expose his misdeeds. But I think better of it. The last thing I want to do is ruin Grandma's dinner, especially after I promised Tara I wouldn't. So, I take a breath and hold my tongue. "Likewise," I say primly.

I eye him suspiciously as he takes his seat beside me. If I thought he smelled good sweaty after a workout, he smells frustratingly delightful now—like a steamy shower fantasy. He's definitely just showered, because he smells like that green bar soap. Manly. Slightly spicy. Far too alluring. Apparently, this is the scent of a coldhearted cheater who shows no visible signs of remorse.

My body is a traitor. The mere proximity of him sends a hum of energy to every limb, all the way down to my toes. I resettle in my seat, turning away from him as Patricia flashes him a stern, motherly look, which I can tell is silently screaming, *How dare you be late to your own grandfather's engagement dinner?*

I refuse to look at him as Martin resumes his speech.

"As I was saying, I've loved Flo since first grade. Since the day she stole my cap at recess and refused to give it back. She'll probably argue with me on the semantics, but we went steady for most of elementary school, until she broke up with me for Ned Reeves." He eyes her with a nostalgic smile.

Grandma Flo whacks him on the arm from her seated position. "I broke up with you because you kissed Peggy Penton."

The two of them chuckle and Martin continues on. "Anyway, we had a couple years apart . . . quite a few." His voice cracks. "We lived most of our lives as dear friends, but I've always cared deeply for her. I loved Roger as well." He takes the time to look at each and every member of my family. "I promise to take as good care of her as he did for fifty-seven years."

Everyone *aww*s, clapping politely before raising a toast to Grandma Flo.

I'm in shock as I raise my wineglass, clinking it robotically against Scott's. Martin has been in love with Grandma Flo since first grade. As adorable and country-love-song-worthy as that is, all I can think about is Grandpa. I think about all the times Martin was over when Tara and I were at their house. I think about how much Grandma talked about him. The fact that I even knew him so well as a friend of hers makes me question if there was something more going on. Martin had a wife too, but she passed away at least ten years ago, from my recollection. Is it possible she was cheating on Grandpa with Martin? Did she love Martin? The entire time?

I've always held my grandparents' relationship on a pedestal. Grandpa used to bring her flowers every Friday. Though he was outwardly crabby about it, he always made special meals for her, even when she went through a phase when she would only eat a raw, plant-based diet. I'm left to wonder if it was all a sham. And now I have to deal with Scott the Cheater's presence.

I try to gauge the rest of my family's reactions to Martin's speech, but no one else appears bothered. Mom is busily chatting with the waitstaff about how they avoid cross-contamination in the kitchen. Tara is in deep conversation with Grandma. Dad is still engaged in what looks like a bromance with Martin's son.

I don't know if it's the wine, but I'm prickly with heat, squished between Grandma's new love and the Cheater. I stand abruptly, knocking my napkin off my lap as I shuffle into the dim hallway next to the bathrooms. The wall is cool against my fingertips. I squeeze my eyes shut, taking a deep breath in and out, trying to push the antisocial monster within me back under temporary lock and key. *Just get through dinner,* I tell myself. *Then you can go home, curl up in bed, and avoid all reality.*

On my inhale, my nose catches a whiff of that green-bar-soap scent. Without even looking, I know Scott is afoot.

I pry my eyes open, confirming he is, indeed, right in front of me.

"You alright?" he asks huskily, studying my face. "You look a little pale. I can grab you some water if you want." He's teetering back and forth on the balls of his feet, hands in his pockets.

"I'm fine. Just needed space," I say, too flustered to come up with a remotely cutting response.

He gives me a head tilt, which tells me he doesn't buy it, but decides to let it be.

"You weren't at the gym today. Or yesterday." The words fall out of my mouth before I can stop them.

What appeared to be a look of concern melts away, replaced with a satisfied grin. "You missed me at the gym?" He is so damned full of himself, he probably has his own selfies framed on his bedside table.

I scoff. "No, I didn't miss you."

"You definitely did. Just a little." He laughs effortlessly, his gaze shifting to my phone in my hand. "I see you finally found your phone. Not in my possession," he adds.

I clear my throat and straighten my spine, ignoring the latter half of his comment. I'd rather die than admit I was wrong. "You're the one who started coming to the gym at the exact same time as me."

"The gym at my fire station is under renovation for the next few months. Excalibur Fitness is right in between the station and my apartment." He pauses for a moment, leaning in closer. "And because you're dying to know, I've been working day shift the past two days. I've been going to the gym at night instead."

I scrunch my nose. "Please spare me the gruesome details of your daily routine. I could care less."

"Hey, you're the one who stalked me into the changing room."

"I was looking for my phone."

He gives me an incendiary look. "And you got a little more than you bargained for."

I force away the hot flashback of being crushed between the locker and his hard body. "And it's never going to happen again. It was a momentary lapse in judgment, obviously. For both of us."

"Alright." His eyes linger, amused, like the smug bastard he is.

"It's not," I say again, for good measure.

"Sure. Whatever you want."

I glower at him, unable to decipher whether he's being sarcastic or not. I internally choose my words, readying myself to finally confront him about his not-so-single relationship status, when he interrupts my thoughts.

"So, your grandma and my grandpa. How weird is that?"

I'm taken aback by his tone. Instead of his usual sneering sarcasm, it sounds normal. Like a casual conversation between friends or acquaintances. I blink a couple times. "It's really weird," I admit.

"I'm sorry for your loss. I know your grandpa passed a couple years ago." His voice is calm and measured. From the way his eyes search mine, as if somehow understanding my pain, I think he's being sincere.

"Thanks." I suck in a shaky breath, trying to stop the tears from spilling over. There is no way I'm doing this in front of my cheating gym nemesis, even if he is being a semi-decent human being for once. I draw in another breath, composing myself before returning to the private room.

* * *

APPARENTLY, GRANDMA'S SEATING arrangements successfully broke the ice between the two families, because everyone is happily mingling now, except me. I'm as close to lying down as you can get in a restaurant chair. My body is halfway off the seat, slouched and lopsided, legs stretched in front of me.

Admittedly, I'm being a poor sport. But only because I've suffered enough emotional shrapnel tonight. Truthfully, Martin's sociable family has exhausted me, as lovely as they may be. All I want to do is go home, curl up under my duvet, and watch mind-numbing reality television.

It doesn't help that my stomach is churning, and not just because of this whole situation with Grandma Flo, Martin, and Scott, or the fact that I've eaten too much fettucine. I've been staring at my phone for the last ten minutes, rereading a text that came in unexpectedly.

NEIL: Hey.

With just one text, I'm fastened on an involuntary roller coaster. One that dips and turns, leaving me winded and breathless, and not in a good way.

I haven't heard from Neil since the last time he texted me to complain about Cammie and their "shitty sex life," which I didn't respond to. Only in the last month did I finally get to the point where I didn't wait with bated breath for his text.

"Are you on Tinder again? Chatting with Zayn?" A deep voice sounds from over my shoulder.

Scott has returned to his seat after spending the past twenty minutes near the bar, socializing and filling the room with his seriously infectious laughter. Who knew the Cheater could laugh with such pure, unrestrained delight?

He reads the text over my shoulder. He's so close, I can feel the faint breeze of his breath tingling the back of my neck.

I clutch my phone, pressing it to my hammering chest. "Excuse you. None of your business."

"Just wondering why you're on your phone at your grandma's engagement party."

"It's not like I'm sitting here swiping left and right. I'm answering business messages." In all reality, I've answered precisely one email. I'm predominantly agonizing over whether to respond to Neil, while simultaneously researching the benefits of Kim Kardashian's Skims shapewear over OG Spanx.

"Looks like you're texting *Neil*."

I whip my head around, so as to ensure no one else in my family heard him say Neil's name. They haven't, clearly, or else they'd have already swarmed me, staging an intervention. "No, I'm not."

He leans in, amused, twirling the unused teaspoon on the table. "So did you Netflix and chill with Zayn?"

"No."

"Why not?"

"Because we couldn't agree on which was better, the UK or the

US *Office*," I lie. Truth is, I never actually responded to Zayn. And why does Scott even care?

"Which do you think is better?"

"The US. Obviously."

He sits back slightly, giving me a disapproving head shake. "Gotta say, I'm with Zayn here. You just can't beat dry, British humor."

"And this is why we don't get along," I snap.

He gives me a lazy smirk. "I think we get along sometimes."

An electric current courses through me again, so much that I can feel the heat in my cheeks. But it's a lie. Because he's a scumbag. The only logical thing to do is turn away from him and avoid him for the rest of the night, and the rest of my life.

Just as I'm about to make my escape, Tara plunks down in Martin's empty seat to my left. "I think the ginger-haired waiter is in love with me," she mutters. "Don't look."

I sneak a peek at the waiter, who is absolutely checking her out as he pours Mom's tea. The poor kid doesn't look a day older than seventeen. "Did you flirt with him?"

"God, no. He's a teenager. Though I don't blame him for shooting for the stars. I mean, I am a vision in this romper," she says cheekily, gesturing to her champagne sequin getup.

I give a weak laugh and she changes the subject. "Did I ever tell you about the time I ate an entire box of Krispy Kremes?" she asks, rubbing her toned stomach.

"No."

She begins to ramble on about the events that led her to eat a half dozen donuts. Something about a lobster dinner, Seth, and taking public transit. To be honest, I'm only half-listening, because

Scott is now engrossed in happy conversation with Grandma Flo to my right.

My anger bubbles to the surface, knowing he's pulling the wool over my sweet grandmother's eyes. Clearly she thinks the world of him. Everyone does. And little do they know, it's just an extraordinarily chiseled façade.

Scott nods, cheeks rosy, as Grandma Flo whispers something in his ear. Our eyes meet again as he says something else I don't catch.

The next words that come out of Grandma Flo's mouth are muffled, because Tara's voice is louder. She's at an animated part of her story now. "And then the guy had the audacity to ask what party I was going to. And I was like, no, bro, these donuts are just for me . . ."

Meanwhile, Scott and Grandma Flo throw their heads back with laughter, as if they're the best of friends. They probably have friendship bracelets at this rate. I'm waiting for them to bust out a synchronized, *Parent Trap*–style handshake.

This is too much. I can't sit around witnessing fake-Scott in action for a second longer. I stand abruptly, purse in hand, wobbling slightly from the alfredo sauce cramps. I don't even bother to say a word to anyone as I hustle out of the room. I take one quick scan over my shoulder, shooting Scott a disgusted look before fleeing the restaurant like a bat out of hell.

It's not like me to leave a party unannounced. But after everything, I desperately want to be alone right now, preferably horizontal.

The sidewalk is littered with people strolling leisurely, enjoying the warm, breezy spring air.

As I confirm my Uber, Tara bounds down the stone steps, her barrel curls bouncing with each stride. "Are you okay?"

I sigh, glancing down the street for any sign of the 2016 white Honda Civic I ordered. "It's nothing. I'm just tired. My introvert is coming out."

"Are you sure there's nothing wrong?"

I pin her with a grave expression. "Scott Ritchie, Martin's grandson? He is Squat Rack Thief."

She covers her mouth with her palm. "What? Actually?"

"Yup."

"That's the guy you made out with in the gym locker room?"

I give her a curt nod.

She raises her brow, coming to the realization. "And he has a girlfriend . . ."

"Yup. He's a disgusting pig. Surprise, surprise."

Her shock transforms into a scowl. "This is why I don't trust the male species anymore."

"Tell me about it." I pause, taking in her anger. "But don't say anything. I don't want to ruin the dinner. That's why I'm leaving." I take stock of my Uber as it pulls up in the nick of time.

"I really want to go in there to give him a piece of my mind," Tara declares, turning on her heel as I open the car door.

"No!" I shout after her. Revealing Scott's infidelity at an engagement party feels petty and juvenile. It also makes me look like the scorned and jealous "other woman," which I'm not.

But it's too late. She's already inside.

chapter nine

'M NEVER EATING *dairy again*, I vow. Unfortunately, lactose intolerance was destined to befall me. Dad's entire family suffers from it.

Making quick work of unfastening my bra from under my dress, I carelessly discard it on the living room floor before sprawling on the couch in a food coma. I'm about to fire up Bravo when my phone lights up on the coffee table. My throat constricts. I hope it isn't Neil.

And it isn't. It's an Instagram direct message. From Ritchie_Scotty7.

Oh hell no.

I pick up my phone and open the message.

RITCHIE_SCOTTY7

Hey Crystal. Your sister told me you were upset.

I stare at his message for a few moments before violently shaking my phone. He isn't even the slightest bit unique. In fact, he's a textbook cheater, desperately sliding into a girl's DMs.

And how am I supposed to respond to that message? I decide to remedy the situation by avoiding the shit out of it. I'm not enabling his behavior further.

Tossing my phone aside, I reach for the remote and turn on a rerun of my beloved *Real Housewives of Orange County*. Halfway through, amid an all-out screaming match between Tamra and Vicki, my phone lights up again.

RITCHIE_SCOTTY7

> I see you read my message. Are you planning to respond? I'll even accept an emoji response.

I almost catch myself snorting at the message, because I can picture his punchable face and hear his deep voice as I read the DM. I spend the entire rest of the episode shamefully stalking his Instagram. He doesn't have tons of photos, but I analyze each one forensically.

In his profile photo, he's wearing aviators against a sunny, azure sky. He's holding a huge, leggy goldendoodle in his lap. The doodle is literally smiling. With teeth. Apparently, I was wrong in my Instagram rant. He does like puppies. In fact, he's seemingly obsessed with his dog, because his Instagram bio reads *Dog dad to Albus Doodledore*.

Against my better judgment, I continue to hate-scroll. There is no sign of Diana, the figure skater girlfriend Martin and his mom were talking about. Instead, there's a plethora of nature pictures, some solo photos of Albus Doodledore on hiking trails, and a couple shots of fire trucks and other guys in firefighter gear.

There aren't even any shirtless gym-bro selfies. In fact, there's only one shirtless photo, of him with another friend on the edge of a dock on a lake. I zoom in with surgical precision, so as to ensure I do not accidentally *Like* the photo. His abs are unmistakable. And this photo is from 2016. Damn. He's lived *years* of his life this beautiful. It's almost unjust.

There is no photographic proof of his womanizing ways, even after checking his tagged photos. No club pictures with big-breasted models, or bikini-clad women on yachts. Sure, his friends are all fit and attractive. But I'm not about to judge someone for having attractive friends, so I abandon the task, tossing my phone aside.

Only minutes later, it lights up yet again. But this time, it's a text from Tara.

TARA: Hey, hope you're feeling better. Just wanted to let you know I'm staying late to help Mom clear all the flowers from the restaurant, etc. PS. The waiter is sticking around and I have it on good authority from the hostess that he's working up the courage to ask me out. Going to have to let him down easy. Wish me luck.

CRYSTAL: Good luck! And I feel bad I'm not there to help. Tell Grandma I'm sorry for leaving.

TARA: No worries! There's not much to do. And I think you should talk to Scott. FYI. He wants to apologize.

I roll my eyes. Apologize for being caught? Beg me not to tell anyone? No, thanks.

CRYSTAL: Tara, I don't want an apology from him. I don't care.

I toss my phone back on the table. The mere fact that he wants to be righteous and "apologize" pisses me off even more.

I scroll through my texts, revisiting my random text from Neil. I still haven't responded.

Crystal, do not give in, I tell myself over and over, eyes fixed on the exposed ceiling.

To distract myself from the temptation of responding to either man, despite my growing curiosity, I throw on some gym clothes and head to Excalibur Fitness—the one and only place I can find any peace. My cramps have subsided in my rage, and I'm desperate to throw around some weights.

• • •

EXCALIBUR FITNESS IS vacant of all human life, except for me. Then again, it's midnight. Most people in their right minds aren't pumping iron in the middle of the night.

The sound system isn't even on, extending the tranquility. It reminds me of when I used to work at Pottery Barn in the mall as a teenager, coming in to open the store in the early hours of the morning and closing late at night. The stillness of a place that is normally bustling with people is off-putting to some, but it's the ultimate serenity for me.

Pre-workout, I snap a photo of my running shoes and dumbbells for my Instagram story, captioning it, "Late-night session. Blowing off some steam!"

Catching my breath, I massage the slight blister forming on my calloused palms after two sets. I close my eyes, concentrating on the air passing in and out of my lungs, when the gym door *whooshes* open.

Scott pushes through the turnstiles.

He's still in his perfectly tailored sport coat from dinner, while I'm wearing a hideous neon workout top that highlights all my worst angles. I desperately need to do laundry.

By the pink flush of his cheeks and the rate at which his chest rises and falls, I'd wager a guess he just ran from the restaurant. "Can we talk for a minute?"

I set the barbell down with a grunt. "I think the better question is, how did you know I was at the gym?"

My menacing, probably downright unnerving expression stops him in his tracks. He takes a small step backward, maintaining a couple feet between us. "Your Instagram story."

"Are you stalking me on Instagram now?" Dad would surely freak out if he found out his fears have come true, that someone actually did stalk me.

"Well, it sounds creepy when you say it like that."

"Why did you follow me here?"

He lets out a long sigh, taking a step toward me. "I'm really sorry—"

"Scott, save it. I have no desire to be some secret sidepiece when you're not getting it from your girlfriend."

"Crystal." His face is pained. "This is a massive misunderstanding."

"How? Your tongue just accidentally fell into my mouth when you have a girlfriend?" I'm on fire now, blood boiling, itching to roast him within an inch of his life.

He snaps his head back, bringing his hands to his temples. "I don't have a girlfriend. I never would have kissed you if I did."

"Then why do your grandpa and your mom think you do? Diana the figure skater? You don't need to lie. I'm not going to out you. I have better things to do with my time."

He takes another step forward, closing the gap between us. "I *had* a girlfriend. We broke up two weeks ago. Not long before I met you, actually. I hadn't told my family before tonight."

It's a good thing I'm not holding the barbell, because I absolutely would have dropped it on my toes. This is just too convenient. I shake my head in denial. "Scott, you don't have to make up some elaborate lie. Good night." I stubbornly turn to begin my next set of ten.

"I'm not lying." Scott rounds the rack, standing to the side, waiting silently. "Crystal," he says firmly as I hit my last rep.

"What? Just go away," I plead, setting the barbell back on the rack with a lazy *thud*, still unable to fathom why he didn't vanish into thin air the moment I let him off the hook.

"Is that really what you want?"

I meet his eyes for a long moment, trying to determine whether he's being genuine or not. I want to believe him. I want to treasure our kiss. I want to tell him, *No. Stay*, but I stop myself.

Whether he's being truthful or not, it doesn't change anything. He literally just broke up with his girlfriend. It takes me twice as long to mourn the end of a juicy season of *Game of Thrones*, let alone a human being I was romantically involved with. And it doesn't help that Diana is a literal Disney princess on ice. Judging from a quick social media stalk, she fully embodies the character of Belle from *Beauty and the Beast*. Aside from her tiny figure skater frame, she has Belle's soulful doll eyes, porcelain skin, and perfectly symmetrical heart-shaped face. What guy wouldn't rush back to a girl who looks like that if given the chance?

I don't want to be some fill-in, giving him a momentary reprieve from how heartbroken he actually is but isn't aware of yet.

I've only just emerged from Rebound Land with Neil—and I won't be returning.

"Yes, just go," I say, squinting in a sad attempt to blur him out of existence.

He sighs, raising his hands in surrender. "Okay. Fine. But I wasn't lying. I don't have a girlfriend. I wouldn't do something like that."

My expression remains unchanged. After a few beats of thick silence, he bows his head in defeat and walks out of the gym.

10:47 A.M.—INSTAGRAM POST: "SIZE POSITIVE CAMPAIGN—KNOWING YOUR WORTH" BY **CURVYFITNESSCRYSTAL**:

Okay, buckle in. This post is about to get serious.

Would you ever tell a friend: "You're disgusting," "You're ugly," "You're not smart enough," "You're not good enough for him"? My guess is NO. Unless you're a really shit friend, or a sociopath. If you'd never say these things to a friend, then why would you say them to yourself?

Your self-worth isn't just about your weight, or your fitness level. It's also about the health of your mind, soul, and heart. If there's one thing I've learned over my fitness journey, it's that negative attracts negative. Get that toxicity out of your life. And yes, that includes people. If you're toxic to yourself, you will attract toxic individuals into your life. Don't allow people to put you into positions that make you feel less than. Take control of your own

life and don't be afraid to put people in their place when
necessary.

So, do me a favor and write down a list of all the things you like
about yourself. Your bomb hair. Your amazing legs. Your sense of
humor. Anything. Stare at that list and memorize the shit out of it
like it's your elementary school speech. Reread it every day.

If you have one of those days where you like what you see in the
mirror, or you've had a kick-ass workout, or you're happy with the
way you've handled something, write it down and keep it for
whenever you have a negative thought. We tend to remember the
bad over the good.

Love,
Crystal

Comment by **Train.wreckk.girl**: I needed to hear this today. ♡
Thank you.

Comment by **Melanie_inthecity**: Yes!! Don't give people the ♡
power to dim your sparkle.

• • •

"WHAT HAPPENED WHEN you went back into Mamma Maria's?"
I ask Tara, finally emerging from my room after uncharacteristi-
cally sleeping in.

She's lying upside down on the couch, reading her latest paperback, a historical romance, from the look of the cover. She makes me wait a couple beats before looking up from her book, eyes widening at the sight of my hair. I closely resemble a mangled killer doll in need of a good exorcism and I don't want to talk about it.

"Mom, Dad, and Grandma were worried, wondering what happened. I told them you were upset because Scott was a dick," she explains.

"Okay . . ." I gesture for her to continue as I perch on the edge of the couch.

"I think Scott overheard, because he awkwardly came up to me after. I was telling him about my New York Public Library disaster and his eyes glazed over one minute in—and you know that's a damn good story," she adds defensively. "I thought he was just an awko-taco, eyes darting around, looking all sad. Turns out, he was concerned about you. He wanted to know why you left. I figured you should be the one to explain it to him, so I just said *Ask her yourself* and left it at that. Then Nathan, the waiter, discreetly left his number on a napkin on my plate. I took it. I figure if I'm still single in ten years, I'll text him."

"You won't be single in ten years," I reassure her, collapsing back into the couch, momentarily glancing at the random Instagram no-tifications popping up on my most recent post promoting my Size Positive campaign. "Scott showed up at the gym, by the way."

Her eyes widen. "Seriously?"

"He claimed he didn't have a girlfriend," I say through a snort. "Said they'd broken up. Conveniently before I met him when he stole my squat rack."

"Why would he say that if it wasn't true?" She stares at me, blinking.

"Because that's just what these guys do. They spin lie after lie. Aside from getting their dicks wet, all they care about is image."

"What if he's telling the truth? What if he's actually super into you?"

"It wouldn't matter. He's been a total douchebag to me at the gym. Even when he kissed me, it wasn't some romantic kiss. It was an *I want to screw you against a locker* type kiss." The latter half of my statement isn't true. But I refuse to remember how tenderly he looked at me. How gentle he was when he touched me.

She gives me a look of derision as she sets her book facedown on the coffee table. "I don't buy it. He went looking for you at the gym. That's pretty extreme. He isn't Neil, you know."

"Maybe he's just trying to clear his conscience," I continue, conveniently ignoring her. "He feels guilty for being a cheater. He's probably trying to cover his own ass. I doubt he wants his family to know he's a secret man-whore. And now that our families are related, he's probably doing damage control."

"He wouldn't do that if he was just trying to *clear his conscience.* I'd assume cheaters don't have a conscience."

I shake my head, doubtful. "People will go to great lengths to save face so they don't have to feel awkward. And even if he isn't lying, I'm not getting involved in post-breakup drama, especially with a dude who's now joining the family."

In addition to my declaration of no more hookups, I make a new vow to myself. I will never be anyone's rebound. Ever again.

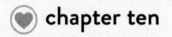 **chapter ten**

H E'S LOOKING AT you like a lost puppy," Mel whispers as
we head to the rower.

I spent the first half of our gym session filling her in on the
events of last night. Like Tara, Mel is also a traitor, it seems. She's
aboard the Scott Ritchie train with a nonrefundable ticket. In fact,
her enthusiasm for him heightened ten notches when he politely
returned her water bottle after she forgot it at the assisted pull-up
machine. I tried to tell her he doesn't deserve a cookie for merely
existing, but she dismissed me.

At no point in our entire workout has he stolen any of my machines. In fact, when it appeared we were headed for the same
cable machine, he stopped and veered left. He hasn't even given
me his usual disarming smirk from across the gym.

"Did you say he was a firefighter?" she asks in between rows.

"Apparently," I mutter, suppressing invading thoughts of him heroically dodging a perilous, fiery blaze to herd defenseless golden-doodle puppies to safety, while shirtless, of course.

She not-so-subtly ogles him from across the gym. "Don't you think he looks like that guy from that Nicholas Sparks movie . . . the one who married Miley Cyrus?"

"They're divorced now," I say, suddenly feeling defensive of Liam Hemsworth for absolutely no logical reason at all. "And you can put your pregnancy test away. I'm not dating Scott. But if you think he's so attractive, maybe you should date him—though I'd advise against it."

She snorts. "I have a boyfriend. Peter, remember? He looks like Henry Golding. That's enough handsome for me."

I refrain from drooling at the thought. "Henry Golding, hashtag too beautiful for this world."

We giggle, and I pretend not to admire Scott's endurance from afar as he does what looks to be a painful number of cleans and presses.

When Mel's gaze follows mine, I avert my stare and clap toward the rower. "You're doing amazing. A couple hundred more meters and you'll be free."

"I think you should just see what he's about. Rebound or not. Use his body for sex, even," she suggests, completely disregarding what I've just said.

My neck prickles with heat at the mere mention of having sex with Scott. If our locker make-out was any indication of how incredible it would be, I would probably be ruined for life. "I'm not about *the other woman* life, thanks."

As Mel finishes her last few meters, I accidentally meet Scott's eyes as he takes a break. My cheeks flush instantly at his kind smile.

This time, it isn't that cocky grin. It appears genuine. It screams *I'm sorry.*

What a mess I've made. Why hasn't modern science cracked time travel yet? I'm desperate to launch myself back in time so I can avoid our hot-and-heavy make-out. I hate the awkwardness. In fact, I'd take the petty rivalry any day over this.

Making a concerted effort to ignore his entire being, I keep my eyes locked forward as Mel and I head for the exit. Before I go through the turnstile, footsteps jog up behind us.

It's Scott, looking no worse for wear after an intense CrossFit circuit. "Crystal? Can we talk before you go?"

Mel gives me a sly look and a rushed wave. "Later, girl," she calls over her shoulder, deserting me in the sun-filled entranceway with Scott. I make a mental note to plot an extra-difficult workout for her next time as revenge for her callous abandonment in my time of need.

I turn to him, folding my arms across my chest, gym bag dangling from my shoulder.

He glances at the floor before bringing his gorgeous eyes back to mine. The sunlight illuminates the gold flecks among the dense green. "What's it going to take for you to accept my apology?"

"I accept your apology. Happy?" I say robotically, purely to get him off my back. I have more important shit to do today than stand here and argue with him.

He blinks down at me. "Really? Because you're looking at me like you want to castrate me with a butter knife."

"Maybe you deserve harsh punishment." I let those words linger a few moments before he swallows, as if fearing for his life. "And just because I might accept your apology doesn't mean your girlfriend should," I add.

He sighs, averting his gaze to the ceiling, as if praying to the gods above for assistance. "I don't know how to prove to you I don't have a girlfriend."

I shrug, giving him nothing as another gym patron impatiently walks around us, shooting us a cross-eyed glare as if we've single-handedly inconvenienced his day. We inch to the left so we're no longer blocking the entire entrance.

Scott runs his hand across the back of his neck. "Look, why don't you just ask Flo? I told my grandpa about my breakup last night. I wouldn't lie to him."

I give him a bored stare before turning for the exit. "Maybe I will."

• • •

GRANDMA FLO HAS always been a hoarder. She isn't as extreme as some of those people on that TLC show with rotting garbage and dead cat carcasses among stacks of newspapers from 1978, but it's still worth an intervention.

There are at least fifty editions of *Oprah* magazine under her side table, along with endless baskets overflowing with yarns of all colors and itchy-looking textures. She also has an expansive collection of those creepy Precious Moments figurines adorning the mantel above the fireplace. I stare down a particularly demonic-looking one masquerading as a delicate ballerina as I wait for her to bring me tea. It sits next to a dusty framed photo of Mom and Uncle Bill in their youth, botched haircuts and all.

There's a smaller picture frame to the left that houses my and Tara's wallet-size school portraits, side by side. Tara is twelve and is the spitting image of Dad, only with a delightful toothy grin and thick, sideswept bangs. Meanwhile I'm at peak awkward stage at ten, mid-blink, sporting thrice-layered assorted-color tank tops from Hollister. When asked why in God's name she'd display this photo of me, of all photos, her response is always something to the effect of "It captures your essence," and I'm left to question my entire life.

"Be careful, it's piping hot." She sets the mug over the coaster on the coffee table, littered with Joann Fabrics coupons.

"Thanks, Grandma." The floral couch squeaks as I lean forward to take the steaming mug. "So how are the wedding preparations coming along?"

She settles into her La-Z-Boy, crochet slippers pointed to the ceiling. "Most of the big details are already set. Tara is organized as all get-out. There are just some small things, like the centerpieces, that need sorting."

I give her an uncomfortable nod after blowing on the scorching tea. Aside from clearing up the Scott conversation, I'm desperate to ask whether she and Martin were together before Grandpa died. But there is no tactful way to go about it.

"I'm surprised you decided to go for such a big wedding," I say instead.

She shrugs, tugging at her blouse. "Grandpa and I never really had a wedding. He didn't care about the glitz and the glam. You know how he was. Wasn't much for being the center of attention." She's right. Grandpa didn't even like being photographed, let alone having an entire day all about him. "So anyway, when it came to a wedding, he decided it would be better if we just put the money toward a house. So that's what we did."

"Were you okay with that?"

"I kind of had to be. It was his money," she says matter-of-factly. She likes to remind me of the old-school ways. As if it's the way things should be.

Grandma was a stay-at-home mom, while Grandpa worked in the financial district, controlling the funds exclusively. Grandma didn't even own a purse until he passed away.

"So does Martin want a grand wedding too?"

"He didn't have much of a first wedding either. He and Sheila eloped. In Vegas, if you can imagine. I suppose we both wanted it. And it helps Tara out so she doesn't have to lose her deposits." Her voice trails as she absentmindedly fidgets with the hem of her blouse. "Do you think it's crazy? Me getting married at seventy-seven?"

When she puts it that way, it's hard to say no. Despite my suspicions about the overlap between Martin and Grandpa, it suddenly seems wrong to call her out on it. Realistically, I want her to be happy and guilt-free, regardless of the past.

I shake my head, forcing a smile. "No. I think it's great. Are you guys going to move in together?"

"Eventually. But we're having a heck of a time deciding on where. I don't want to move out of this house, and the stubborn man doesn't want to move from his. He suggested downsizing, but . . ." She casts a sad gaze around her cluttered living room. "I just don't know about that."

I cringe at the inevitable task of sorting through all of this junk. God knows what creatures we'll unearth. "I'm sure you'll figure it out before the wedding. There's no rush."

"So," she says, taking a sip of her own tea, eyes glinting. "What did you think of Scotty?"

My shoulders fall with relief. I'm thankful I didn't have to bring it up. "I actually wanted to talk to you about him. But first, I wanted to apologize for leaving your dinner so early. I wasn't feeling well."

She nods, as if she already knew. "No sweat, dear."

There's a pregnant pause before I come out with it. "Does Scott have a girlfriend?"

The corners of her lips curl upward, amused. "Why? Do you fancy him?" Before I can even respond with an exaggerated *No*, she continues on. "I thought he'd be perfect for Tara. But she might be better off with someone who will dote on her and shower her with his undivided attention. Scott is too busy for that. But *you*—oh, I could see him with you. Imagine your children!" She hoots and clasps her hands together at the mere thought of us procreating.

My eyes widen and I lean back, away from her. "Anyway." I clear my throat, trying to steer her back to my original question. "I thought Martin said he had a girlfriend?"

"That's what everyone thought. But Scotty told him after dinner they'd recently parted ways. Something about the distance being too hard on them. Marty said he seemed down about it. Poor thing."

I'm rendered silent for a moment, clutching my mug. I'm relieved to find out Scott wasn't lying about being newly single. He's not a cheater after all. But it still doesn't change the fact that he's just gotten out of a relationship and he's "down" about it.

"But," Grandma continues, "if you ask me, he has nothing to worry about. He won't stay single for long. He's quite the catch. All-

American. Handsome. Nice to Martin. Family oriented. Heroic. Works a lot though . . . but that means he'd be a good provider. What if I set something up? Are you free tomorrow night?"

"Thanks, Grandma. But I don't know if he's *my* type." I conveniently leave out that we're gym nemeses and we loathe each other.

"What's that, dear? You're mumbling." She holds her hand to her ear theatrically.

"I don't think he's my type," I repeat.

She gives me a knowing once-over, as if I've just said something completely ludicrous. "Oh, honey. He's *everyone's* type. And you're getting on in age, you know."

Grandma Flo is a product of the fifties, not that it's an excuse to be ignorant. But she still firmly believes women should be married in their twenties. Being in your late twenties and unmarried is bordering on spinster status, as per her humble opinion.

"Unless you're still interested in being one of those career types. I can really picture that for you," she says, still unable to grasp the concept that women can balance both family and career.

I pretend to check my phone, ignoring the fact that my own grandmother envisions me dying alone. "I have to get back for a virtual meeting with my client," I lie. "But I'll see you tomorrow for your bloodwork appointment?" I'm the one who takes Flo to all her various appointments, given I have the most flexible schedule in the family.

She nods, watching me as I stand. "I'll be ready with bells on."

As I sit in her driveway behind the steering wheel, I find myself back on Scott's Instagram page. Maybe I owe him an apology. It's the least I can do for giving him a hard time and wrongfully accusing him of philandering.

CURVYFITNESSCRYSTAL

You were right. Sorry for not believing you.

By the time I pull into the parking garage of my apartment building, Scott has responded.

RITCHIE_SCOTTY7

You talked to Flo?

CURVYFITNESSCRYSTAL

I did. She confirmed your singleness.

RITCHIE_SCOTTY7

Does that mean you no longer wish death upon me?

CURVYFITNESSCRYSTAL

To be determined.

RITCHIE_SCOTTY7

So when are you taking me on a hot date?

I scoff when I read his text. What is it with guys and their inability to stay single?

You've only been single for a little over two weeks. You're probably still crying into your pillow over her, I want to type in all caps, bold and underlined. But instead of a dramatic response, I give myself a minute to calm down.

CURVYFITNESSCRYSTAL

Never.

RITCHIE_SCOTTY7

Can I ask why not?

I'm tempted to just tell it like it is: it's too soon after his breakup. But I don't. He is Squat Rack Thief, after all. I take pleasure in making him squirm.

CURVYFITNESSCRYSTAL

Because.

RITCHIE_SCOTTY7

"Because" isn't an acceptable response.

CURVYFITNESSCRYSTAL

I'm allowed to turn you down without an excuse.

RITCHIE_SCOTTY7

That's true. But I'm pretty sure you kind of like me. You even pretended your phone was missing so you could attack me in the changing room.

CURVYFITNESSCRYSTAL

🙄 You're so full of yourself. That's one reason I can't go out with you.

RITCHIE_SCOTTY7

One reason? There are more?

I smile, knowing I've intrigued him.

CURVYFITNESSCRYSTAL

Yes.

RITCHIE_SCOTTY7

Care to share?

CURVYFITNESSCRYSTAL

Stand by, this might take a while to type.

RITCHIE_SCOTTY7

Lol . . . Eagerly awaiting your novel.

CURVYFITNESSCRYSTAL

Aside from reason 1—the fact that your ego is the size of Boston . . .

2) We go to the same gym and our families are joining. What if things didn't work out? We'd have to see each other. It would be weird and awkward for everyone involved.

3) I can only be wooed with classic joke pickup lines. You've failed to give me one I can't refuse.

4) I'm not looking to be someone's rebound.

RITCHIE_SCOTTY7

1) I'm really not conceited. It's all an act. Part of my façade. But don't tell anyone.

2) It's only a date. Not a marriage proposal. If the date doesn't go well, we can just be friends like mature adults.

3) Just wait for it.

RITCHIE_SCOTTY7

Do you like raisins? How do you feel about dates?

CURVYFITNESSCRYSTAL

RITCHIE_SCOTTY7

Oh, come on. That's a great one.

I can't help but notice he still hasn't addressed reason number four. The glaring reason. The real one that's authentically keeping me from taking him up on his offer.

CURVYFITNESSCRYSTAL

It's not the worst I've ever heard in the history of awful pickup lines.

RITCHIE_SCOTTY7

Alright. Challenge accepted.

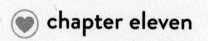 **chapter eleven**

9:34 A.M.—INSTAGRAM POST: "SIZE POSITIVE
CAMPAIGN—MYTHS ABOUT BEING CURVY" BY
CURVYFITNESSCRYSTAL:

Nothing grinds my gears more than the stigma against people who
are curvy. Here are a few myths I'd like to address.

1) Curvy people must be unhealthy—Even health professionals
get this one wrong. I can't tell you how many times doctors have
blamed an injury on my weight, even though my twisted ankle had
literally nothing to do with it. Did you know you can have a BMI
in the "healthy" weight range and still be unhealthy af? My sister
(sorry, Tara) is a size six and her personal diet consists solely of
potato chips.

2) Curvy people are lazy and unmotivated—Whether someone is "lazy" and "unmotivated" has nothing to do with size. Anyone, regardless of size, can struggle with binge eating or could be going through something that causes them to lose the motivation to live a healthy lifestyle.

3) Curvy people are sad, lonely, and have low self-esteem—Sorry, but size doesn't define who we are. I don't live my life thinking about my weight all the time. People of all sizes have varying degrees of confidence. Look at my girl Lizzo.

4) Curvy people only exercise to lose weight—I hold this one near and dear to my heart. Just because you see me in the gym doesn't mean I'm there to burn a calorie deficit and lose weight (and no, I'm not saying that shouldn't be someone's goal). But I personally hit the gym to lift heavy things. Period.

Comment by **trainerrachel_1990**: PREACH GIRL 🙌 ♡

Comment by **rileyhenderson**: Agreed. I get weird looks at the ♡ gym and people always offer to help me, assuming I can't do things because I'm fat.

Comment by **Cafi80**: Your platform is totally great! Don't ♡ get me wrong! But I feel like it's targeting us skinny girls. I work so hard to achieve my abs and my body . . . I work harder than people who are overweight, because I'm seeing results and obviously others aren't. I feel like your platform discounts all my discipline.

Comment by **Arthur.Dilstraa**: lmao kk keep kidding urself ♡

• • •

I STUDY THE generic fruit bowl painting above Grandma Flo's head. It's bland, understated, and uncontroversial, the ideal décor for a medical clinic where emotions tend to run high.

Case in point: we just witnessed a scary lady with a bleached blond pixie cut verbally assault the receptionist for not having her updated home address in the system.

"Grandma, are you sure you don't need me to drive you home after this?"

Grandma Flo waves me off, casting a disapproving stare at Pixie Woman, who is now mumbling vague threats under her breath as she stomps to a seat across from us. "Oh, honey, I'm fine. Martin is picking me up," she says flippantly, as if this had been the plan all along.

Pixie Woman glares at us, lips pursed. "This place is a zoo. Run by incompetent floozies." She's hoping Grandma and I will join her on the soapbox and air our grievances too.

I flash her a sympathetic smile of solidarity in an effort to ensure our safety. Her scowl and twitchy eye tell me she's a loose cannon, ready to cause bodily harm to anyone who dares step in her way. I turn back to Grandma. "I really don't mind taking you home. It would save Martin the trip."

She shakes her head again, catching the September 2019 edition of *Oprah* magazine before it slips off her lap. "He wants to bring me to the craft store afterward to pick up that wool—"

The little bell hanging above the entrance behind us chimes, alerting the receptionist that someone has entered. The scowl all but disappears from Pixie Woman's face. When I dare look at who has turned her into a swooning teenage girl at a One Direction concert, I meet a familiar pair of green eyes.

"Oh. Hey, Crystal." Scott waves. He's wearing a casual navy-blue T-shirt that reads *Boston Fire Department* in bold letters. His jeans hug him so perfectly that I'm convinced mere mortal eyes aren't worthy of this view.

Grandma Flo beams. If I didn't already know she was seventy-seven years old, I wouldn't believe it after witnessing her spring out of her seat like a jack-in-the-box to pull him into the throes of her embrace. I can't help but smile at how massive he is compared to her tiny five-foot-two frame. "Scotty, thank you so much for coming."

"What are you doing here?" I ask, casting an accusatory glare at a mischievous-looking Flo.

Scott's gaze flickers to Grandma Flo as he unknowingly sits next to Pixie Woman, who is shamelessly gawking at him like he's a Magnum ice cream bar. "You called yesterday and said you'd need someone to take you home from the clinic."

"Oh, did I?" Grandma Flo places her palm on her cheek.

I nearly crack my neck whipping my head in her direction. "I thought Martin was picking you up?"

She shrugs, unable to stop grinning. Her acting skills are appalling. "You know me, I get a little mixed up in my old age," she says, as if she isn't of sound mind and doesn't know the answers to eighty percent of the clues on *Jeopardy!*

"Florence McCarthy," Brandy, the nurse, calls from the doorway leading to the examination rooms.

Grandma clasps her hands and stands, gleefully exiting the awkward situation that is entirely of her own making.

I roll my eyes, making a concerted effort not to give her a piece of my mind ten seconds before she's about to undergo a cholesterol and heart test. "Want me to come in with you?"

She nods, glancing at a very confused Scott. "Both of you should come. It could take a while."

The nurse leads us down the stark white hallway into an equally sterile examination room.

I can tell by the furrow of Scott's brow that he hadn't the slightest idea about this little "run-in" Grandma Flo orchestrated. I feel guilty she's wasted his time. I wonder if he's had to rearrange his entire schedule to drive in from downtown. It also feels awkward, given I turned him down via text only yesterday.

Brandy gets Grandma set up in the chair and begins to roll up her sleeve. "Remember what I told you last time? We're going to do some routine bloodwork to check those cholesterol levels."

Scott and I stand near the wall side by side as Grandma and Brandy chat about this morning's episode of *Live with Kelly and Ryan*. When his arm nearly grazes mine, I internally scream, unable to still my fidgeting. I keep bouncing back and forth between adjusting my shirt and my hair, and picking my nails to stubs, all of which do little to dull my anxiety. Must he stand so close to me? Is personal space a foreign concept to him?

My body is in turmoil, unable to decide what it wants to do. Part of me is dying to get half an inch closer, to feel even just a fraction of the electricity of our changing room encounter. But I'm still bothered. Just because Scott Ritchie turned out not to be a vicious cheater doesn't take away the fact that I don't do hookups anymore, especially not with my gym nemesis—a guy who waltzes around the gym like he's the second coming of Christ himself. That kind of arrogance doesn't sit well with me.

"I can't believe her," I mutter in displeasure.

Scott chuckles, arms folded against his broad chest. "She thinks she's so smooth."

"Feel free to leave if you want. I can just bring her home."

He shakes his head, meeting my gaze. "Nah, I'm good."

"Well, there's no point in both of us hanging around." Realistically, him leaving is better for the both of us, as well as the state of my makeup, which is melting off my face like the Wicked Witch of the West when doused with water.

His expression remains unbothered. In fact, his lips are curled up ever so slightly. I think he might be enjoying this. That makes one of us, at least. I seriously wish I'd doubled up on the deodorant this morning. I try to sneak a look at my armpits, but I'm directly in Scott's peripherals. There's no way to do this discreetly.

We're standing in identical crossed-arm poses, listening to Grandma rattle off her diet and exercise routine over the past month.

Scott's easy smile doesn't leave his face. Until Brandy brings out the needles. When she wraps the little rubber band just above Grandma's elbow, Scott sucks in a deep breath, loud enough for me to hear. As Brandy raises the needle, he immediately sways, turning to face me. His complexion has turned unusually pale. In fact, it's ghostly white.

"You alright?" I ask, elbowing him in the ribs.

He nods, averting his gaze upward as she begins to insert the needle. "I, uh, just really hate needles."

I'm silent for a moment as I register this completely unexpected fact. "Scott Ritchie has a fear of needles?"

He nods, eyes still fixed on the ceiling, his Adam's apple bobbing.

"Really?" I ask, expecting him to snap out of it and admit he's joking.

When he accidentally catches sight of the second needle, he nearly gags.

"Scott, dear, do you need to leave the room?" Grandma asks from the chair.

He shakes his head, reaching for the nearby sink, gripping the edge. "Nope. I'm good," he says through clenched teeth.

"What is it about needles you don't like?" I ask.

He contorts his face, as if I've just asked an outrageous question, like why would one dislike diarrhea, or STDs? "They hurt."

"Says the guy who fights fires."

He hunches his shoulders. "I wear fireproof gear."

I eye him for a moment, unconvinced that fighting fires and needles are remotely comparable. "I think you should go sit in the waiting room."

Grandma Flo nods. "Yes, why don't you go with him, Crystal? Make sure he's okay."

I may not like Scott as a human, but I don't want him passing out in public over a tiny needle. I roll my eyes as I lead him out of the examination room.

He takes a deep breath when we reach the relative serenity of the waiting area. I direct him to a chair out of Pixie Woman's line of sight. She leans around the drywall column to catch another thirsty glimpse of Scott. He plunks into the chair, covering his eyes with his hand, his long legs outstretched.

I bend forward in front of him to examine his face. It's still pale. "I'll be right back."

Ronnie, the receptionist, glances up at me with a bored stare, as if people nearly passing out in the office is just a typical day, which it probably is. "Can I help you?"

"Do you guys have anything for grown men who feel faint? Something sugary?"

She gives me a silent nod and wheels her chair backward. Without even standing, she reaches into the mini fridge and produces a juice box.

"That's perfect. Thank you." I gratefully pluck the tiny box from her limp hand.

I haven't physically held a juice box since sixth grade, before it became wildly lame to bring a packed lunch to school. I'm amazed at how tiny they are.

"Here, this might make you feel better." I insert the tiny straw, tossing the plastic on the side table for now.

He opens his eyes, squinting. "Apple juice?"

"It'll help. Shut up and drink it."

He complies, drinking quietly from the straw. I'll admit, watching a six-foot-two alpha male fireman drink a children's juice box is strangely attractive. Why am I more attracted to him when he's vulnerable and in need of medical attention? I push that thought aside. It's a deeper issue for another time.

Within three sips, he finishes it to the last drop. "Thanks, Crystal." He manages a weak smile.

"Do needles really affect you that much?"

He places his fingers over the bridge of his nose. "Yup. I avoid them. At all costs."

"Is it the blood you don't like?"

"No. I'm fine with blood. It's the needle itself."

"You're telling me you never get the flu shot? You'd prefer worshipping the porcelain God, puking your brains out, over a measly needle?"

He nods.

I pull back from him dramatically, giving him a funny stare. "You're an anti-vaxxer, aren't you?" I whisper conspiratorially.

His color is back now. He gives me a half smile, which makes my heart flutter. "Definitely not. I believe in modern medicine. I just really hate needles."

"Never would have expected that."

"See? I come full of surprises." He holds me captive with his dimples.

I don't know if it's the juice box, or the fact that he's terrified of needles like a young child, but I'm marginally charmed.

He waves a hand toward me. "It's only fair that you tell me something you hate."

"When people don't clean the machines at the gym," I say pointedly.

He shakes his head, unsatisfied. "Nope. Doesn't count. I already knew that."

I sigh, succumbing to the temptation of learning more about him. "One for one?"

"Sure."

"Okay . . . I also hate restaurants with laminated menus. They're always sticky and it freaks me out."

He runs a hand along his chin in deep thought. "Related, I hate bumper stickers."

"The last sip in a water bottle."

"When I'm trying to send someone a GIF with an accompanying message and they send a message before the GIF goes through and it's all out of order."

I can't help but cackle at that one. "Facebook friend suggestions. Like, no, ex-boyfriend's new girlfriend. I do not want to be friends."

"People who floor it at green lights. What's the rush?"

I interrupt our game, nodding toward his well-fitted T-shirt. "Did you come here straight from work?"

"Nope. Got the day off. I usually work three or four twelve-hour shifts and then get the rest of the days off."

I cringe, feeling guilty yet again that Grandma schemed to get him here on one of his days off.

"What do you do when you aren't fighting fires?"

He runs his hand over his jaw. "I mostly spend some quality time with my dog, Albus, get my groceries, go to the gym, catch the odd game with friends. You?"

"That sounds awfully adult." I silently appreciate the simplicity of his answer while purposely not reciprocating my response.

He gives me an easy smile. "I'm a thirty-year-old man. I'd hope so."

"How long have you been at the fire department?"

"You're suddenly very interested in my life."

I make a concerted effort to flatten what I assume is a border-line manic grin. "No. I'm not. Just trying to learn your weaknesses so I can exploit you."

He shrugs. "Fair enough. I've been with the fire department since after college. I was lucky and got in pretty much right away."

"Did you always want to be a firefighter?"

He crushes the juice box in his fist and closes his left eye, aiming it into the trash can across the room. It lands with a perfect *clunk*. He glances at me triumphantly. "My grandpa always talked about it, so it was in the back of my mind. But I didn't think about it seriously until high school."

I cast a stealth glance at his biceps, unable to stop the question from rolling off my tongue. "Have you ever been in one of those naked first responder calendars?"

The corners of his lips turn up. "Why? Want a copy for your wall?"

"Don't flatter yourself," I scoff, refraining from requesting this potential calendar enlarged in poster size.

Before I break down and inquire, Grandma Flo comes striding through the lobby, her monstrous red purse draped over her elbow. Her gaze narrows to Scott. "Scotty, are you alright?"

He stands, as good as new again. "Yup. Nurse Crystal healed me." He flashes me a wink.

"I gave him a juice box from reception," I explain, standing to follow them toward the exit.

She pats him on the bicep affectionately as he graciously holds the door open for her. "I'm terribly sorry to have troubled you,

Scotty. I get all mixed up with the plans sometimes with so many appointments, you know? But I'm perfectly fine to have Crystal bring me home."

I expect him to be visibly annoyed that he's just wasted an hour of his time, was presented with his phobia, and nearly fainted in the process. But he doesn't appear rattled. When he gives her an easy smile, I wonder if anything truly fazes him. "No worries, Flo. You can always call if you need me."

We're on the sidewalk outside the clinic. Scott looks frustratingly relaxed, in no rush to go anywhere. As the two of them make small talk about the weather, all I can think about is that calendar. Is he in one or not? I make a mental note to google it the moment I'm in private. And then I chide myself. *Stop thinking about how his eyes look like blades of grass on a summer day. Or better yet, his cut biceps. It's irrelevant. All of it.*

Scott is arrogant. Impossibly charming without being smarmy. Probably a player who'll go back to his ex after getting what he wants from me. Exactly the kind of guy I don't want to touch with a ten-foot pole.

"Well, tell Gramps I say hi," he says to Grandma Flo, hands in his pockets as we head toward my car.

I'm walking at a brisk pace compared to a meandering Grandma Flo because I've got shit to do today, like filming a nutrition Q&A. I don't have time to dillydally making forced conversation with my enemy in a parking lot.

"Oh, that's right. He wanted me to remind you to come over for the Blackhawks versus the Bruins next week. If you're off," Grandma tells him.

"I'll be there." He dips his chin as she gets in the car.

I twist my keys around my fingers before opening the driver's side door. "You're a Blackhawks fan?"

"Is there any other way to live?" he deadpans.

"Reason number five," I mutter.

A pleased look overcomes him. "I find it fascinating that not one of those five reasons actually includes not being interested in me. So far, all I'm hearing are weak excuses."

I try my hardest to maintain a chill façade. So much so that I'm left with absolutely zero chill on the inside. I hate myself for getting flustered over him and his persistence. His cockiness is growing old. Our eyes lock and I clear my throat. "Fine. Reason number six: I'm not interested in you."

"If that were true, I'd accept it. But I'm not convinced." *That makes two of us.* He searches my face for a moment, giving me a chance to backpedal.

"Don't hold your breath, Scott. I don't date guys like you. Period."

He lets out a strangled laugh, glancing at a car passing by. "But you'll accost me in changing rooms, though, right?"

I freeze, anger spiking. It's bad enough he won't let this go, but to say it in front of my conservative grandma? I scowl and shut the car door so Grandma Flo can't hear us. "We aren't talking about that. Stop bringing it up."

"Are we just acting like it didn't happen?"

It's not necessarily that I want to act like it didn't happen. But talking about it seriously affects my resolve. If I'm going to survive the four months until Flo and Martin's nuptials without breaking my vow to myself and diving headfirst into trouble, I need to squash this sexual energy between us, and quick. "Yes. We are. As far as I'm concerned, it didn't happen at all."

He snaps his head back, his jaw tensing. "Alright. Fine."

"Fine."

He shakes his head, unable to leave it. "I am curious, though. You made such a big deal over me having a girlfriend, which means you care on some level. Am I wrong?"

He may not be a cheater, but it certainly doesn't exclude him from being a player. Scott's flirting is so natural, it must be the result of ample practice. And realistically, he has every right. He's a single guy. He can do what he wants. But nothing positive can come out of this for me except inevitable tears and heartbreak. Just like with Neil.

I level him with a hard gaze. It's time to drop the truth bomb. "Scott, you're arrogant. You're used to getting what you want in life because you're hot and you know it. And the only reason you're getting rattled right now is because I'm telling you *no* and you don't wanna hear it. Either that or you're too much of a Neanderthal to take the hint."

His jaw is slack in bewilderment, as if I've said something insane. "Is that what you really think?"

"My opinion hasn't changed in the last three seconds." I struggle to spit those words out, because I remember how he's petrified of needles like a child, and how he was kind enough to pick up my grandmother from her appointment on his day off. Unfortunately, all of that is clouded by his cockiness.

He scoffs, hands on hips, stance wide. "It's funny . . . you're making snap judgments about me when you preach this message of self-love and no stereotypes. You're a hypocrite, Crystal."

I flinch at his words. He isn't wrong. But I can't forget his asshole attitude when he refused to leave my squat rack, among his series of affronts against me. It's not my fault his personality happens to match the stereotype.

He starts stomping off, but after a couple angry strides, he pivots. "And by the way, you can rest easy knowing I'm not pursuing you. My Neanderthal brain got the hint. Loud and clear."

• • •

GRANDMA FLO IS stark silent when I haul ass into the car and slam the door. She's definitely overheard our argument through the window. She knows something happened between Scott and me, and I'm embarrassed. I brace for a lecture on the drive back, but she doesn't say a word about it. Instead, she prattles on about her wedding plans, which include having Tara and me as her bridesmaids. Apparently, I still get the pleasure of donning the ill-fitting peach maid of honor dress I purchased for Tara's wedding. Lucky me.

"Thanks for the ride, dear," she says when we reach her driveway. "Remind me, next time you come in, I need help with my iPad. I can't figure out how to turn off those darn *dings* every time I get a message. Scares the jeepers out of me every time."

I muster a fake smile. "Sounds good."

Just as she's about to close the passenger door and wave me off, she pops her head back in. "You know, you weren't very nice to poor Scotty in the parking lot."

And there it is. "He's not always nice to me either."

Her glare is terrifying enough to scare a hardened criminal into submission. "That's not an excuse."

"But—"

"Apologize to him, Crystal."

chapter twelve

IT'S BEEN THREE days since my unintended confrontation with Scott, and despite repeated orders from Grandma Flo, I have yet to apologize. In fact, I'm all-out avoiding the gym during the times I know he might be there—eight in the morning or after six in the evening—depending on whether he's working days or nights.

With each passing day, the guilt of my truth bomb sets in. I shouldn't have said what I said, even if there was a kernel of truth to it. Scott may be a cocky, infuriating human, but he didn't deserve a verbal assault, nor did he deserve to be called a Neanderthal.

I've thought at length about texting him to make things right, but I don't because, apparently, I'm an emotionally inept individual. Telling him I'm sorry would be the right thing to do, but my pride can't take it. I already falsely accused him of unhygienic gym practices *and* adultery. Now I've preemptively struck once again.

There's no way he'll accept some flimsy apology, which is why I make the wise decision to leave it be.

It's better this way, I think to myself as I journey to meet Grandma Flo at her florist appointment. Tara was supposed to go, but she got called into work.

When I pull into the parking lot at the dodgy strip mall that houses the florist, Grandma Flo waves manically from the sidewalk, like a kidnapping victim flapping their arms for help on the side of a remote highway after making a daring escape. She crowds me as I get out of the car, ready to pull me into a hug, as if we didn't just see each other a few days ago.

"Sorry I'm late," I say. "A virtual session with a client went a little longer than expected." I leave out the fact that I left in such a frenzy, I forgot to put on a bra. I realized this when I zoomed over a speed bump and my double D boobs practically hit the sunroof. It occurred to me that I could carry on braless, but there's no taming them in a thin tank top. In the absence of underwire support, there's a high risk of a nip slip if I bend a certain way. Grandma Flo would condemn me until the end of time, so I doubled back.

"No matter. My appointment is over." She waves a vague hand and takes the liberty of hiking my tank top to my chin to cover my cleavage. She smiles, satisfied I no longer look like a jezebel.

I knit my brow, checking the time on my phone. "I'm only ten minutes late. Did they take you early?"

She gives me a brief nod. "I was thinking we could do something fun. Spend some quality time together." She gestures like Vanna White to the unit next to the florist. The black sign reads *Battle Axe* in a bold, white, graffiti-esque font.

"Grandma, that's an axe-throwing establishment." I feel the need to clarify, because there's no way my crochet-queen grandmother is interested in axe throwing, the very same activity undertaken by people who exclusively wear plaid and think they're hard-core.

"It's on my bucket list," she informs me casually, as if it's a perfectly normal activity for frail, elderly women. She proceeds to tug at my arm, yanking me toward the door with more force than expected.

When the door opens, the scent of cedar, freshly churned dirt, and testosterone slaps me in the face. A massive lumbersexual dude sporting a man-bun and a predictable flannel shirt gives us an inviting wave from behind an expansive wooden desk. There are no words exchanged between him and Grandma. They just smile at each other conspiratorially, igniting my suspicion.

I eye him sideways as he points to a sinister, all-black hallway to the left. He motions for us to follow him. "You're all set up in lane two," he tells Grandma Flo.

"Excuse me?" I cast an accusatory glare at her as we emerge into a large, open room.

There are ten spaces, separated by wire fences. Each section contains its own wooden bull's-eye and platform. The space on the far right is occupied by a group of hipster college-age guys. They're definitely *not* here with their grandmas.

Everything in here is either wood, plaid, or stuffed (there are two taxidermied deer heads mounted on each far wall). This is so not my scene. Nor is it Grandma Flo's.

Why would she go to the effort of pre-planning this, pretending it was an impromptu decision?

And that's when I hear it. Two boisterous voices. Two men emerge from what appears to be a hallway leading to the restrooms.

Scott and Martin.

• • •

I'VE BEEN AMBUSHED. No wonder I have trust issues.

Martin plows forward to fold me into a hearty embrace. He smells like a library, old paper and smoky mahogany. Through my shock, I return his hug. It's everything a typical grandpa hug should be, wholehearted and reassuring.

Or it would be, if Scott wasn't serving me menacing looks from behind Martin's shoulder. Based on the fact that he's grimacing at me as if I'm a vile presence, suffice to say that he's not over our last encounter.

"Hi," I squeak, breaking my hug with Martin.

There's a pause as Scott and I size each other up. My tenacity lasts all of ten seconds before I look away like a weakling. I'm not up for the challenge. In fact, I'm about to blurt out an apology for the emotional turmoil he may or may not be suffering from my wrath, until I zero in on his hand.

He's wielding an axe. When his gaze narrows to my face, I'm convinced he's about to launch it smack-dab into the center of my forehead. He's certainly calculating how much force he'll require for a clean shot, or plotting something equally sinister. He's practically Jack Nicholson in *The Shining*.

Without so much as a greeting, he turns his shoulder and stomps into the cage. Grandma Flo and Martin don't acknowledge the obvious tension between us. They're too busy observing with bated breath as Saint Scott saunters onto the platform. He wastes no time before expertly overhand-pitching the axe toward the target with one hand. It pierces the center of the bull's-eye so smoothly, it almost looks effortless.

As the grandparents clap and holler, fervently praising Scott's superhuman athletic ability, I gulp. I must keep watch. From all angles. He's liable to murder me in cold blood. This seems like the perfect place to do it. It would be easy enough to fake a slip of hand and pretend it was nothing but a tragic, bloody accident.

"Spend a lot of time practicing?" It's my half-assed attempt to emit a neutral vibe as he waltzes past me, tossing another axe in the air.

He catches it like it's a baseball and not a bladed weapon. He's seemingly pleased with himself for demonstrating his precise assassin skills. When he comes face-to-face with me, the smirk drops, replaced by pure animosity. "Yup. In between being a womanizer and a Neanderthal." His tone is casual enough so as not to alarm our grandparents. It just comes off like an oddly placed joke. He turns his gaze to Grandma, gently handing her the axe.

Surprisingly, she's better at this than I would have expected for a woman wearing extra-wide, orthopedic loafers. On her third try, she manages to sink the axe into the wood, despite not hitting the target.

After congratulating his bride-to-be, Martin claps me on the back, giving me a gentle push forward. "Crystal, you need to give this a whirl. It's a good stress reliever." *I bet it is. For crazed lunatics.*

Scott snorts. "Yeah, *Crystal.* Why don't you come relieve all that pent-up anger? It might even help with those aggressive mood swings." He holds me captive with his stare as he dislodges Grandma Flo's axe from the target.

"Uh, it's fine. I'm fine right here. Martin, you go first," I stammer, sweat pooling at the base of my back.

"I insist. Ladies first." Martin kindly steps aside, ushering me toward Scott.

Scott holds out the axe, handle first.

I swallow a golf ball–size lump in my throat, eyeing him with trepidation. I take it hesitantly. It's lighter than it looks. "Do the staff not give any safety demos?" I ask, delaying.

Grandma Flo nods. "They did. Before you arrived. But it's okay. Scotty will show you the proper form."

Scott flashes her a painfully fake smile, clearly disturbed by the prospect of being within a three-foot radius of me.

"I'm good." I nervous-cough, wobbling as I hop onto the platform. I'm naturally competitive. I can't fail and show weakness, especially after Scott's show-off performance and covert jabs. Here goes nothing. I close my left eye, swinging the axe over my head.

"Holy shit!" Scott's strong grip catches my hands a millisecond before the axe is released, rudely prying the handle from my fingers without an ounce of delicacy. His eyes are wide, like those of an antisocial loner living off-grid in a one-bedroom cabin with no electricity.

I whip around. "Dude, what's your deal?"

He holds the axe out of reach. "Your form was all wrong. Are you trying to kill someone?"

I roll my eyes in offense, making a dramatic show of suffering. "Just because I'm a woman doesn't mean I'm automatically an uncontrollable liability with a weapon. I can handle myself, you know. I played tennis in high school," I add, knowing damn well tennis and axe throwing are not remotely similar.

He doesn't respond. Instead, he gruffly clasps my shoulders, physically spinning me around to face the target. I have to admit, being manhandled is kind of hot. "What hand do you use?" he demands. His tone is glacial, contrasting the warmth of his chest as it grazes the width of my back.

Jesus. "Uh, I'm right-handed."

With his calloused fingers, he shoves the axe into my right hand from behind. He positions my palm on the base of the handle before folding my left hand over it to hug my grip. Then, he kicks my left foot out to line up with a black mark on the platform. "Now, when you let the axe go, do it at eye level. Not an inch higher or lower," he instructs as he guides my arms upward.

All I can do is nod. I'm surprised I'm even still breathing with his body practically enveloping me like this. I try to rid my mind of errant thoughts as I follow through in one smooth motion. The axe lands, sinking into the edge of the target.

I turn to thank Scott for his shockingly advantageous assistance, but he's no longer behind me. My first assumption is he's dramatically ducking for cover, but instead, he's smile-nodding in animated conversation with Grandma Flo as if I don't exist. The man can turn his charm on and off like a light switch.

We cycle through our turns for the next forty minutes. Scott nails practically every shot, as does Martin, who happily reminds us that firefighters wield axes as part of their equipment. It's an unfair advantage, as far as I'm concerned. Grandma Flo improves by the end of it, despite her concern she's thrown out her shoulder.

When our time is up, the four of us walk out in single file, spilling onto the blazingly hot sidewalk. "Wasn't this just the loveliest time?" Grandma Flo's gaze jumps back and forth between Scott and me hopefully.

Has she not noticed how we've avoided each other like the plague the entire time? Aside from when he so courteously helped me with my form.

"Yeah, it was fun," I say. Truthfully, axe throwing is kind of exhilarating. The satisfaction of hitting the target is addicting. And even though Martin regaled us with long-winded tales of yesteryear when he was a firefighter, I actually found myself amused by his stories.

"We'll catch you kids soon. Nice to see you, Crystal. And Scotty, tell your mother I said hi." Martin waves as he lumbers into the driver's seat of his Lincoln. As they back out of their parking spot, Scott walks off in silence, presumably to his car.

I stand there like an idiot, staring at his back for far too many paces before the guilt becomes too much.

"Scott?" I call out.

He stops, waiting a few beats. Then he slow-pivots to face me, arms crossed in a wide stance.

My legs carry me halfway through the parking lot, stopping a couple feet in front of him. When his fiery eyes meet mine, my mind blanks, rendering me incapable of forming a proper sentence. "I, uh, I wanted to, um . . . to thank you."

His forehead creases. "Thank me for what?"

"For helping me with my form," I spit out. I'm such a coward.

"Didn't do it for you. I did it in the name of public safety."

I dip my chin, squinting into the beating sun. "I also wanted to say . . . I-I'm sorry."

His face flickers with momentary satisfaction before he pulls it back to an expression worthy of a drill sergeant. "You're sorry for what?" Damn, he is not letting me off easy.

I bite my lip. "I apologize for the other day. For stereotyping you. For assuming you were a man-whore. And for calling you a Neanderthal. It was uncalled-for and hypocritical."

There's a prolonged pause as he searches my face. I think he's waiting to see if I'll walk back the apology, but I don't. Finally, he runs his hand along the back of his neck and nods. "Thanks."

More silence. The longer he stares at the cracked pavement, the further I sink into guilt.

"I really messed up. I have some trust issues I need to work through," I say, bowing my head.

When I look up, his face softens slightly as he meets my eyes. "It's fine."

"So, are we cool now?" I ask hopefully.

He rocks back on his heels, unfolding his arms. "I guess so."

I nervously twirl a piece of my hair around my fingers. "That doesn't sound overly convincing."

"Crystal, I'm fine. Are you convinced now?" He gives me a forced Chandler Bing smile.

I release an exasperated sigh. "Why do you have to be so difficult? Do I need to give you my firstborn child? Sell my soul?"

He's pensive for a moment, as if he's actually considering it. Then his lips finally turn into that self-satisfied smile I know all too well. As aggravating as it may be, I'm relieved it's made a reappearance. "Meet me at the gym tomorrow," he instructs.

"The gym?"

"Yup. We'll be doing my choice of workout, though," he says as he starts toward his car.

I'm tempted to say yes, simply because I don't shy away from a challenge. And maybe because seeing him work out is a sight to behold. But I already know it can't lead anywhere good. I ponder this proposition until he's almost at his car. "And if I do your mystery workout, I'll be forgiven? Just like that?" I call out.

Even from a distance, his eyes offer a glimmer of amusement. "Don't underestimate me, Chen. You'll be working for it."

chapter thirteen

WHEN MEL INVITED me to her place for a "working lunch," I eagerly accepted. Admittedly, I was exceedingly curious to see if her apartment was as glamorous as it looks on Instagram, sans filter. And just like her, it truly is.

The moment she opens the door, she shoves a sparkling tray full of various fancy, bite-size sandwiches in my face. An array of macaroons, scones, and mimosas awaits me in her gleaming, all-white kitchen. She claims she gets it from her mom, who is the "ultimate Stepford host extraordinaire." Either way, I'm now appalled by my own hosting skills, which are limited to store-bought trays and chips, no bowl.

Mel lives in one of those modern buildings in the Theater District with floor-to-ceiling windows you can probably see directly into from a neighboring building. Even though it's a deranged stalker's dream, it's perfect for her Instagram aesthetic. I beam and point when I spot the dusty-rose velvet chaise by the window where she takes a lot of her photos, as if I'm on a *Sex and the City* tour scoping out Carrie Bradshaw's iconic front stoop for the first time.

Spending the afternoon with Mel is a much-needed distraction from thinking about Scott and how I'm supposed to meet him at the gym later today to mend fences. Yes, I want to ogle him without restraint. But that's neither here nor there. I'm doing this for peace. For the sake of our families. End of story.

I'm about to ask Mel's opinion on Instagram's new algorithm and my nosedive of engagement in the past few weeks when a lanky, bare-chested dude lumbers into the kitchen. He wears nothing but boxers covered in cartoon hot dogs. His wild blond hair sticks straight up, as if he's been through a wind tunnel.

"Hey, you." He treats me to a flirtatious smile, chest puffed out. He's boyishly cute, if I were a decade younger and still drinking Bud Light from a funnel.

Mel rolls her eyes, giving him a dead-eyed stare. "Julian, grow up."

"Relax, Mel. I'm just being friendly." He shoots her a defiant look and begins to rifle around in the fridge, but not before winking at me. He slightly resembles a photo I've seen online of Mel's late adoptive father, with his baby-blue eyes and narrow face.

Mel casts him an indignant look over her shoulder. "This is my charm-void of a brother, Julian. Julian, this is my trainer and good friend, Crystal." She pauses and leans in. "I wouldn't live with a college student by choice. Trust. But my mom is making him stay with me while he tries to *figure his life out* in the city."

"Sounds familiar." I chuckle, glancing at Julian, who is impatiently tapping his foot, waiting for the toaster to finish cooking his bagel.

"At least Tara's twenty-nine." Mel's lips turn to a slight frown. "I wish I had a sister."

"Sisters are great. But only sometimes. When they're not stealing your shit." Tara has never stolen my clothes, given our size difference. But she's always swiping my makeup and hair products. I refocus my attention on my laptop, while internally mourning the expensive salon-quality shampoo she polished off as of yesterday.

I'm working on catching up on the comments on my recent Size Positive post. Despite the trolls and hateful fatphobic comments that I can barely read before I start to shake, I'm pleased so many people are loving it. It makes all the negative comments worth it.

"Which preset looks better?" Mel asks, shoving her phone two inches from my face.

I lean back, squinting. There are two side-by-side shots of her wearing an adorable polka-dot dress. It's the same photo, but one is filtered slightly darker.

"First, that dress looks fire on you. But I like the lighter one."

"Same. My boobs look bigger in that one too." She double-checks the photo. "I think I might start using the pink preset. I noticed I've been getting more Likes on them."

I'm about to offer to send her some of my favorite presets when I receive a notification.

Ritchie_Scotty7 is now following you.

My stomach somersaults.

Before I can even contemplate following him back, I receive a notification that he's liked my most recent post, a video of my ab workout from the day he stole my phone.

Within a minute, I've received over twenty notifications. All from him. This is a surefire sign all is not lost. That he doesn't completely hate me.

Ritchie_Scotty7 has liked your post.
Ritchie_Scotty7 has liked your post.
Ritchie_Scotty7 has liked your post.
Ritchie_Scotty7 has liked your post.
Ritchie_Scotty7 has liked your post.

• • •

I NEARLY REGRET showing up at the gym when Scott emerges from the changing room sporting a smug-ass grin, as if he already knew I would come. I had half a mind not to show at all, but after those notifications, which were like little teasing reminders of his sexy existence, I couldn't get him out of my head. I kept glancing at the time, willing myself to resist putting on my cutest, most flattering gym ensemble, stay at home, and ask Tara to help me craft a written apology instead. Unfortunately, my willpower is zilch.

My face flushes the moment we lock eyes. He looks like he's just stepped off the cover of a *Men's Fitness* magazine. In an effort to refrain from gawking at his square-jawed beauty, I catch my orangutan hair in the mirror as I stretch my calves in the Gym Bro Zone. I have deep regrets about not using hairspray today.

"Well, well, well. Look who actually showed up," he leers, his humongous bottle of water dangling from his index finger.

"You liked every one of my pictures," I say, deflecting.

"Sorry, I blacked out. One minute, I was looking at your profile, checking out your ab video. And the next, I was liking your selfies from 2014."

"You're insane." I secretly admire his honesty, while pretending I haven't googled his high school athletic accomplishments.

"Are you going to follow me back?" he asks. "It would be a step toward forgiveness."

I shrug. "Maybe I will. Maybe I won't. But if I were to follow you back, it would be purely for your dog."

He beams like a proud parent.

"Are you a Harry Potter fan?" I ask.

He stands over me. Even from an upward angle, the man is so hideously attractive, I'm convinced sorcery is at play. "Hell no. But it was already his name when I adopted him from the shelter. Didn't have the heart to change it. Figured it would confuse the poor guy."

My heart flutters involuntarily at the thought of him saving helpless dogs in shelters. I imagine them moments from being euthanized before he busts in and whisks them away to a sprawling farm . . . His expectant stare brings me out of my reverie. I give my head a literal shake, turning away from his mesmerizing gaze.

"So, are we just gonna stand here or are we working out?" I try to lower my voice to a serious tone. It fails miserably. I sound like a child trying to impersonate their stern father.

He snorts, pulling a small slip of paper out of his pocket, scribbled with what appears to be a workout routine. I'm pretty sure I see the word *Revenge* at the top of the page, ominously underlined multiple times. "Oh, we're working out."

He's not bluffing.

He puts me through a killer CrossFit circuit involving a malicious number of rounds on the assault bike, burpees, barbell front squats, and box jumps. Again with the hostile acts of aggression, probably to tire me out so he can launch some sort of surprise attack. It doesn't help that he's racing me, ensuring he's faster than me through every circuit. When I complete my burpees before he does, he looks certifiably devastated.

We're quiet throughout in between panting and gasping for air. I blame my excessive sweating on the little smiles he's giving me. Working out with someone who could pass as a movie star is more challenging than expected.

It's strange to be instructed by him. I'm so used to being the one telling others what to do. Now I know how it feels to be bossed around while on the cusp of fainting, or hurling, I'm not sure which.

"I'm done with this. I think I'm gonna puke," he pants, bent over, palms resting on his knees.

"Hey, this is all your own doing. Your sick little revenge fantasy." I lean my elbow on the squat rack. "I don't think I'll be able to walk tomorrow."

"Things guys like to hear after a date." He gives me a mischievous grin and quickly backtracks when he sees my jaw drop. He holds his hands in front of him. "I'm just kidding. Please don't kill me."

I reach out, giving him a lackluster punch in the chest. "You're a pig. And this is not a date."

He shrugs, wiping the sweat from his forehead with the fabric of his shirt.

We sit face-to-face on the floor. Legs stretched out in front of me, I press the bases of my shoes against his to deepen my stretch. His feet are nearly double the size of mine. Holy shit.

A series of images of a gigantic penis of the same length flash through my mind at warp speed. My throat instantly dries like the Sahara when I recall him hard against me during our changing room make-out, lending serious credence to this size association. I think I'm going to require intensive therapy to get these images out of my head. I try to swallow, but I end up coughing. "What size are your feet?"

A devious smile forms on his face. "Why do you want to know?"

I give him a dramatic eye roll as I cough again. "You're the worst."

"You walked right into that one." He hands his water bottle to me. "I'm sorry, though. Really. I've developed a crude sense of humor after a decade of working in a firehouse."

I gratefully take a sip, gaze wandering to the gym bros crowding the squat rack to cheer their buddy on. "So, have you forgiven me yet?"

He appraises me, tilting his head side to side, contemplating. "Nah, not yet. You got through those burpees too easily."

I roll my eyes. "Would me begging for mercy and puking on your shoes be satisfactory?"

He doesn't respond. He's too busy looking out the window. "Hey, let's get out of here."

chapter fourteen

BLINK. "WHY? AND where?"

"Dunno." Scott shrugs and stands. "But it's a beautiful day out there and I don't think we should waste it inside. I say we go for ice cream. On you, of course. Since you're still groveling for my forgiveness and all."

"Don't you CrossFitters exclusively eat paleo?" I'm in shock, while trying to maintain the illusion that I'm a serene being. If buying Scott ice cream can earn his complete and total forgiveness, I'll buy him all the flavors on the menu.

"Not me." He shakes his head, giving me a curious once-over. "Do you not eat ice cream?"

"I'm lactose intolerant."

He clutches his chest, as if I've told him I only have a month to live. "Wow. What did you do to deserve that?"

"I don't know. But it seriously sucks."

"Good thing I know a good place with sorbet. It's down the street."

I cast one last hesitant gaze to the door so as not to appear too eager.

Turns out, the quaint ice cream shop down the street is one of those places with a million flavors and toppings, as well as those artisanal chocolates. After agonizing over my decision for far too long, I settle on a tropical swirl sorbet, and Scott orders the same.

"Is this together or separate?" the monotone teenager wearing a T-shirt that reads *Dab King* drones from behind the counter.

"Together." It feels weird saying it. It crosses my mind that the teenager probably thinks we're a couple. I relish that thought for a few seconds too long before reality hits me in the face again. I'm not thinking about him in this way. We're purely platonic gym nemeses turned acquaintances. Obviously.

"You know you could have ordered an actual ice cream, right?" I say as the teenager passes our sorbet dishes over the counter.

"I feel bad eating it in front of you. Wouldn't want you to get secondhand cramps, or whatever happens to your stomach." He tosses me a wink as I decline to take the receipt. Only he can make an indigestion joke remotely charming.

"That's true. You don't want to see me cranky."

"Is that not your natural state?" he deadpans.

I bump him with my shoulder on the way out of the shop. I walk ahead a few paces, forcing my mouth into a neutral position. I'm smiling like a child at Disneyland and I refuse to let him see it. I'm enjoying non-hate-filled banter with him far more than he needs to know.

We make our way to the waterfront. The sun casts a glittery

layer on the surface of the water. There's a sunset cruise boat docked ahead, just waiting to be boarded by tourists.

"Isn't Albus lonely during the day when you're at work and at the gym?" I ask, scooting over as a man walking a tiny terrier in pink boots scurries past us on the sidewalk. I wonder if Scott has boots for Albus Doodledore.

"Nah. My roommate, Trevor, and I work opposite shifts a lot. He's at the same station as me, so he's typically at the apartment when I'm not. He takes him for walks and stuff."

"Sounds like a good friend."

"When he's not busting my balls over the Blackhawks, he's a decent guy."

I'm momentarily distracted by the sight of him licking sorbet off his spoon. "I don't know if this acquaintanceship is going to work out. I just don't trust Blackhawks fans."

He points his spoon at me. "Hey, who says we're acquaintances again? How do you know I've forgiven you?"

My stomach clenches. "Have you not forgiven me?"

"I have. I don't really hold grudges." He treats me to a comforting smile.

I snort.

"What? Do you hold a mean grudge?"

"No."

He eyes me leerily. "I have a feeling you hold on to things."

"Nah. But my sister does. She found out a couple weeks ago her asshole ex was still using her Netflix. So instead of changing her password like a normal person, she messed with his account algorithm by watching the first three minutes of over twenty romcoms. Then, she waited for him to be on the second-to-last episode of *Stranger Things* before switching his account's maturity settings to G-rated."

He tosses his head back in hearty laughter. "That is pure gold."

"Oh yeah. He was pissed. That's what I'd call a serious grudge." I pause, smiling at the memory. "Are you a *Stranger Things* fan?"

"Nope. I don't really watch movies or TV at all, actually."

I stop dead, slow-blinking. "At all?"

"Not really. I watch TV sometimes. Preferably twenty-minute shows."

"But why not longer shows? Or movies? What do you have against them?"

He gives me a shy smile. "I fall asleep. Every time."

As we resume walking, I picture him cuddled up on a couch watching a movie. His chest looks very inviting . . . "Maybe you just haven't watched a good movie," I say, snapping out of it.

"Nah. I just get comfortable and end up dozing off if I'm not moving. A girl once broke up with me because I fell asleep at the movie theater on a date."

I let the sorbet melt on my tongue, savoring the taste almost as much as I'm savoring the sight of his adorable smile. "I can see why she had absolutely no choice but to dump you."

"Hey, I took her to see some chick flick. Why should it matter whether I watched it or not? As long as she liked it."

"It's part of the moviegoing experience, Scotty. Otherwise, she might as well have gone to the movies alone and not had to share her snacks with you."

"Maybe you'll just have to force me to watch one," he says with a sparkling grin.

I squint at him. "Do acquaintances watch movies together?"

"I don't see why not."

I throw my empty sorbet dish into a nearby trash can. Of course, he has to try to shoot his into the trash like he's LeBron James.

"So you do the fitness and personal training thing full time?" he asks as we continue walking.

"Yup. I've been doing it since college."

"It's crazy how many followers you have. I'm really impressed."

"Thanks." I don't love talking about my Instagram success, because I feel like a fraud. When people ask how I gained my following and how they can make money from Instagram as well, I never know how to properly respond. I don't know what prompted my following, aside from a dash of luck, research, and hard work. It sounds lame to say "Just be yourself," but it's truly what worked for me.

"What made you want to start your account?" he asks.

"I was into sports growing up. Then I got really into the gym in college as a way to de-stress. Obviously, the gym life isn't for everyone, but it was really therapeutic for me. When I realized how toxic the fitness industry can be, especially online, I wanted to set a positive example for other women." I pause for a moment as we dodge a group of cyclists breezing by us. "Like . . . for me, my body type will never be skinny, so losing weight was never the goal. I just love lifting and pushing myself. And I wanted to help other women like me who don't always feel so confident, or who don't know where to start with the gym. Getting paid to promote brands I love isn't too shabby either."

I watch him, fully expecting him to launch into a well-meaning rant about how I'm not "big," or worse, offer unsolicited advice on weight loss, like so many others I've had the pleasure of interacting with.

But he doesn't. So I continue. "Society tells us women aren't fit unless we're a size two with washboard abs."

He arches a brow. "They obviously haven't seen you kill it in the gym. You're an animal."

I blush. "Thanks. I mean . . . I just think being healthy isn't just about your size or your weight, but your mindset and your mental health too."

He nods thoughtfully. "I completely agree."

"Says Mr. Abs of Steel."

Scott playfully bumps my shoulder with his. "I wasn't always into the gym."

"Oh, come on. You've had abs since at least July of 2016." Upon realization of my inadvertent admission, I sneak a sideways glance at him.

His lips twist into a funny smile. "That's very specific. How do you know that?"

My cheeks burn. I'm mortified, until I remember he liked all my photos since 2014. "Your Instagram," I admit with faux confidence.

"So you did creep on me."

I shrug. "I had to make sure you weren't a serial murderer. I don't know about you, but I'm kind of picky about new acquaintances."

"I am honored to have made the cut." He pauses, his face growing serious. "Actually, though, I used to be super lanky and awkward as a kid. I wasn't even into sports or anything until I got to high school."

"Really?" I ask, unable to picture him without muscles.

"Yeah. We kind of struggled for a few years back when we lived in Illinois. Cheap fast food and no money for organized sports. Kids were assholes."

I close my eyes for a moment, trying to conjure the image of Scott as an outcast. I think back to my prepubescent self in middle school. There was a year my friends decided I wasn't "cool enough" anymore. I'd stand alone at recess, circling the perimeter of the fence, head down, too shy to approach other kids. "Never would have guessed school was hard for you."

His eyes gloss over slightly and he grits his teeth, as if he was going to elaborate but thought better of it. "Anyway, by the time I got to high school, we were doing better financially. My dad got a really good job here in Boston, and my mom was happy since it was close to both grandparents. So we moved and I got to start over here. Filled out with puberty, I guess. Then joined sports."

"And then you suddenly became hot overnight?"

He smiles, keeping his eyes ahead. "Nah. I was still socially awkward as hell in high school. Could barely talk to girls, let alone have a girlfriend."

I can't help but absorb his earnest smile like a sponge. On the surface, Scott has all the confidence in the world. But in reality, it's an illusion. He's just like the rest of us mere mortals, stressing over stupid things we've accidentally said out loud. It makes me feel even worse about prejudging him. It isn't his fault he's a gorgeous specimen.

"I don't find you awkward at all. The opposite, really. Unless I'm just equally awkward."

"I didn't say I'm *still* awkward," he says, flashing his bewitching smile.

"Always so cocky."

"Well, now that you know my darkest secrets, what do you do other than go to the gym?"

"Not a whole lot, to be honest." It's on the tip of my tongue to take back that statement completely. Do I really want to tell him I'm practically a recluse? It's always been drilled into my head that being a wallflower is somehow lesser. That being outgoing like Dad is more desirable. But after Scott's raw honesty, it feels wrong to be anything but truthful.

"You're a homebody?"

"Oh yeah. I have Lululemon leggings specifically designated for home and for going out."

"That is . . . a very expensive habit," he teases.

"What can I say, I'm an introvert."

He eyes me with curiosity. "So just how introverted are you?"

"I'll put it this way: If I have plans for more than two consecutive nights, I'll probably stress about it all week. Oh, and if someone cancels plans, it feels like I won the lottery."

He smiles. "Now I know how to get you to like me. I'll just make plans with you and then cancel them." Strangely, the idea of Scott canceling plans on me doesn't sound nearly as appealing as I wish it did.

Talking to Scott is easy. More than easy. I feel light and joyful. We have a similar sarcastic, dirty-minded sense of humor. I don't feel the necessity to pre-plan what I'm going to say next. It just flows out. And if it's awkward, he doesn't seem to notice, or at least, he doesn't make it obvious.

By the time we loop around the pier, I've already made a list of ultra-long movies he needs to watch, in their entirety, obviously. Scott seems happy to accept the challenge. He is also keen to ask me random questions, like who my favorite singer is (Lizzo), or where I want to go on vacation (New Zealand). I've also learned more about him.

His favorite color is blue. He doesn't like cats, or pineapples on pizza. He had a pet turtle named Bob as a child. He also has two older sisters (one in the UK and the other in Arizona), who he claims tortured him growing up (he has a scar on his left knee to prove it). Since his dad passed away, he's the only guy among his mom and his sisters.

By the time he gets around to telling me about his unhealthy obsession with *Bill Nye the Science Guy*, we finally reach the Excalibur Fitness parking lot.

He lets out a long sigh. "Wish I could keep telling you embarrassing facts about my life, but I should get back to Albus. I'd ask you to come back and hang out, but it's probably too soon for him to meet you."

"Are you always this picky about Albus meeting your acquaintances?"

"Of course. I can't just bring random people into his life. He's still impressionable at his age."

"By the way, this wasn't a date in any way, shape, or form," I remind him. "It's simply an apology sorbet outing between two former strangers, turned nemeses, turned acquaintances whose grandparents are getting married. A truce."

"Are you confirming we're not mortal enemies anymore?"

I nod.

He gives me a satisfied grin and pulls me into a casual yet warm hug.

7:35 A.M.—INSTAGRAM POST: "SIZE POSITIVE CAMPAIGN—FOR THOSE ON THE FENCE ABOUT FITNESS" BY **CURVYFITNESSCRYSTAL**:

I haven't always been a boss bitch in the gym. Truth. Just ask my 15-year-old self. I'd just gotten dumped by my very first boyfriend—some gangly kid named Bobby with a 2.0 GPA who was best known for eating an entire brick of marble cheese on a dare. I was quite literally sobbing on the treadmill over him after school and actually slipped on my own tears and flew off the back (skinned my chin and both knees). I think I was unconscious for a couple seconds, because I woke up to the most popular guy in school (think Peter Kavinsky on steroids) holding my hand and rubbing my back. LOL.

Then there was also the first time I attempted a pull-up without testing my grip strength. I fell ass-first onto the hard floor. And then that time I attempted a push-up after doing a chest superset. I full-out face-planted.

Why am I sharing my embarrassing gym stories? It's for everyone who is nervous about getting into fitness. It literally can't get worse than the above stories. Seriously. And even if you do embarrass the crap out of yourself, just remember, every gym regular has a story, no matter how pro and "fit" they may seem. They've all been there. Trust.

If you're on the fence about incorporating fitness into your life (whether at the gym or at home), or simply getting back on the fitness train after taking a break, just try it out again. I'm not saying everyone needs to exercise to be happy. I'm not saying you need to get in the gym and lift weights. Fitness has brought me and many others a lot of joy. But it's not for everyone, and that's okay. I'm simply advocating for you to make the time to do something for you. Even just go for a walk around the block and clear your mind. Or curl up with a comfort book. I guarantee you won't regret it!

Remember: The worst part about working out is putting on your sports bra.

Comment by **_averyking**: It can be frustrating getting back ♡ into fitness, but it's so worth it.

Comment by **greenjay4**: not surprised your teenage ♡ boyfriend dumped you.

Comment by **KathyHilliker**: LOL these stories killed me. ♡ Thanks for putting a smile on my face!!

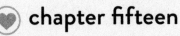

chapter fifteen

A STOCKY MAN WITH bulging steroid biceps, in a matching yellow helmet and suspenders, grinds his junk over Grandma Flo to the rhythm of "Pony" by Ginuwine. It's the last thing I thought I'd ever bear witness to. I am in desperate need of eye bleach. Stat. Unfortunately, this image is burned into my memory for all of eternity.

Compelled to preserve the spectacle to scar future generations to come, I took multiple videos. The footage is shaky at best. It's difficult to hear the music over the high-pitched squealing in the background, partially thanks to the martinis. Grandma Flo's howling laughter is unmistakable as she snakes her hands up and down the man's bare, generously oiled chest while her lifelong best friends, Annie and Ethel, crowd around, snapping blurry photos with their massive iPads.

It was Annie and Ethel's idea to attend Ladies' Night at a strip club for Grandma's bachelorette party. Tara kindly ordered an array of phallus-shaped sugar cookies of all colors, girths, and lengths. Given Grandma Flo's pearl-clutching tendencies, I was certain the whole thing was going to go tits up—that she'd find the night's activities crude and "unbecoming." But all my fears were hung out to dry when she mock–deep throated one of the penis cookies for a photo, without prompting.

Who is this woman? This surely can't be the same Grandma who washed my mouth out with Dove bar soap when I was ten after I uttered the word *hell* on a Sunday—"the Lord's Day"—of all days. It's certainly not the same woman who strong-armed my religiously indifferent parents into sending Tara and me to Bible camp for three consecutive summers. I'm beginning to think she's been kidnapped by aliens, replaced by a much cooler replica—up until she matter-of-factly informs Tara she'll "never keep a man" if she doesn't learn how to cook.

I stealthily slip outside for a breather, parking myself on the sidewalk, crunching one of the penis cookies I snagged. Aside from the threat of an unwanted lap dance, the club was starting to feel cramped and hot from one too many martinis. The music, strobe lights, and fog machine didn't help, not that the plumes of cigarette smoke, the steaming garbage, and a hint of sewage outside are much of an improvement.

In my tipsy state, I have this nagging urge to show someone the video. And the only other person who will fully appreciate its eccentricity is Scott. We've been texting back and forth since our sorbet hangout last week. Our texts have been constant today while at our respective grandparents' bachelor parties. Scott has apparently achieved "best friend" status with Dad. He's even sent me selfies of the two of them golfing together to prove it.

RITCHIE_SCOTTY7

Wow. I can't unsee that vid. Ever.

CURVYFITNESSCRYSTAL

Right? It should be illegal.

RITCHIE_SCOTTY7

It's your own fault. I volunteered to step in. Then you guys would have had a real fireman over 5 feet tall.

CURVYFITNESSCRYSTAL

LOL.

Truthfully, the vision of Scott grinding over Grandma Flo is probably more disturbing than the professional stripper. I shudder at the thought.

RITCHIE_SCOTTY7

Haha, I'm kidding. I'm not good on the pole. Better in photos.

CURVYFITNESSCRYSTAL

Are you in a calendar or not?

RITCHIE_SCOTTY7

Damn, you are so thirsty to know.

CURVYFITNESSCRYSTAL

I'm not. Forget I asked.

RITCHIE_SCOTTY7

Hint, I'm the month of June.

Your dad is pretty drunk FYI. His face is very red lol.

CURVYFITNESSCRYSTAL

Tell him to stop drinking. He gets the Asian flush!

RITCHIE_SCOTTY7

I'll try. He's a riot. I'm slowly getting him to reveal all your childhood secrets.

CURVYFITNESSCRYSTAL

...

RITCHIE_SCOTTY7

He told me about when you ran across the stage naked at your preschool grad. Bold move.

CURVYFITNESSCRYSTAL

Stop talking about me!

RITCHIE_SCOTTY7

Impossible.

CURVYFITNESSCRYSTAL

In my defense, that dress was itchy. I have a thing against itchy fabric.

RITCHIE_SCOTTY7

Your dad just gave me permission to date you.

Oh and marry you, apparently.

CURVYFITNESSCRYSTAL

> I'm so glad my dad is securing my future because
> I'm oh so incapable. Pass along my sincere
> gratitude.

My phone vibrates with an incoming FaceTime. From Dad.

His rosy, smiling face pops up on the screen in front of a wood-paneled wall with a dartboard.

I wave at the camera. "Hi, Dad."

He gives me a toothy smile. "Crystal!" he shouts over the loud classic rock music in the background.

Scott's head suddenly appears in the frame beside Dad. "Tell your daughter what you just told me."

Dad looks directly into the camera. "Scotty has my permission to ask for your hand in marriage."

I give an exaggerated raised brow. "Do I get a say in this?"

In typical social butterfly fashion, Dad gets sidetracked and abruptly disappears from the frame, abandoning his phone in Scott's capable hands. I can see Dad in the background, high-fiving one of Martin's friends. Scott looks like he's walking away from the crowd to take refuge in a quieter area of the bar.

"Hey, I'd make a damn fine husband. I'm very low maintenance," Scott declares with confidence.

"I don't get that impression. You're quite needy . . . passing out in clinics, constantly needing your ego stroked and such."

"Minor details. I really only require two things. Regular sex and food."

"That's a tall order," I tease.

My skin prickles at the sight of his dimples. "Wanna get married if we're both forty and still single?" he asks.

"What? Like a marriage pact?" I clear my throat at the horrifying-but-not-so-horrifying thought of giving *him* regular sex and home-cooked meals. You'd really have to twist my arm . . . not.

He shrugs casually, as if he's merely asked me to play on his rec league baseball team. "Lots of friends have them."

I give him a slow head shake. Before I can respond, he begins to squint at the camera, his lips curving upward in pure amusement. "Are you holding a penis cookie?"

I nearly choke on a tiny piece that accidentally went down the wrong pipe. "Maybe."

"It's, uh, very veiny," he observes. "Are those black specks supposed to be pubes?"

"Indeed. And it's delectable, I'll have you know. I have extras. Maybe I'll even bring you one. If you're good."

A wide smile overtakes his entire face. "There are so many things I could say right now."

"Please don't."

He makes a zipper motion across his mouth. He leans in farther toward the camera. "Where are you?"

"Sitting on the curb outside the strip club."

"Why aren't you inside? Are you okay? That's not a great area of town." His voice deepens with concern.

"Just feeling a little spinny. I'm good. I think I'm gonna call an Uber and head home early."

"Stay there, okay? I'll come wait with you. I'm about two blocks away at the pub."

I arch my brow. "You seem to be an expert on the location of the strip club. Are you a frequent customer? A VIP?"

He scoffs. "Ha ha, very funny. You told me you were at Diamonds earlier. I've been there once for my buddy's bachelor party. Thanks, though."

"Mm-hmm . . ." My voice trails off as I peer around, the distant wail of a siren growing louder. There's a seedy-looking dude in zebra-print pants and a thick gold chain loitering in front of the dingy alleyway to my left, casting his shifty eyes every which way.

"Stay where you are. I'll be there in a few minutes," Scott orders before the call goes dead.

• • •

"MISS, SPARE SOME change?" a raspy voice sounds.

My eyes snap open. Did I just fall asleep? And for how long?

Bleary-eyed, I turn to spot a rail-thin homeless man wearing two jackets approaching on my right. He looks terribly hungry and in need of a warm meal. "I'll check." I scramble to search the forgotten depths of my purse. God knows what lurks down there. I have no idea if I even have any change. Who carries cash with them anymore?

Fingers hopelessly tangled in my headphone cords, I uncover one lone, half-squished Skittle and a two-year-old receipt from Trader Joe's. Just as I manage to locate a rogue dollar, a shadow towers over us.

It's a monstrously tall, muscular figure with ashy hair winging out of a black ball cap. This guy fills out a Henley like a sexy, rugged, recluse farmer who just so happens to have bulging biceps from slinging a bale of hay or two. Sleeves rolled up to accentuate his forearms, he spends his days taming wild horses and aimlessly riding his tractor over terrain of varying degrees of difficulty. He stubbornly refuses to sell the land that's belonged to his family for millennia to evil corporate developers from the big bad city. My focus sharpens slightly as the streetlight catches his green eyes.

I wheeze. It's Scott. Suddenly, I wish I'd worn something lower cut than my turtleneck bodysuit. At least I'm wearing semi-flattering jeans and heels.

Scott hands him a crisp twenty-dollar bill. "Here, man."

The man bows his head, gratefully reaching for the bill. "Thank you. God bless."

"Have a good night!" I call after him, now practically horizontal on the sidewalk. It isn't just the alcohol that's knocked the wind out of me. It's Scott's decency. His kindness. Most people just dart right past homeless people without a second glance. Had I been sober and in a rush, I probably would have too.

Scott kneels down, studying my face while still keeping a watchful side-eye on the man in the zebra-print pants. "You shouldn't be out here alone like this."

"Why not? I'm fineeee. I was gonna call an Uber or walk home. I only live a few blocks away," I slur, unable to refrain from staring at him like he's a full bag of Sweet Chili Heat Doritos.

"Where's your mom? Or Tara?"

"They're still inside. Probably getting lap dances. One guy looks like Tom Brady. We're obsessedddd with the lad." For reasons unknown, I've randomly decided it's as good a time as any to bust out a British accent.

"Are you pretending to be British?" His voice shakes with suppressed laughter.

"A Geordie. You know, from the north. My new client is from there," I dutifully explain. "She was talking about her weight in stone the other day. I had to use a stone-to-pound converter. And then she talked about how she used to hook up with a lot of guys in university. She called it *pulling*."

Scott's face contorts in confusion. "Pulling?"

"Yeah, like, *I used to pull all the lads*." I giggle, clapping my hand over my mouth, fully aware I've royally butchered her amazing accent.

"Wow. Please say that again. It's such a turn-on," he teases.

"*I'm feeling like a real radgie*," I mimic her, containing my laughter.

He half-smiles. "Alright, Crystal from Northern England. I think it's time for me to take you home."

"Is that a promise?" I ask, brutally failing to make my voice low and sexy. It sounds like I have laryngitis and possibly swallowed a couple hairballs. Maybe I am more than tipsy.

"You know what I mean." He rolls his eyes and grabs my hands. His forearms flex as he pulls me up. "Can you walk or do you want me to get you an Uber?"

"*Pffttt*. Of course I can walk." It's a half-truth. I can walk. Just not in a completely straight line. But who needs to walk in a straight line?

He wraps his big arms around my waist and guides me down the sidewalk, preventing me from pirouetting into oncoming traffic. I try my best to remain as discreet as possible while sniffing him, marinating in his intoxicating green-bar-soap scent. I want to ask him how he maintains his freshly showered aroma after a full day of golf. Is it witchcraft? Blessed genetics?

"Alright. You're not making it on foot." He whips out his

phone and clicks around. "Your chariot will be here in five minutes. What's Tara's number? I'm texting her to tell her you're going home."

I shrug, pausing to lean against a spiderweb-laden lamppost. Who knows people's phone numbers anymore? "There's a three . . . and a four. Maybe a seven."

He sighs, extending his hand. "Give me your phone."

I manage to locate it in my purse without struggle. "Here. But you better not go on my Tinder again."

He raises a brow as he pulls up my texts. "Still Tindering, huh?"

"Nah. Haven't been doing that lately. It's too sad."

He looks up from my phone. "Too sad?"

I toss my hands in the air, momentarily distracted by a jeep whizzing by blasting music. "I don't want to do random hookups anymore."

He nods, hurriedly completing the text. He leans in to drop my phone back in my bag. "Looking for something more serious?"

I take my shoe off to massage the blister forming on the side of my foot, still using the lamppost for support. "I guess so. I don't really know what I'm looking for, to be honest. My last relationship ended badly. Makes me scared to date anyone at all."

"Ah, right. Trust issues." He holds me captive with his mesmerizing stare, his gorgeous eyes glowing under the streetlight. They're so vibrant, you could see them from space. "Is that why you won't go on a date with me?"

I shove my foot into my shoe again, taken aback. I'm going to need both feet planted on the ground for this. Since our argument in the clinic parking lot, he hasn't seriously brought up dating again. Despite our flirting, I assumed the topic was off the table. "I didn't know you were still interested."

He lets out a soft laugh as he drags his hand through his hair, an act that never fails to disarm me. "Seriously? I only text you a million times a day." He pauses. "I'm interested, Crys. But you made it clear you just wanted to be friends, so I haven't brought it up."

"Aside from trying to lure me into a marriage pact," I remind him.

"Believe me, I'd rather date you long before I'm forty. But I'll take what I can get."

Goose bumps erupt on my arms as he comes into sharp focus. I stare at him for a few moments, imagining what it would be like to go on a date with Scott Ritchie. My stomach flutters at the mere thought, until it's washed away with a twist to the chest I call "reality." I can't repeat the mistakes of the past. "I can't, Scotty. And it isn't because I'm not interested."

He deflates a little. "Then what is it?"

I drag my palms down my cheeks. I have no idea how he's going to take this. "Lots of reasons. Mainly because our families are joining. And you just got out of a relationship."

His mouth opens slightly as he studies me for a few breaths. His brows relax with what looks like a blend of confusion and relief. "Really? That's why?"

"I like you. I really do. But I don't want to be your rebound while you pine over your ex. I was a rebound with my last ex, Neil, and then he went back to the girl he dated before me."

His forehead creases. "Diana and I didn't get along the majority of our relationship. We should have been over months before we actually ended things. Trust me, I won't be going back to her."

"It's not that I don't want to . . . I just don't want to get hurt again. Maybe I'd chance it if you were just a random guy I met at the gym, but our grandparents are getting married. I don't want things to be weird if it doesn't work out." I turn my eyes away, trying to find a spot on the pavement to stare at, but everything is still spinning. Scott senses my loss of balance and wraps one arm around my waist, stabilizing me.

I desperately want to believe him when he says things are over for good with Diana. But then I remember how Neil used to say how "done" he was with Cammie. He'd go on and on about how glad he was to be rid of her, and how she never crossed his mind. Looking back, it's clear he was compensating for the fact that he did think about her, probably all the time while he was with me.

I don't question that Scott is genuine. He's practically bursting at the seams with good intentions. But feelings are complicated. It's only been a few weeks since they broke up. He could be more heartbroken than he's letting on, or than he even realizes. He needs time to work out his underlying feelings before I end up suffering the consequences.

Scott squeezes my shoulders affectionately, his fingers gently stroking in a circular motion. "Why are you so sure it won't work out?"

"Because it never has before, for me. Especially not with guys who've just gotten out of relationships."

"Okay. I get it. But can I just ask, how long 'til it's no longer a rebound?"

I glance at the midnight sky for answers, but end up toppling to the side, straight into Scott's chest. His grip tightens. "I don't know? At least three months." I haven't the faintest clue where *three months* came from. It has no historic relevance in the deep recesses of my mind. It's completely arbitrary.

He nods in consideration. "Three months from the date I broke up with Diana, huh? That takes us to exactly August sixth. The day of our grandparents' wedding. Will you at least consider a date then? We could take it really slow. To be really sure."

I light up like a Christmas tree. Heat courses through my body as I fight to suppress my toothy smile. It gives me hope that he's serious. Serious enough to wait for me. "You'd really wait that long?" I ask. "I mean, I wouldn't blame you if you got bored and stuck your fingers in a few more pies."

He doesn't laugh at my shitty joke. In fact, his expression is so pure and earnest I'm reduced to a quivering specimen in the middle of the sidewalk. "Crystal, I won't." He pauses and digs his phone out of his pocket. "I'm setting the date in my calendar. August sixth. Get ready for it."

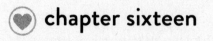 **chapter sixteen**

RITCHIE_SCOTTY7

There's something wrong with my phone.

CURVYFITNESSCRYSTAL

??

RITCHIE_SCOTTY7

It doesn't have your number in it.

CURVYFITNESSCRYSTAL

GIF of Michael Scott's unimpressed face

RITCHIE_SCOTTY7

> Seriously though, when are you going to let me out of DM purgatory and give me your actual number? Or do I have to wait until August sixth for that too?

CURVYFITNESSCRYSTAL

> Maybe.

RITCHIE_SCOTTY7

> I bet you text me and hang out with me more than anyone else.

He isn't wrong. In the weeks since the bachelorette party, we've texted constantly, mostly communicating in random GIFs. He's always down to run errands with me after our increasingly regular gym sessions, like going to the pharmacy to pick up tampons. He was even thoughtful enough to buy me a package of clearance Mini Eggs when I was PMSing.

There was also the time he helped me with a massive grocery run for my summer meal prep. He carried my four hundred dollars' worth of food all the way up the stairs to my apartment in one trip, because more than one trip is allegedly sacrilegious. Once inside my apartment, he proactively changed my fire alarm, which had been malfunctioning since I moved in (which he was quite disturbed to hear).

He's still flirting with me, hard. And I'm flirting back, despite playing hard to get in the name of taking things slow.

> **CURVYFITNESSCRYSTAL**
>
> You'll get my phone number in due time.
>
> Are you messaging me from work?

RITCHIE_SCOTTY7

Sure am. Just got back from a medical call.

> **CURVYFITNESSCRYSTAL**
>
> Aren't you supposed to be fighting fires? Saving lives? Doing CPR?

RITCHIE_SCOTTY7

Are you personally requesting CPR?

Yes, yes I am.

> **CURVYFITNESSCRYSTAL**
>
> *GIF of Judge Judy giving a slow, condescending head shake*

RITCHIE_SCOTTY7

What are you up to tonight?

CURVYFITNESSCRYSTAL

Working on some content for my posts for next week. You?

RITCHIE_SCOTTY7

I was gonna see if I could enlist your help on a top secret, high-priority mission.

CURVYFITNESSCRYSTAL

Does it require leaving my apartment?

RITCHIE_SCOTTY7

. . . Yes. You'd have to put on your "going out" Lulus.

I've just settled onto the couch with Tara, where I damn well planned to remain for the entirety of the evening, being a miserable curmudgeon. But the glimmering prospect of hanging out with Scott is impossible to ignore.

CURVYFITNESSCRYSTAL

??

RITCHIE_SCOTTY7

I need to know you're committed to the mission before I give you a detailed briefing.

CURVYFITNESSCRYSTAL

Ugh, fine. I'm committed.

RITCHIE_SCOTTY7

I need a new dresser. From IKEA.

CURVYFITNESSCRYSTAL

And you need my help constructing it? Lol.

RITCHIE_SCOTTY7

Haha, no, I got that part covered. But my mom says I have no style. Would be nice to have someone steer me in the right direction.

I've been to his apartment once to pick up a foam roller he generously offered to lend me. His place fit the blueprint for two young, unattached men who have zero sense of style. Barren.

Plain. Minimalist. I've been tempted to bring a plant or a few throw pillows to liven the space, but according to Mel, that's what a girlfriend would do. And I am definitely not a girlfriend.

CURVYFITNESSCRYSTAL

I do like home décor . . .

RITCHIE_SCOTTY7

K I'll pick you up at 6:30 after work.

• • •

YOU CAN LEARN a lot about a person by going through the entirety of IKEA with them. It's a true test of one's patience, spatial awareness, level of maturity, and self-discipline. Particularly in the final section, where they so rudely tempt you with cinnamon rolls and Daim chocolate caramel candies. Why are you trying to break me, IKEA?

As it turns out, Scott has the patience of a saint. We're trapped behind a family with three rambunctious children, all under approximately seven years old. They're screeching because their parents shunned their demands for soft-serve ice cream cones. I wince, digging my fingernails into my palms as the youngest one lets out an earsplitting howl, all while Scott whistles cheerfully beside me, as if we're taking a leisurely stroll through a lush, tranquil meadow on a breezy, sunny day. His stride is confident, unhurried, and so entirely sexy, I could watch hours of CCTV footage of him doing nothing but walking.

He also appears to have an excellent sense of direction. He's whizzing through the showroom like a total pro, undeterred by distractions. The last time I was here, on a solo mission for a mere picture frame, I ended up hopelessly disoriented, despite the large arrows on the floor. Then again, Scott is a career fireman. I assume spatial orientation while running into unfamiliar burning buildings is a prerequisite for the job.

Despite this, Scott is immature in the mattress section. And so am I. One by one, we test them, assessing the level of bounce, support, and overall plushness.

"I need this bed," he says, eyes closed, as we lie side by side on a marshmallow-like queen-size mattress.

When I turn toward him, the mattress dips more than expected, causing me to inadvertently roll into his shoulder. My stomach flutters at the mere warmth of his body. Hello, bliss.

He gives me a flirty side-eye. "Trying to cuddle with me?"

"No." I abruptly roll away to put the appropriate amount of space between us again. I overcompensate and nearly tumble off the mattress entirely. Talk about being on the edge of glory.

"I think you were."

"I think you just wish I were." Truthfully, his chest looks cozy and inviting. All I want to do is nuzzle into his neck. But I manage to pull myself back to reality and maintain my restraint, despite how barren, cold, and lonely it is in my own personal space bubble.

"I never knew IKEA was such a good time," he says, changing the subject.

I give him a warning look. "It's all fun and games until you hit the warehouse. Then it's all-out anarchy."

He laughs and sits upright, holding his hand out for me. "Alright, let's go pick a dresser." Without thinking, I take his hand. But the moment our fingers touch, a jolt of electricity sends a shock wave rolling down my spine.

Hand locked firmly around mine, he carries on down the aisle, perma-smiling.

I sigh as I follow him through the aisle, unable to stop concentrating on the pad of his finger circling around the soft part of my hand below my thumb. I gloriously fail to fend off semi-sexual or romantic thoughts. I do a quick scan for something, literally anything, to lift my mind out of the gutter. My eye catches a beautiful living room display.

"Did you know I'm kind of obsessed with houses and décor?" I ask.

He eyes me with interest. "I figured as much, based on your furniture. You're practically an antique hunter."

"When I was little, I used to get my dad to drive me around the neighborhood at night so I could see into other people's houses."

Scott halts in the middle of the aisle, to the horror of the elderly man behind us. I make room for the man to step around us, accidentally backing into Scott's chest. I let go of his hand and spin around.

Scott smiles, settling his hands on either side of my waist, as if they belong there. "You're telling me you used to peep into people's houses at night? And your dad aided and abetted?"

For a brief moment, I gawk up at him, taking in the full extent of his height towering over me before backing away. Cheeks pink, he studies my face, a smile playing across his lips.

I nod, as if it isn't a big deal. "Pretty much. He mostly used it as an opportunity to blast his Shania Twain CD. She's his forever girl crush."

He throws his head back, clutching his chest with booming, uninhibited laughter. "Didn't expect Will to be a country fan. And you're basically one step below serial killer status." He pauses as we turn toward the dresser section. "Did you have binoculars too?"

I playfully whack him on the bicep.

"Now I know to close my blinds."

I fight the urge to laugh while maintaining a serious expression. "I don't do it to creep on people, obviously. I just like looking at other people's décor, the layouts of houses."

"You'd get along with my mom, then. She watches HGTV constantly. She's in love with the Property Brothers," he says as we approach the dresser section.

After gentle prodding, I persuade him to select the six-drawer HEMNES chest in a dark gray stain (ample space for all his lacy delicates, I argue). We then manage to locate the correct model number in the warehouse with relative ease. Based on how much fun he's having wheeling around on those flat carts, I conclude the warehouse is his favorite part of the entire store.

"Get on," he orders, nodding toward the cart with a completely straight face.

I level him with my sternest authoritarian glare. "No. Let's just go check out."

He persists. "Get on the cart."

I sigh, relenting. My feet could use a break after going through this maze of a department store in the hideous leopard ballet flats that were two for ten dollars at Target. Life lesson: you can't count on five-dollar flats for proper arch support.

I settle onto the cart, my back to him. His face is so close behind me, his alluring aftershave fills my nostrils, sending a buzz of electricity to my toes. I desperately want to lean back into him. Is this what dating Scott could be like? Laughing and doing dumb shit together while doing the most mundane of errands?

I'm practically doubled over with laughter as we fly down the wide aisles, one after another, only very narrowly dodging innocent bystanders.

As we whiz by a bookshelf display, a frazzled, gray-haired IKEA employee gasps in horror. "Ma'am, it's against store policy to sit on the carts unless you're under ten years old." As Scott abruptly stops the cart, she practically fires lasers at me with her hawkish eyes like I'm a shameful criminal.

"Sorry," I murmur, promptly stepping back onto the floor.

Scott and I stifle our amusement before he speeds down another aisle ahead of me, nearly ramming the cart into a couple loading a long, skinny box.

By the time I catch up to him, he's profusely apologizing to a blond woman with thick bangs. She stares at him, doll-like blue eyes wide, lips pulled back, miffed, as if he'd nearly crushed them flat.

I palm Scott's shoulder as I inch forward. "I am so sorry for him. I left him unsupervised for one second. I really need to get him a leash—"

When the man whips his head around, the air expels from my lungs. The overly tousled hair. The piercing ice-blue eyes. Neil.

Neil rips himself from the embrace of the woman, whom I now recognize as Cammie. She looks different with her new, thick bangs. Neil takes a step backward, nearly tripping on the front bed of Scott's cart as he swivels to face me, mouth open. "Crystal."

Cammie's eyes narrow, examining me. I have no idea if she

knows who I am. I wouldn't be surprised if he never told her about my existence at all.

"Neil . . . Hi," I manage. Barely. Blood rushes to my ears. The distant chatter around us echoes, as if we're in a fishbowl.

Scott flashes me a worried glance and backs up his cart. He's standing next to me now, shoulders pulled back, arm grazing mine. His touch grounds me, preventing me from being sucked into Neil's twister.

"What are you doing here?" Neil asks, voice octaves higher than normal. He's doing a piss-poor job at masking his shock. A single bead of sweat trickles down his forehead, illuminated by the warehouse lighting. I think he's about to wet himself at the sight of Cammie and me in the same place, and quite frankly, so am I.

"I, uh . . ."

"We're picking up a dresser," Scott cuts in. The way he says *we're* isn't lost on me. It's daring, but I'm thankful.

Seeing the two of them face-to-face is interesting. Neil isn't a weakling. But Scott still towers over him by about five inches and forty pounds of muscle.

"We're getting new living room furniture, for our new place," Neil informs us, glancing nervously at me.

"New living room furniture?" I register their cart stacked with boxes.

Cammie dips her chin in a nod, maintaining her doe-eyed, innocent vibe.

"We just moved in together," Neil admits. It strikes me as odd yet unsurprising that they'd be moving in together a few weeks after he texted me, likely to complain about her.

"Really? Us too." Scott's tone is overly jovial. I can tell he's being fake, but only because I know him so well. He must sense my unease, because he throws his arm over my shoulder, pulling me snug into his side. Warmth flows through me instantly, rendering me impenetrable. With Scott by my side, Neil couldn't do anything to knock me off course if he tried.

"Oh." There's a flicker of righteous annoyance in Neil's eyes before he pouts, evidently displeased his second choice is no longer available. "I didn't know you were dating anyone new."

I'm tempted to offer a cutting remark, like *Sincere apologies for forgetting to mention it the last three times you texted me*, but I have zero desire to be petty. So I settle on a casual shrug, as if it's no big deal.

Scott clears his throat to fill the awkward tension as he tightens his grip around my shoulder. "Well, babe, we better get going."

"Yeah, we should." I don't even bother to say goodbye to Neil and his new live-in girlfriend. I walk until they're both out of sight. A couple aisles down, I stop, waiting for Scott to catch up with the cart.

When we're out of earshot and heading toward the monstrous lineups at the checkout, Scott speaks. "Crys, I'm really sorry if I overstepped, I—"

I turn to him, my fingers grazing his forearm. When his muscle tenses beneath my grip, I drop my hand back to my side. "No, you didn't overstep. Thank you. Seriously."

"I take it that was the ex?"

I nod, mindlessly running my fingers over the random kitchen accessories in the checkout aisle. "Yeah."

"No offense, but he's a prick. You have no idea how much I wanted to deck him in the face." Scott keeps his stony stare on the line in front of us.

His protectiveness fills me with comfort. I inch closer to him, our shoulders touching. "He does have a very punchable face. But what made you want to deck him?"

"Because he's the reason I have to wait months to date you. And I hate the way he looked at you."

"How did he look at me?"

"Like he owned you or something. Like you were a toy someone else was playing with." He steps closer. So close, his breath grazes my hair. "You're worth so much more than that, Crystal." Somehow, he's managed to pinpoint my exact feelings when I'm near Neil. Worthless. It's not like he's maliciously trying to make me feel that way, but after being his second choice for so long, I've almost gotten used to it.

I bow my head. "Thank you. It was really weird seeing him with her . . . she's the one he left me for. The woman he dated before me."

Scott's jaw tenses. "That's really shitty. I know that must be hard on you."

"Yeah. Though I should have expected it. Even while we were together, I always felt like he wasn't fully over her. He'd always find weird ways to bring her up. One time, literally fifteen minutes after we slept together, I caught him creeping on her Insta."

He cringes. "Ouch . . ."

"The worst part is, I'm not a naive person. At least, I didn't think I was. And yet, I believed everything he told me for so long. It really messed with me."

"I completely get it. It's hard when someone turns out to be exactly who you hoped they weren't."

"Have you ever had a bad relationship?" I ask, growing acutely aware that this conversation probably isn't the most suitable for an IKEA checkout line. But then again, no one around us seems to be paying any attention. The woman in front of us has her nose buried in her phone, while the couple behind us are strangely captivated by ice cube trays.

He nods, swallowing a lump in his throat. "Yeah. My last girlfriend."

I suck in a breath. I've never asked him about what happened with Diana, mostly because he's never brought her up. "What happened?"

"We met last year. She was a figure skater. Things were really good in the first month, until she got offered a job touring with Disney. She wasn't sure if she wanted to take it, since our relationship was so new. But I encouraged her. Didn't want her to give up her dream for me. I thought long distance would be a breeze, but we didn't talk a lot while she was gone on tour, especially not in the last few months. And it didn't help I was always working and picking up extra shifts. We ended up fighting all the time because of the distance." He pauses, grimacing. "Anyway, we finally broke up after she visited for the weekend. I stupidly assumed things would go back to normal if we saw each other. But they didn't. And she admitted she'd started catching feelings for a guy she skates with. Cliché, huh?"

Definitely cliché. I frown. "I'm sorry. Did anything actually happen between them?"

His eyes shift to his feet momentarily. "She said nothing happened. But I don't know if I believe that."

"Do you think it'll take you a long time to trust again?"

"No."

"Really? Doesn't it still hurt? That she had feelings for someone else?"

His eyes hover over mine. "Of course it does. But just because one person broke my trust doesn't mean everyone is going to, you know?"

We stay silent the duration of the trip back to my apartment. Scott seems to be in his feelings after our conversation about Diana. I'm riddled with guilt for ruining his cheery mood.

I'm also disappointed in myself. Sometime after nearly cuddling on the mattress and riding the IKEA cart like a child, I nearly broke the pact I made to myself. I was tempted to give in, kiss Scott, and let myself be his rebound, and vice versa.

But after seeing Neil and Cammie shopping for furniture together, practically on their way down the aisle, I'm reminded of the fact that I was nothing to him but temporary reprieve from the pain. A palate cleanser. A way to get off. Someone to reinforce the fact that he still loved another woman.

If I want to be a role model to my followers and practice what I preach in my Size Positive campaign, I need to know my worth. Being Rebound Girl once again is simply not an option.

chapter seventeen

DON'T KNOW HOW you have so much willpower. I'd have broken that three-month rule and jumped his bones already." Mel huffs, out of breath from forty-five of fifty ball slams I've mercilessly assigned.

"It's under two months now, if we go by the date he actually broke up with his ex," I explain. "And it's not a hard, set rule. I just figure it's a healthy amount of time in between relationships."

In the two weeks since our IKEA hangout, Scott and I have met at the gym at least four or five times a week, aside from the days he has double shifts. Sometimes he helps film my videos, or gives me new workout ideas to demo and share with my followers.

He takes up the majority of my weekends too. We spend hours together watching sports at his place, walking around Boston Common and the harbor with Albus, spending time with Grandma

Flo and Martin, or embarking on our strange new habit of browsing home décor stores.

Yesterday, he accompanied me to dinner at my parents' place (Dad so kindly extended the invite), where he proceeded to make friends with Hillary. I'd warned him she'd probably pee all over him, but he scooped her into his big arms and let her lick his entire face with her repellent, lizard-like tongue. This act solidified him as "the perfect man," according to Mom, who is the newest passenger on the Scott train, along with the rest of the family, who forcefully insist I date him ASAP.

"Fifty!" Mel slams the medicine ball to the floor one last time before leaning against the wall.

"Good job, girl. Your form was really good throughout." I give her a high five as we start toward the changing room.

She grins with pride before chugging the remainder of her water bottle. A month ago, that circuit would have been far too difficult, and today, she crushed it like a boss. "Anyway, I get why you're being cautious, especially with your families involved."

I hold the changing room door open for her. "My thoughts exactly. I kind of rushed into my last relationship . . . if you can even call it a relationship. It's nice to take things slow." Admittedly, keeping my feelings for Scott at bay is increasingly more difficult with each interaction.

Mel gives me a serious expression as she slips past me toward a bench. "Speaking of which, you better not be a flaky twat at the end of all this and take it back. You need to date the shit out of him. He has serious BDE. You can't let that slip between your fingers."

"BDE?"

"Big dick energy," she explains, to the shock and horror of a gray-haired lady with a perm generously applying her gel deodorant on the bench next to us.

"How can you gauge someone's BDE?" I ask, lowering my voice to a whisper.

"It's all in the gait. In the way he walks. Super cocky, like he could handle himself on the streets or among your dude friends at a barbeque. He'd be sweet to your mom and then ravish the shit out of you in the bedroom." She pauses, still not bothering to lower her voice as she straddles the bench. "Like, take the guy from *Twilight*, for example."

"Robert Pattinson?"

"The man has no gait. Not an ounce of swagger, which is surprising considering he has the whole *tortured novelist who has locked himself in a desolate cabin to overcome his writer's block* look going on."

I used to feel some type of way about Robert Pattinson. Then again, I was fifteen years old and still sleeping with a stuffed animal. "I kind of see what you mean. He always looks like he's on the cusp of emotional ruin." I fight to suppress my guffaw as the permed lady storms off, away from our inappropriate discussion.

Mel opens her locker, chuckling. "By the way, did I tell you Berry Cloth & Co. reached out to me for a collab? They're sending me some pieces for their fall Extended Collection."

I flutter my hands, both shocked and elated. "Shut up. Really?"

"Yeah. I've been trying to get them to notice me for forever. Finally they did."

"I'm so pumped for you. They have really nice stuff. Though

their larger sizes are always more expensive. Which is the worst," I say, shoulders slumping.

She scowls. "The Fat Tax. I know. It's wrong. I actually brought that up when I spoke to the marketing girl, and she fully agreed."

"There are hardly any brands out there for curvy people that don't cost a fortune."

She nods in thought before pursing her lips. "That's exactly why I started my Instagram account. Hey, would you want to do a guest video showcasing your closet? Maybe some of your workout clothes?"

I register my current getup with revulsion—a baggy ripped Bruins T-shirt with holes in questionable places, my awful non-Align leggings that do absolutely nothing for my ass, and matted hair in a messy bun. "I doubt *mom of two-year-old quintuplets* is the aesthetic you want to promote."

Mel rolls her eyes. "I've seen your closet. You have the cutest clothes. You don't wear them, for whatever reason."

I sigh, mentally recalling all the forgotten outfits that haven't seen the light of day since the turmoil with Neil. "I-I don't know."

She gives me a sympathetic nod. "Okay, well, I don't want to pressure you. I just thought it could be nice to switch it up. Do a collab or two."

The guilt sets in immediately. Mel has promoted the crap out of my platform, even though she's paying for my services. Because of her, I've gained multiple new clients and hundreds of followers. The least I can do is scratch her back too. "Okay. I'll do it. I have some pieces that could work."

She lights up. "It's going to be great. I promise."

TRANSCRIPT OF **MELANIE_INTHECITY**'S SPECIAL GUEST VIDEO FEATURING CRYSTAL CHEN (**CURVYFITNESSCRYSTAL**):

MEL: *Hi guys! Melanie_inthecity here with a very special guest, Crystal Chen, a role model in the body positivity movement. If you're into fitness, you probably already follow her account, Curvy-FitnessCrystal.*

CRYSTAL: *[Jazz-hands wave] Hey everyone! Thanks so much for having me, Mel.*

MEL: *Of course. I've posted about it on my channel before, but in case some of you are new, Crystal and I met because I booked her as my trainer last month. [Turns to Crystal] You take pleasure in making me work out until I nearly puke, don't you?*

CRYSTAL: *Hey, I'm just trying to get results. And you're doing amazing, by the way. [Looks at camera] She started off not being able to do one push-up. Now she can do twenty.*

MEL: *[Scoffs] Barely. But anyway, I love your style. [Camera pans to a rack of Crystal's favorite outfits] I see a lot of comfortable, yet super-chic outfits. Lots of jersey dresses, denim jackets, and very neutral tones.*

CRYSTAL: *Yeah. I mean, I'm also not a size two. Girls like us can't just walk into any store and pull whatever we want off the rack. Anyone who isn't straight-sized knows that tailoring is your friend. But it can get expensive. That's why I love fabrics that are versatile.*

MEL: *Can you tell me how you choose pieces?*

CRYSTAL: *Back in college, I used to buy tons of clothes from Forever 21 and those types of stores. They're great prices, but I found they weren't as durable.*

MEL: *Right. It's hard to find high-quality clothing that's affordable.*

CRYSTAL: *So, lately, I've been trying to buy less, but higher quality. [Thumbs through clothing rack] I have a couple neutral staples, like this pencil skirt, or this gray dress, a plain white T, black jeggings, all things that can be matched with anything.*

MEL: *I totally agree. Having your staple pieces is so important. I'm a big fan of a simple black dress.*

CRYSTAL: *Yeah, for sure. I mean, my job is fitness, so truthfully, I spend a lot of time in my Lulus. But with summer coming, I want to start wearing more light dresses.*

MEL: *Do you have any advice for fellow curvy women?*

CRYSTAL: *I don't ever want to speak for all curvy women. I'm just speaking from my own experiences. But society tells us we can't wear certain things. So many brands don't actually carry sizes larger than ten. And if they do, they're more expensive. But there are some amazing brands out there. I can link them below in the comments. But really it's about finding your own personal style. As with fitness, you have to figure out what works for you and your body. As important as confidence and embracing your body are, you have to be comfortable with what you're wearing to feel confident.*

MEL: *I think that's great advice. It goes for all women, regardless of size.*

CRYSTAL: *For sure.*

MEL: *Let's check out your closet.*

[Mini montage of Crystal modeling various outfits]

MEL: *Well, thank you so much for a peek into your closet. It was great having you! [Turns to face camera] Thanks for watching, guys. Make sure to follow Crystal for amazing advice on how to embrace your body and live your best healthy life!*

Comment by **_RobinAnne_Mc**: You guys are adorable! Love Crystal. More vids together please. ♡

Comment by **Danthegamer_384**: Melanie is fake af. Go blow up your lips more. ♡

Reply by **CurvyFitnessCrystal**: **@Danthegamer_384** Do you have nothing better to do than make rude comments on other people's appearance? ♡

Comment by **CourtneyG-1324**: y do we feel the need to constantly give fat people reassurance that they look good in clothes that don't fit them properly ♡

Reply by **Aquariusgirly**: **@CourtneyG-1324** people like u are the reason. Crystal and Mel u look amazing!! ♡

Reply by **CurvyFitnessCrystal**: Thank you **@Aquariusgirly**. ♡

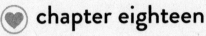 **chapter eighteen**

T HE DUMBBELL HITS the rubber mat at my feet with a louder-than-intended *thud*. Patty, the chronic complainer, clasps her chest as if I've stolen her virtue. She's perched on the bench nearby like a queen, dabbing her perfectly dry forehead with a royal-blue gym towel.

Scott treats me to a discreet eye roll, gently placing his own dumbbells next to mine. We're cooling down with a few strength-training sets after a deadly Girl Power Anthem–themed spin class. Unsurprisingly, Scott was the only dude in the class. I assumed he'd be too macho for it, but with much pleasure, he basked in the not-so-subtle attention from ladies.

"You okay?" he asks. "You're doing that thing with your jaw. The thing you do when you're pissed."

I make a point to soften my frosty expression, while refraining from grinding my teeth to stubs. "Yeah. People are dicks."

"What's going on?" He sits on the mat and pats the space beside him.

I sit next to him, blowing a stray hair out of my face. "I did a guest video on Mel's Instagram Live feed yesterday. Some of the comments got a bit out of hand."

"What do you mean by *out of hand*?"

I pull up the saved video. Our fingers brush ever so slightly as I hand my phone over, sending a tiny spark of electricity sizzling through me.

Scott doom-scrolls for a couple seconds, shaking his head before tossing the phone back into my lap. He stares into the void for half the Excalibur Fitness ad before meeting my gaze. His expression isn't one of pity. It's soft and sincere, as though he really cares. "Crystal, I'm so sorry you have to deal with this. You know these people—"

I raise my hand to stop him. "I know. It's been this way ever since I started my account. Honestly, it's fine." I pause, realizing how that sounded. "I mean, it's not *fine*, obviously. But I've learned to deal with it. I don't care what asshole strangers from the bowels of the internet have to say about my body."

He holds eye contact. "I know. And it's amazing. But isn't there a way to block them?"

I shrug, momentarily admiring the female bodybuilder's impeccable biceps as she passes behind Scott. "Not really. I used to try, but it's impossible to block so many accounts. Honestly, I'm more concerned for my followers than myself." And it's the truth. I know what I can handle. But I live in constant fear of my followers reading those hateful comments.

A vein flexes in his forearm as he reaches to touch his toes. "I know. You worry about everyone. I know you're strong, but I guess I just . . . I can't help but worry about you too. I know you say the comments don't bother you, but they must get to you sometimes, don't they?"

My lips press together, as if blocking the words that are so desperate to escape. Admitting that fact means I'm not living up to my body-positive message, and that's a tough pill to swallow. "Sometimes, yeah." The admission feels like a forty-five-pound plate has been lifted from my chest.

"Did I ever tell you about that asshole kid in middle school?"

"No."

Scott gives the dumbbell a small, mindless push to the side. "I started at a new school halfway through sixth grade. I was late on the first day because my sister Kat had a meltdown before we left the house. Anyway, I showed up during gym class. They were doing basketball drills, shooting layups and stuff. I was up against this kid named Alex. He was massive for a twelve-year-old. Was basically the size of a teenager." Scott's eyes grow darker as he continues. "I scored before he did and he got pissed. Tossed the basketball at my face and broke my nose."

"Jesus. What a psychopath."

"Oh yeah. He bullied the shit out of me after that."

I hang my head. "I'm so sorry. Why did he pick on you?"

"I was the new kid, I guess? Scrawny. An easy target. He terrorized me every recess. Held me down and made me eat sand. Basically used me as a punching bag." Scott's easy smile is replaced with a severe scowl as he focuses on a ripped spot on the mat.

I recall our sorbet date, when I discovered he wasn't always the picture of confidence. It's jarring and heartbreaking to imagine a devastated and humiliated adolescent Scott, compared to the (overly) confident man he is today. No one would dare challenge his cocksure, alpha presence now. While I'm amazed at the transformation, my gut twists. Kids can be serious assholes.

He lifts his ball cap and rakes a rough hand through his mane. "Anyway, sorry I'm so worked up about it. I guess I just know how you feel—" He backpedals, cringing. "I know it's not the same thing . . . getting bullied by a jackass twelve-year-old compared to what you're going through—"

"No, I get it. I appreciate you sharing that," I cut in, taking in the residual pain in his eyes. I place a gentle hand on his forearm and his muscles flex under my touch.

"Do you ever feel like you'd be happier if you . . ." The words trail off when he realizes the weight of what he's about to say. He looks away, as if he's afraid of my reaction.

"Do I ever want to delete my account?" I finish for him.

He meets my gaze. "I'd never suggest that. I know how important it is to you. But I can't imagine dealing with that day in and day out. It's cyberbullying, Crys."

I sit up straighter. "I'm fine." My tone is harsher than I intend it to be, which doesn't seem to bother him. "And I fully understand your concern. But I'm an adult, not a kid. I have off days, true. But I believe in my message. If that means I have to deal with assholes, I'll take it if I can help one person feel better about themselves."

He places his hand on my shoulder and I lean into it. Again, it doesn't feel like pity. It's support. It's comfort. "Alright. Well, I'm always here for you. If you ever have an off day."

Warmth blooms in my chest at his touch. For years, I haven't relied on anyone but myself to feel confident and worthy. I've never needed a shoulder to cry on when the trolls unleash their fury, and I don't intend on changing that. But just knowing he's here to help lighten what's been a solo burden for seven years makes all the difference.

• • •

I'M CREEPING OUTSIDE the Boston Fire Department, Engine 10, Tower 3 (whatever that means) with a stack of glass Tupperware in my arms.

It's the last place I thought I'd end up after a fruitful gym session. I managed to shoot a full week's worth of videos. When I woke up this morning, I had more vigor than the Energizer Bunny, partially because I slept for nine hours, but mostly because of Scott.

After our spin session yesterday, a delivery showed up at my door. It was a bouquet of lush pink, white, and purple tulips. The card read:

Crystal,

You're beautiful.

—Scott

I melted like a snowball in hell after reading that card. It's probably the kindest gesture I've ever received. The message was simple, but the words were just what I needed to hear to snap me out of my spiral of negativity. This was physical proof that I was truly special to him. That I really mattered.

So when Scott mentioned in passing he'd forgotten to pack dinner today, I felt the overwhelming urge to come to his rescue.

I'd already made myself a lemon poppy seed summer kale salad and turkey wraps anyway, so I figured I'd bring him my extras, lest he starve to death.

There are four massive garage doors open, housing three bright-red fire trucks. I step into the engine bay tepidly, entirely out of my element. It smells like a mechanic's shop, ripe with oil, gasoline, and testosterone.

The last time I was at a fire station was for my second-grade field trip. One of my classmates, a girl named Alyssa, who galloped around the yard at recess under the delusion she was a horse, threw up her pizza Lunchable in the fire truck. According to Facebook, she's married with two children now, living in a picturesque ranch bungalow.

As I let that thought soak in, I spot a tall, muscular guy with neatly trimmed dark hair and a full sleeve of tattoos adorning his right arm. He's fiddling with some sort of contraption on the side of the truck. He flashes me a smoldering smile as I approach.

"Are you lost, ma'am?" He exudes a very overt brand of charm that's probably an instant panty dropper for most women with the gift of sight.

My cheeks burn. I'm highly regretting my decision to show up without notice in the first place. I should have texted Scott first. But now that I've been spotted, it's too late to turn back. "Uh, I'm looking for Scott Ritchie."

He raises his brow with interest as he gives me a not-so-subtle once-over. "Scotty? He's upstairs in the lounge." I'm about to tell him I have no idea where the lounge is when he extends his hand. "I'm Trevor."

"Crystal," I say with a polite handshake as the name settles in recognition. Trevor is Scott's roommate and godfather to Albus.

We haven't met yet, because every time I go to Scott's, Trevor is either at work or with a lady friend. According to Scott, Trevor is a perpetual bachelor. In fact, he affectionately referred to him as a "cynical womanizer because daddy issues," which strangely encapsulates the vibes I'm getting.

Trevor gives me an amused, cocky smile, as if he already knows who I am. I wonder how much Scott told him about me. Then again, how much would a guy tell his friend about a girl he's cock-blocked from?

"Scott's roommate," I confirm.

"Sure am. I'm guessing Scotty's told you all good things?" He casually leans against the side of the fire truck, arms crossed, tattooed biceps prominent, apparently in zero rush to usher me to Scott.

But before I can respond, a brawny, bald man with deep-set brown eyes comes barreling around the truck. "Word of advice, don't look this guy directly in the eye. Most women don't bounce back."

I snort as Trevor punches him in the arm. "Duly noted."

"Did you say you're looking for Scotty?" the man asks.

I flash him an awkward smile and nod. He waves for me to follow him through a small door off to the side and up a narrow cement staircase. Trevor follows close behind.

"I'm Kevin. You Scotty's girlfriend or something?" He glances at the Tupperware in my arms.

I snort again. "No. I'm a girl who happens to be his friend. My name's Crystal."

Kevin gives me a sly smile, obviously unconvinced. We pass through a minimalist boardroom adorned with photos commemorating firemen I assume have passed while on duty. Upon seeing these photos, it dawns on me just how serious Scott's job is. Every day, he rushes headfirst into all kinds of dangerous scenarios. Being a fitness trainer, my biggest worry is dropping a weight on my toe or pulling a muscle. Comparatively, Scott could lose his life at any time. He's a hero. And yet, you'd never know it to talk to him, because he never brags about it.

Kevin leads me a couple steps down the hallway into an open area with a flat-screen television and a monstrous suede sectional sofa, sizable enough to seat at least twelve. Scott is lying on the couch, arms crossed, ball cap over his eyes. By the slow way his chest rises and falls, he appears to be sleeping.

Trevor gives me a funny look, as if to say, *Wait for it*. He grabs a random tennis ball from the table and launches it straight into Scott's hard stomach.

Scott bolts upright, brows furrowed, disoriented, as Trevor, Kevin, and I snort with laughter. "What the fuck, man?"

"You have a very special visitor," Trevor tells him, watching the tennis ball bounce onto the floor.

Scott leans forward, squinting at me as if I'm a mirage. "Crys?"

I give him an embarrassing jazz-hands wave, like that of a dad trying to be hip in front of his tween daughter and her friends. I make a mental note to never do it again as long as I live. "Looks like you're working hard. Or hardly working, I should say." I cringe. My uncool dad vibes are out of control right now.

Scott stands, rounding the couch toward me. "I just got back from a stressful call an hour ago, smart-ass."

I avert my gaze from his gorgeous eyes to the Tupperware in my hands. "Brought you some dinner. So you don't starve."

"Seriously?"

I nod, handing the glassware to him. "Kale salad and turkey wraps."

His lips curl upward as he steps forward to pull me into a one-armed hug. "You're amazing. Thank you."

An involuntary shiver ripples down my spine from the tingle of his voice in my ear. "It's no trouble. I had extras." I glance at Trevor and Kevin, who are shoulder to shoulder, observing our exchange in amusement. "Anyway, I better get going. Tara and I are supposed to have Mel over tonight for a movie." I really should turn to leave, but I don't. I rock backward on the balls of my feet, loitering, because I want to soak up his magnetic presence for a little while longer.

Scott hesitantly chews his bottom lip. "Hey, let me give you the grand tour."

"You don't have to. You look like you were pretty busy there," I tease.

He bumps my shoulder. "Hush. I'll even let you sit in the fire truck."

Kevin whistles. "Only special ladies get to go in the fire truck."

Scott's cheeks flush. "It's true."

I hold back a massive grin. "Okay, sold."

Scott leads me through the building, introducing me to everyone who walks by. All the guys are easygoing, friendly, and highly interested in my presence. One of them asks me if I liked the flowers yesterday, which warms my heart, because now I know Scott talked about me at work.

After we razz Scott about his love for the Blackhawks, he shows me where they store their gear and tools. He even lets me hold his fire jacket and pants, which must weigh a good fifty pounds.

"How long do you have to put on all your gear?" I ask.

"About thirty seconds, ideally." He smiles when he sets his helmet onto my head. "You look cute in that."

My cheeks burn instantly as the helmet falls forward, shielding my eyes. "Don't call me cute."

"Sorry, I just speak the truth." He lifts the helmet back off with a cheeky smile and nods toward yet another narrow doorway.

When we return to the garage area, he gestures at a gleaming fire truck. "Ever been in one of these?"

I inch closer. "When I was eight."

He points to the handlebars on either side of the metal stairs leading to the entrance. "Hold on to the handles as you go up."

"You have to promise not to stare at my ass," I say, one foot on the first stair, fully aware he's staring. I'm thankful I'm wearing my best leggings, which accentuate my booty.

"I promise nothing." He methodically makes a point of absorbing my backside from every angle.

I hoist myself into the truck, which doesn't actually feel that spacious inside given all the screens and gear. I immediately go for the driver's seat.

"Which is the button for the sirens?" I ask, pointing at the console.

"Don't touch anything." He swats my hand away playfully before I have the chance to wreak havoc.

He settles into the passenger seat, my Tupperware in his lap. I hand him a fork from my purse and silently watch in anticipation as he takes his first bite, like a contestant nervously awaiting judgment from a celebrity chef on the Food Network.

"Thanks, Crys. This is really good."

"Glad you like it."

He catches my gaze and holds it. "I love it."

The moment those words come out of his mouth, goose bumps erupt everywhere, most noticeably on my arms. My throat instantly dries. It's as if he's told me he loves me, even though he merely loves my salad. I clear my throat, straightening my spine, desperate to change the topic. "So aside from sleeping, what do you guys do when you're in between calls?"

"Chores, usually. Lots of cleaning, making sure all the gear is good to go. We do training too. Oh, and meetings. But sometimes it's slow, so we just shoot the shit or watch TV, depending on who's supervising."

"And you love it?"

"Yeah. Love the action. Every call gets my adrenaline going. I mean, we get a lot of bullshit calls, but we treat each one the same. You never really know what you're gonna get when you show up." Seeing his face light up when he talks about his job is beyond attractive. "And it makes me feel close to my grandpa. Gives us something to bond over."

"You must really look up to Martin, following in his footsteps," I say, mesmerized by his passion.

"Yeah. We've always been pretty close." His voice breaks slightly. "Especially after my dad and my grandma Sheila passed in the same year. About ten years ago. Makes you want to cherish the people you have in your life when stuff like that happens."

My stomach turns to rocks at the revelation. "In the same year? I'm sorry, Scott. That's awful."

"My dad had a random heart attack. My grandma passed a few months later. Her health kind of deteriorated after my dad died."

"Your dad must have been really young."

"Yeah. No one saw it coming. He was really active. Always out running and biking. Trying to set new personal bests." He pauses and takes another bite.

"Sounds like someone else I know," I say affectionately.

His ashen expression revives itself, as though he doesn't want to dwell. "Anyway, enough about that. You'll like this story . . ."

As Scott downs the salad, he describes a medical call from a man who is a frequent caller. He wears a literal tinfoil hat and calls 911 at least three times a week, claiming a foreign government is leaving coded messages in the form of burning paper bags on his doorstep.

I giggle as he promptly moves on to the turkey wrap. He groans loudly on his first bite, sending a course of heat throughout my body. I shift, resettling in my seat, trying to think of literally anything else, like the stray piece of lint on my leggings.

"This is my new favorite food," he declares.

"What was your favorite food before?"

"Ribs. Yours?"

"Clementines."

His eyes widen in elation. "Those tiny Christmas oranges? They're like crack."

"Right? No one else appreciates them."

"I like them. As long as there's none of that white stringy stuff."

I roll my eyes. "The pith? You have the eating habits of a small child, Scotty."

He grins and takes another bite. "I have a sophisticated palate, thank you very much. And this shit is amazing." When he smiles, I'm immediately reminded of how different our relationship is now, compared to a month ago. We still banter constantly, but there's a tenderness in his eyes now when he looks at me. Like he truly cares.

"I have a serious question for you," I say hesitantly after a few moments of silence. "And you're not allowed to lie."

"Okay." He seems unbothered by my tone.

"Did you hate my guts at the gym when we first met?"

"No." He shakes his head, as if offended I'd even ask. "I don't hate anyone. And I definitely didn't hate you."

"You didn't have much of an issue stealing that squat rack from me. I even called you Squat Rack Thief until the engagement dinner."

He bursts out laughing, his deep chuckle sending vibrations throughout my body. "Honestly, I was so stunned you were even talking to me that I didn't really know what to do. I kind of just froze up. And I was actually gonna be late for work. Guess I came off like an asshole, huh?"

I set my head back on the headrest. "I mean, it was a quintessential asshole move. I was so pissed at you."

He grins, like it's a personal achievement to grind my gears. "Oh, I'm aware. I still remember the look you gave me. Pretty sure you could have frozen an entire country."

"What about when I was putting Mel through sled pushes? Did you purposely steal our floor space?"

He swallows his bite. "Sure did."

"Why?"

He waits a couple seconds, tightening his lips before speaking. "Because I thought you were cool. I wanted an excuse to talk to you. I didn't know how else to do it."

I'm momentarily stunned at how severely I misjudged him.

"You didn't want to come up to me and strike up a conversation? You know, like a normal, mature human?"

"I told you, I have a history of being socially awkward. I don't approach women on the regular without a pretext."

"I think people see you a lot differently than you think."

His gaze lingers on my face. "I think the same about you." He pauses. "Wanna know the first thing I noticed about you?"

"Please don't say my eyes." I shyly cover them with my hands. My entire life, my eyes have been a hot topic. People have always fetishized my "light" eyes, which makes me uncomfortable.

He reaches forward, his fingers circling my wrists, gently pulling them down to my lap. "No. Not your eyes, even though they're beautiful. They were second . . . or maybe third after your ass in those leggings." He smirks, watching my face with an expectant grin.

I should be pulling away, but we're both leaning closer. The air has changed around us. I'm hypersensitive to everything. The one wayward hair falling into my eye. The softness of my shirt against my skin. The feel of the seat below my thighs, which are tingling with heat. "Then what did you notice first?"

"Your beauty mark, right here." His finger brushes the little dot right below my left eye, close to my nose.

We're practically knee to knee. I don't know if it's just me, but the space around us shrinks with each passing second.

He lets his hand fall over my knee, giving it a light squeeze, sending a trickle of electricity to the forgotten places in my body. Our faces are close enough that I can feel his warm breath against my cheek. If I closed those last few inches, I could kiss him. His gaze flickers to my lips. I catch myself leaning in slightly, until our foreheads connect. We stay like this for a few long breaths as I listen to the steady drum of my heart. Finally, he tilts his head downward, his lips grazing mine with the lightest touch.

I'm about to press closer as an equal and very willing participant when an awful, high-pitched alarm goes off, sending my blood pressure sky-high. We jump back simultaneously.

"Shit. It's a call. I gotta go." His easygoing face suddenly transitions to that ultraserious expression from when we first met. He bolts out of the passenger seat, taking care to gather the Tupperware containers.

I shuffle out of the truck after him as everyone races to the back room behind the fire trucks to gear up.

He stops for a beat, pulling me in by the nape of my neck. He then rewards me with a soft kiss on my forehead. "Thanks for bringing dinner, Crys." It isn't a quick peck. It's a full-on press of his lips to my skin.

Then he bolts away to the back room, leaving me mystified and practically immobile.

As I walk back to my apartment, my forehead and lips sear from the warmth of his kisses. From the touch of our foreheads together in the fire truck. From the look in his green eyes that stirs up all the feelings I'm trying to suppress until August. I don't know if I can wait that long.

chapter nineteen

STILL REELING FROM our kiss in the fire truck, I pick up snacks on my way home for girls' night. A rom-com and a deep-dive risk analysis on the merits of abandoning or abiding by my three-month rule are just what I need right now.

But by the time I get home, Tara and Mel have changed the plans without bothering to consult me. They're in crisis mode. Tara is "distraught" over her new bob à la Khloe Kardashian, which she's convinced has ruined her face (it hasn't). And worse, Mel had an epic fight with her boyfriend. I hide my face in a pillow and dramatically pretend to sob when they announce the new plan to "dance our troubles away" at the club.

Half a drink in, and the reason clubs are no longer my scene becomes oh so apparent. Instead of wearing my trusty Lulus, I'm in a one-piece jumper that's giving me a perma-wedgie. Wherever I go, my sense of smell is assaulted by a mixture of B.O., heavy perfume, and the rose incense diffused throughout the velvet-wallpapered space.

Mel and Tara are in their element, dancing and flirting with strangers, acquiring enough free drinks to render them halfway eligible for a stomach pump.

One of Mel's friends, Kelly, has met us here. She's equally as gorgeous as Mel. Asian and tall, almost lanky. Unlike Mel and Tara, who are dolled up in four-inch heels and dresses plastered to their skin, Kelly is wearing Birkenstocks and a baggy T-shirt that reads *NOPE*, paired with silky pajama-like pants that do not match in any way, shape, or form. It's ratchet as hell, but I dig it.

Apparently, everyone else does too. Even though Kelly isn't flaunting her assets, she's attracting the attention of literally every guy in this club. They're descending on her like moths to a porchlight. She's one of those girls who emits this welcoming, free-spirit, manic pixie vibe but will crush your heart all the same. She probably leaves a trail of salty tears and broken hearts wherever she goes, which is fitting, because she's a travelgrammer.

Even though I'm being a miserable wench keeping a watchful eye over the proceedings, I'm pleased Tara is letting loose. After breaking up with Seth, I wasn't sure she'd ever make a full recovery. Watching her slow-grind against a guy who looks eerily like the Weeknd gives me renewed hope.

Mel pulls me from my safe space on the sidelines and onto the crowded, sweltering dance floor, nearly sploshing me with her rum and coke.

"I'm fine here holding the purses and making sure you guys don't get roofied," I explain, hoping my mom mode will ward her off.

"Come on! You're being a buzzkill!" she shouts over the house music, slapping me square on the boob.

I sigh, appeasing them for a couple songs. As I sway awkwardly to the music, I'm having a hard time understanding how I used to do this on the regular back in college. Dancing with Tara, Mel, and Kelly isn't the problem. It's everyone else that I can't stand. Everywhere I step, I'm shoulder to shoulder with twenty-year-olds aggressively fist pumping. Do they even know the origins of the fist pump? Unlikely. They were literally ten years old when *Jersey Shore* premiered on MTV.

I'm officially done when a guy with a rattail grabs my waist, even after I turned him down politely on three separate occasions. He's shamelessly relentless. One of those creatures who don't understand the words "I'm not interested." I'm like a bird in flight, taking refuge in a random booth across from a couple in the midst of a sloppy make-out session involving a lot of tongue and groping hands everywhere.

As I soberly observe everyone gyrating on the dance floor from the safety of the booth, all I can think about is how I don't want any stranger, good-looking or not, to touch me right now.

In fact, the only person I want to hang out with is Scott, who, ironically, was merely an infuriating stranger only a month ago. Despite the short time we've known each other, the level of effortless comfort between us makes it impossible to imagine what it was like when I didn't know him.

I look forward to turning over, bleary-eyed in the early morning, reading Scott's texts, especially his random messages while he's on night shift and I'm sleeping. The odd time when there isn't a text from him, I feel a smidge of disappointment.

I can't stop thinking about the way Scott's dimples appear at the slightest smile, the glint in his eyes when he looks at me, how he doubles over with laughter at the smallest things, how easy it is to open up to him about anything, from the serious to the ridiculous, and how nice it feels to *be* in his presence, even if we're not saying anything at all.

Rage-chugging the remainder of my sour drink is the only thing that remotely helps expunge invading thoughts of being with him in the fire truck today.

My feelings for him are confirmed when his name appears on my phone. I instantly light up, spellbound and humming with electricity, as if someone has just turned on the twinkle lights.

SCOTT: Just got off a call at this lady's house. Guess how many ferrets she had in her apartment.

CRYSTAL: One too many?

SCOTT: Higher.

CRYSTAL: 20?

SCOTT: 23!!

CRYSTAL: WHAT???

SCOTT: Right? Disgusting. *GIF of immaculately dressed Tim Gunn flicking his dainty wrist in disgust*

CRYSTAL: Ferret people are weird.

SCOTT: Yup. A girl in my school had one. She brought it for show-and-tell one day in fourth grade. She let it eat out of her mouth . . . haven't looked at a ferret the same way since.

CRYSTAL: Lmao.

CRYSTAL: Guess what? I'm at a club with Mel and Tara.

SCOTT: A club?

CRYSTAL: Yeah. They're grinding on the dance floor right now with randoms. I'm just here to spectate and ward off the creepers.

SCOTT: Why aren't you out on the D floor too?

CRYSTAL: I was . . . then a guy with a rattail ruined it.

SCOTT: Want me to come kick his ass?

CRYSTAL: How kind of you to offer. But I'm good. I prefer being a wallflower.

SCOTT: Haha I don't blame you. I can't stand clubs.

CRYSTAL: Really? I imagined it would be your hunting ground. Your natural habitat.

SCOTT: Wow, you make me sound like a massive creep.

My phone vibrates from his call, so I duck into the bathroom.

"Hey," I yell over my ringing ears, even though the bathroom is ten times quieter, aside from the flushing of toilets and the squealing of two drunken girls sharing a stall.

"Do you still think I'm a huge fuckboy?" he asks.

I lean against the sink. "I never said that. I'm just sayin' . . . You look like a Marvel superhero. I'd think someone who looks like you would take full advantage of your genetic gifts." I make my voice light and teasing, remembering how upset he got the first time I falsely assumed.

"Superhero, huh? Someone once told me I look like a Hemsworth. I'm better looking, though."

"Don't get too cocky," I tease him. "You don't have the Aussie accent to heighten your sex appeal." He merely has strong, protective biceps I want to curl into until the end of eternity. But no matter.

"Well, blimey," he says in an awful fake accent.

I shudder with laughter as I catch my reflection in the smudged bathroom mirror. I pat down my now frizzy hair. "Scott, that was British, not Australian."

"Oh, shit. You're right. Guess I should stick with my Midwestern accent."

"It suits you." I'm cut off when the two drunk girls emerge from the stall screeching about a "bitch" named Brittany.

Before we hang up, I promise Scott I'll call him when I get home. It's sad how eager I am to talk to him again.

Luckily, things pick up after I emerge from the bathroom. The girls and I find a more tolerable spot to dance, and by the end of the night, I've nearly lost my voice from dramatically singing (screeching) "Wrecking Ball."

I call Scott back the moment I kick off my heels when we return home.

"Are you in bed now?" he asks.

"Yeah. Just climbed in. Are you?"

"Yup."

Silence. I wonder if he's thinking what I'm thinking, that I really wish he was here. My breath quickens at the mere thought of the warmth of his body beside mine. Aside from the fact that I've physically resisted the urge to climb him like a tree at every opportunity, particularly when he's in all his muscled glory at the gym, I undoubtedly like him. A lot.

In fact, he's my favorite person. Hanging out with Scott is always light. Even when one of us is in a particularly bad mood, we're clutching our stomachs in rip-roaring laughter fifteen minutes later. Laughter is a staple when we're together. I don't think anyone else has ever made me cackle to the point of tears and stomach pains, as if I've done an entire ab-ripper routine. And whenever he's not around, I miss him.

I want to be with him. Every time I see his face, I nearly lose my resolve, just like in the fire truck. The more I think about it, the more I'm starting to realize how different he is from Neil. Looking back, Neil talked about Cammie constantly. I knew deep down he was still in love with her, but I chose to ignore the signs. And yet, Scott doesn't ever talk about his ex, unless I bring it up. And he doesn't dwell on it for long.

Maybe this could be different. What am I waiting for? Why am I delaying the inevitable?

I draw in a breath, readying myself to declare *To hell with the rebound rule. I don't want to wait anymore* with gusto, until he interrupts my train of thought.

"I have a very important question to ask you, Crystal Alanna Chen." His tone is dead serious.

I swallow nervously, staring up at the ceiling. "Mm-hmm?"

"Do you sleep with your socks on or off?"

I snort, unable to stifle my laughter. "Obviously off. What kind of sick individual sleeps with their socks on?"

He lets out a dramatic sigh of relief and pauses for an awkward second. "Uh, my ex-girlfriend, actually. It was kind of a deal breaker."

"Is that the real reason you ended things?" I try to keep my tone light, even though I'm taken off guard that he's brought her up without my prompting.

"That was a factor. But besides how things ended, we didn't click. It's hard to describe. She was really great on paper. Had everything going for her. But then I'd make a joke and she wouldn't really get it. Different sense of humor, I guess."

"Is humor important to you?"

"Always."

"Why?"

He pauses for a moment. "My grandma always said you should laugh at least once a day."

"I love that." I turn onto my side. "What was she like?"

"Hilarious. She had one of those infectious laughs. Like . . . even if you were having the worst day, she would just laugh and make everyone feel better. One time the whole family went to visit during the summer when I was eleven. She served the entire family yogurt and berries, but she replaced the yogurt with mayonnaise." He begins to laugh and it's pure nostalgic joy.

"That is so genius. What a power move."

"Oh yeah. It was great. My oldest sister got sick all over their living room."

I smile, reveling in the sound of his laughter. I could listen to it all day. And there's no reason I shouldn't. *Just say it. Before you chicken out.* "Hey, Scott?" My voice cracks.

"Yeah?"

"I was thinking, remember that rebound rule? What if we—" A strange break in the line cuts me off. "Hello? You there?"

"Shit, sorry, Crys. I'm getting a call. Gotta go." His tone is rushed, almost frantic.

My face twists in a mixture of worry and confusion. "Uh, okay. 'Night."

The line goes dead.

What just happened?

chapter twenty

SHOULD NOT BE in public like this.

It looks like I've done years of hard time in solitary confinement. My eyes are bloodshot. My skin is pale, practically translucent. I'm dehydrated and my hair is so matted I'm surely going to require scissors to remedy the situation. All night, I tossed and turned, kicking my duvet on and off, unable to stop my mind from churning out scenarios, none of which boded well for me.

Did Scott actually receive a call? Or did he sense what I was about to say about forgoing the three-month rule, change his name, and defect to a remote desert island?

Maybe he was disappointed by our kiss in the fire truck yesterday, which has yet to be acknowledged by either of us. I'd assumed he'd make some sort of cocky remark about it last night on the phone. But he didn't, which is off-brand for him.

And if there was a real call, who would be contacting him at two in the morning? After my time on Tinder, I've learned any call or text after ten-thirty at night is to be considered a booty call, or an emergency. He'd just completed a twelve-hour shift, so I doubt he'd be getting called back in. Could it have been Diana? He'd literally brought her up in conversation minutes before.

Or could it have been another girl? He'd told me he would wait until the wedding, implying he wasn't going to date anyone else. But maybe that long a dry spell is a tall order, especially for a guy who looks like an A-list action movie star masquerading as a normal dude to avoid the paparazzi. I'm reminded of this every time we're in public. Women do quadruple-takes, either flirting or freezing upon sight of him, no in-between. One lady even slipped him her number in the line at the pharmacy while he was temporarily holding my purse. If he wanted to get laid, he'd hardly have to lift a finger.

It doesn't help that he hasn't texted me back all morning. My heart sinks as I re-analyze my ignored text from earlier to ensure it can't be misinterpreted out of context. I'd teased him about the Blackhawks loss—our usual banter—nothing to be personally offended by. So why is he suddenly ignoring me?

Tara is quick to remind me of how Neil would ghost me for days, claiming he was "so busy" when realistically, he was an unemployed, struggling musician, getting high on his couch. In her humble opinion, I'm overreacting. "Scott's probably just adulting," she told me confidently before I left for the gym. But given he's texted me nonstop for the past month, reporting the most mundane of things, like the fact that he's pouring a glass of milk, it strikes me as uncharacteristic. Something feels wrong. I feel it in my gut.

Just as I finish my cooldown on the treadmill, Scott finally texts.

SCOTT: You're coming over tonight.

He hasn't fled the country after all. Maybe things are fine. Maybe he hasn't been intentionally ignoring my very existence.

CRYSTAL: Um, I don't remember you inviting me. Nor do I
   remember accepting an invitation.
SCOTT: I have snacks.
CRYSTAL: . . . Fine.

On the promise of snacks, I head to Scott's after dinner after editing a new workout video tutorial. The entire way there, I find myself nervously picking my nails to stubs in anticipation of an explanation. I have no idea how to play this. Should I pretend to be chill about it? Or should I pounce and ask him about the call immediately?

By the time I arrive, I'm still undecided. When his door opens, a massive ball of beige, curly fluff bounds toward me, leaping at my face. After all of two seconds, Albus Doodledore has managed to coat my hands entirely with slobber. He flops his gangly body onto the floor, hyperventilating, tongue out, over the moon to see me.

"Hello, hello, nice to see you again." I laugh, returning Albus's nearly human smile. His bushy tail sways back and forth like windshield wipers at full speed. I kneel down to give him a generous belly rub, which he takes full advantage of, rolling onto his back. It's become our ritual whenever I come over.

"Nice to see you, too, I suppose." I pretend to regard Scott dismissively, trying to ignore the way he towers over me, and how his muscular chest strains under his fitted navy-blue Henley rolled at the elbows. The man can seriously wear the shit out of a Henley.

He closes the distance between us. "That's how it's gonna be, huh? The dog consistently gets a better greeting than me."

My body fights the urge to grab his ridiculously beautiful face and kiss him. But when I remember how he hung up on me after randomly bringing up his ex, I think better of it. Instead, I cross my arms over my chest, inadvertently pushing up my boobs, accentuating my cleavage. "My deepest regrets. Would you also like your belly scratched?"

His gaze flickers briefly over my chest before settling back on my face with a devilish smile. "I mean, I wouldn't say no."

My face heats. He's being his normal, deliberately flirty self, which only heightens my curiosity about last night's mystery call. Suddenly, the entranceway feels far too small. In need of air, I inch past him, into the living room.

Scott's apartment is clean and simple. It's older, with original wood flooring and crown molding around the ceilings. There's a sizable living room, filled with masculine leather furniture and a flat-screen television. Basically a frat boy's starter pack. A cutout wall separates the living area from the slightly outdated kitchen. As always, it's surprisingly clean for two men who work long shifts.

Scott follows my lead into the living room, watching as I perch on the arm of the couch. There's a lingering silence, casting a barrier between us that's never been there before. As I mindlessly stroke Albus's head, I wonder if he feels it too.

I can't suppress my curiosity any longer, nor can I stand the awkwardness. "So . . . who called you last night?" I finally ask.

His eyes immediately go to his feet, deliberately avoiding the weight of my penetrating gaze. He runs a hand over the back of his neck before clearing his throat. "Trevor."

I frown, immediately suspicious. He never avoids eye contact. "Why'd he call?"

"To tell me he let Albus out before going to work." His voice is clipped, like he's desperate to move on from the topic.

It strikes me as odd that Trevor would call him at two in the morning over something so trivial. Why not send a simple text?

I want to press him farther, interrogate him FBI-style, because my gut tells me he's lying. But what else can I say without sounding unhinged? I have no actual proof otherwise, and I can't go all *jealous girlfriend* when we aren't even a couple.

Instead, I settle on an innocent, "Did you have a busy day today?"

He's still avoiding eye contact as he shrugs, hands deep in the pockets of his dark-wash jeans. "Uh, it was okay. Did some errands."

I tilt my head, unconvinced.

He registers my suspicion, finally meeting my eyes. "What? You don't believe me or something?"

"I hadn't heard back from you this morning. I thought that was kind of weird."

He watches me for a moment, the tension in his jaw softening. "Sorry, really. I had a lot going on."

"Do you want to talk about it?"

"Nah, not right now. Appreciate it, though." His vague response does little to quell my nerves, and he senses it. "It's nothing for you to worry about right now. I promise." He steps forward, reaching for a strand of hair falling into my face. His fingertips brush my cheek as he places it gently behind my ear, eyes locking to mine. They're soft and sincere. I know him well enough to know he wouldn't deliberately hurt me.

I want to respect his request for privacy. We may be close, but it's not like I have an automatic right to know everything that's going on in his life. I search his face for any sign of deception, but fail to find one. If he's lying to me, he deserves an award. "Okay."

I flop onto my usual spot on his couch while he rifles around in the kitchen. When he returns to the living area, he's bearing fruit. Literally. There's a carton of clementines tucked under his right arm.

He remembered my favorite snack.

"No way. Where did you find these? They're out of season." Grateful, I reach to pluck two from the box, almost entirely forgetting his sketchy behavior.

"I have my ways."

My cheeks burn as his eyes linger for a moment longer than casual. "So, what do you wanna watch?" I ask, clearing my throat. I settle in the left-hand corner of his couch, making a concerted effort to loosen my grip on the clementines, lest I inadvertently juice them with my bare hands. "Something twenty minutes or less?"

He sets himself down beside me, man-splaying, long legs stretched out under the coffee table. "Ha ha, very funny. I promise I won't fall asleep. You have my permission to take any means necessary to keep me awake."

I shoot him a mischievous smile. "Any means necessary?"

"Within reason," he warns, pretending to inch away from me.

"I think it's time to work on your stamina. We'll watch . . ." I rack my brain for a morbidly long movie. "*Lord of the Rings*," I say evilly, knowing full well it's a trilogy, which yields about nine combined hours with him.

He smiles, amused. "I didn't take you for a big nerd."

"Oh, I'm a die-hard fan," I lie, just to get a rise out of him.

He tries not to laugh. "Yeah? Do you even dress up in character and go to conventions?"

"Biannually. There's one next week, actually. Was gonna see if you want to come with me."

"Oh, uh—" He's not quite sure where to go from here, so I let him off the hook.

"Scott, I'm kidding. I'm not really a fan. It was the longest movie I could think of." *Which means more time with you*, I leave out.

Clearly relieved, he chuckles, running a hand over his stubble. "Hey, I would have gone. I would have hated every minute and judged you just a tiny bit, but I'd go."

"Really?"

"If it was something you really liked, of course I would." My heart turns to goo instantly. "Maybe I'd even let you dress me up." He bounces his brow and I can't help but laugh at the overtly sexy mental image of Scott with long silky locks, wielding a sword. It's less ethereal Orlando Bloom and more haven't-bathed-in-weeks Henry Cavill in *The Witcher*, and I'm very much here for it.

After we queue up the movie, I turn sideways to stretch out my legs. But there's no room with him directly beside me in the middle cushion. Instead of scooting over, he drapes my legs over his lap.

He doesn't look at me, or acknowledge it. It's just casual, as if this is the norm. And it feels like it is.

"Can I make a prediction?" he asks as Frodo departs on his quest.

"Go for it."

"The uncle is Frodo's real dad."

I give him a sarcastic stare. "Really?"

"I'm right, aren't I?"

"No. Not even close. This isn't *Star Wars*."

He ponders for a moment. "Okay. Gandalf is Frodo's father."

"Scott, rest assured. There is no baby daddy drama."

He fake pouts. "Well, that's a missed opportunity."

Scott's plethora of outlandish theories doesn't stop at Frodo's father. They're far ranging, like "the blond elf" and Gandalf are secretly in love, or Samwise Gamgee is going to betray Frodo, or the ring is a covert listening device for Sauron. In fact, the only correct theory he's thrown out is that Aragorn is the rightful king.

Truthfully, paying an iota of attention to the movie is humanly impossible while he runs his hand over my legs. I'm answering all his questions from straight memory. In fact, the only thing that keeps me sane and distracted from the blooming heat in my lower half is aggressively peeling clementines. By the time the fellowship forms, I hold out a freshly peeled clementine to a confused Scott.

He's too busy gesturing to the TV like an outraged sports fan to notice straight away. "How is that little weirdo with the bug eyes still following them?" His eyes widen and his mouth falls open when he takes stock of the clementine in my hand. "You peeled that for me?"

I nod. "I painstakingly peeled off every last bit of the white stuff for you."

He presses his palm to his heart with an openmouthed smile. "Holy shit." He takes it from my hand gently, inspecting its juicy bareness before giving me an approving look.

He adjusts my legs on his lap, giving my thigh a squeeze before popping a slice into his mouth. Then, he turns to place one into mine. It's almost erotic how his fingertips graze my lower lip, sending a spark rippling down my spine. My entire mouth tingles with heat.

I channel my sexiest, most sultry self, going in for a slow, seductive bite. I'm basically vintage bikini-clad Paris Hilton, rubbing my soapy bits over a Bentley before indulging in a Texas BBQ Carl's Jr. burger, as one does. Unexpectedly, a spray of citrus launches out. As if in slow motion, it soars upward, landing directly in Scott's left eye.

Smooth, Crystal. Smooth.

He immediately lurches forward, pressing his eye closed.

"Oh, crap." I swing my legs off his lap, covering my mouth with my hands.

He squints at me through splayed fingers, shuddering with silent laughter. "It's cool. I'm just blind. It's no big deal."

I try to peel his hand away from his face. "Let me see your eye."

He rubs it. His lid flutters wildly as he attempts to open it all the way, to no avail. "Crys, it's kind of burning."

I pause the movie and dash to his bathroom to grab a washcloth, wetting it with warm water. By the time I return, he's managed to open his eye again. I press the washcloth over it. "I am so sorry. I think that's the worst thing I've ever done to a guy."

"Yup. Getting an acid burn in the eye is definitely a first for me." He tilts his head as I remove the washcloth, revealing his gorgeous, evergreen eyes.

"Excuse me while I perish from embarrassment."

He chuckles. "It's fine. It isn't burning anymore. I'll forgive you eventually."

I eye him, cheeks still red-hot. "The good news is, you've stayed conscious for over half of the first movie."

"Because I have so many questions."

"I think you might be a *Lord of the Rings* fan. Makes one of us," I say. I hit *Play* again, resettling on the couch.

He brings my legs back over his lap like they belong there. "Which character would I be?"

I pretend to think, but the answer is pretty obvious. "Aragorn. One hundo percent."

"Why?"

"Well, you both have some nice flow, for one. And you're a firefighter. So you're brave, daring, and chivalrous. When you want to be," I add.

He nods in quiet agreement, clearly thrilled. "What about you?"

That's an easy answer. "I'm definitely a hobbit. Hardworking, patient, fair, and loyal. Prefers to stay close to home. Strong moral code, sense of right and wrong."

"Can't argue with that. I'm pretty sure you have the Excalibur Fitness Center policies down to a science."

I roll my eyes, tossing a throw pillow at his head. He ducks.

When he brings his head back up, there's a mischievous glint in his eyes. "You really wanna go there?"

I nod, accepting his challenge.

Before I even have a chance to speak, he pins my legs over his lap and begins tickling my sides mercilessly. My legs wriggle and thrash as I try to slither out of his strong grip. I squeal in between breaths, unable to do anything but give him a swift swat in the chest. "You're the worst. What did I do to deserve this?"

"You mean other than blind me with acidic fruits?"

Point taken. I'm quite prepared to give my body over to suffer the consequences, so much so that I readily let him climb all over me. He places his weight on me, pinning my wrists to the arm of the couch for a brief second. This view is spectacular—his corded forearms planted on either side of my head, caging me in. I have the perfect view of the thick swoop of his eyelashes.

He watches me for a few moments before his gaze flickers to my lips. If I lifted my neck even slightly, I could kiss him. And I want to. I want to taste him again. Desperately. He swallows, his thumb tracing the line of my jaw, cupping my chin. He tilts my head up, letting out a soft sigh before his lips brush against mine, stealing my air and all my resolve.

Our lips meet again and again, sinking into a flurry of sweet kisses, gentle bites, just sampling and testing each other. I run one hand over the stubble of his jaw, while the other combs wildly through his thick, wavy hair, which feels like silk in my hands. I paw at him, wanting him closer.

He rolls off me and into a seated position. "Come here," he commands, as if he can read my mind. He tugs me by the arm onto his lap.

I position my legs on either side of his thighs, feeling his enthusiasm for the situation as I settle onto him. His groan fills my ears and it makes me feel light, like I could float up and away with him.

There's a fragility in the way he's looking at me, truly at me. As if he's inviting me in, allowing me to see into the depths of his soul. Every guy I've ever been with would already have my pants off right now, but he's treating me like I'm something to be cherished, savored.

Being with him feels anything but fleeting. It's like plunging headfirst into a deep pool, knowing there's no way out.

A small smile falls upon his lips as he moves my hair behind my ear. "You're so beautiful." His breath comes out in shallow pants before he presses another soft kiss to the side of my mouth.

He runs a flurry of small kisses along the edge of my lips before coaxing them apart. His tongue melds with mine as his hand moves to the back of my head, tugging my hair gently. I'm surprised there's any oxygen left in the entire apartment.

This feels different than our first kiss. While our steamy changing room make-out was mind-numbingly hot, akin to unlocking every secret fantasy I've ever had, it was lust spurring me on. The perfect storm of lust and loathing for a nameless gym patron with the body of a god.

This kiss is something else, because I know Scott on a deeper level that takes my breath away. I know he's an outgoing introvert. Crowded places don't faze him, but if he can avoid them, he will. I know how sad he gets when he sees lost dog posters—he lingers, reading them at least twice with a heavy sigh. I know how he likes his cereal, with very minimal milk, due to his aversion to soggy foods. And I know how funny he thinks something is based on the placement of his hand to his chest and how far back he tosses his head.

Just knowing all of these things, among a million others, intensifies our fusion. Like the stakes are higher than ever with every move we make.

His fingers move from my hair to my back, running up and down my spine. I arch myself, moving in a slow rhythm against him, remembering how perfectly we moved together. Eventually, the tips of his fingers edge around the curve of my waist, under the front of my sweater, darting upward, over my stomach.

"Is that okay?" he whispers against my mouth.

More than okay. I nod and he continues, his hands slowly making their way around the undersides of my breasts underneath my bra. He molds them in his palms, skimming the peaks with the pads of his fingers, his breath quickening with each passing second. A tingling sensation rockets through me, rendering me desperate to drive myself even closer to him.

When I roll my hips, he lets out a deep groan into my ear, grasping my thighs to ground me to him. Suddenly, I hate these leggings and the thin layer they cast, dividing me from what I really want.

As if he can read my mind, his fingers dip under the waist, teasingly tugging them down. His hand curves over my ass underneath my leggings, giving me a firm squeeze. His chest heaves as he meets my wild, primal gaze, which is silently telling him to push me around and have his way with me.

Then, out of nowhere, he stills underneath me. Letting out a ragged breath, he pulls his hand north of my waist. A vein pulses in his forehead. He looks hungry, starving, as if he's doing all he can to resist.

"Crys . . ." he says between labored breaths, "we can't do this."

"What? Why?" I stiffen on top of him as disappointment avalanches through my body. He's rejecting me. The only reason I'm not side-aerialing off his lap is because he's still firmly gripping my waist, as if silently telling me not to move.

His face looks pained as he drops his head. "Because. We're waiting. Taking it slow. Remember?"

I've never hated myself more than I do right now. Why did I do this to myself? Was the old me of merely a few weeks ago really that visually impaired? Did I not want my Marvel-Chris crush to send me to the edge with just his touch? Sure, I didn't want to be his rebound. I wanted more than just sex. But current me, with his massive erection pressed against me, doesn't even care. I want this, regardless of the consequences.

I curve my hand along his jaw, my fingertips scratching his stubble as I pull his face closer to mine. "Screw it."

His massive hands close around my comparatively tiny wrists. I feel like I'm in shackles, which does little to quell my all-out carnal lust for him right now. Our faces are literally an inch apart. I desperately want to close that last inch, but he won't let me.

"I don't want to fuck you." His starved, gravelly voice drops an octave. I'm stunned for a moment, not just because he sounds like the velvety narration of an erotic fantasy, but because he's full-on rejecting me right now. Sensing my shock, he tightens his grip on my wrists. "That came out wrong."

"No. I heard you," I say, attempting to rip my wrists out of his death grip, to no avail.

"Just listen. I want to. Badly." His eyes nearly plead with mine. "But you told me you needed time."

"That was weeks ago. I've had time," I assure. "Why are you suddenly so against it?"

"Because you were right. If we're going to do this, we need to trust each other, with no doubts. We're not there yet."

I frown. "Do you not trust me?"

"I do. But I don't know if it goes both ways."

I'm helpless because he's right, which is exactly why I implemented this time rule to begin with. To save myself from being a shiny object, a distraction to get over Diana.

I release a small sigh. "I'm sorry. I hate that I overthink everything . . . I wish I could jump in, headfirst."

"I don't want you to until you're ready. Really. And it's not just you." He dips his chin, avoiding eye contact. "I had a talk with Martin too."

"Really?"

"He wants us to be careful, especially in the lead-up to the wedding. He doesn't want any drama. This wedding means a lot to him and Flo."

I understand the apprehension. Tension between Scott and me would put a damper on the occasion. But I'm surprised by the sudden shift in attitude toward our union. Last I checked, Martin and Flo were practically begging us to date. I'm tempted to pry further, but I get the sneaking suspicion Scott isn't interested in sharing more. So I just nod. "Yeah, makes sense. We'll cool it."

After a few beats, he looks back up at me, eyes alight, as if he's just come across a rare sale on his hideously expensive protein powder. "But that doesn't mean I can't take you on a couple dates in the meantime."

"You want to court me? The old-fashioned way?" Grandma Flo would be so pleased.

Scott's cocky smirk returns. "Why not? But there will be old-fashioned conditions."

"Conditions?"

His fingertips run a featherlight trail along my cheekbone, sweeping across my jaw and down my neck, tracing my collarbone. His green eyes are a kaleidoscope of want, need, desire, everything I want. "No touching," he whispers in my ear as he sweeps my hair to one side, exposing my neck.

I'm hardly breathing. In fact, I'm practically immobile. I feel nothing above the waist, probably because every nerve between my legs has catapulted itself front and center.

His lips graze mine. "No kissing."

I squeeze my legs together. I'm going to die. I'm going to spontaneously combust on this couch right now.

His hand traces straight down my front, over my breasts, down the hill of my stomach, circling around my inner thigh over my leggings, so close to where I want him. He leans closer, his breathing strained. "And no sex."

"What?"

He smooths his finger over me exactly where I'm craving pressure. "No. No sex of any kind. No kissing. No touching."

"You've already failed. You're touching me right now," I manage as his fingers continue to work their magic. When he presses harder, I nearly spin out of control. My vision tunnels and a delicious heat blooms everywhere. I shift slightly, desperate for that contact. Literally one more touch and I'll be a goner, over the edge. Good night and goodbye forever, world.

And that's when he dares to take his hands off me completely. It's as if I'm inches away from the finish line and someone viciously grabs the back of my shirt, pulling me away from victory.

A wicked smile falls over his lips as he sits back from me. The bastard knows exactly what he's doing to me. "Starting now."

I can barely see straight. I cough due to my bone-dry throat. I sound like a cat hacking up a furball. "You're really committed."

"I have to be if this is gonna work. Otherwise, we'll end up hooking up long before August. I don't want either of us to regret anything. You were right . . . about our families. If things didn't work out, Flo would probably murder me in my sleep. We owe it to ourselves and everyone else to take things slow." He's completely right. If we were to continue on this trajectory, we'd hook up and my insecurities from Neil would resurface and probably swallow me whole.

Sure, I'm frustrated, like a coiled ball of yarn in desperate need of detangling. But I'm also entirely smitten. The fact that Scott is doing this demonstrates how much he truly cares. When I think about how outrageously amazing this man is, my entire body calms, as if it knows how perfectly in sync he is with me on every level. In fact, I'm struggling not to force him into marriage right here and now.

"You have no idea how much that means to me . . . I don't know what to say."

He smirks again, raising his brow. "You don't have to say anything. Just show me how much it means to you. On August sixth."

 **chapter twenty-one**

3:20 P.M.—INSTAGRAM POST: "DO YOU FEEL
LIKE A FRAUD IN YOUR OWN LIFE?" BY
CURVYFITNESSCRYSTAL:

And no, I don't mean fraud as in when you text your friends "omg
dead dying lmfao rofl" with a completely straight face. I'm talking
about serious thoughts, like "I got lucky," "I don't deserve my
success," "Someone is going to figure me out."

These are real things I've thought to myself, and still think to
myself occasionally. I'm only human. It all started way back when I
exclusively wore neon workout clothes, listened to trap music, and
hit my first couple thousand followers. I thought I was
"unworthy," especially compared to all the fit trainers out there

with ripped abs. These feelings of inadequacy doubled by the time I got my first big collaboration with Nike. They offered to send me a literal headband. An inch-wide pink piece of elastic band. And I cried and curled up in the fetal position, so sure they would call me out on being a phony.

Similarly, I'm always seeing my clients disregard their progress. As harmless as this may seem, you're actually disregarding all of your hard work and holding yourself to impossibly high, unattainable standards.

But there is good news. Did you know most people (ahem, mostly high-achieving women) who feel impostor syndrome do so because they're simply driven to succeed? If you're feeling some type of way about your success, my advice to you is stop trying to chase perfect. No one wants perfect, because it doesn't exist.

Comment by **Train.wreckk.girl**: I love this. Impostor syndrome is all too real! ♡

Comment by **trainermeg_0491**: I think these thoughts all the time. You're right. Perfection isn't possible. We should really be easier on ourselves. ♡

Comment by **NoScRyan**: You can't call yourself high achieving when you're a trainer and you're overweight. ♡

• • •

SCOTT: Albus has a question for you.

Five seconds later, he sends a photo of Albus sitting upright in a human position with a tiny sign that reads *Date tomorrow night?*

If a goldendoodle named Albus asks you on a date, you kind of have to go.

CRYSTAL: Yes.
SCOTT: Wow. I'm hurt you're so quick to say yes to him and not me.
CRYSTAL: What can I say? I like wizards.
SCOTT: I should have had him do my bidding weeks ago.
CRYSTAL: What do I wear?
SCOTT: Something nice. Don't worry, next time I'll bring you somewhere you can wear your leggings.
CRYSTAL: Damn, you're already banking on there being a next time? What if I'm super boring? Or weird?
SCOTT: I'm boring too. And I already know you're weird.
CRYSTAL: What if I chew with my mouth open? Or talk during important movie scenes? Or spend too much money?
SCOTT: All tolerable.
CRYSTAL: What if I have a needle fetish?
SCOTT: No comment.

• • •

"WHERE ARE WE going?" I ask, adjusting the hem of my floral sundress.

Scott is taking me on what he's been calling a "top secret" date all day. As cute as it is, the anticipation is killing me. I've never been one for the element of surprise. I'm one of those people who read every movie spoiler. I always know who's going to win *The Bachelor*, thanks to Reality Steve.

"Just wait for it." Scott flashes me his mesmerizing smile, one hand on the steering wheel, the other on the center console. It's readily accessible, purely to taunt me.

At one point, I try to grab his hand. But he promptly bats me away, flashing me an intoxicating wink, reminding me of the *no touching* rule. As thankful as I am for Scott's efforts, I'm like a child who's been told they can't have the candy right in front of them. I want to test his limits.

I fight to suppress nature's urges as we drive through a relatively newer suburban neighborhood toward an area with brand-new custom builds.

I stare at the homes in awe, stifling my amusement. "Did you bring me here to creep in the windows?" I'd passively mentioned how curious I was to see what these homes looked like on the inside a couple weeks ago on our way back from dinner with my parents.

He gives me a throaty laugh. "Yup."

"This is officially my favorite date ever," I tell him as he pulls to the shoulder of the road.

"Ever?"

"I think so."

"You're such an oddball," he says through a massive grin.

I attempt to channel the picture of tranquility as we walk side by side, shoulders grazing ever so slightly. We journey down the not-yet-paved dirt road, past some of the gorgeous Craftsman homes that appear to be complete, at least on the exterior.

"I love these homes. I just wish I could see inside," I lament.

He nods toward one of the largest homes in the cul-de-sac. "Let's go in."

I stop in the middle of the road. "We can't just *go in*."

"Since when are you against trespassing in places you're not supposed to be? You have no issues with changing rooms." He gives me a wry smile. "And I bet they aren't even locked."

I take a quick glance around. There's not a soul in sight, given the houses aren't yet occupied. Normally, I wouldn't be caught dead trespassing on private property, but Scott's cult-leader-level charisma makes me want to drink all his Kool-Aid and bend some rules.

We jog up the steps to the front door. It's locked. I don't know whether to be relieved or disappointed. I'm about to run back to the street when he continues around the back of the house. Before I can even yell at him to give it up, he's managed to pry open the basement window. His lips tug upward in defiance. "Come on."

I watch tepidly as he sneaks in, wedging his broad shoulders through the window, landing gracefully inside.

He evaluates the unfinished basement and then glances up at me, arms outstretched. "Get over here," he orders, low and gravelly.

I take one last look around to ensure there are no witnesses before sliding through the window, legs first, straight into his arms. I revel in the feeling of his hard body against mine. "We broke in."

He grins, proud of our criminality. He holds me for a beat, his hand stroking the small of my back. The intensity of his eyes holds me in place. His gaze flickers to my lips and I brace myself for a hot, adrenaline-rush kiss—derived from the excitement of breaking the law. He bends his chin, lowering his lips an inch from mine, hovering for a moment before abruptly turning his back. He jogs up the stairs two at a time, callously depriving me of his touch.

The moment my feet hit the main floor, we're off. We run from one room to another, practically flying through the house, our laughter echoing off the barren walls. The home is essentially finished, aside from a few piles of extra wood planks and sawdust sprinkling the floors. This particular model boasts gleaming brown-gray hardwood, an all-white, gleaming kitchen, and a beautiful open layout. There are four bedrooms upstairs, with a huge claw-foot tub in the master bedroom en suite.

We climb into the tub, sitting opposite each other. His long legs take up the entire space, making it impossible not to tangle together.

I laugh, unable to get comfortable. "This arrangement doesn't work. You're too tall."

He waves me toward him. "Come here. Sit with your back to me."

I dry-swallow, digesting the fact that he wants me to sit between his legs as if we're a pair of handsy teenagers in the back of a pickup truck at a drive-in movie. I raise my brow at his highly erotic suggestion. "We'd be touching."

"Nah. Doesn't count. It's for practical purposes." He flashes his mesmerizing grin. "I won't touch you. I promise."

I eye him suspiciously before spinning myself around faster than an amateur break-dancer. I settle in between his strong legs, leaning against his chest. Eyes closed, I take in his delicious scent, wishing I could bottle it and spritz it around everywhere I go. I bet I could even patent it and make millions.

It's a bit awkward with his hands at his sides, settled on his knees, not touching me. But if this is as close as we can get, I'm not going to complain.

"I want a house like this one day." I close my eyes as I clasp the cold edges of the tub, letting out a small, mildly pornographic moan. The muscles in his thighs clench around me and he promptly shifts back slightly. I smile, because I know I'm not the only one struggling here.

"If you had a house like this, you'd never leave," he chuckles.

I let my head fall against his firm chest. "True. And neither would you."

"How would you decorate each room?"

"I've always wanted a velvet green couch. Maybe some sort of gold, green, and beige-y theme in the family room. The kitchen's perfect as it is, white and gray. I've always loved darker colors for the master. And then fun colors for the kids' rooms."

"Oh yeah? How many kids?"

I purse my lips in thought. "Two. A boy and a girl."

"I'm having at least three. And obviously at least two dogs," he says, deadpan.

I nearly choke. "*At least* three children? You'll require a mom van."

He shrugs, as if cool with it. "The full seven-seater."

I laugh, picturing him as a suburban dad in a minivan. He gives me more of a sporty SUV vibe, but the image is hilarious nonetheless. Now that I've envisioned him as a sexy-as-sin domestic dad, there's no unseeing it.

"I want a pool." He waves his hand toward the round window beside the tub, which overlooks the sizable, un-sodded backyard. "We had a pool when we moved to Boston. Though my dad always complained about cleaning it."

"Who needs a pool when you have a bathtub like this?" I re-settle, making myself at home against his chest, pressing farther against him.

He swallows against the back of my head, but he doesn't move. In fact, I feel the full brunt of his enthusiasm. His breathing goes ragged against me.

I smile, pleased with myself, continuing on as if none the wiser. "Baths are essential to my health and well-being."

"Yeah? What do you like about them?" His voice comes out strained.

I tilt my head in consideration and turn back around, repositioning so we're facing each other again. "They're relaxing. With a candle, music, bubbles, oils . . . and soap. Just lathering myself . . ." I lean back against the opposite end of the tub, imagining the warm water lapping against my bare skin, the mixture of the fruity, citrus scent of my soap and the blossom scent of my candle.

"Show me," he commands, eyes locked to mine.

"I start up here . . ." With achingly slow precision, I methodologically run my hand down my neck, over my breasts, and over my stomach. It might be evil, but I want to break him. I want to watch him lose all restraint.

His heated expression spurs me on as I dip under the hem of my dress, bringing it upward. My fingers tease around my inner thighs, and between my legs. My skin is on fire from his eyes alone. "Sometimes I'll do this." I slip my hand under the thin lace of my panties.

He practically lurches forward when I make contact with myself. From the way he's clenching his fists, eyes dark, focused on my fingers under the lace, I'd say he's on the brink of losing the battle.

I moan, fingers continuing to swirl around my warmth to relieve the pressure. Up until now, the changing room make-out was the hottest moment of my life. But him watching me like this, vulnerable in front of him, officially takes the title.

Just the way he's looking at me, as though he's fully with me, is all-consuming. It's different than I've ever experienced before, to the point of being petrifying. I want to lose myself completely in him and no longer exist. I don't think I could ever be the same, not after this. By the way my heart aches for him in this moment, I know if he hurts me, I'll be completely wrecked. I'll be broken beyond repair. And strangely, the risk feels worth the reward.

I grip the side of the tub with my free hand, swiveling my finger, the pressure building with each second.

"You're so wet," he pants over me, the silky evidence of his effect on my fingers. Our chests are rising and falling, the tension thickening with each passing second he's not touching me. In fact, his hands are clasped on the sides of the tub, knuckles white, confirming that the hold he has on me has nothing to do with the physical world.

His voice alone makes me shiver. I watch the cords in his forearms flex and shake. He grunts as he loses restraint, reaching to place his hand over mine. I have no idea what he's about to do, but I'm fully on board with a first-class, one-way ticket.

Eyes locked to mine, he moves my own finger in and out of me at a tantalizingly slow pace.

"Aren't you breaking the rules?" I manage teasingly, stifling a moan.

"Partially."

I'm unable to come up with a word to describe the sight of him pleasuring me with my own hand. We've broken our *no touching* rule, but he's still semi-abiding by avoiding kissing my lips and not touching me anywhere else except to guide my hand, which is maddening in itself. He leans in to press a slow kiss to my temple, our breath blending together as he moves another one of my fingers in, his own hand grazing my warmth in the process.

"Oh god," I gasp, clenching around myself as the jolt of pleasure hits me. I'm numb to anything and everything except what he's doing to me.

He pumps my fingers faster and harder, holding on to the base of my neck with his other hand. A bloom of heat shoots from the base of my spine, rocketing to all the forgotten places of my body. My inner walls pulsate, closing in around my fingers, faster and faster as the tension builds to an unmanageable level.

"Let go for me." His low, raspy voice in my ear is all it takes for the knot to finally untangle.

A blinding shock wave rips through me, fast and unexpected. I'm shaking as I clasp his hair in my fingers, desperate to anchor myself to him as the tidal wave hits me, over and over, slamming me home. I never want this to end. I never want to forget how it feels to have Scott look at me the way he's looking at me right now, his eye contact unbreaking as he watches me unravel in front of him.

He lets out a strangled moan, pressing his lips to my forehead, threading his fingers through my hair, cradling me as I struggle to catch my breath. "Christ. I want you so badly right now."

"How badly?" I eye him, still riding the residual waves of my high.

He lets out an exaggerated sigh before grasping his hands on the sides of the tub. "Bad enough that we need to get out of here. Now."

I flash him a wicked smile, nodding toward the very strained zipper of his jeans. "You already broke the rules. Why not let me help you out? It's only fair."

His teeth are clenched as he pauses, hanging his head. "We

can't. I'm two seconds away from breaking all rules and shoving you onto that counter."

My cheeks flush. "I'm not opposed."

"You're killing me." He lets out a muffled groan as he steps out of the tub, his excitement very prominent, at eye level.

I'm immobile for a few beats, just staring at it, mouth open, wishing he didn't have a superhuman level of discipline.

"Hey, my eyes are up here." He smirks at me, obviously pleased with himself. Then he turns, making his way out of the en suite, whistling, as if nothing happened.

When I don't follow immediately, he pokes his head back in. "All good?"

I give a wild nod, drastically failing to remain unfazed by his soul-rocking smile. *Yup. Cool. Just pretending I wasn't about to jump your bones and ravage you in return for the best orgasm of my life. Kindly fetch me a straitjacket, because I'm incapable of practicing basic self-control.*

chapter twenty-two

I'S BEEN A week since *the bathtub*. In the days since, Scott has been trying to pretend that everything is completely and totally okay by practicing rigorous self-control and ensuring a safe distance between us. Two couch cushions away. Avoidance of small spaces. At all times. In fact, he nearly dropped his water bottle when our fingers lightly touched upon exchange, as if my skin was lava.

As much as I'm keen to abide by the old-fashioned "courting" arrangement, I am a millennial, after all. Instant gratification is beyond tempting, particularly when he brushes against me, dutifully spotting me as I do my squat sets.

But today, I have no time to reflect on my pent-up sexual frustration, because I've been tasked to gallivant around the greater Boston area to pick up décor items Grandma Flo found dirt cheap on Facebook Marketplace (her new obsession), as if she needs an excuse to buy more junk.

Centerpieces and miscellaneous décor are about the only things Grandma is not inheriting from what was formerly Tara's wedding. Apparently, Tara's décor lady issued a partial refund after she broke down crying in her office days after the wedding was canceled.

Fetching items from random people online is always an adventure. And Scott has volunteered to join me, despite delaying me by an hour and a half with no explanation.

When I pick him up, he mumbles a bored "Hey," but makes no eye contact.

He's hardly speaking, aside from one-word answers. He's the opposite of his normal, happy-go-lucky, smiles-when-he-talks self. He doesn't even crack a smile when I blast "Thong Song" by Sisqó at maximum volume. Listening to the dirty anthems of our millennial youth in ridged, thick silence is hella awkward. And it's not just my imagination that he's also pressed as far as possible into the passenger window, scrolling on his phone for thirty long minutes while we're stuck in traffic.

I sneak a sideways glance at him while committing the ultimate crime of lowering the volume on Beyoncé. "You know, you didn't have to come if you were going to be a miserable twerp the entire time."

He arches his brow at me for a split second. "A miserable twerp? That's a new one."

"I stand by it." I tighten my grip on the steering wheel. "Seriously though, just say the word and I'll drop you back off."

He keeps his stare locked straight ahead. "No. I want to hang out with you." His tone does little to reverse my clouding doubt.

But though I'm curious about why he's acting like an emo sixteen-year-old boy tormented by thoughts of his mortality, I have little time to dwell, because we've reached our first stop. We're picking up a box of unused votive candles from a man sporting a hideous beige turtleneck that might as well be a federal offense, as Mel would say. His name is Spike. Why Grandma thought it would be safe to send me to the address of a man named Spike is beyond me.

On our way to the second destination, we've advanced to making stilted small talk about the oppressively humid weather like sixty-five-year-old retirees. Or random coworkers who have absolutely nothing in common forced together on some dreadful business road trip, which strangely sounds kind of hot.

I try to push his behavior to the back of my mind as I journey inside to retrieve faux greenery from a seemingly cheery lady with bountiful mom-energy who insists I come in and peruse the other décor for sale. But when I hear pounding and exorcist-style screaming coming from a door to what I assume is the basement, I bolt, feigning digestive distress. When I return to the vehicle, alive to tell my tale, Scott barely even looks up from his phone. Had I perished inside that house, he'd have been none the wiser.

Thankfully, the third stop is uneventful, save for the heavy, hideous candelabras Scott has to Tetris into the trunk of my car.

The final task is to pick up lanterns and fairy lights from a farmhouse wedding venue that has closed its doors for good.

When we arrive, it's abundantly clear why the venue is out

of business. It literally looks like a scene from *The Texas Chainsaw Massacre*. The barn is dilapidated, and quite frankly, I wouldn't be surprised if it's haunted. There are a bunch of sketchy-looking farm tools left for dead, decomposing around the premises among weeds extending to my belly button. I don't even want to think about how many wild creatures are lurking about. It doesn't help that the encroaching darkness is casting eerie shadows every which way.

Scott puts his hand out in front of me as we approach the barn, as if expecting some sort of attack. "Are we sure we're in the right place?"

When we knock on the barn door, there is no answer. I don't think there is another human being for miles. It's located on a property deep down an unkempt dirt road, if you can even call it a road, what with the dense bush on both sides. In fact, it doesn't even appear on Google Maps. I'm surprised we found it in the dark of night.

I cast my gaze around, listening to the swish of the leaves blowing in the wind. A long string of lanterns droops in between a big oak tree and the roof of the barn. I seriously pray those are not the lights I've been sent to fetch.

I call Grandma Flo.

"Grandma?"

"Hi, dear, how are you?"

"I'm okay. Look, Scott and I have gone around to get your décor and—" I cut myself off the moment I remember Scott's talk with Martin and his request that we take things slow in the lead-up to the wedding. While I've been tempted to ask Flo about this sudden change of opinion, we haven't had any one-on-one time over the past week.

"How do the candelabras look?" she asks excitedly, apparently unbothered at the mention of Scott.

"Um, they're nice," I flat-out lie. "Anyway, I'm at—"

"Did you get the greenery for five dollars? I really don't think it was worth ten."

"We compromised at seven," I lie again. After the exorcist sounds, the last thing I wanted to do was stick around and barter. "Anyway, I'm at the last stop at that wedding venue to pick up the lanterns and lights. But there's no one here."

"Really? Give me a minute."

I can hear the clicking of her furious taps on her iPad. Scott has gone wandering around the premises while I wait, vulnerable and alone, searching for any sign of movement among the shadows. I fully expect something to emerge from the bushes and attack me, whether person, animal, or pissed-off spirit with unfinished business.

"The lady just responded. They forgot we were coming to pick it up and they're out of town. She said you can grab it all for free, given the inconvenience."

I sigh, relieved when Scott comes back around the front, waiting. I force my gaze from his biceps straining against his navy fire department T-shirt back toward the height of the tree. "It's literally still strung up in the trees. I don't think I can get up there," I say, taking stock of how high the lanterns are. Scott follows my gaze and shakes his head, silently telling me *Don't even think about trying it* with his eyes.

Grandma Flo sighs with disappointment. "I just loved those lights. They're a fortune in the stores."

"You know what? Don't worry. We'll figure it out," I reassure her.

"Thank you, Crystal. Love you, honey. Tell Scotty I said hi."

"Will do. Bye, Grandma. Love you." I turn to Scott, who's standing with his arms crossed, seemingly dazed. "Think there's a ladder somewhere around here?"

He turns, appraising the premises as if in slow motion. "Maybe. I'll take a look. Stay here."

I put my phone back in my pocket and wait, staring up at the massive tree. It must be fifteen or twenty feet tall, at least. Too tall to climb. Then again, I've never been one to shy away from a challenge.

• • •

THIS WAS OFFICIALLY the worst idea of my life. It's up there with the top three most moronic things I've ever done, including the time in kindergarten when I confidently ate a purple glue stick like it was a chocolate bar. I was sure of myself, scaling the tree like Spider-Man. I didn't notice how high I'd climbed. And I'm not even within reach of the lanterns yet. Apparently, my fear of heights was also unknown to me. Until I looked down.

Scott made it worse when he emerged from the barn with a rickety-looking ladder that I doubt could hold more than one undersized, malnourished child, and berated me for climbing up.

Clutching the tree branch for dear life, trembling with lip-biting fear, I'm unable to let out a full breath or keep my eyes open. For the past fifteen minutes, I've tried to psych myself up for the descent, but I'm immobilized. The thought of moving my foot, or any part of my body, makes my stomach dip, as if I'm about to plummet to my death.

I never imagined I would die like this, falling from a tree outside an abandoned barn. Grandma is going to be devastated, both because of my untimely demise and because of the lack of magical lanterns at her wedding.

Scott leans the ladder against the foot of the tree and tests it. He squints up at me. "Stay exactly where you are."

I keep my eyes squeezed shut until his voice gets louder and louder, signaling his increasing proximity. When I dare to open my eyes, he's three feet below me, one foot still on the ladder, hand extended.

"Sweetheart, listen to me."

"Don't call me that," I snap. The last thing I need is to digest bizarrely timed pet names when death is nigh.

He doesn't appear fazed by my tone. "You need to let go of the branch very slowly and step down so you can grab my hand, okay?" His voice is slow and measured. He breaks eye contact as a few droplets of rain sprinkle over us. I hadn't noticed the clouds coming in.

Within seconds, the dark sky opens up with a crack of ominous thunder. Rain cascades over us. It's cold, falling in icy sheets.

My hand begins to shiver around the now-wet, slick tree branch. I practically begin to hyperventilate as the rain splatters off me. "No, I can't let go."

"You'll be okay. I'm not going to let you fall. You just have to give me your hand. We're going to go down together."

"No. I'm going to die up here. I'm okay with it. I accept it. Tell my family I love them. Play Lizzo at my funeral," I order. I clamp my eyes shut again as fat, juicy droplets seep under my lids, rendering me half blind. I'm officially convinced nature has it in for me.

"Alright. Which song? 'Tempo' seems funeral-appropriate." He cracks the first smile I've seen out of him all day.

I briefly flash him the stink eye. "Yeah. If you want to give Grandma Flo a heart attack."

"Crys, you're not going to die."

"I am."

"You're not. Do you trust me?"

That is the question, isn't it? Technically, I'm still sketched out about that two a.m. phone call, as well as his weird mood today. But I do trust him, with my life. I know he won't let me fall to my death. So I make a pact to myself. On the count of three, I'll let go of this branch and step down.

One.

Two.

Three.

His hand wraps around mine, filling me with warmth and comfort despite the cold rain pelting us.

Climbing the tree was fast, but my descent is twice as fast on the ladder. He strokes my now-dripping hair and prattles on casually, as if I'm not being rescued from a tree by a member of the Boston Fire Department. Something about how Albus Doodledore ate his new lifting shoes. Truthfully, I'm not really listening, because I'm too busy freaking the heck out with each terrifying step down this rickety-ass ladder.

I don't dare open my eyes until Scott whispers that we're back on the ground. When the decrepit barn comes into view, I realize I'm clutching him around the torso so hard I can feel his ribs. He has to firmly pry my hand away from him to loosen my grip. My fingernails have probably left permanent indents all over his abdomen. Yes, despite the terror, I shamelessly take full advantage of this poor excuse to touch him.

"Jesus, you've been working on your grip strength. You almost broke my ribs," he tells me through clenched teeth.

"I'm sorry."

"Don't be sorry." His even tone calms me slightly. "But why did you try to climb that tree when I told you not to? Couldn't you have just waited for me to find the ladder?"

I untangle my arms from him, taking a step back to shoot a wistful glance at the lanterns swaying in the rain. At least I made a valiant effort to save Grandma Flo a few dollars. "I was desperate."

"Don't worry. We'll find others. Let's get out of the rain."

By the time we reach my car, we're utterly soaked.

The seat squishes as Scott leans in, cranking the heat. "Glad I got to hang out with you today, even if you almost broke your neck." The soothing sound of his voice in my ear does something to my body. Everything tenses and prickles, and I'm pretty sure it's not just the chill of my wet clothes.

I lean my forehead against the steering wheel for a moment before turning the windshield wipers to full speed. "I'm an idiot. Thanks for rescuing me. I shouldn't have done that."

When I look up, he gives me a small shrug, as if to say, *Shit happens.*

"Still up for an extra-long movie tonight?" I ask, backing out of the laneway. The other day, he'd agreed to losing his *Titanic* virginity. Apparently, he's never seen the movie in full. Like a typical boy, he's only ever watched the scene where Jack paints topless Rose like One of His French Girls.

I expect him to say no, but surprisingly, he nods. "Yeah, I am."

I white-knuckle the steering wheel, unable to contain my invading worries. "You sure? Because you've been weird with me all day."

He gives my shoulder a reassuring squeeze. "I'm sure, Crys. I wouldn't want to be with anyone else today."

• • •

MY APARTMENT BUILDING is quiet, save for the squeak of the original hardwood underneath our wet steps, and the droplets of water ricocheting off the hallway floor outside my door.

My chest heaves as I wring my hair out, as well as my dress and jacket, both of which are now pressed to me like a second skin.

Scott doesn't bother to wring his clothes out. He just watches me, forehead creased, as if he wants to say something.

When I lean against the door, he takes a step forward, closing the distance between us. I let out a shaky breath when he sets his palm on the door beside my head. His eyes drift from my face and downward.

"Do you want me to dry your clothes before we start the movie?" I ask, breaking the awkward silence.

His eyes reach mine again. "Yeah. Thanks."

We head inside. Save for the beam of light from the stove illuminating the kitchen, the living room is empty and dark, which tells me Tara's on night shift. Our clothes squish as he follows me down the hallway toward the closet, which contains my stacked washer and dryer.

With each step, my heart rate quickens at the mere thought of us stripping out of our wet clothes. It's beating so loudly, I'm convinced Scott can hear it.

I halt and he crashes into my backside upon my abrupt stop. "I have nothing for you to wear in the meantime." My words come out shaky, not just because I'm shivering, but from the mere proximity of him and the hardness of his chest practically flush against me.

Silence lingers before he speaks over my shoulder. "True. No worries. I'll head home and change." I expect him to back away, but he doesn't.

I ache at the thought of him leaving right now. I don't think I could physically let him, no matter how loud my logic screams *Stop*.

Thanks to a complete lack of self-control, I back into him. I expect him to back away and remind me we're not allowed to touch. But he doesn't. He readily accepts me, pulling me tight against his chest, as if he needs me there. Warmth fills me everywhere, to the point that I'm no longer shivering from the rain.

We stay like this in the hallway for a few breaths as he nuzzles his face into my neck. He presses a trail of small, prohibited kisses onto my shoulder before he spins me around so we're face-to-face.

Our gazes connect, searching, before I dissolve into a puddle on the floor. He glides his fingertips up and down my spine. He leans his forehead against mine, just as he did in the fire truck.

"I have a confession," he says.

I gulp, bracing myself for the worst. "What?"

"If I don't kiss you in five seconds, I'm gonna lose it," he tells me in a low whisper.

I think of the rules we're about to break. Literally every single one we've ever made. Those thoughts hover for all of one second before I banish them to the murky depths of my mind. Goodbye, logic. You won't be missed.

I glance upward to meet his fiery gaze. "Then do it."

I haven't even finished saying *it* when his mouth collides with mine.

chapter twenty-three

H IS LIPS MEET mine with zero hesitation.

When he sighs into my mouth, it feels like relief, like he needs this long-overdue connection as much as I do. I hungrily press closer, sliding my tongue against his. Our mouths open and close against each other in an agonizingly slow rhythm. His tongue explores my mouth patiently, as if we're going to be here all night. And maybe we are.

His finger trails my spine, curving over my bottom. The moment I let out a moan in response, a switch flips. Our kisses meet hungrily, with force and intensity. He tastes like the peach drink he was drinking in the car. Apparently, that's my current favorite flavor, because I'm sucking and tasting, wanting everything from him. He meets my demands at the ready, filling and claiming me with his mouth.

We're in a marathon of tongues, teeth, and grinding against

each other in the hallway before we finally gather the wherewithal to move into my bedroom, peeling off our wet clothing as we go.

As I begin to shimmy his wet T-shirt upward, he stills against my mouth, hesitating. His eyes search my face, as if battling between what we want and the rules. "Are we really doing this? Breaking the conditions?"

I reassure him by practically clawing the fabric over his head to reveal the artwork that is his glorious six-pack. "Please."

He pauses. "Even though we aren't waiting, you know how much I care about you, right?"

I eye him, unable to stop myself from relishing this. "I care about you . . . so much it scares me," he continues.

His fingers trace my jawline, hovering over my lips. "I think about you all the time. Every day, all day. All I ever want to do is be with you. Even if we aren't doing anything at all." His eyes are the color of a pond filled with lily pads, floating peacefully along the water's surface. He doesn't appear nervous in the slightest.

I barely have time to mutter a lame "I think about you all the time too" before he presses a kiss on my lips and tugs my wet dress over my head.

When my dress pools to the floor at my feet, my breath hitches. Even though I love my body, I've always been shy around others, especially guys. But in front of Scott, I feel entirely beautiful.

Every inch of my skin vibrates as his finger skims the edge of my jaw, down my neck, over the slope of my breasts, down the curves of my stomach, curling around to hook at the edge of my lace panties.

I feel cherished, worshipped, and cared for in a way I never have with anyone else. In this moment, I know this is right, regardless of rebounds and intertwined families.

"You're perfect. Every part of you," he whispers. His voice is rough as his eyes roam downward, drinking me in, adoring me fully and completely. I can tell how much he means it by the way he looks at me.

He cups my cheeks with both hands, his lips crashing down over mine with intensity and passion. My tongue slides back into the newly familiar comfort of his mouth before he sinks to his knees, grasping the backs of my thighs before his lips make their way down my stomach. He pulls my panties down swiftly, seemingly losing restraint before he stands again, towering over me, treating me to the perfect view of his abs, shining from the rainwater.

I have no idea how I'm even still upright, because my entire body is complete liquid under his fingers. Touching myself in front of him in the bathtub was hot, but the heat of his actual skin is an inferno. When the backs of my calves hit the edge of my bed, he slowly lowers us down, losing his pants and boxers along the way, corroborating Mel's Big Dick Energy hypothesis once and for all.

His forearms rest on either side of my head as his lips meet mine with abandon. Then he stills over me for a moment as the steady drum of our hearts syncs, faster and faster. His lips journey down my neck, past my breasts, over the hill of my stomach, all the way down. He pushes my legs apart, teasing his tongue around my inner thighs before slipping his fingers into me, his thumb dancing and circling outside. I shudder as our moans collide together, my hand clasping the sheets.

Everything is spinning. The moment he smooths his tongue against me, I lose it completely in him and all the ways he makes me feel. My back arches upward as he holds me down against the mattress.

My fingers clench his hair, pulling him as close as possible as he continues to swirl around and around with the perfect amount of pressure. When I feel the vibration of his guttural, primal groan against me, everything goes white. Crashing. Pulsating. Wave after wave. I couldn't tell anyone my name, my age, or where I am in this moment.

By the time I'm ready to open my eyes again, he's hovering over me, kissing me again, gentler this time. I moan when he pulls away, wanting nothing but him close to me for the rest of my life.

I meet the safety of his gaze again. He stills on top of me, jaw tight in a way that tells me he's losing all control. I want to be the one to push him over the edge, to test him, and most importantly, show him how badly I've wanted this.

It dawns on me that we need a condom. My upper half dives sideways for the side table to grab one. When my fingers find a packet, I practically whip it at him. He laughs, catching it before ripping it open. He slides it on faster than I've ever seen a man do.

Brushing the wayward hairs from my face, he presses a soft kiss over my beauty mark as he reaches down to part my thighs again. He holds my gaze. "Are you sure?"

All I can do is nod, distracted at the impressive sight of him.

"I didn't hear you. Tell me louder," he commands, not breaking eye contact.

"If you're not in me within five seconds, I'm going to lose it," I warn him, parroting his own words back to him.

He grins, swiftly hooking one of my legs around his waist. I open my legs slightly wider to guide him in. He pushes into me achingly slowly, exactly the way he kisses. He slides in inch by inch, moving back out ever so slightly, almost teasing. When I move against him, signaling I want more of him, he fills me completely.

He shudders over me when he feels me adjust and close in around him. He brushes his thumb over my cheek and over my lips. I run my fingers greedily over the ridges of his back, digging my nails in the deeper he goes.

"Holy shit. You feel so good." He glides in and out, his breath like hot waves against my neck.

It's more than how good this feels. It's how he looks at me, all of me, washing away all my worries and fears. It's how he gets me, knowing exactly what I want before I vocalize it. I've never felt connected with someone like this before. It's a completeness I've never experienced. A fullness that tells me I'll never feel empty again when it comes to this man.

With each movement, our bodies slide together like two pieces of the same puzzle, joining and melding. In this moment, I don't know how I could ever be without him again.

As we find the perfect rhythm, moving faster and harder together, he never takes his eyes from me. He never stops communicating with me, telling me how beautiful I am or how good it feels. And when he tells me he's close, my entire body unspools beneath him, over the edge, past the point of no return.

• • •

I WAKE UP TO the awful hissing, sputtering sound the kitchen faucet makes when the hot water is running. I press the pads of my index and middle fingers to my eyes. When I extend my legs under the covers, there's a dull ache everywhere below the waist. It feels like I've done a killer leg day.

I rub the sleep out of my eyes, cracking them open only slightly to take in the stream of light bursting through the space in my blinds I always make a note to fix but never do.

Why do I feel like a nineteen-year-old the morning after a wild rager where I took down too many tequila shots off the bodies of strangers? I didn't even drink last night.

The faint sound of Tara's laugh and the deep, gravelly voice that prompted it echo from behind my bedroom door. I grip the duvet with a clenched fist when the realization crashes over me.

Stuck in tree. Cold rain. Breaking all the rules in the book. Mind-blowing sex. With Scott.

The memory comes back full force, like an ultra-HD movie. I remember everything. How he looked at me like he truly gave a shit. The deliciously sweet taste on his lips. How he touched me with such precision, as if we'd been together for years. His rough voice when he told me he couldn't wait any longer. And how unapologetically loud, masculine, and guttural he sounded when he finally let himself go.

We fell asleep after the first time. Then we woke up again an hour later and had sex again to make up for lost time. It was slower, with me on top. We took our time, memorizing every inch of each other's bodies, rocking in a near tantric rhythm, not wanting the window of bliss to end. When it was over, he wrapped me in the safety of his big arms, his embrace giving me an overwhelming peace I've never experienced before.

There's a loud vibration on my side table which interrupts my incessant fond memories. I sigh, rolling out of the comfort of my cocoon to check my phone. I squint at my screen. A text message from *Diana*.

My stomach bottoms out. The blissful tingles flittering around my body all but disappear when I register the unfamiliar feel of this phone.

This isn't my tacky bedazzled phone case.

It's not my phone plugged into my charger. It's Scott's.

chapter twenty-four

MY THROAT CONSTRICTS. I'm entirely frozen. From his lock screen, which is a precious photo of a smiling Albus Doodledore, I can't see what she's texted him. I hover over the screen, itching to type in his password, which he's readily admitted is his birth year.

I flex my fingers, willing myself to do it. But I pull back. I can't bring myself to snoop through his phone. It feels like a massive invasion of his privacy. And to be frank, I'm terrified of potentially unlocking the brutal truth.

I stare at her name for a few more moments, blinking in disbelief until I lose my resolve and creep on Diana's social media from my own phone.

And that's when I see it, on Twitter.

Diana Tisdale—Boston, how I've missed you! Happy to be home. ♥

Diana is back.

In Boston.

The tweet is from a week and a half ago. The very same night Scott received the mysterious phone call.

I scour her Instagram, searching for a tiny grain of evidence that can help me put the pieces together. However, Diana has only posted two photos since her return, neither of which give me any clue at all.

None of this makes sense. I trust Scott with everything I have. I've put myself out there. I've shown and told him how much I want him. I've slept with him two months earlier than intended. And now this?

As much as I don't want to believe he's hiding the fact that they're back in touch, this text and all his weird behavior tells me otherwise. My mind races with the possibilities. Are they getting back together now that she's back in town? Or are they just talking casually? It doesn't make much sense, given that Scott claims they're no longer friends. What could have possibly happened upon her return that would launch him into such an awful mood yesterday?

It feels like the Neil situation all over again. Weeks before we broke up, I began to suspect Neil had resumed talking to Cammie after they each posted photos from the same coffee shop. I only know this because I went full-blown CSI on the photos. Have I really been hoodwinked a second time?

After ten minutes of stewing, unsure how to play it with Scott now that this text cannot be unseen, I finally garner the energy to throw on a baggy sweater and leggings and stumble into the bathroom. Luckily, my face isn't smudged full of mascara and blotchy foundation as it would have been in my college days. I'm bare-faced. My lips are red and swollen, and I have an obvious, violet hickey on the right side of my neck.

By the time I round the corner into the kitchen, Scott is standing in front of the stove in his dried clothes from yesterday, as if he's meant to be here. As if this is a usual morning. I'm not surprised he's one of those people who wake up looking flawless, with only slightly tousled hair as evidence of his status as a mere mortal. I bite my lip, recalling how soft it felt in between my fingers last night.

Tara is being Tara, still in her scrubs from the night shift, casually spectating from the kitchen table as Scott cooks eggs in the large skillet.

I brace myself for the awkward morning-after interaction. Instead, Scott actually lights up when he sees me. "She's alive." He flashes me an easy smile, as if we didn't just spend hours connected together in more ways than one.

I think about the R-rated sounds he made last night. Will I ever forget them? Will they replay in my mind like my favorite soundtrack (of all time) every single time I see him?

"Hi," I croak. Against my better judgment, I unearth the ill-advised jazz-hands wave.

"Scott made you breakfast. Scrambled eggs with no milk." Tara gives me a supremely satisfied smile. From the wild look in her eyes, she's definitely fighting the urge to shout *I told you so* at the top of her lungs. I have no idea what time she returned from work last night, but I know that the walls in my apartment are anything but thick.

Mortified, my gaze flickers back to the pan. "Really? You hate scrambled eggs."

He shrugs. "I know, but you like them." My heart practically combusts and I'm tempted to forget all about that text.

A heavy silence fills the kitchen as he plates the eggs. This should be perfect. He hasn't peaced out into the dark of night the moment he crawled off me. He's stuck around to cook me breakfast. I should be smiling like a loon right now, but all I can think about is Diana's text.

Tara clears her throat. "I'm, uh, going to my room," she announces, shuffling off to give us some space. I can't decide whether I'm grateful or horrified.

Scott holds out a plate and fork in his extended hand. I stare at his hands for a moment, and then his lips, recalling their exceptional talent. In fact, my body owes them public recognition plaques for their service, innovation, leadership, and stellar initiative.

Dazed, I take the plate and pierce a clump of eggs with my fork, standing beside him. Just like last night, his body radiates heat, and I'm drawn to it like a fly to shit.

He leans back against the counter. "You okay?"

I blink up at him in rapid succession, willing away the too-recent memory of our bodies tangled together, satisfying each other's needs willingly, without judgment or restraint. I need to call him out. Right now. But I chicken out.

My expression hardens the longer he looks at me, because I know why he hung up on me the other night. I know why he was in an awful mood yesterday, glued to his phone. I need to ask him about it, but I decide to broach one elephant at a time.

I tilt my head knowingly, dry-swallowing the lump in my throat. "We had sex. Two months early."

His face doesn't change. In fact, it stays flat. "Wait—what?"

I go still for a moment before the corners of his lips turn up into a devious smile. I swat him on the arm. "You're such a dick."

He lets out a low chuckle. "Sorry, that was a bad joke." He pauses for a moment. "Actually, I feel like an asshole. I shouldn't have let it go that far."

I can't tell what he's thinking, especially now that I know he's back in touch with his ex. And it's driving me insane. So insane, to the point of insecurity. "It was okay, right? Last night?"

He doesn't respond right away. In fact, his smile disappears into gray neutrality. It's still completely unreadable.

Fuck my life. I loved it. He hated it. I nearly pulled my hamstring for nothing. All I want to do is crawl into a ball and remain motionless.

Finally, his smile returns. "*Okay*? You'd rate that as just okay?"

"No. It was good. Really good. Was it for you too?" I cover my face with my hands, peeking through the cracks between my fingers.

He cocks his neck back. "Are you kidding me? Last night is ingrained in my memory. Etched into a sacred stone tablet."

I can't help but snort, hand to stomach. It isn't sexy in the slightest, but I'm relieved beyond measure. I wasn't flying solo last night on my journey to heaven after all.

He takes my plate and sets it gently on the counter before wrapping his arms around me, pulling me into his warm chest. I nestle my head against him, trying to capture this moment. I want to remember how it feels to be in his arms. I take in his musky scent, which, even after a full night of serious cardio, is still alluring as sin. I revel in the security of his muscly arms enveloping me with just the right amount of squeeze. Not tight enough to crunch my bones and loose enough to wriggle free.

We stay like this, rocking back and forth in the kitchen, before I finally come to my senses. I can't pretend I didn't see the text, as much as I wish I could. This can't last. This isn't reality. I can't tiptoe around this any longer.

I shrink out of his arms. It's cold without his body heat. Instinctively, I wrap my arms around myself. Frankly, it's a poor substitute. "Scott . . ."

"Yeah?"

"I know about Diana."

His jaw tightens as he frowns at me. "What are you talking about?"

"I know she's back in town. I know you're talking to her again."

He runs his hand through his thick hair. "I'm not talking to her, Crys."

"Then why is she texting you? I didn't mean to see it . . . I thought it was my phone."

He sighs. "She texted me the other day, saying she was coming back to town and wanted to come get a necklace she left at my place. That's literally it. She was supposed to get it last night . . . but I obviously wasn't home. I never mentioned it because I honestly didn't give it a second thought."

I slow-blink, registering his words. "So, nothing is going on between you guys now that she's back?"

"You really think I would cheat on you with her? After everything?"

"What am I supposed to think? We aren't technically together. You could do anything and it wouldn't really be cheating."

He sidesteps away from me. "I told you I wouldn't see anyone else."

"How can I believe you? You're being so sketchy with me. It doesn't make sense. If she just texted you for a necklace, why were you acting so moody?"

He reaches forward, cupping my cheeks with his massive hands. "I'm telling you, it has nothing to do with Diana." His shoulders slump, which tells me he's at the end of his rope.

"Then what is it?"

He stiffens, letting his hands fall to his sides. "I can't tell you."

I laugh manically out of pure frustration. "That's highly convenient." How on earth does he expect me to trust him when he refuses to enlighten me on whatever this deep, dark secret is?

He bows his head. "I know it sounds ridiculous."

"Then tell me. Please. Is it bad?"

He takes in a deep breath and lets it out slowly, as if choosing his words carefully. "You're going to hate me."

My stomach twists as I take in his watery eyes. This is bad. And try as I might, I fail to scrounge up any possibilities in my head. "Scott, tell me."

"My grandpa might be sick."

I blink. "Sick? What do you mean, *sick*?"

"He hasn't been feeling well for the last few weeks. That's the phone call I got. He needed someone to bring him to the ER."

I exhale loudly, hand pressed to my chest. I'm light-headed. Thank god Scott has fed me, or I'd have passed out.

"They ran some tests and they found a tumor. He has to go

back to find out if it's cancerous. My mom and I are bringing him this afternoon."

Cancer. The word echoes in my mind, bouncing around, taunting me like an out-of-control Ping-Pong ball. The same disease that killed my grandpa. And now, it could be happening all over again to Martin. My heart is broken for Scott and his family, who are now kind of my family too. When I think about them having to endure the pain of losing Martin, the same way we lost my grandpa, I want to scream.

And then the realization hits me. "This is why you were suddenly adamant that we take things slow. Isn't it?"

He nods. "I couldn't move forward knowing I was hiding that from you. That's why Martin told me to cool it with you. Until we knew for sure."

"But why did you keep this from me? Does Flo know?" I demand.

He shakes his head. "No. He doesn't want her to worry for nothing. That's why I couldn't tell you. He made me swear I wouldn't."

The anger bubbles into my throat like bile. My family would never keep secrets like this. We'd get through it together, just as we did with Grandpa the moment we found out his diagnosis. "Because you didn't trust me to keep a secret?" Realistically, I know for a fact I never could have kept that from my family. But I'm furious nonetheless.

He dips his chin in regret. "I couldn't ask you to keep such a huge secret from Flo. I knew that would destroy you."

My mind spins at the thought of Grandma Flo's face when she finds out. I hold my hand out in front of me, preventing him from coming closer. I can't even look at him right now. "Scott, please leave."

His face twists, pained. "I wanted to tell you so badly. I told my grandpa this wasn't right and that he needed to tell Flo today. Before I bring him to the specialist—"

I hold my hand out to signal him to stop. "Please. I need space right now." As much as I want to hold him and take away all his hurt, all I can think about is Grandma Flo and how devastated she's going to be. I need to be there for her, right now.

Scott nods, taking one last dejected look at me before he opens the front door. "I'm so sorry, Crys."

chapter twenty-five

W E'RE ON THE way there," I tell Grandma.

The moment Scott left, Tara bolted down the stairs in tears after overhearing my confrontation with Scott. She and I contemplated going to Grandma Flo's house immediately, but decided against it, in case Martin hadn't told her yet. Luckily, Grandma called not long after to inform us she was going to the hospital to await the results.

While Tara and I are both angry about being kept in the dark, our feelings hardly seem to matter, given the circumstances. As badly as Martin handled the situation, his obnoxious, loud self has grown on me immensely in the past two months.

He and Scott are so much alike in some ways, it's almost creepy. At family gatherings, they're the last to take food, waiting for everyone else to serve themselves first. They're both thoughtful, remembering small, seemingly innocuous details about everyone's lives. They'll both go to any lengths to protect their families, even if it means keeping secrets. The very thought of losing Martin, however strange and new he may be to the family, is something I can't entertain in my head for longer than a fraction of a second without being overcome with dread.

Driving to the hospital, finding a parking spot, and locating them on the correct floor is a complicated, blurry endeavor. But I know we're in the right place when I nearly collide with Grandma Flo and Mom as I enter a waiting area.

There are massive purple bags under Grandma's weepy eyes. She's slouched, pale, and overall worn. It reminds me of the long, difficult months when Grandpa was going through chemotherapy. She barely ate or slept. I'm pretty sure the awful experience prematurely aged her by years. It's beyond cruel that she may have to go through this all over again.

"Patricia and Scotty are in the doctor's office with him now," Grandma says as Tara sorrowfully embraces her.

"How are you doing?" I ask as a group of nurses rushes past down the white, sterile hallway.

"Alright." Her eyes are teary as she motions for us to sit in the uncomfortable waiting room chairs. Like most hospitals, it smells faintly of body odor and disinfectant. It's relatively quiet on this floor, save for random distant beeping, hushed chatter, and the little girl giggling on her mom's lap a couple chairs over.

"When did he tell you?" Tara asks as we take our seats.

"He came by earlier this morning and told me over coffee," she says neutrally, making it difficult to determine how she's feeling about it.

I give her a sympathetic gaze. "Are you mad he didn't tell you until today?"

"I am. We're meant to get married next month, move in together." Grandma's lips tighten as she fidgets with her gold charm bracelet. "But then I think, what's the point? I don't have time to be angry about stuff like this at my age. He had the best of intentions, even if he was wrong."

I take in her words as the realization washes over me—Scott's had to carry this burden for nearly two weeks. No wonder he's been moody and distant. It isn't his fault Martin asked him to lie on his behalf, wrong as it was. He was in an impossible position, forced to choose between his family and his new relationship. Had I been in the very same situation with Grandma Flo, I realistically would have made the same choice: family.

I cross and uncross my legs a million times as the minutes pass, eyes focused mindlessly on the local news reel on the TV. I'm barely digesting anything, because nothing else seems to matter right now.

Grandma and Mom are in and out of their seats, trying to busy themselves by pacing the hallway. Tara is reading quietly on her Kindle. I wonder if she's even processing any words. From the way her knee is bouncing up and down, she appears as anxious as I am.

After over an hour, the fatigue from last night with Scott, combined with the emotional roller coaster that was this morning, finally begins to sink in. Despite the lack of comfortable seating, I fold my legs over the arm of the chair and manage to close my eyes.

• • •

"YOU LOT LOOK like you're at a funeral." Martin's familiar, boisterous voice snaps me out of sleep.

As I rub my eyes, planting both feet back on the ground, his figure lumbers into the waiting area. He's smiling like he's merely here for an annual physical. One would think that would mean good news, but I get the feeling he's the type who would smile either way. To delay everyone's pain for as long as humanly possible.

Grandma Flo nearly knocks the coffee table over as she rushes into his arms. "Is it cancer?"

He embraces her wholeheartedly before giving her a soft kiss on the forehead. Then he shakes his head, casting a triumphant smile at Mom, Tara, and me. "It's benign. The tumor isn't cancerous."

The entire room changes color. It's no longer lifeless, blue, and void of hope. It's vibrant, sunny, and full of light. The space that was so stuffy and depressing just seconds ago is suddenly alive, fueled by everyone's relief. We've been given a priceless gift. The gift of more time with someone we love.

It's a good thing Martin has his arms around her, because Grandma Flo would have otherwise hit the floor, face drenched with a blend of what I imagine are happy tears and the painful memories of losing Grandpa.

The tightness in my stomach releases when I stand to hug Martin. I don't know if I've ever felt more thankful for anything in my life. "I'm sorry, Crystal," he says.

"For what?"

Martin pulls back regretfully, squeezing my shoulders. "It's my fault . . . what happened with Scotty. Please don't blame him. I asked him to lie and it was an unfair request. I see that now."

"I appreciate that," I say, letting out a massive sigh, just as Patricia and Scott come around the corner.

Scott is still in his same clothes from this morning, which are technically the same ones from yesterday. His wavy hair looks like it's been brushed five different ways, and his eyes are bloodshot.

He stops a couple feet in front of me, as if unsure of what to do next. "You came."

I wait a few beats before practically lunging at him like a flying squirrel, desperate to be back in his arms. Just like Martin did with Flo, Scott wraps his arms around me, tighter than he ever has before. His entire body seems to relax in our embrace.

After this ordeal, after our family was quite literally granted a second chance, I never want to let him go. I don't care that we got into a massive fight. I don't care about the hurt feelings. And I don't care that we're in the middle of a hospital waiting room full of onlookers.

"Of course I did. I'm so sorry for being so mad at you," I whisper into his neck.

He glosses his thumbs over my cheeks, pressing his forehead to mine. "I never should have kept that from you. It killed me to do it."

"Scott, it's okay. I know."

"I swear to you, I will never keep something like that from you ever again. I care about you so much—I don't even know what to do with myself. I can't lose you." He tugs my hand, holding it to his chest. The steady drum of his heart vibrates against my palm. It's the most raw and honest moment of my life.

I practically melt into him, because I believe him wholeheartedly. "You won't. Ever," I whisper, tracing my finger over his stubbled jaw.

His eyes flicker to my lips as he drops his forehead to mine again, tightening his muscly arms around my lower back, securing me to him. He lets out a long sigh as I run my hands over his shoulders, up his neck, and through his hair.

There's a heaviness to his gaze, and it isn't just lust. It's overwhelming affection. The intensity of the moment steals my breath, rendering me putty in his arms. I want to capture this look and keep it forever.

I give him a small nod to continue, watching as the incredible relief washes over him before he drops his mouth and presses his soft lips to mine.

Everything goes silent. The beeps of the hospital machines, the urgent voices around us, and all the broken rules and worries of the past fade into obscurity in the background. All I can hear is the gush of blood flowing to my ears as we struggle to pull ourselves closer, tongues melding in a mixture of gentle and rough. There is no twister unleashing havoc, tearing my heart apart. Instead, he grounds me into a calm state of being. And it makes all the difference.

I pull back momentarily to drink in his gorgeous eyes. "Screw August sixth?"

He gives me a wicked smile. "Screw August sixth," he repeats before capturing my mouth again.

chapter twenty-six

2:31 P.M.—INSTAGRAM POST: "SIZE POSITIVE CAMPAIGN—DEALING WITH THE HATERS" BY **CURVYFITNESSCRYSTAL:**

You guys! The response to Size Positive has been insane!! I'm SO glad this campaign has resonated with so many of you who are finding joy in ditching the scales and becoming more and more in tune with your bodies. QUEENS.

Unfortunately, people are still dicks. There has been an increase in assholes in the comments, as I'm sure you've noticed. Here are a couple tips on how to deal with the haters:

1) Ignore them—It's easier said than done. Sometimes I respond when I really feel it's necessary to set someone straight. But

remember they're just thirsting for attention. It's best not to give them the satisfaction.

2) They have no bearing on your life—If you surround yourself with good people and a good support system, the comment of some idiot doesn't matter in the long run.

3) They are the miserable ones—Darkness is attracted to light. People who are sad and toxic can't handle when other people are happy and successful. Don't let them drag you down.

Comment by **MarleyYogaInstructor**: You're so right. Darkness ♡ is attracted to light like moths to flames. People will do anything to drag others down into their own unhappiness. They're jealous.

Comment by **Stannerjr**: hahahahh ur pathetic. ♡

• • •

THERE IS NO adequate word to describe the past few weeks with Scott. *Fantastic, amazing, blissful, wonderful, remarkable.* None of them properly encapsulate the kaleidoscope of feelings that reach in and take hold of my entire being when I'm with him.

The feeling is similar to that giddy, post-workout high, except it doesn't dull the moment the running shoes come off and you resume normal life as a reclusive couch potato. The magic lingers, like simmering liquid.

It's the evening before Grandma Flo and Martin's wedding,

the day we were supposed to wait for. And I'm so glad we didn't. Since we found out Martin is cancer-free, Scott stays over every night he isn't on night shift. Albus happily third-wheels. He enjoys running at full tilt on the carpet in my apartment. Apparently, he can't run without slipping on the parquet floors at Scott's place.

Scott also brings me boxes of clementines on the condition I peel them for him. He's made a special Lizzo Spotify playlist for when I'm in his car. Most mornings, he brings me coffee from the little cafe around the corner from my apartment in return for healthy, meal-prepped lunches.

But despite practically worshipping Scott's entire kindhearted and genetically gifted being, I'm still petty and competitive as hell. And so is he.

We're doing a warm-up cardio circuit consisting of a minute and a half of exhausting high-knees. Like the egotistical alpha male he is, he doesn't bother to hide that he's trying to outdo me. Typical. We lock eyes in a challenge, both exerting well past the point of a relaxed warm-up.

Unfortunately for me, gravity is not on my side, despite my ultra-supportive sports bra. Unless I want my boobs to slap me in the chin, I can't continue at this speed. "This is so unfair. My boobs are out of control. I'm gonna throw out my back," I pant, coming to a full stop.

He leans against a nearby cable machine with a faux innocent expression. "Babe, this isn't a competition."

I level him with a knowing stare. "It is. You always make it one."

"You do realize you're the competitive one. I'm just here, going at a leisurely pace. Just enjoying the view."

"What view?"

He shrugs, green eyes falling to my chest.

My mouth falls open. That bastard.

His grin is Disney villain–worthy. "The faster I went, the faster you'd go, and the higher they'd bounce . . ."

I pretend to punch him in the chest, flustered. "You're diabolical."

He grabs my wrist and pulls me flush to him, the heat of our bodies melding together. He gives me a chaste peck on the nose as he presses harder against me, sending a shiver to my lower belly. "I'd prefer *genius*."

I bring my lips over his, letting my tongue explore him at a languid pace that is definitely not appropriate for a public gym. He lets out a heavy sigh as I pull away abruptly, just to torture him. "I need to film my workout. If you'll excuse me." I flash an evil wink over my shoulder before sauntering off.

When I begin to film my dumbbell arm tutorial, he keeps his distance, knowing not to interrupt me mid-filming for fear of my mighty wrath. Instead, he sends me a text.

SCOTT: Do you believe in love at first set? Or should I do another ten reps?

CRYSTAL: Wow. 🙆

SCOTT: New rule: you can't wear those leggings in front of me anymore.

He's now watching me from the other side of the gym as he hoists himself upward, dangling effortlessly from the pull-up bar. He proceeds to show off his superhuman strength, doing some fancy ab workout involving twisting his legs up in the air every which way in a controlled manner.

> CRYSTAL: No can do. Not after you tricked me into giving you a show.
> SCOTT: Sorry. No regrets.
> CRYSTAL: And I've asked you nicely not to flex your muscles in front of me either, but you don't listen. So the leggings are staying.
> SCOTT: Tease.
> CRYSTAL: 😉

By the time I'm finally satisfied with each segment of the video, there's a new text from Scott from a few minutes ago.

> SCOTT: Need your help in the changing room.

I take stock of my surroundings. In the entire gym, there is only a woman on the elliptical watching something on her iPad, and a young couple taking turns on the window squat rack.

Excalibur Fitness gender-assigned changing rooms be damned.

I hold my breath as I creep into the men's changing room, smiling to myself at the memory of the last time I was in here, under very different circumstances.

As I slink around the lockers, I spot Scott man-splaying on the bench. He's shirtless, ripped abs prominent and glistening with a coat of dewy sweat. It's a critical public safety hazard. No wonder shirts are required by the gym's dress code.

He gives me an incendiary look, standing abruptly to pull me to the back of the changing room, near the showers. I'm about to ask what he's doing, but he covers my mouth. He nods to the right, signaling there's someone in one of the private changing room stalls.

When the stall door opens, Scott swiftly pushes me into the shower, pulling the curtain to conceal us. We're still, barely breathing as we listen to the man's gruff voice. It sounds like he's on the phone. "Whatever it takes, Janice. I don't care what it costs. Don't forget I bought you a Beamer for your birthday," he grumbles.

We shake in silent laughter. The man's conversation fades as he moves toward the lockers in the front.

"What are you doing?" I whisper.

Scott responds by closing his lips over mine, greedily taking all my air. He pulls back and playfully tugs my ponytail. "What I wanted to do the day you followed me in here and accosted me," he whispers before his lips blaze a hot trail down to my neck.

The thrill of being in here and the possibility of getting caught are a serious turn-on. I turn to liquid instantly, my entire body vibrating with anticipation, desperately craving what he has to offer.

His kisses are eager as our tongues collide. He bites my bottom lip, holding it for a second too long before I moan into the salty taste of his mouth. Usually, his kisses start off slow. In fact, Scott usually starts everything slow. The aching buildup is his specialty. But this is different. This is pure need.

He hooks his fingers under the fabric of my tank top, practically tearing it over my head. We make quick work ridding ourselves of the rest of our gym clothes and shoes. As soon as we do, he runs the shower to muffle the sounds we can't contain.

His fingers move over every inch of my body, lathering me with soap, dipping between my legs, massaging me in a maddening circular motion. My head falls back against the cold tile when his fingers begin to loop exactly where I'm aching for him. When he mouths *You're beautiful*, the pleasure triples, because I know he means it.

I grab his face with both hands and press my lips to his, showing him how much I care about him in the only way I can. I can't physically utter a word right now. Everything comes out in small, undiscernible moans.

He presses his free finger to my mouth, telling me silently to be quiet as the steam billows around us. I nod, but my promise is broken the moment his hand presses harder against my core.

"Fuck," he whispers in my ear as his fingers smooth in and out of me, torturously slow.

In return, my hands dance around the hard, impressive ridges of his back, his stomach, and down, stroking his length. I revel in the sight of him, eyes stormy and wild with pure need, abs clenched and shaking in desperation.

When he can't take my hand anymore, he brings his lips to my neck, pressing kisses all the way down my body, until his face is right where I want it. He smooths his tongue, rolling it over me in a perfect circular motion. Then he brings my leg up, deepening the angle.

I clasp his hair, still trying to muffle myself, to stop from crying out his name. It happens fast. I feel it coming, crashing, tunneling everything around me until all I see is him.

When it's over, Scott comes back up, kissing me again before he presses himself to me. "You're gonna have to be quiet this time. Promise?" he whispers, moving his thumb over my lips.

I nod dutifully as he drives inside of me so unexpectedly hard it's impossible for me not to scream. He shudders, letting out a guttural groan of his own as he pins my wrists against the tiles above my head. He pulls my leg around his waist to hit me deeper, burying himself inside me.

Purposeful force and passion join us together, over and over, to the point where I can't even remember how it feels to be without him. He's so much better than any hope, dream, or fantasy I could conjure in my head. And he's real.

He's whispering how beautiful I am. How much he desires me every minute of the day. He's here with me, cementing all the endless reasons he's stolen my whole heart.

The sprinkle of the water ricochets off the tiles as we chase our release together.

• • •

FULLY SATIATED AND no longer requiring an early-morning leg workout tomorrow, I lie in bed scrolling through the photos Mel took of Scott and me on a beach outing last week. Mel has been asking me for weeks when I'll give my followers a glimpse into my relationship with Scott. From a business perspective, she's of the opinion that filling my grid with couples' workouts will expand my audience. She isn't wrong. For some reason, people love the catalog shots of perfect couples in matching cable-knit sweaters posing in pumpkin patches, cutting down perfect Douglas fir Christmas trees, or gazing into each other's eyes in front of a crackling fire.

Business aside, I've always been an open book with my followers on a personal level. I genuinely consider many of them to be friends. Keeping them out of the loop of my relationship feels strange, as though I'm somehow being dishonest with them about a huge part of my life.

I've been hesitant to reveal Scott mostly because he isn't interested in Instagram fame in the slightest. Despite being supportive of my business and eagerly helping me with my content, he rarely even uses his own account.

While Scott and I are certainly not that perfect couple in matching pajamas, the beach photos of us are seriously adorable. We're laughing hysterically because he'd just pulled my bathing suit out of my crack, preventing it from riding up too far (one-piece swimsuit problems).

I'm struck with overwhelming happiness as I scroll through. Maybe Mel has a point. Why not share my joy with the people who've faithfully followed my journey for years? Besides, Scott is a stone-cold fox, a walking thirst trap, and that's putting it lightly. The world deserves some eye candy.

I zero in on my favorite shot of us side by side, his arm firmly around my waist, rippled six-pack shadowed at all the right angles. We're smiling at each other, completely lost in the moment.

Before we go to sleep, I finally debut Scott to my followers.

chapter twenty-seven

S COTT AND I accidentally sleep until ten in the morning, despite the fact that hair and makeup are scheduled to be at the
hotel promptly at nine.

Bleary-eyed, I check my phone while simultaneously pulling on
a wrinkled sundress from the floor. I have a flurry of notifications
on last night's post.

The notifications are plentiful, popping up one after another,
but I don't have a spare second to check them. In fact, I leave my
phone at home, because Grandma Flo made it clear the wedding
day is to be "unplugged."

The entire chaotic race to the hotel, I'm sweating through my
Spanx thinking about how Tara is probably plotting to roast my
organs and sell them on the black market for being an hour late.

But instead of fire and brimstone, I'm the least of Tara's worries. She hasn't even noticed I just arrived, given the first frantic thing out of her mouth is "Have you seen the rings?"

Apparently, Tara has every right to stress. First, the photographer arrived in desperate need of liquids and Advil. She regrettably admitted she was suffering an epic hangover. Then it was discovered the baker mixed up the cupcake order, having made the grave error of buttercream frosting instead of cream cheese. The florist is still entirely unaccounted for, as is Dad, who was last seen two hours ago socializing with family by the pool, but is now AWOL. And Hillary has revenge-peed on Mom's dress after being ignored for seven full minutes.

It's quite the sight. Me in crisis mode, despite being in full hair and makeup. I'm high and half blinded from the salon-quality hairspray fumes as I dash barefoot around the entire hotel premises, checking items off of Tara's list. The bottoms of my feet are charcoal black and it's only noon.

"Crystal, the floating candles go in the stem candle holders, not the pillar holders." Tara aggressively hip-checks me in front of the head table like we're rival contestants on a reality TV game show competing for a hundred grand.

"Jeez, sorry." I flash Scott, who was tasked to quadruple-check the name cards, an expression that screams *Save our souls*.

"How does it all look? It's too plain, isn't it?" Tara casts a self-conscious gaze around the candlelit room, clipboard in hand, nostrils flared. She can barely bring herself to look at the newly installed bold-print carpet that apparently triggers her gag reflex. She's been especially prickly since I forgot the guard-with-your-life instructional binder at home this morning. It's complete with a detailed list of tasks for every minute of the day (*4:35—Remove greenery from archway and spread evenly on head table*), typed in nine-point Times New Roman font, single-spaced, with narrow margins, and printed front to back.

But every time the urge to snap back at her becomes oh-so-tempting, I remind myself *she* was supposed to get married today. The entire family agrees she's entitled to her extra feelings, especially after our quasi-traumatizing bridesmaid dress fitting last week. Tara had a mini-meltdown in the dressing room when reality set in that she was no longer the bride. It took half an hour to coax her out of the changing room, where she'd been starfishing on the floor, sobbing, draped like a mummy in peach chiffon.

Despite the emotional turmoil, Tara has done an outstanding job with the entire wedding. Everything is so expertly organized, I wouldn't have believed she could pull it off on her own. "I think it looks great," I say, observing her nervous eye twitch. I take a full pace backward, for my safety.

She groans. "Oh, come on. Give me your real opinion."

My brows knit together as I take another scan around the ballroom. "I told you, it looks beautiful. Magazine-worthy."

"You're always so vague and general. Like you don't want to hurt my feelings because you think I'm on the verge of a mental breakdown. Sometimes I don't even know what you like at all." She tosses her hands up in the air with a literal growl and tornadoes in the opposite direction.

Despite the stress, everything comes together behind the scenes at the last minute. And it's all worth it to see Grandma Flo walk down the aisle.

It isn't just the fact that she's wearing a gorgeous short-sleeve gown, with Chantilly lace running from the bodice and extending to a teacup cut falling elegantly at her ankles. Or that her hair is swept to the side in twenties-style waves and clipped with an antique broach that belonged to my great-grandmother. It's the radiant smile she's wearing, and the way her eyes twinkle when they catch the sun filtering in through the opulent stained-glass windows.

Seeing her and Martin walk back down the aisle side by side as husband and wife makes my chest swell to the point where I feel guilty about being bothered over their relationship. If this isn't a clear sign that movie-worthy love exists at any age, I don't know what is.

Like the wedding ceremony, the reception follows Tara's stringent timeline. Bride and groom entrance, soft classical music, and speeches evenly interspersed between each of the four courses.

Scott and I are crammed at a long, rectangular table that holds the vast majority of the immediate family. Grandma and Martin sit at a sweetheart table at the front of the ballroom. They're being adorable, as usual, until Martin begins hand-feeding Flo her dinner like she's a wounded baby bird.

Aunt Shannon is going hard tonight, pushing her latest pyramid scheme venture: the healing power of crystals. As a person who sells fitness, I've tried hard not to judge people who abide by the crystal lifestyle. But it's damn difficult to refrain when she's flaunting her whimsical pendant necklace, trying to coerce everyone into buying the three-hundred-dollar gem she swears cured her chronic arthritis.

Dad is in all his glory emceeing, delivering punchy one-liners. The man can seriously work a room. It's a vibe.

"Think your dad would emcee our wedding?" Scott whispers after a particularly well-delivered line about Grandma's dry turkey that has the room in stitches.

Warmth engulfs me from head to toe when I register what he's said. A brief picture of Scott and me saying *I do* flashes through my mind. It's the happiest moment of my life, and it hasn't even even happened yet. Now that I've seen it, it can't be unseen.

Every single time I think about how perfectly he fits into my life, how desperate I am to see him after work, and how my entire body hums with pure joy at the mere mention of him, I simply can't imagine life without him. We haven't said "I love you" yet. While I've been tempted to blurt it out on numerous occasions, or write it on a sign and stand outside his window, I'm stubbornly waiting for him to say it first. Despite his cocky façade, he wears his heart on his sleeve. If he hasn't told me yet, he must not be ready. And the last thing I want to do is rush him.

"Don't get too ahead of yourself. You need my dad's permission first," I tease, clapping as Dad swaggers off the stage, returning to our table at the end of his speech.

Scott gives me a confident wink before polishing off the remainder of his drink. "*Pfft.* Not worried. He already gave me his blessing long before we even started dating. Planted that seed early."

I chuckle at the drunken memory of FaceTiming Dad the night of Flo's and Martin's respective bachelor parties. "What did you even say to get his approval?"

Scott's momentarily distracted by the sight of the waiters delivering the entrées. Merrily leaving me hanging, he carefully unrolls my cutlery from the cloth napkin and neatly folds it on my lap. When his fingertips lightly graze my thigh, I shiver involuntarily.

"Well, I said you were stubborn, self-righteous, territorial, especially at the gym . . ." he says, pretending to list my flaws. "Generally, a little unhinged. Your dad fully agreed. Said you'd always been that way and there was little chance of changing you. He practically begged me to take you off his plate."

I give him a playful whack on the chest. "God, your ego really is the size of Boston."

He squeezes my thigh under the table, a knowing grin spreading over his lips.

"Crystal, are you still on Instaworld?" Uncle Bill asks for the forty-seventh time as he demolishes his roast chicken leg with his bare hands as if he's at KFC. Along with inquiring about how old I am, he condescendingly asks me about Instagram every single time I see him. I don't know whether he's genuinely curious, or if he's teamed up with Dad to make a point. Either way, it's highly ironic, given Uncle Bill's addiction to reposting politically touchy and gently racist memes on Facebook with stunning frequency.

"Instagram," I correct through a bite of salad. "But yeah, I am. Business has never been better, actually."

Dad sighs heavily, taking his seat across from me. "Though her mother and I keep telling her about the importance of getting a proper job. Something more stable over the long term."

Mom nods in agreement as she bounces Hillary on her lap, the dog occupied happily licking the crumbs on the edge of the table with her lizard tongue. This has to be a violation of the health code.

My hand immediately tenses into a fist, only softening when Scott wraps his arm around the back of my chair. "I do have a proper job," I respond politely, so as not to make a scene.

"But how long is this Instagram fad going to last? What happens when people move on to another platform?" Dad asks, obviously unaware of how awkward this conversation is in front of the entire family.

"I'll adapt," I cut in, meeting Dad's curious stare. "I have a degree in business and marketing, and multiple certifications in fitness and nutrition. I don't need Instagram to spread my message."

"Millennials," Dad chides, eliciting a rumble of laughter around the table. "I just don't understand."

I catch Dad's eye and hold it. "Dad, you don't have to understand it."

As he sets his napkin next to his plate, Dad's face is unusually blank. Unreadable. I can't tell if he's pissed or embarrassed that we're hashing this out in front of the whole family. He clears his throat, and finally, his lips curl into a smile. "You're right. I shouldn't be so hard on you."

I take in a sharp breath. I definitely didn't expect that. Dad may not have come out and said it directly, but I think that was his weird signal of approval, which he's withheld the entire seven years I've had my Instagram account. Until now, I'm not even sure I knew I needed it. And it feels good.

Scott leans forward across the table to Dad. "Your daughter is the hardest-working person I know. I don't know about anyone else, but I can't wait to see what she accomplishes this year."

My heart swells at his unwavering support, especially when Dad nods and says, "Me too. Really."

The moment dinner ends, Scott pulls me onto the crowded dance floor. If I didn't know any better, I'd assume this was the wedding of a twenty-year-old couple, what with the DJ's strobe lights and all the Ritchies (plus Dad) tearing up the dance floor to some oldies.

Dad has just attempted the worm, which tells me Flo and Martin's open bar bill is going to be staggering. I make a mental note to keep a watchful eye. He has a history of getting a little overeager when there's music, booze, and people. At the last family wedding, he split his trousers while getting "Low" to the age-appropriate musical stylings of Lil Jon and the East Side Boyz.

"This is the best wedding I've ever been to," Scott yells enthusiastically over a Whitney Houston song as he loosens his tie. I don't know if it's the expertly tailored, dapper suit, but I can't tear my eyes from him for longer than a minute. I'm used to drooling over him in a casual T-shirt, jeans, and a ball cap. But tonight, his hair is pushed back in a way that makes him resemble an old Hollywood movie star. I desperately want to haul him off the dance floor, find a darkened corner, and grope him with abandon.

When he twirls me, I channel *Dancing with the Stars* and spin into his chest, utterly and completely content. Not even Uncle Bill accidentally stomping on my foot and spilling his beer on me five minutes ago is enough to dim my smile.

Hair caked to my face with sweat, I take a quick breather to get another drink, leaving Scott to dance with his sisters, both of whom are intensely enthusiastic about synchronize-dancing to the "Cha Cha Slide" and "Y.M.C.A."

Whiskey sour in hand, I return a few minutes later to find Scott chatting with a long-legged redhead whom I recognize immediately as Holly Whitby, the granddaughter of Grandma Flo's friend Ethel. Holly and I grew up together, thanks to our grandmothers.

We were close friends as kids, but grew apart when I got into sports and she entered the beauty pageant circuit. She's something of a local Boston celebrity, having participated in prestigious international pageants. Of course, I only know all of this from stalking her Instagram. I haven't actually seen her in person since high school.

She was always gorgeous, with a nearly perfect symmetrical face, pouty lips, and angelic ice-blue eyes. But now she looks straight off a runway in Milan with her voluminous hair and lush lash extensions.

Holly leans in close to Scott, who nods politely.

"Dance with me," she orders over the music, extending her dainty wrist.

His startled gaze flickers to me, with a sweet smile, not that I ever doubted him. Unbothered, I wave a hand toward her, signaling for him to go ahead and dance with her. He gives me an *I'd rather not* face.

Holly follows Scott's gaze and glances over her shoulder, jolting when she sees me. "Crystal?"

I smile. "Holly. So nice to see you."

We simultaneously go in for an awkward hug. As we pull away, her face remains twisted in confusion. She whips her head back to Scott. "Wait, *Crystal* isn't your girlfriend, is she?"

When Scott dips his chin, confirming, Holly doesn't hide her bewilderment. She turns to appraise me. "Wow. You've—you've done really well. I mean . . . good for you." Her tone is anything but authentic. But it also isn't bitchy or malicious. It's genuine surprise. "We'll have to catch up sometime soon. Maybe do lunch," she adds.

The fleeting thought crosses my mind: *Does she have a right to be shocked? Does everyone feel this way when they see us together?*

As the toxicity of my thoughts begins to burrow into my gut, I shut them away, pulling myself back to reality. "Yeah, lunch sounds good," I tell her, maintaining a friendly tone, despite my clenched jaw.

Scott holds his hand out, straight past Holly, toward me. "Come dance." I instinctively let him lead me into the thick of the crowd.

His arms envelop me as we sway to a slow song I recognize but can't name. The new lanterns we ended up buying thanks to my failed tree-climbing ordeal are strewn from the ceiling, casting a golden glow off his face. "I have no idea who that was. She came up to me while I was talking to your mom," he tells me, as if he has to justify himself.

I stop him. "Scott, don't worry about it. She's Ethel's grand-daughter. She's a nice girl."

He runs his hand up and down my back protectively, pulling me closer into his chest. "You okay?"

"Yeah, I'm totally fine," I say, even though I don't know if I am.

I try to shake off Holly's astonishment over me being Scott's girlfriend. I try to forget about the way she looked at me. Or how she literally congratulated me for scoring him. But for some reason, the sting is unrelenting, to the point that I no longer know what song is playing or who is dancing around me.

Scott presses his lips to my forehead when the song ends. "Wanna go back to my place soon? And by *soon* I mean in exactly fifteen minutes? I have to work at six in the morning."

I manage a half grin through the intruding negativity. "I really want to be horizontal with you right now, but I should probably stay back and help my mom and Tara with the cleanup."

He gives me a chaste peck on the cheek. "No worries. Gym tomorrow after I get off work?"

I nod. "Sounds good. But seriously, go home and get some sleep."

• • •

CLEANING UP THE décor at the end of the night is a painful endeavor that involves me limping around barefoot and tipsy, putting my lifting skills to good use. In fact, Tara has designated me the "muscle," responsible for carrying all the heavy items from the reception room to Mom and Dad's car.

By the time we return to my place, I'm entirely exhausted from the day and desperate to put on my trusty elastic-waist pajama pants.

As I settle into bed, I'm finally able to check my phone for the first time since last night. When my screen illuminates the darkness with its blinding blue glow, I jolt.

There are literally thousands of notifications. All on the beach photo.

chapter twenty-eight

Can't believe a guy that looks like that would date a chick like ♡
you. Guess some guys just like them insecure.

I've reread those words at least fifty times. Now they're a permanent screenshot in my head. It's a complete manifestation of all the
thoughts I pictured going through Holly's head when she realized
I was Scott's girlfriend. And there are thousands more similar
comments, all from total strangers.

He's with her for her Instagram money. He's totally got side ♡
chicks . . .

He deserves so much better!!! He's sooooo hot. ♡

She could eat him for breakfast. ♡

The sheer number of vile comments and DMs rolling in on this photo every second is unprecedented. Usually, my posts reach the height of their engagement within the first few hours they're posted. But nearly twenty-four hours after I originally posted the beach photo, the barrage of notifications on my phone hasn't slowed. In fact, this photo has received at least five times more attention than most of my Instagram posts.

My heart sinks lower and lower into despair as I continue to scroll through the thousands of comments and DMs. It's like a twisted addiction. Like I'm willingly injecting poison into my veins, despite knowing the catastrophic consequences. The smart thing to do would be to turn off my phone and succumb to a good night's rest. But I can't tear myself away, for some sick reason. I read through the comments until the strain becomes unbearable. Until my eyes are heavy, dry and gritty like sandpaper.

After less than two hours of sleep, the first thing I do the next morning is sit up, grab my phone, and pick up where I left off.

I try to remind myself there are three times as many supportive comments as there are negative ones, but it does little to quell the sickness festering in my stomach.

OMG so happy for you!! ♡

Beautiful couple 🤍 ♡

SMOKESHOW. ♡

He is so in love with you, you can see it in his eyes. ♡

Even as Tara prattles on about an awkward encounter with the wedding DJ last night while inhaling a Pop-Tart, I'm still glued to my phone at the kitchen table, hunched over like Igor in that ancient black-and-white Frankenstein movie, bracing myself for another abusive comment.

She ditches her plate in the sink and hops onto the counter, legs dangling. "Anyway, so he added me on Snapchat. When we got home last night, he'd sent me a snap of only his face. At an upward angle, which I'll never understand. Why do you want three chins? And there wasn't even an accompanying message. Like . . . if you want sex, you can at least say *Hi*. Or *Sup*." She pauses, taking a breath. "Is this what I have to look forward to in the dating world? If so, I think I'll go purchase the first of my thirteen cats."

I give her an unenthusiastic shrug. "Nah, DJ Heavy J is definitely lazy."

She sighs, examining her eccentric flamingo slippers. "Is Scotty coming over today? Do I need to put on a bra?"

"Maybe later tonight. I'm going to the gym with him when he gets off work," I tell her, dazed as another nasty comment pops onto my screen.

Just the thought of seeing Scott tonight makes my gut clench. The last thing I want is to explain the photo. I don't want him to see it, for the simple reason that I'm embarrassed. Not just about what people are saying about me, but about the comments directed at him, especially after he's opened up about his childhood bully.

My stomach is riddled with unrelenting anxiety as I spend what feels like an eternity deep in the bowels of the comments. I'm consumed, with no sense of how much time has passed. Has it been one hour? Three? Who can say? I have zero desire to leave my apartment to do errands, or attend my session with Mel later today.

I try to banish the negative thoughts to the deep recesses of my mind, like I usually do. But it's different this time. For some reason, they refuse to budge. There are too many of them, ping-ponging around in my head, sticking like burrs. They're relentless. It's like I'm drowning in them.

I've thought about deleting the post, but that would signal weakness. It crosses my mind to handle this like I usually do, mic drop a thirst trap and move on with my day. But the very thought of posting another photo of myself feels like pouring rubbing alcohol on an open wound.

Right now, the only strategy that seems semi-appealing is to take a hiatus on my account and ride out the storm.

Despite my decision to go dark until it all blows over, I'm still accountable to my clients. The irony of the entire situation sets in after I spend far too long struggling to draft a message to a client about the importance of loving herself, despite her perceived flaws. Is my self-doubt hypocritical? My brand's very foundation is rooted in body positivity. So why have I allowed the comments of total strangers to make me doubt myself when I've come so far in loving my body?

I play back the worst comments and DMs in my mind, about how Scott is too good for me. About how he's either cheating or settling. I keep thinking about Holly's face. The way she looked me up and down, unable to comprehend my association with Scott.

As I head to the gym for Mel's training session, I'm painfully aware of the self-doubt scratching its way to the surface, like a disease-ridden rodent burrowing through a crack in the wall.

Mel waves from her place stretching on the mats in her color-coordinated Gymshark outfit. She's chipper and radiating effortless confidence, as per usual. "Hey, girl." She stops a few feet in front of me and narrows her chestnut eyes, probably mentally eviscerating my latest haphazard ensemble. "You okay?"

I nod curtly. The last thing I want to do is talk about the photo for fear of breaking down in front of the 'roid-pumping frat boys in the Gym Bro Zone. "Just didn't get a lot of sleep last night."

"Did Captain America keep you up all night again?" She bounces her perfectly shaped brows suggestively.

"Nah. Just tired from the wedding," I say, unable to crack a smile.

"Tara sent me pictures. It looked like a blast. You guys all looked amazing. Your dress fit you so well."

"Thanks," I mutter, pointing to the shoulder press, in desperate need of a distraction.

She's taken aback by my abrasiveness. I can tell by her expectant face that she wants to poke further, but she doesn't. I purposely refrain from idle conversation so she gets the hint I'm not in the mood to talk.

I manage to make it through our hour-long session without looking at my phone, even though my anxiety is still bubbling under the surface, ready to boil over.

On our way out of the gym, Mel asks if she can come over to "lay low." Apparently, her brother is finally moving out of her apartment today and she would sooner flash her boobs to all of Excalibur Fitness than do manual labor.

I tell her "Yes," because her company is comforting, even if I have no desire to string more than three words together.

The moment we return to my apartment, I swap my going-out Lulus for my pajama bottoms. We sit in silence through nearly an entire episode of *Real Housewives of New Jersey*. Mel definitely knows something is up, because I've barely acknowledged the episode, which is a juicy one involving the pulling of a busted-ass weave, a nip slip, and a thrown birthday cake.

Usually, I'm right there with her, providing snarky commentary and judging Teresa's latest atrocity of a dress. Instead, I'm watching my phone like a hawk as the comments and DMs continue to roll in, burying myself deeper and deeper into a spiral of sadness.

When the show ends, Mel finally turns to me. "Okay, your doom-and-gloom vibe is seriously depressing me. What's up?"

"What vibe?"

She preens her lashes and levels me with a look that screams *Cut the BS*. "Oh, come on. We got full access to the window squat rack today. Usually you'd be all giddy and weirdly sentimental about it, acting like you've won the lotto. But you've been miserable all afternoon."

I sigh. There's no more avoiding this. Wordlessly, I turn my screen to Mel with the beach photo of Scott and me enlarged.

Her face lights up. "You finally posted it! You guys look amazing in that shot."

I take a moment, biting my nail to the quick. Objectively, I know I look great in that photo. That swimsuit is flattering as hell. So why have I become so obsessed with the opinions of strangers? "Have you read the comments?"

"Do I need to cut someone?" She scoops up her own phone from the coffee table, already scowling before she begins to scroll, like the loyal friend she is. It warms my heart that she's already righteously outraged on my behalf, and she doesn't even know what's going on. As she reads, she lets out a strangled gasp, shaking her head. "I am so sorry. These people are seriously messed up. Like psychologically messed in the head."

I press my lips together. "You should see the DMs. They're even worse." I toss her my phone so she can see for herself. She reads a couple aloud, which only further cements their brutality.

She regards me for a moment. "Screw them. If they have a problem with our bodies, why should we care? I hope you're not taking any of this to heart."

"I guess not . . . I don't know," I lie, even though my heart is as raw as a bloody rare steak. I desperately wish I were tough enough to let the comments roll off my back like Mel does. But after seven years of having my account, my armor is worn and I'm fully exposed.

"Don't let it consume you. And definitely don't respond. It's not healthy to engage with the haters. Trust me, I know."

"I'm not. I'm not posting anything until I figure out how to handle this."

"All influencers go through this and everyone comes back from it stronger than ever. Even the skinny influencers. Selena Gomez was fat-shamed a few years ago. I'm not trying to say it's the same thing, but I do understand—"

"Yeah, it's not the same thing," I interject, tone sharper than intended.

She cuts me a stern look and crosses her arms. I'm officially an asshole.

My throat tightens with regret and I backtrack. "I'm sorry, Mel. I'm just a little overwhelmed."

Her face softens as the seconds tick by. Eventually, her arms uncross and I'm thankful she hasn't written me off as a complete asshat. "Does Scott know about this?"

"I don't think so. He hasn't mentioned it, at least." Thankfully, Scott doesn't regularly check his Instagram account. I also didn't tag him in the photo in an effort to maintain his privacy.

"You're going to tell him, right?"

I shrug.

"Crystal, you need to before he sees it himself. Tonight."

"I know."

Deep down, I know Mel is right. Scott deserves to know. My fingers itch to call him, but upon a brief glance at my phone screen, I see he's already texted me a few minutes ago.

SCOTT: Excited for leg day? Think you'll go for a personal best?

SCOTT: Also, I have a new high intensity workout for us. Promise I'll go easy on you 😊

The juxtaposition of his carefree text with the sting of the Instagram comments makes me feel even worse. It's like someone has trapped me under a heavily loaded barbell.

The last thing I need is pity from Scott right now, despite how comforting I already know he would be. He's seen the hateful comments on my other posts, and we've talked at length about them. But he's never seen comments in relation to himself. He's never straight-up read about how he's *into fat chicks*, or how I'm *so disgusting* and *unworthy*. If the comments I'm so used to can affect me to the point of tears, how badly could they affect him?

And worse, could he start to believe them?

• • •

"I WAS THINKING, since you're not feeling up for the gym tonight, we should just have a night in? I could even pick up some sushi," Scott cheerfully suggests over the phone. He's completely oblivious to the avalanche burying me alive.

He's called me on his way home from work, just as I'm midway through reading a random email from a journalist at BuzzFeed News.

Dear Crystal,

I've been a longtime follower of your Instagram account, CurvyFitnessCrystal. I've been inspired by your journey and I couldn't help but notice your recent post with your new boyfriend. I know you've received a lot of attention on the post and a lot of negative comments. I'm writing an article about it, if you wouldn't mind answering a few of my questions? I have five hours for my deadline, so I'd like to hear your side of the story before the article goes live.

Best regards,
Daphne Jenkins
Health & Lifestyle Contributor

My eyes burn lasers into my phone. What fresh hell? An article about my photo? On BuzzFeed News? Is this a joke?

While this journalist appears to have good intentions, broadcasting the issue draws even more unwanted attention to the negativity. The very fact that someone has deemed it newsworthy only reinforces the ridiculous idea that me being with Scott is somehow "controversial." So much for slinking away into the shadows.

My hands tremble again as I try to blink myself back to the moment. "Sorry. I zoned out. What did you say?"

"I asked if you want to stay in. You still in a sushi mood? You were saying you were craving it the other day."

I cringe, hoisting my blanket up to my neck like a protective shield. I don't want any company, particularly from Scott.

"I'm actually not feeling too well," I say, panicked. My excuse to deny a sushi dinner needs to be believable, or Scott will be suspicious. I make a muffled retching sound, grimacing when it comes out like the distressed cries of a wounded cat.

"Are you sick?"

"I think so," I say weakly, which is a half-truth. I'm void of all energy from the emotional roller coaster of the past day.

"Tell me your symptoms. I'll come over and make you better," he teases suggestively, obviously not picking up on my tone.

"Sore throat. Runny nose. It's not a big deal." I literally facepalm myself when I realize I've made a rookie mistake feigning illness. Scott has a paramedic certification as a firefighter.

"I'm about ten minutes away. Can you stay alive until then?"

"No," I squawk. I'd rather swim in shark-infested waters than be face-to-face with Scott right now. I'm not ready to witness his humiliation, nor am I ready for the inevitable pity. "I mean, don't come. I might be contagious. I don't want you to get sick too."

"I don't care if you make me sick. I'm bringing you soup."

"I don't like soup."

He snorts. "Yes, you do, you liar. You eat it all the time when we go for lunch."

"Scott, listen to me. I don't want it."

He's quiet for a moment. "Okay, fine. You sure you're okay? You sound mad. Did I do something to piss you off?"

"No, you didn't." My voice is pained. I almost wish he had done something so I could justify being such a frosty asshole right now.

"I obviously did. Are you upset I smeared icing on your cheek at the wedding?"

"I'm not mad at you," I say, tone clipped.

"Okay . . . Is there anything at all I can do for you?"

"No. But I appreciate it. Really."

More silence. "Uh, alright. I guess I'll go back to my place?"

"Yeah. I'll talk to you tomorrow." My entire body aches from that call. I can't even fathom the thought of sleeping alone tonight, knowing this journalist is writing an article about me. I end the call, holding my phone to my chest.

I must have drifted into much-needed sleep, because when my eyes fly open at the sound of keys jingling in the lock, the living room is engulfed in a depressing darkness. I rub the sleep out of my eyes with my fists as Tara looms over me like some ominous ghost out of a horror movie. When my eyes adjust, I see she's just come from work, based on her scrubs. She smells like chicken broth, which makes sense when I register the container of Whole Foods soup in her hand.

"Scott texted me and asked me to bring this to you"—she brings her hands up in air quotes—"for your sickness." She levels me with a knowing look. Mel told her all about the Instagram comments. I know this because Tara sent me a million texts, in all caps, not five minutes after Mel left earlier this afternoon.

I take the soup from her hands, giving her a bored, exhausted chin dip. "Thanks. How are you?"

"I ate shit outside Whole Foods and burned a man. Thanks for asking." She hikes up the pant leg of her scrubs to reveal a bloody gash on her knee.

I lean closer to examine it. It looks bad, but not deep enough to require medical attention, even though she'll probably act like she needs it. "What happened? What do you mean, you *burned* a man?"

"I was walking out the doors with your soup and I shit you not, a guy who looked identical to the late Paul Walker—RIP, bless his beautiful soul—came out of nowhere. It was like a movie . . . he slammed right into me." She claps her hands for dramatic effect. "But instead of a romantic moment of prolonged eye contact, the soup went flying."

My eyes go wide. "No!"

She nods. "Yup. It all happened in slow motion. I dove forward . . . somehow under the illusion I could heroically catch the liquid with my bare hands and spare him. But I couldn't. It splattered all over him and he screamed like he was being murdered. Not sure if it was because of the soup scorching his skin or the sight of me diving toward him . . . Anyway, he leaped out of the way and I went knee-first onto the pavement." She grimaces at her knee again.

"Did you at least get his name?"

She shakes her head vehemently. "No. By the time all was said and done, he looked at me like I was a lunatic and ran into the store. And I awkwardly had to limp in behind him to get more soup."

The story is objectively hilarious and quintessentially Tara. I'd usually be in stitches over it. But right now, the muscles in my mouth refuse to turn into a smile.

"You doing alright?" she asks, settling on the edge of the couch near my feet.

I shrug lazily. "I feel like shit."

"How long will you pretend you're sick? Scott's not gonna buy it for much longer," she points out.

"I know. I'm just not ready yet." My eyes snap to a new text.

SCOTT: Did Tara bring you the soup?

CRYSTAL: She did. Thanks a lot.

SCOTT: Hope it makes you feel better. I really wish you'd let me come over. Heading into another double shift tomorrow and I miss you.

CRYSTAL: I'm fine. Please stop worrying. I miss you too.

SCOTT: Okay. Get some rest. Also, don't ask me how I know this because it's embarrassing, but those leggings you like at Lululemon are on sale.

CRYSTAL: Cool, thanks.

SCOTT: Ok, iRobot. I know you're sick but would it kill you to send an exclamation mark? An emoji??? A GIF???

CRYSTAL: 😃 😃 😃 😃 😃 😃 😃 😃

SCOTT: That's a tad aggressive, but I'll take it.

I let the guilt of lying to Scott settle before I reread the email from BuzzFeed News. I google the reporter's name and contact details to confirm she's the real deal. And she is.

I seriously contemplate responding to the email, begging her not to write the story. I draft a response, which takes me the better part of an hour—most of my time spent deleting curse words and uncapitalizing full sentences so as to come across like the mature, emotionally balanced individual I am. But before I hit *Send*, my mind drifts back to my Size Positive campaign. *Love yourself and ignore the haters.*

I delete my draft email and close my laptop.

With or without my comment, this story is going viral. To-morrow.

chapter twenty-nine

**FULL-FIGURED FITNESS INSTAGRAM QUEEN
BODY-SHAMED FOR DATING SIX-PACK HUNK**

Crystal Chen (@CurvyFitnessCrystal), 27, broke the internet when she posted a sexy, now-viral photo of her and her new beau at the beach (photo below) to her 250,000 Instagram followers. Posted on August 5th, the photo has received over fifty thousand Likes and six thousand comments, many of which have questioned her apparent new romance.

As a body-positive advocate, Chen has been on the scene for years, cheerfully spreading the message to women to "embrace their curves and love their bodies." She's been an inspiration for women of all sizes and shapes to engage in weight-neutral healthy lifestyles. Her clients have long raved about her flexible workout programs, which stress the importance of mental well-being in tandem with physical health.

While she didn't specifically name her swoony new beau, he's been identified as Boston Fire Department member Scott Ritchie (@Ritchie_Scotty7), 30.

Chen's followers hope she will continue to share her life with her new partner, while also continuing to serve as a role model in the fitness industry.

*Editor's note: Chen did not respond to BuzzFeed News's request for comment, nor has she been active on her account for two full days.

Cocooned under the protection of a thick, knitted blanket on the couch, I read the article again for the fifty-eighth time. I'm most certainly developing a severe case of carpal tunnel from clutching my phone with a death grip.

Upon my first read of the article, I was livid. I wanted to breathe fire and flip a table, *Real Housewives* style. I knew the journalist was going to write the article, but somehow, it didn't seem real. Not until my name was blasted all over the internet.

It's now been a total of two days since the photo was posted, and it's officially gone beyond viral. In between self-loathing and staring into the abyss, I'm obsessively tracking the coverage, trying to locate every place the articles are reposted and retweeted.

I've also been contacted by all the biggest news outlets, including *Glamour* magazine, Perez Hilton, and the *New York Times*. It was even a Hot Topic on *The View*. When Whoopi Goldberg passionately shrieks across the table on your behalf, you know you've made it. If only it were for a different reason.

I've received an outpouring of supportive messages telling me how "inspiring" I am. But I can't help but feel like my platform's message has been completely overshadowed. It's no longer about body positivity. It's about fat-shaming. Crystal Chen as a victim. The curvy girl who somehow snagged a six-pack hunk.

The logical side of my brain tells me to end my hiatus and reclaim the message. But then again, would it all backfire? Would it just scare other women off from loving themselves, especially when they read the nasty comments? The mere fact that the photo is viral *because* of the negativity further reinforces the inherent struggle of being curvy.

There's really no winner in this—aside from the trolls, whom I don't want to pay an iota of attention to. I need more time to strategize a response. And realistically, I don't have the energy to defend myself, or be anyone's role model right now.

I'm heating a cup of noodles, my new go-to meal, when I catch the time on the microwave. It's six. Scott is probably just getting off his shift. It occurs to me that I haven't heard from him yet today, which is uncharacteristic. Then again, my responses to his texts yesterday were bland at best. It's safe to say he's bothered I haven't wanted to see him after being apart for the past few days, which might as well be an eternity.

Just as I settle back onto the couch, steaming cup of noodles in hand, Scott bursts through the front door without knocking. It's as if the mere thought of him has summoned his presence. He's wearing the dark green hoodie I love, which brings out the deep forest-green hues of his eyes.

I've never seen him like this before, aside from when he thought Martin was sick. Hard, bloodshot eyes. Jaw tense. Hair wild, sticking up, unsure of which way it wants to fall. He stands in place for a few agonizing beats before stomping forward, brandishing his phone in front of my face with one of the articles pulled up. "What the hell is this?"

I sink farther into the couch, immobile, eyes welling. I feel awful he's had to find out about it from some third party. It doesn't help that I'm void of any plausible explanation as to why I haven't told him myself. Every time I went to call him, I chickened out, terrified of what would happen if he read those comments sooner than he needed to. But now that he's right here, obviously having read them, how can I even begin to explain?

His severe expression softens as he sits down next to me, his thumb and index finger pinched over the bridge of his nose, eyes closed. The familiar warmth of his body next to mine settles the dread in my stomach, but only marginally.

The silence is deafening. I think it's about to swallow us both, until he says, "Why didn't you tell me?"

I bury my tearstained face in my hands, inching to the edge of the couch, knowing full well there is no excuse. I should have told him the night of the wedding, or days ago when the BuzzFeed journalist emailed me. Or better yet, when I originally posted the photo. "I wanted to handle it myself," is all I can think to say.

He splays his thumbs over my cheeks to wipe away the free-flowing tears. "Why?"

"Did you see the comments?"

"Yeah, but I had to stop before I smashed my phone. They're bullshit," he says, expression tightening. "Why have you been avoiding me?"

I suck in a shaky breath. "Because I know how much you hate this stuff. I didn't want you to read that crap about yourself, all because of me. I know it's not an excuse. I'm sorry I didn't tell you sooner."

He presses his lips to my temple. "You know none of those comments are true, right? I—" He pauses for a moment, pulling back. "I hate that this is happening to you."

The moment his eyes lock with mine, my lips tremble and the tears overflow yet again. My vision blurs and I find myself lurching forward, sobbing into his chest. I've never done this before in front of him, in front of any guy. I'm like a completely broken version of myself with no way to put myself back together.

I'm weak, in a way I haven't been since junior high. The days I used to hide in the changing room stall to change. My entire high school and college years were spent erasing those feelings, desperately willing myself to feel the complete opposite—strong and confident. Trying to be someone who doesn't give a shit about what other people think, especially for the sake of my followers. Now, I'm faced with the reality that I'm not really that self-assured, happy person. Not to my followers, and now, not to the person who matters most. Scott.

I hate this. I can't go back to that dark, lonely place. I refuse.

My eyes harden at my internal declaration, and I straighten my posture, promptly dabbing away my tears. "I'm good. Really," I say through a sniffle. "To be honest, I think I want to be alone tonight."

His face knots with unease. He looks positively ill. "Alone? You shouldn't have to go through this by yourself." He runs a hand through his hair, exasperated. "There's gotta be something I can do—"

"Scott, please," I cut in, voice quivering. "Stop treating me like I'm some sad, pathetic puppy. There is nothing you can do. I don't need you to go into hero mode right now. In fact, I need the exact opposite. All I'm asking for is one more night alone, just to collect my thoughts and figure out what the hell I'm going to do about all of this."

"Crys, I—"

I stop him, placing my hand over his. "I will handle this myself. Trust me."

• • •

TARA CLOSES HER paperback abruptly and lets out a heavy sigh beside me on the couch. "Do you remember what you said to me the second week after I came to stay with you?"

"Uh, to stop leaving your Pop-Tart crumbs all over my kitchen counters or I wouldn't cook for you anymore?" I mutter, cheek pressed into the arm of the couch at an awkward angle. I've been lying in this exact position since I woke up this morning. There might as well be a chalk outline surrounding my lifeless body.

"Besides that." Tara shifts to the edge of the couch, knee bouncing, eager to enlighten me. "You told me to wash my face and at least pretend to have my shit together."

I can't help but snort at the grim memory. "And you whipped a book at me."

She tightens her grip on the book. "Damn right. You were being a hard-ass. But you know what? It helped. I felt a thousand times better. So if I can stop moping over my fiancé dumping me and my whole future being flushed down the toilet, you can snap out of this. You're acting like a brooding man-child from one of my romance novels. It's not a good look. You've gotta let it all out."

I flash her the stink eye, silently willing her to leave me alone. She doesn't.

This is one of many glaring differences between us. With any given problem, she airs her woes to everyone and anyone within her general vicinity, like the poor, confused technician at the pharmacy a block from my apartment. The more people and opinions, the better (not that she actually takes anyone's advice).

I've never been one to rely on others when I'm upset. For some reason, I prefer to suffer in bleak solitude. I'm basically the Grinch (the Jim Carrey version), dwelling in his lair, monologuing excessively, and loathing all that is good in the world.

It's been a day since Scott left, albeit reluctantly. If I'm being honest, my stomach bottomed out the moment he walked out the door. But the shock of having gone viral, combined with his I-must-fix-you attitude, was overwhelming, almost suffocating.

Being alone with my thoughts, however terrifying, reenergizes me and clears my head, which is exactly what I need to strategize my response to the situation. I can't ghost my Instagram forever.

Unfortunately, literal silence to think is hard to come by. Tara has been blasting "Rumors" by Lindsay Lohan on repeat. She's deemed it my new theme song, and it's both tragically and embarrassingly appropriate. The bop is a classic, but I'm getting a little unnerved.

I'm about to text Scott to check in and thank him for giving me the space I need when Tara shrieks, pausing Lindsay right when she's asking why people can't just let her live.

"What?" I ask.

"Did you see what Scott commented?"

I wrinkle my nose in confusion. Scott never uses Instagram, aside from liking all my photos when we first met. "What? No."

Tara hands me her phone, eyes wider than dinner plates. "You're not gonna like this."

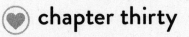 ## chapter thirty

Comment by **CJS_49er**: There's no way this guy is with her ♡
for anything but her money and fame lol. Why would a guy
who looks like that settle? He's definitely cheating!

Reply by **Ritchie_Scotty7**: @CJS_49er You're pathetic and ♡
you should be ashamed. Crystal is beautiful, inside and out. I
feel sorry for anyone who doesn't see that. She's the kind of
person who would give the shirt off her back for a stranger
and has dedicated her life to helping others. Do us all a favor
and get a fucking life. Put your hatred and ignorance toward
something useful for a change.

"You just can't help yourself, can you?" I hiss.

Scott looks a little frazzled as he steps aside to let me in, and I don't blame him. I've shown up at his apartment out of the blue, practically fuming. Admittedly, it's difficult to maintain any level of outrage when Albus Doodledore is galloping around the living area like a tiny horse, euphoric about my arrival. His tongue lolls out of the side of his mouth as he nibbles my fingers.

I clench my fists, shielding my fingers from Albus, which automatically resets my headspace. The simple act reminds me why I'm here, reigniting the fury pulsing through my veins. If I were an animated character, steam would be billowing out of my ears.

"I can explain." He watches as I pace the length of the IKEA coffee table in front of the couch, Albus following nobly at my feet, thirsting for me to toss the slobbery stuffed gibbon he's dropped on my foot.

"Scott, I made it clear I didn't need backup. That I wanted to handle this myself. And you went behind my back and responded to a bunch of comments. You did exactly what I told you not to do. You've swooped in, trying to be a hero I don't need. You've stolen my opportunity to strategize. To regroup. To address the entire situation in my own way. And now I look like some broken damsel in distress who requires rescue and validation by her big, strong boyfriend."

He swallows, head hanging in regret, like a small child in trouble with the principal. "I'll delete them."

My irritation flares. "It's way too late for that."

The comments were only posted two hours ago, and already, BuzzFeed News has written a follow-up article, titled *Six-pack boyfriend of full-figured fitness influencer speaks out, loves her curves.* It paints me in an even more pathetic light than the first.

And worse, just when the comments were slowing down, just when I was becoming old news, buried by the next juicy scandal, the hate has ramped up all over again.

Scott regroups and stands, reaching for my hands. I wrap my arms around myself, avoiding his touch. "I'm sorry. But I couldn't let people bombard us with these asinine comments about how I must be cheating on you, or using you. It couldn't be farther from the truth. I can't let people say horrible things about the person I love."

Love.

Everything comes to a screeching halt. My mind is akin to one of those plastic car-crash test dummies, flying forehead-first into the airbag. I'm jolted. Whiplashed. Frozen. Did he really just tell me he *loves* me? "What?" I manage through my shock, vision tunneling.

His gaze doesn't waver, eyes locked to mine. "I said I love you. More than I can even put into words."

"When did you decide this?" My voice comes out in barely a whisper. As the weight of his words settles onto my shoulders, I lower myself to the couch. He sits next to me, knees touching mine.

There's a long pause, as if he really needs to think this through. "Since you peeled my clementine for the first time. That night we watched *Lord of the Rings*."

Everything inside me clenches. Those three words are everything I've been dying to hear from him over the past month. On one level, he seems to be telling the truth, or at least he thinks he is. But saying it now feels like pity. Why not tell me the moment he felt it? He's had plenty of opportunities since. Why wait until the worst possible moment? I desperately want to believe it's genuine.

But there's a nagging doubt that won't go away, no matter what he says. It's the same doubt that's seemingly clouded everything in my life since the photo went viral.

How can *he* be in love with me if I'm not even sure *I'm* in love with me anymore?

After the whirlwind of the past few days, it simply isn't registering. "Scott, I just don't know."

His patience wanes. "You *just don't know* about what? I just told you I loved you."

"I'm so mad at you. You should have asked me first before you went ahead and responded."

"I didn't ask you because I knew you would freak out. Like this." He waves a fed-up hand in my direction.

"This is social media 101. You never respond to your haters. Ever."

"Even if they're spreading lies?"

"Especially then." A fresh swell of resentment rises in my throat. "Your comments look like my response to the whole thing. It makes me look weak. Like I needed you to go to bat for me publicly. Like the comments affected me. Like I hate my body and I need reassurance from someone like you."

"But why is that such a bad thing? Why do you need to be the one to respond?"

"Because! It's my image. It's my brand."

His lips twist in dismay. "Don't you ever get sick of this? Tired of constantly getting shit on?"

"You know I do. But what choice do I have?" I run my palms down my cheeks in exasperation. It feels like I'm being forced to solve an unsolvable jigsaw puzzle.

"Why don't you delete the stupid picture? It's going to take a toll on you, little by little." He trails off when he notices my grimace.

I should have known this was coming. "Scott. How many times do I have to tell you? I'm not a twelve-year-old in middle school. I'm so sorry about what happened to you. I really am. But this isn't the same thing. Deleting one photo won't change anything."

He tosses his palms in the air, red-hot irritation flaring. "But look at what it's done to you. You're consumed by it. You have been since I met you. I'm concerned for you. This shouldn't define you. You're worth so much more. You are so much more than just this."

"It's not that simple."

His jaw ticks. "How is this supposed to work if you continue to shut me out entirely? Every single time the idiotic internet trolls say shit about you?"

"I don't know!" My voice comes out louder than I intended, and I find myself standing.

He scoffs, standing too, hands on hips. "You know, this is the entire problem with us. It always has been. You don't trust me. You don't trust me enough to rely on me when shit goes wrong. And you know what? I'm done trying to earn your trust. I don't know what else I can do."

"How can I trust you when you go behind my back like this?" I ask honestly, manically gesturing to the space between us. "I told you I was handling it by myself."

He rakes a tense hand through his hair. "But that's just it. You don't have to do things by yourself anymore. That's the entire point of a relationship. You have me now. We're supposed to get through these things together. As a team."

I'm quiet for a few moments. He's right. My first instinct should have been tackling this together. And it wasn't. It was the exact opposite. I kept it from him like a dirty secret, because, deep down, I was terrified he'd believe the comments. I was terrified he'd walk away from me.

He continues. "And if we're actually going to be a *team*, I refuse to stand by and keep letting this shit happen."

I blink. "I can't be known as the fat girl who dared to date a hot guy. I can't. I've worked too hard to get to this point."

He digests my words and shakes his head, like a realization has just washed over him. "So that's what this is about?"

"I haven't felt this bad about myself in years. I need time to figure myself out before I can focus on us."

Scott pulls back as if I've slapped him in the face. He stares at the floor under his bare feet for what feels like a hellish eternity. "So . . . you . . . what? You're just ending things? After I told you I loved you for the first time? After all we've gone through to even get to this point, you're willing to toss it all out the window because of some stupid photo?" he asks, voice low, gravelly, and exhausted.

"Yes." My heart is crushed to dust when the word settles. I can't even argue, or take it back, because it's the truth. If I truly want my strength back, I need to find it myself, not while hiding in Scott's arms as he pets my hair, telling me everything is going to be sunshine and rainbows.

He drops his head in his hands. When he comes up for air, it feels like the entire apartment has been sucked of all oxygen. I've completely crushed him. Dug my heel in and stomped.

Instinctively, I reach forward tepidly to pull him into a hug. He draws in a prolonged sigh, pressing his forehead to mine. I memorize his woodsy scent and the secure feeling of being near him. I try to hold on to this moment for as long as I can.

I close my eyes, and unexpectedly, his lips crash into mine. It's not gentle or smooth. It's anguish. Our tongues fight against each other's, in turmoil. In anger, sadness, and love, all spun up in a tornado of chaos.

Before I open my eyes again, he tears himself from me like he's been burned. He runs his hand through his hair, unsure of what to do next. Our teary eyes meet again as he lets out a strained breath. "Crystal . . . do you even love me?"

I want to tell him *Yes*. Badly. That I've known I love him for weeks now. But what's the point? It will just make things harder. "I'm so sorry." My voice comes out in a whisper.

I meet his gaze, and all I see is sadness. It's like I'm witnessing his heart crumple and split in two. And mine's quick to follow. It's like the full weight of a kettlebell dropping onto my chest, shattering the bone.

When the realization settles that I'm not changing my mind, he turns away.

There's nothing left for me to do but leave.

chapter thirty-one

HAVEN'T LEFT THE confines of my apartment in two days. I haven't even changed out of my pajamas. Tara has undertaken the task of brushing my unruly troll hair every day. It's a painful experience, because she brushes straight from the root—not the middle—like a monster. I'm surprised I'm not entirely bald.

I hate feeling like this. I hate that I've let the haters win. And it makes me feel like my entire platform has been a lie. How am I supposed to preach self-love and body positivity when I've allowed myself to get so caught up in the negativity?

By now, I'd hoped to have some grand epiphany. To come up with a game plan to move forward with my Instagram. But instead, I'm in zombie mode. Just existing. Eat, sleep, repeat.

After I refuse to leave the couch, Tara calls in reinforcements. Mel barges into my apartment with a full carton of clementines. Immediately, I begin to ugly-cry, Kim Kardashian–style. In Mel's defense, she doesn't know the sentimental meaning of these adorable, innocent citrus fruits. All I can think about is the smile on Scott's face when I peeled them for him.

"God, you are a mess, Crystal," Mel says, not bothering to hide her displeasure as she takes in the absolute disaster that is my normally tidy apartment. She frowns at the dirty dishes piled in my sink, the used tissues littering the coffee table, and the soda cracker crumbs smeared into my couch. Because of my state, Tara has started cleaning up after me, but her initiative is still spotty at best.

Mel inches onto the tiny patch of couch that isn't covered in crumbs. She pats my back as I go back and forth between sobbing and blowing my raw nose.

I finally come up for air. "I'm sorry, Mel. I've been a selfish asshole. How are you doing?"

She shakes her head, vaguely waving me off, as if her life is the last thing she wants to discuss. "I'm fine. Really. I got a partnership with this super-cute swimwear brand."

"I'm so happy for you," I tell her genuinely. Despite my own sadness, digesting someone else's good news is actually a welcome change. "How are things with Peter?" I ask after a couple moments of silence. I don't know Peter on a personal level, aside from the time Scott and I went on a double date with them at the rock-climbing gym. He's one of those guys with a resting bored face who's under the delusion he's too intellectually superior for pedestrian activities like rock climbing. He also exclusively watches television for educational purposes, never for entertainment. Scott called him "cardboard" and bet me they wouldn't last longer than a few more months, given their lack of literally anything in common.

Mel's shoulders rise and fall, as if exasperated. "I dunno. Okay, I guess. We still can't agree on anything. Ever. Like, the other night, I was really looking forward to hanging out when he got off work, but he said no because he wanted *alone time*. Even after I tried to entice him with a blow job."

Tara juts her chin forward. "You offered a blow job and he still didn't want to come over?"

"Nope. And I rarely offer blow jobs. I thought for sure he'd pounce on it. Do you think that's a bad sign?"

Tara frowns. "I mean, I've never met him. I can't judge his life and motivations. Though I've never known a guy to turn down a blow job."

I grimace, dazed. "Scott is the only person I've ever wanted to be around all the time, even when my shits-to-give reserve was low."

The past few days without Scott Landon Ritchie have been dull. It's like the vibrant, warm preset filter has been stripped away, leaving only gloomy darkness. Everything is empty. His spot on my couch, his side of my bed, the lack of his infectious, full-body laughter echoing through my apartment.

I miss watching outrageously long movies together. Him asking a million questions, confused because he fell asleep for ten minutes and missed a crucial scene.

Mel discreetly brushes some of the cracker crumbs off my couch. "Have you talked since?"

"No." Scott hasn't bombarded me with calls and texts, and I don't know whether I should feel relieved or worse about it. Though he did leave one voicemail, which said *"Crys, I . . . I'm so sorry about responding to those comments. When you're ready, please call me."*

"I still don't get why you're taking space from him. Especially after he told you he loved you," Mel says.

"But he told me at the worst possible time. And when he first said it, I didn't even believe it. That's how far gone I am right now."

"Seriously? Of course he loves you. I really don't know why you're doing this to yourself," Tara adds, joining us after tidying the kitchen. Instead of curling up on the end of the couch, she nestles herself on top of me, feet dangling on Mel's lap like a gigantic baby.

As much as I want to call him at any given moment to tell him I love him, that I'll go back to my old, confident self, I can't.

"Not until I'm back on track," I say. "I can't risk breaking his heart again until I shake this. And I'm still a little mad at him."

Tara shoots me a furious stare. "It isn't Scotty's fault your confidence took a dip. It's the trolls'. You can't blame him for that. He was just trying to protect you. Sure, he went about it all wrong. But he also had the best of intentions. And if I'm being honest, I kind of agree with him. I'm worried about you too."

I glare at her. "Seriously?"

"Look, you've become obsessed with this body-positivity thing to your detriment. You've let a bunch of idiotic, jealous internet haters affect you so badly that you've lost your relationship over it."

"He still went behind my back," I remind them stubbornly.

Mel rolls her eyes. "There were some nasty comments about him too, you know. Why is he not allowed to stand up for himself, if not you? It's not all about you."

She has a point. There were awful comments about him too, not just me. Have I really been that selfish?

I bury my face in my hands, ashamed of my misplaced blame. "Well, it doesn't matter. The only way to avoid this is to delete my entire account. And giving my platform up isn't a question."

"Whatever you decide, you can't continue on like this. It's not sustainable," Mel warns.

"It has to be."

Mel passes me more tissues as I begin to hiccup. "You don't need to be so strong and confident at all times, Crystal. Even if you're a trainer. The curvy community doesn't need you to defend them. We're perfectly fine. What we need is you to be the best you can be."

I sigh. "And that's the worst part. After all is said and done, I don't feel my best. And it feels like I'm living a lie. How can you be so positive all the time, Mel? It's like you don't let anything bother you, ever."

She levels with me, stone-faced. "Therapy. Ever since I got Insta-famous, or whatever you want to call it, I see my therapist once every two weeks and she's a miracle worker."

I tilt my head, considering. "Maybe I could look into it."

"And I am positive, most of the time," Mel continues. "Just like you are. I may not give two shits about the comments anymore, but I still have days where I don't love everything about myself. It's normal."

Tara nods, resting her head on my shoulder. "You're putting unfair pressure on yourself, Crystal. Everyone doubts themselves sometimes. It's part of being human. Especially after what you've been through."

I struggle to take in their words. "I guess so."

After Mel leaves, I find myself scrolling through my *Feedback* email folder. It's where I save all the final messages from my clients after they've completed their programs. I pull up one from Jennifer—one of my favorites.

Hi Crystal,

I can't believe how fast these few months have gone by. I can't tell you how much your support has meant to me. I never had the confidence to go to the gym and lift weights. That all changed when we had our first meeting and you told me that no one else is actually paying attention. You gave me that kick-ass playlist and for the first time, I felt empowered.

I've progressed so much both in the gym and mentally. You've convinced me that eating one bad meal isn't going to erase my progress. I no longer count calories or obsess over weighing my portions. I'm happy now, for the first time in years. Some days are better than others . . . but as you said, as long as the good days outweigh the bad days, that's what counts.

I can't recommend you enough. You're more than just a fitness trainer. I'll always consider you one of my best friends.

Love you!
Jennifer

I spend the entire evening reading these emails. If there's one common thread among all my past clients, it's that they were well on their way on their journey to self-acceptance. Sure, they didn't love themselves every single second of every day. And I reassured them that was okay. That as long as there was more love than loathing, they were on the right track.

Maybe I was onto something.

chapter thirty-two

M Y WAKE-UP CALL comes the next day when the UPS man delivers my new sponsored athletic wear. The repulsion in his eyes at the sight of my pale, cadaver-like face and stained pajamas as he asks for a signature is a gut punch. So much so that I feel compelled to fake cough and give the unsolicited explanation that I'm the victim of a mysterious, possibly deadly plague. *I'm not suffering from a severe case of self-loathing! I swear! Don't judge me. OkaythanksBYE.*

If there's any hope of going back to normal, I have to start somewhere. I need to return to the gym—the place that used to be my sanctuary from all things bad, ugly, and stressful. Not only for the sake of my business and livelihood, but for myself. For my soul.

The moment I step through the turnstiles and inhale that familiar scent of sweat, disinfectant spray, grit, and determination, the anxiety of leaving my apartment begins to dissipate. There aren't a ton of people here, given that it's midafternoon. I take a quick glance around, recognizing a couple faces. The Walkman guy with the goatee. The bodybuilder woman clenching her rock-hard butt in the mirror. Thankfully, the one person I'm desperately trying to avoid is nowhere to be seen.

When I'm face-to-face with my favorite squat rack by the window, the guilt floods in. That's the thing with strength training: breaks delay progress, regardless of muscle memory.

By my second set, I'm crimson-faced, frustrated, and on the verge of tears. I feel the strain. The immediate soreness and Jell-O sensation in my legs from days of inactivity.

I'm glistening with sweat, contemplating giving up and retreating to the sanctuary of my bed, when a woman I don't recognize approaches. She's middle-aged, with tanned skin and gorgeous deep brown eyes. My attention immediately zeroes in on her neon-colored Lizzo concert T-shirt, which reads *Feelin' Good As Hell.*

"Great T-shirt," I tell her.

She smiles, glancing down to stretch it out. "Thank you! Got it at her concert in the winter. The woman can seriously perform. And in heels."

"Right? I don't know how you can rock heels for that long without ruining your feet."

She nods in vigorous agreement, still lingering. "I hate to bother you . . ."

I draw in a breath, fully expecting her to ask me if I'm the girl from the viral photo.

"I don't want to sound super creepy, but I was watching you do your squats and I couldn't help but think, holy shit, that woman is freakin' amazing. How much are you squatting?"

I stare at her in disbelief, for so long that she must think I'm deranged. After days of agonizing over what strangers think of me, the unsolicited compliment feels foreign. "Uh . . . thank you," I stammer.

"I don't think I can even squat the bar," she laments as she examines the weight on the bar behind me. "I'm Rhonda, by the way." She extends her hand in a friendly greeting.

"I'm Crystal." I return her handshake before nodding to the squat rack. "And when it comes to squatting, it really depends on your body weight. That will determine how much you're naturally able to push. But it's like any other muscle training. You have to start off slow. Really slow with squats. Let your body get used to the dynamic movement."

She rests her body weight on the rack as she nods with interest, so I continue.

"Squatting is a full-body workout. You're not only working out your legs. You're fully engaging your core and your butt too."

"You sound like an expert."

I'm struck by the realization that I really do know my shit. "Technically, I am. I'm a personal trainer."

"No wonder you're lifting so heavy. I've been meaning to book a few sessions with a trainer, just to get started on some weight lifting. It's only my second day today and . . ." She glances around the Gym Bro Zone like a lost sheep. "I'm feeling a little overwhelmed."

I tilt my head sympathetically, recalling the terror and embarrassment of entering the gym for the first time so many years ago.

I scan the space, taking in the sight of the intimidating gym bros grunting to our left. My eye catches the cable machine, where Scott committed Paper Towel Gate. The thought makes my gut ache, but only for a couple seconds before I'm transported back to Rhonda.

"Honestly, those guys look intimidating. But they're really nice when you get to know them. Always willing to help if you need it," I reassure her. As much as I rag on their frat-boy ways, they're always friendly, greeting me whenever they see me.

She doesn't look convinced, and I don't really blame her, as a newbie. After rereading my client emails, I want to help someone again. "I have two more sets and I'll be done. Then I can show you some things, if you want?"

She smiles eagerly, but quickly shakes her head. "It's okay. I don't want to take up your time if you're busy."

"You aren't at all. Just give me a couple minutes."

After my last set, I show Rhonda one or two basic moves on the machines. I usually start brand-new gym-goers on the machines so they can get a good base before moving on to free weights.

Rhonda tells me about how she's a recently divorced high school guidance counselor. She moved to Boston from a small town near Atlanta. She's been "on a self-acceptance journey," as she describes it. While she doesn't have the budget to go all *Eat, Pray, Love*, she has indulged in a new haircut and new wardrobe.

When she tells me I've inspired her to start lifting weights, I have to sit down on a bench to collect myself. It's the first time in weeks I've felt hope, up close and personal, right before my eyes. Hope that another's success and happiness can motivate me once again. Hope that this viral incident won't define me for the rest of my life.

Meeting someone who's learned to accept and respect herself again after her life was turned upside down is inspiring. Maybe I can learn a little something from her too. So I offer to train her free of charge.

"WATCH YOUR FORM. Straighten your back a little . . . there. You got it."

I swell with pride as Rhonda embarks on her third set of squats. I started her off with just the bar, but after only a few sessions, she's already progressed to one hundred and twenty pounds.

Even though Rhonda's a decade older than me, she and I have become fast friends. She's still job hunting, so our sessions are usually in the afternoon. In between her workouts, when she can catch a breath, she updates me about her divorce woes, the fierce custody battle over her two hairless cats, Tim and Tam, and how liberating it is to pee with the door open in her new apartment.

"I've even bought a bunch of period panties," she announces proudly, doing a mini shimmy. "Chuck always hated them. Banned them when we first started dating. I mean, I know Fruit of the Loom isn't sexy. But damn, those things are comfortable."

"My ex hated them too. Not my last one. The one before. Neil."

"Ah, the guy who used you as a rebound?"

"Yup. The one before Scott."

Her forehead pinches as she registers my immediate mood shift. "What happened with Scott?"

I bite my bottom lip, and despite my loner instincts, everything floods out. Fast and furious. Like someone's cut a slit through my umbrella in a torrential downpour. I open up about the viral photo. Letting it all out feels like a massive weight has been lifted from my shoulders.

Rhonda listens like a true guidance counselor, seated atop the riser, long past our scheduled hour-long session. "This is why I hide from the internet at all costs." Her teasing expression is quickly replaced with sympathy. "I'm sorry you feel like you've lost your platform and some of your confidence over the photo. That's awful. Humans aren't made for that kind of scrutiny. No one should have to go through that."

"It hasn't been fun. But I'm managing. I hate feeling like I've sold lies to people. I've encouraged people to love themselves no matter what. I'm starting to think it's a lot to ask. Loving yourself all day, every day?"

She shrugs. "I don't think confidence and self-worth is something you magically attain. And you don't simply hold on to it forever like a tangible object. It's fluid. You can be confident in every aspect except one. Or something could happen and all your confidence can be shattered in an instant. Like the Instagram photo. It doesn't mean you don't inherently love yourself to the core."

I take in her words for a moment. "How do I get my confidence back?"

"You've gotta find it on your own terms. You rediscover things you love about yourself and nourish them. And not just the things society tells you that you should love. Beauty isn't objective, you know, as much as society tells us it is."

I purse my lips. "I don't know if I agree with you."

"Why not?"

"Because people seem to like the same things, predominantly. Everyone thinks Scarlett Johansson is hot. The Hemsworth brothers. Idris Elba. Heart-shaped faces. Light eyes. You name it."

"Only a segment of Western society," she notes. "Curves used to be revered. And personally, I don't know what people see in those Hemsworths. Ripped abs don't do anything for me. Like, give me some dad bods already, Hollywood!"

I chuckle, picking at the lint on my leggings. She has a point there. Different regions of the world have different beauty ideals. And beauty standards change with time. "Maybe."

"Everyone sees beauty differently, Crystal. What's worse, that same society taught us as little girls that we're not beautiful because we're not white and skinny. I mean, did you ever have a Barbie doll that looked like you when you were a kid?"

"No."

She gives me a pointed look. "Exactly. And all these massive corporations that told us we weren't beautiful—that we weren't objects of affection—are suddenly screaming at us to love ourselves."

"And if we don't love ourselves, all the time, we're the problem." I nod, coming to a stark realization. I became part of that machine, selling that idea to my followers.

After my session with Rhonda, I return to my apartment and lie on the living room floor, staring at the ceiling. To be honest, I can't even remember when I first heard the terms *body positivity* and *self-love*. I'm guessing it was around the time I started my fitness platform. I latched on to those terms with all my might, because I thought they were powerful. *Of course I deserve to love myself. Screw society*, I thought.

Taking my own advice from my recent Instagram post, I grab a piece of paper and make a list of all the things I like about myself. Not just the things I like because society has deemed them valuable. I also make a list of the things I don't like.

Interestingly, my "Likes" list is twice as long as my "Dislikes" list. I also put a bunch of things into both lists. I stare at the lists as it all begins to seep in.

Confidence and love for yourself are ever-changing. I'm allowed to feel good sometimes, and not so good at other times. Who's to tell me I should be ashamed for not feeling my best after being humiliated online only days ago?

With this in mind, I get back on track with my workouts over the next few days, slowly but surely. Every time I return to the gym, my confidence returns, piece by piece.

I'm beginning to respect the image I see in the mirror, even if I don't love it all the time. The other day, I caught my reflection after doing a challenging set of Romanian deadlifts. I actually smiled, not just because I was having a good hair day, but because I was proud of myself. And that was probably the happiest moment I've had in a very long time.

Of course, there are setbacks with every step forward. But as long as I'm honest with myself in my dark moments, as long as I'm moving forward, finding little ways to counter the negative with positive, that's all I can really ask for.

7:30 P.M.—INSTAGRAM POST: "I'M SORRY" BY **CURVYFITNESSCRYSTAL**:

Hi, everyone. This post is hard. I owe you guys a sincere apology. Not just for being MIA. But I'm sorry about my Size Positive campaign. I'm sorry about every time I told you to love yourself ALL THE TIME. I'm sorry about all the times I used words like "body positivity" and "self-love." Basically, I'm apologizing for my entire platform up until now.

I am no longer an advocate for terms like "body positivity" and "self-love." And here's why:

Growing up as a chubby half Asian girl, I never saw myself reflected in the media as an object of affection or beauty. I didn't conform to societal standards of beauty. I wasn't supposed to love myself.

And then it was like a switch. The term "body positivity" was everywhere. Suddenly, popular brands that previously only used size-zero, airbrushed models were using curvier women in their ads. Curvy blondes were telling me I needed to LOVE MYSELF and everything would be okay. That I wasn't allowed to have any ounce of self-doubt, ever.

Of course, loving yourself is the ultimate goal. I'm not saying not to love yourself if you do (seriously, I respect that so much). But this concept takes longer for some. It's a lifelong journey. I hate this onus on people whose bodies don't conform to society's standards to change the perception that's been drilled into our heads. Suddenly, it's not socially acceptable to feel bad about yourself, ever.

I'm sorry, but I can't say I love every roll and all my cellulite all day, every day. At the same time, I don't need to self-loathe and hate myself either. It's about accepting and respecting yourself, while realizing there is so much more to you than just your body.

Things are going to change on my account. I'm still going to be offering my programs, doing workout tutorials, etc. But my message will be different. You will no longer see the comment section in some of my posts. Instead, I made a private Facebook group for all my clients and vetted followers to congregate.

I really hope you guys will join me in my new group and follow along for the ride. 🦾

Crystal

Comment by **trainerrachel_1990**: I love this!! You're so right. ♡ We're taught to hate anything that's not society's beauty standard, and then at the same time, we're being told to suck it up and love it anyway and made to feel bad about it.

Comment by **fitnessgoalsbymadison**: Wow. This message is so ♡ powerful. I'm along for the ride with you.

Comment by **gainz_gurlie**: Crystal this is amazing!!!! I'm so ♡ glad you've embraced body respect.

Comment by **DarcyChapman12**: I miss your posts. I hope ♡ you're back for good?

chapter thirty-three

RANDMA FLO FINALLY cajoled Martin into moving into her Hoarder House of Horrors (as Tara calls it). The place is still piled with junk to the ceiling, but Martin convinced her to throw out at least some unnecessary items, including but not limited to her collection of old, stained lampshades (she was convinced she would make use of them), three KitchenAid mixers (all unused and in mint condition), and two deluxe birdcages (she never owned birds) to make room for his things.

"How's Scotty lately?" Martin asks while hacking at his overcooked steak.

While my parents know about my breakup with Scott thanks to Tara's big mouth, I've been hesitant to share the news with Grandma Flo and Martin, knowing they would be devastated. Grandma Flo would surely lose her marbles over the prospect of me dying all by my lonesome.

I haven't seen Scott in almost a week and a half. Acknowledging how long it's been since I've been able to talk to him brings my entire mood down.

As proud as I am that I'm finally seeing the light at the end of this shit tunnel, I'm starting to think maybe Scott had a point. Maybe this would have been easier with him by my side.

Before I'm forced to respond to Martin, Mom distracts everyone by resetting a high-strung Hillary in her lap. "No more steak for you," she says, poking Hillary in the back.

I zone out as the family chatters on about Flo and Martin's upcoming honeymoon in Hawaii, as well as Martin's great-niece's acceptance into medical school. All I can think about is how much I miss having Scott by my side, his hand protectively squeezing my thigh under the table.

When dinner is over, I drift onto Grandma Flo's rickety deck and sit, taking in the remainder of today's sunshine. I make a concerted effort to avoid direct eye contact with the terrifying lawn gnomes scattered about the lawn. When we were young, I took pleasure in convincing Tara they were alive, akin to Chucky the redheaded serial killer doll. I squint, covering my eyes as I settle onto the retro lawn chair, a relic as old as I am.

Dad is quick to follow me outside, beer in hand. "Did you find the steak was overdone?" he asks, in typical Dad fashion. He always opens a conversation with a random question.

The setting sun casts a radiant golden light off the brown lawn, desperate for some rain in this particularly dry summer. "Yeah. But it was okay."

He nods, staring straight ahead as he takes a seat in the lawn chair beside mine. "Did I ever tell you how I started my cleaning company?"

I let out an exaggerated breath. Right when I start to get my mojo back, Dad has to swoop in with a lecture about financial stability. "Dad, I really don't want to hear another sermon about getting a real job."

He ignores me, waving a vague hand. "I'd just finished high school. Didn't have the money for college. I was working at the laundromat downtown one night when your mom came in." He pauses, eyes filling with nostalgia. "She was with one of her girl-friends. Her hair was teased, all bushy like a poodle. It was the style back then," he says, nudging me with his arm before taking another swig of his beer.

"Anyway, she made eye contact with me and smiled. So I smiled back. I thought she was beautiful. Out of my league com-pletely." A chipmunk scurries across the deck and hurls itself off the far end. "I think it was five days later when she came back. She didn't have any laundry with her this time. I thought maybe she forgot something from last time. But she walked straight up to me and asked me on a date."

I snort. I can definitely picture Mom doing that. Despite her quiet demeanor, she goes after what she wants, elbows out, head-first.

"I had forty dollars total to my name. But she wanted to go on a date, so I took her to McDonald's and bought her a combo. Then she held my hand and kissed me." He shudders with soft, easy laughter.

"Classic." My cheeks warm at the foreign thought of a young Mom and Dad kissing in a McDonald's.

"After that day, I knew I wanted to marry her."

I think about being in Scott's arms, knowing I wanted to spend the rest of my life with him, no matter what it looked like, no matter the obstacles. "What does this have to do with your cleaning business?"

He puts his hand up. "I'm getting to it. On one of the first times I took your mother to a nice restaurant, I was late. She was already there when I arrived. I told the waiter I was meeting my girlfriend, and he gave me a strange look and said, 'She's not here.' I only had to look over his shoulder before I saw the top of your mom's head in the booth a couple rows back. I waved at her, and he gave me a look I'll never forget. He said, 'That can't be your girlfriend.' He didn't say it to be cruel. He was genuinely confused. This happened all the time, especially in those days. People didn't understand how a white woman would date an Asian man."

I suck in a deep breath, shocked. I'd never thought about it before. As a half Chinese, half white woman, I've experienced racism and ignorant comments, asking some blunt variation of *What are you?* But I've never been told I can't date someone because of it.

"I didn't know that," I say, resettling in my seat.

He meets my eyes again. "Your mom used to think subtle racism didn't exist. But it did. We had a lot of comments from people, little jokes even from our own friends that weren't supposed to be insulting. But they were, because it reinforced the fact that me not being white was something they thought about whenever they looked at us. Even your mom's parents were a little hesitant at first."

"But Grandma Flo loves you, and so did Grandpa."

"After a while," he admits, running his hand over his chin. "I felt like I had to do more than a white guy to win them over. It didn't help that I didn't have two dimes to rub together. So I started the business . . . almost to prove to myself I was good enough for her."

I meet his eyes, unable to accept this. My heart breaks, thinking about how someone so confident like Dad could feel unworthy because of his race. Nothing could be further from the truth. "But you were enough. You always were."

"That's what she told me. She didn't understand why I'd let it get me down so much. We argued about it. But eventually I realized, no matter what, people are going to be cruel. And if I wanted to live a positive life, I needed to do what I could to protect myself."

"Like what?" I ask.

"Not allowing bigots into my life. Speaking up when someone says something offensive. But there's a difference between speaking up and letting their ignorance have power over you." He sighs. "Took a while to come to terms with. But I didn't need anyone's approval, nor did I need to feed into negativity and let it define me."

The words *I didn't need anyone's approval* reverberate in my mind. Scott said this too, but it feels different coming from Dad. Someone who's actually been the one people have a problem with—the one who doesn't fit society's stringent mold. I'd been naive enough to think I was the only one going through this. That no one else could understand what I was feeling.

He continues. "But the biggest thing that got me through it all was your mother. Sure, I could have done it alone. But it was a lighter burden when I let her in. She didn't always understand. But she tried to. She listened. And she helped me see the positive when I was down. She was my rock. Still is."

I squint at him. "I know why you're telling me this."

He shrugs innocently, winking as he takes a sip from his beer. "I'm just telling you one of my stories. Whether you relate it to your own life is your prerogative." He stands up to pull me into a hug.

When his arms wrap around me, my eyes begin to water as I realize I'm face-to-face with someone, my own father, who's gone through what I'm going through. And he's come out on the other side. He didn't let hate ruin him, or his love for Mom. It made them stronger. Together.

"Don't let anyone else dictate your worth. Ever. Not even your old man when he harps on you to get a job. And especially not strangers," he says, stepping back to hand me a random tissue from his pocket.

"Dad?" I ask, sniffling.

"Mm-hmm?"

"I hate it when you bring up me getting a job. I'm happy about where I've taken my business. Especially lately. I don't need the constant critique."

He freezes momentarily before letting out a sigh. "I know."

"Then why do you do it?"

He bows his head, kicking at a dried leaf near his feet. "I'm sorry. I didn't think I was hurting you. I thought I was helping."

"You're not, though. I think our ideas of success and stability are very different."

"Then we'll agree to disagree. I promise to stop with the comments. I haven't brought it up since you laid down the law at the wedding, have I?"

"No. And I appreciate it."

He stands, patting my shoulder. "Anyway, remember what I said. You're not alone. And I am so proud of you and the woman you've become."

"Thanks, Dad." I linger on the deck as he steps back inside, replaying his words.

Had Dad succumbed to those ugly comments and let them define him, he and Mom never would have happened. They never would have had their so-called botched, yet perfect wedding in the rain right here in Grandma Flo's backyard. They never would have had their eventful honeymoon in a bedbug-ridden hotel in the Adirondacks. They never would have had Tara and me. Or thirty full years of a beautiful life together.

The life I could have with Scott. The life I desperately want.

chapter thirty-four

OESN'T LOOK LIKE there's any sign of smoke. Thought this was a fire call?" Scott's familiar, husky voice echoes through the empty gym.

I hadn't expected Scott and the fire crew to arrive at Excalibur Fitness so fast. As soon as I spotted the red truck pulling up outside, I bolted into the utility closet in the yoga room.

I crouch in a cloak of darkness, peeking through the tiny crack in the door, like the true creeper I am. My heart pounds as I will myself to remain stone-still. The mountain of yoga mats beside me threatens to topple over and bury me alive seemingly every time I breathe. It doesn't help that the broom has fallen over, whacking me on the head on three separate occasions in the span of a minute. Who knew grand gestures could be so dangerous?

When I started planning this, I knew it needed to be elaborate. Scott deserves it, after everything I've put him through. I need to prove to him that I'm sorry. That I'll never let fear and insecurity dictate our relationship again. That I love him too. When I stumbled across old, unused footage from my workout tutorials, I knew exactly what to do.

"Maybe it's just a faulty alarm," a deep voice I know to be Trevor's responds.

Thanks to Trevor, this entire crazy plan has been made possible. And surprisingly, he was beyond extra about it, meticulously analyzing all possibilities and backup plans from start to finish to ensure a flawless execution. For a womanizer who recoils at the very idea of a monogamous relationship, Trevor is a closet romantic. It's unfortunate all his talent is wasted.

"What is this?" Scott asks, voice growing closer.

When heavy footsteps enter the yoga room, my throat dries and constricts. Scott is in full gear. I think my soul has left my body. Though a crack in the door doesn't grant me a full view, he's far too sexy for human eyes. Not even the massive, thick jacket and pants can disguise his towering, broad physique. He takes his helmet off, setting it under his arm, revealing that long, pushed-back hair flow I drooled over upon first sight of him.

His expression is one of focus and confusion as he studies the wall. The projection takes up the majority of the far wall with *the* picture. The picture that ruined everything. The picture of us on the beach. The picture that made national news.

He shoots an accusatory glare at Trevor. "Is this some sort of messed-up joke?"

Trevor shakes his head, giving Kevin a conspiratorial glance. "Just give it a minute."

Scott glares at them, gesturing to the photo. "This is a setup, isn't it? Are you guys trying to stage an intervention or some shit? I know I've been depressed, but this is—"

"Stop being an asshole and watch," Trevor orders, quickly losing patience. He reaches for the remote on the little projector table and clicks *Play* before sauntering into the dark hallway with Kevin and the rest of the crew.

The video begins to roll. The beach photo disappears, replaced with a video of me looking into the camera.

"Hey, Scott." My voice fills the room. "I'm sorry to drag you here under such mysterious and dramatic circumstances. I know we didn't leave things on a good note. I am truly beyond sorry for hurting you. I know this whole thing made you doubt my feelings for you and my trust in you. I have a couple things I need to say to you. But first, take a look."

The video cuts to a clip of me doing cable rows. It's the perfect shot, until a large figure walks in front of the camera, blocking the majority of the screen, save for half my face.

"Here. So you don't forget to wipe down the seat." Scott's eyes widen when he recognizes his own voice.

When he exits the frame, I'm left sitting on the cable bench, just blinking. What I didn't know at the time, which he later admitted, was how much he wanted to continue talking to me. "I had no clue how to continue the conversation without sounding like a massive creep and embarrassing myself beyond repair. So I walked away," he'd told me one night as we reminisced about how we first met.

The video cuts to me on the mat doing an ab workout. Scott watches in disbelief when his own figure enters the shot, kneeling in front of me with that cocky grin. "What did you do with my phone?"

"I don't know what you're talking about," I say, sitting up. We're locked in a face-to-face glare for a few moments before the banter continues on. There's a massive smile on my face, which shocked me upon first seeing the footage, because I was sure I was giving him a fierce stare-down at the time.

The video keeps going, even during the times it goes black when he put my phone in his pocket. I'm bugging him about Tinder and asking him to justify why he needs his phone. Then we're bartering to give our phones back. The video cuts on a still of his face, close up, when he refused to relinquish it, choosing instead to creep on my Instagram to find out my name.

Then the video switches to a workout we did together some weeks after we agreed to the three-month rule. I think we must have forgotten the camera was on us.

We're recovering on a mat, legs splayed in front of us, just shooting the shit, as we always did. I'm calling him an anti-vaxxer (which he fiercely denies) and bugging him about how I kicked his ass in burpees (which I did). I can barely breathe, both from the workout but also because he's grinning uncontrollably at me. The video stops, frozen on the shot of me mid-laugh.

Then, the video switches to a montage of Scott making funny faces at the camera before getting serious and shooting my workouts. There are a few shots of him giving me a kiss, and even one where we're trying to take a photo together on my couch, not realizing it was on video mode.

The video transitions to a session with Mel. I was documenting

Mel's push-up form. It's from the day after we found out Martin was healthy. The camera pans to Scott a couple feet away, doing box jumps. "Hi, babe," I call out. My hand enters the shot, waving at him.

The camera pans back to Mel, who gives me a funny smile. "You guys are too cute."

My chuckle fills the room. "Stop."

"You love him," Mel teases.

"I do," I say. I then switch the camera mode onto my smiling face. "I love him."

Scott appears stunned. He's staring at the screen, captivated, as more video and photos roll by of us at Flo and Martin's wedding. Then the photo of us at the beach reappears.

He turns in my direction when I crack the closet door open. At that precise moment, the broom falls, whacking me on the head yet again as I emerge from my hiding spot.

chapter thirty-five

H E'S LIKE A frozen statue. A deer in the headlights. Not even the fact that the yoga mats spilled out of the closet like an avalanche fazes him. His gaze darts from me to the projected video on the gym wall.

"I have some explaining to do." I twist my fingers together, unable to fight my nerves, while praying my broom-induced injury won't turn into a goose egg. Any sense of chill I had is completely gone. "First and foremost, I love you. And I hate that I never told you when you asked, because it was the truth. I've loved you for an embarrassingly long time, as you saw in the video."

My gaze follows the bob in his throat as he swallows. He looks like he's in complete anguish. In fact, I'm convinced he's about to turn around and walk away from me for good. But he doesn't. He stays in place and dips his chin for me to continue.

I had my entire speech prepared, but now that he's right in front of me, all my thoughts stream through like water from a bursting dam. Whatever's about to come out of my mouth is going to be anything but smooth.

"The truth is, what happened was more than just the viral photo. Growing up, I had this weird complex where I never felt quite good enough. And it wasn't only because of my size. It was everything. I never thought I was good enough at sports, or smart enough for school, or funny enough for my friends." I pause to take in a breath. "That all changed a bit when I started building my platform. I started gaining acceptance from complete strangers, and I thought, wow, I really love myself now."

His face softens more and more as I continue to ramble.

"I've tried to dedicate my platform to helping people feel the opposite of how I've felt. It was like an escape from how I was truly feeling inside, especially when I was with Neil. And it worked, for the most part . . ." I wring my hands in front of me, unable to stop fidgeting. "But as my platform grew, the comments kept getting worse. I didn't want to say anything. I've preached the entire time to ignore haters. It became an obsession, because I was desperate to change people's minds. I was desperate to prove myself, in a way, and I let it become my identity."

Scott takes a small step forward, as if he wants to say something. But he doesn't. He just lets me speak.

"When the photo blew up, it was like a manifestation of everything I was afraid of. That somehow, I wasn't worthy. I'm sorry I didn't consider your feelings. I'm sorry I didn't acknowledge how awful it was for you too. I was being selfish. Completely." He nods, which I take as acceptance. "I understand why you were worried about me and why you responded to those comments. And I think I've figured out a compromise. A way to disengage from the negativity, while still having a personal connection with my clients and supporters."

"Good, I'm glad to hear that," he says genuinely, still keeping his distance.

"Scott, I know I can never make it up to you. It took me longer than it should have to realize that I trust you more than anyone. It was myself I didn't trust, because I was holding myself to an unattainable standard. And I know that now." I pause. "I realized . . . loving myself isn't realistic at all times. I'm allowed to feel self-conscious and sad at times, but also confident and happy at other times, as long as I'm accepting and respecting myself. And I want you on my team."

He readjusts the helmet under his arm. "That's a lot to work through. I'm really proud of you." His tone is soft and genuine. "But for the record, it was wrong of me to respond to the comments. I've felt like shit about it for days. I know how passionate you are about your platform and I never want to stand in the way of that. I overreacted because of my own experience as a kid. But I never should have projected it onto you. I know you can handle it yourself."

"You're already forgiven."

He runs his hand over his stubble. "I-I can't believe you staged a fire call." He turns to the window where the crew are not-so-subtly watching our exchange. "You guys were all in on this?"

They nod and each give an enthusiastic thumbs-up.

"I think this is the most extra thing I've ever done," I admit with a half laugh, fighting the urge to reach out and touch him. To feel his huge arms around me. "I know this is a lot to take in." He opens his mouth to speak, but I continue. "I wanted to tell you how much I love you and the person you are. I know I should have told you earlier, when I first realized it. I miss your stupid pickup lines. I miss watching movies alone when you fall asleep beside me. And I miss laughing with you until we cry."

"You really miss my pickup lines?" A flicker of that cocky grin returns, but only for a fleeting second. He rocks back on his heels before inching forward, towering over me, just as he did that first day we met when he was callously stealing my squat rack. Heat radiates from his body.

"I do. Even the worst ones."

The smoldering smirk is back. Even his dimples make an appearance. It's understated, as if he's genuinely both relieved and happy.

The moment I smile, the creases on his forehead soften. Any lingering tension leaves his jaw. There's no doubt, his entire being is magnetic. So much so, my feet instinctively move toward him.

He doesn't step back from me. In fact, he rushes forward, bridging the gap, his strong arms folding me into his tight embrace. He cups my face in his hands, beaming into my eyes before he bends to capture my lips with his. I wrap my arms around his neck, pulling him closer to me.

The feeling of his lips against mine, after all this time apart, is like that first drop of water hitting your tongue after a killer Cross-Fit workout. His kiss is a revival. It's full of life, relieving me of all the chaos and noise spiraling around my mind, crippling me for far too long. It all just stops when he touches me, settling into perfect serenity. It's quiet. It's crystal clear. I can hear all of my own thoughts, for the first time in years.

When Scott rests his forehead against mine, I whisper, "I'm sorry it took so long."

He presses his index finger to my lips. "I would have waited forever for you. I love you."

chapter thirty-six

DESPITE MY CINEMATIC grand gesture, Scott and I aren't able to gallop into the starry night, hand in hand. He's obligated to complete his full shift, like a responsible human. But it's fine, because immediately after his shift ends, he's at my door, lush green eyes quite literally sparkling, with a brand-new carton of clementines tucked under his arm.

I marinate in the sight of him in his well-fitted T-shirt, biceps prominent like those of a mythical god. He leans against my doorframe with his cocksure grin, as if he's never even left.

"You know, you don't have to buy these for me all the time," I say, even though I never want him to stop for as long as he walks the earth.

"I do. Who else is gonna peel 'em for me?" He flashes me a mesmerizing smile as he strides in, setting the carton on the coffee table. He pauses, waving a hand to the television screen, which has

The Godfather, yet another ridiculously long movie, queued up and ready for our viewing pleasure. "I see you already selected our entertainment."

"Yup. Though I give you an hour before you fall asleep. Tops." I step toward him, my entire body whirring with suppressed energy, desperate to explode, nullifying all the negativity I'm leaving behind.

He smirks, closing the gap to bring me into the warm, secure blanket of his embrace. In return, I wrap my arms around his torso like a koala, silently telling him I'm never letting go. My knees threaten to give out as I bask in his familiar alluring scent, fresh laundry and soap.

He presses a soft kiss to my temple. "But you still love me."

"I do love you." I perma-smile the moment the words tumble out, because I already can't wait to say them again. Over and over.

His dimples are prominent as he runs the pads of his fingers down my backside, giving me a firm squeeze. "Hey, you've been spending some extra quality time with the window rack, haven't you?"

"I had to do something to fill my time. It was actually nice, having it all to myself. Without you stealing it on me."

His brow cocks and he treats me to an even firmer squeeze. "Oh, right. My sincerest regrets. I forgot the rack was off-limits to everyone except Crystal Chen."

"Hey, that day I claimed it fair and square," I remind him with a teasing poke to the chest. "It's not my fault you didn't see my stuff."

He tries to suppress his amusement. "Okay, confession time. I might have seen your stuff there and stolen it anyway."

I clap a hand over my mouth, half vindicated, half scandalized at the revelation. "I knew it!"

His chest vibrates with sunny laughter as he splays his fingers through my hair, cradling the back of my head, his other hand settling on my cheek. "I'd shown up at Excalibur twenty minutes before that. I'd never been there before and wasn't really sure about it. It was almost double the price of the gym down the street. But I was in a rush to squeeze in a workout before my shift, so I thought I'd just pay for a day pass." He captures me with a serious gaze and continues. "Right when I was about to pay, I saw you. You were cooling down on the treadmill and you were so fucking stunning. I was all flustered like a kid. Pretty sure I tried to tap the credit card machine with my driver's license. Not my finest moment."

"I can't believe that . . ." I manage through the shock of his revelation. He admitted he was attracted to me from the beginning when I visited him at work, but I never knew he'd noticed me before the squat rack incident.

I suck in a breath as he grazes my beauty mark with his thumb. "I knew I'd be a goner the moment I first talked to you. And I was. So, after I finished my squats, I went back to the front desk and asked for the yearlong membership instead of the day pass."

"Very presumptuous of you."

He arrows a knowing look at me. "I know my type."

"And what's that?" I ask as my fingers trace the hard ridges of his back.

"Strong-willed, confident, kind, and challenging." A soft laugh escapes him. "My mom says I have a thing for anything guaranteed to be a massive pain in the ass."

I bury my smile in his chest and inhale his calming scent before sneaking a glance upward. "You know, even if you never went to my gym, we would have met anyway through Flo and Martin."

He tilts his head, taking it in. "That's true. It was meant to be. Though I did have fun bugging the shit out of you at the gym . . ."

I playfully squeeze his arm. "How come you never told me you got a membership because of me?"

"Because. I'd just gotten out of a relationship. I wasn't sure how you'd react back then if I told you."

"Good point."

"But I was planning on it. Was gonna save it for when I was really in the doghouse," he says against my ear.

Heart more swollen than a steroid bro's biceps, I press a kiss to the corner of his mouth. "I love you. You know me so well."

"I also know you don't *really* want to watch a movie right now."

I tilt my head like an innocent lamb as he feathers light kisses over my neck. "I don't?"

"Nope. I made other plans."

"Like what?"

"We have an intense full-body workout scheduled. For right now."

My body tingles in anticipation as I poorly feign hesitation, unable to resist running my hands over his chest, practically clawing at him. "Just how intense are we talking?"

"High intensity. Multiple rounds. No breaks." He gives me a deadpan look for all of two seconds before his lips curl into a wicked grin. His heated gaze locks to mine as he moves me backward, down the hall to my bedroom, and onto my bed.

I smile, soaking up the splendor as his body molds to mine, as if we've never been apart. Like muscle memory.

I've never felt more loved than I do right now in this very moment, by myself and by him.

I may not be everyone's cup of tea, and neither is Scott. We laugh at stupid things. We'd rather die than put on real clothes and leave the house, unless it's to go to the gym. There are no theatrics. No crazy, impulsive, fairy-tale adventures.

It's simply us, day in and day out, doing life together. And every day is a new personal best.

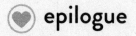 **epilogue**

CURVY FITNESS INSTAGRAMMER SPEAKS OUT AGAINST BODY-SHAMERS, INSPIRING WOMEN AROUND THE WORLD

In August, fitness Instagrammer Crystal Chen posted a sweet photo with her new boyfriend, Scott Ritchie, who happens to have a six-pack. What Crystal didn't expect was the onslaught of backlash that followed.

"The vast majority of the comments were nothing but loving and supportive. But I had to sift through a lot of awful messages. Some said Scott was only with me for my money, or that he was cheating on me," she tells BuzzFeed News.

Chen moves on to say, "I'm human. I felt guilty letting the haters affect me, because I had just launched my Size Positive platform which preached self-love, no matter your body type, race, or ability.

"The truth is, I no longer use terms like 'body positivity' and 'self-love.' Instead, I now use 'body respect' and 'self-acceptance.' Why? Because loving yourself ALL THE TIME is unrealistic. We all have days where we doubt ourselves. And that's when we need to focus on acceptance and respect for ourselves, not hate or love. I can love my body and still have moments of doubt without feeling guilty about it. I'm sick of being 'too fat' for society, and then demonized if I don't 'love myself anyway.' It's an unhealthy cycle, and it took this experience to see it.

"Scott received a lot of hate too after the photo was posted. Messages from people telling him he could do better, calling him a 'chubby chaser.' He also got praised for 'seeing my beauty' beyond size. It's a nice sentiment, but he loves my body. He tells me I'm beautiful even when I'm a sweaty mess at the gym, or when I've just woken up. And I love him even more for it. And the best part: I know it's true. I've always known it.

"It's easy to say 'Oh, the haters are just jealous and miserable.' Maybe that's true. It's a shame people can't see beyond size, or color, or class. And it's taken time to realize that I can't single-handedly change people's minds."

Crystal goes on to express hope that her story will inspire others. "I want everyone who doesn't conform to mainstream beauty standards to know that they are worthy of an epic love story too. We all are."

*Editor's note: Since conducting this interview, Chen made the announcement to her now 650,000 followers that she and Ritchie are engaged, set to be married next spring. For shots of the intimate proposal and custom ring, be sure to visit her Instagram account.

8:34 P.M.—INSTAGRAM POST: "DOES THIS RING MAKE ME LOOK ENGAGED?" BY **CURVYFITNESSCRYSTAL**:

Today started off like most normal days. My pup, Albus, tried to hump my leg as I interpretive danced around my kitchen to "Soulmate" by Lizzo (your new anthem, you're welcome). Then, Scott and I went to the gym for leg day.

After my workout, I started filming a tutorial on hip thrusters. Mid-video (which was going flawlessly), Scott randomly intruded into my shot with a funny smile. I promptly scolded him for tarnishing my video (historically, this is his modus operandi when he wants to aggravate me). I was about to threaten legal action, but then he got down on one knee and busted out a ring.

He said a million amazingly sweet words (swipe to see the video). Apparently, he stressed beforehand, thinking maybe he should do something more elaborate. But it was perfect. It was so completely us.

After I said (shrieked) YES, both our families burst out of the back room of the gym, where they'd been impatiently hiding out for over an hour. I think this will go down as one of the happiest moments of my life. So far. 😉

Crystal

Comment by **Melanie_inthecity**: I am deceased. MY BABIES ♡ ARE ENGAGED!!! *breathes into paper bag*

Comment by **BostonKelly89**: That ring is stunning. I am so so ♡
happy for you girl. Meet me in Fiji for your honeymoon 😌

Comment by **Samantha_Tay1991**: OMG that video tho . . . he ♡
loves you so much. You're meant for each other!

Comment by **FairyDustWeddings**: DM us for wedding ♡
collabs! Xo

Comment by **Ritchie_Scotty7**: You're so beautiful. Inside and ♡
out. I will never stop trying to outdo that moment just to see
you smile. I can't wait to spend the rest of my life with you,
until we're 90 in matching tracksuits at the gym. I love you
forever, Crys.

acknowledgments

Publishing *Set on You* with a major publishing house was a pipe dream I never imagined possible. It is an understatement to say I couldn't have done it without the support, love, and expertise of so many people along the way.

Thank you to Kim Lionetti, my rock star agent, who is a staunch advocate of so many love stories written by diverse authors. I am eternally grateful for all your support, guidance, expertise, and willingness to answer all of my random questions throughout this process. I will forever credit you for taking a chance on me and making my dreams come true. I still pinch myself whenever I see your name in my inbox. Thank you so much to the rest of the amazing BookEnds Literary team.

I am beyond thankful to my dream editor, Kristine Swartz, for believing in this story and championing it every step of the way. One of my fears was that someone wouldn't understand the nuances of my character and her lived experience as a biracial

Chinese woman. I can't underscore enough how much I've cherished not only your expertise, but your personal connection to these characters. Thank you to the incredibly talented Berkley dream team for making my very first publishing experience so seamless.

To the bookstagram community, where my love of contemporary romance began: One cannot underestimate the loyalty and rallying support of people on the internet you've never met (who have quickly turned into real friends). Your DMs expressing excitement for my books make my day (no, my life). It is in this community where I found my amazing beta and sensitivity readers. Special thank-you to Kelly for your eagle eye. You helped make this book what it is today.

I am so grateful for my writer friends for all the support and for talking me off multiple ledges. I am so appreciative to the #Berkletes for all the belly laughs on Discord while I should have been writing. You are hands down the best writer friends I could ever ask for.

Thank you to my best friends, Sam and Robin: You two are the first people who lay eyes on all of my garbage first drafts (sincerest apologies). You two are who I text or call when I'm spiraling over a plot issue (as I tend to do). Thank you for keeping my writing endeavors a secret before I had the courage to tell people. Sam, thank you for reading all my ridiculous, half-baked stories for the past fifteen years. You were my first fan and I will never forget it.

To my parents: First, I hope this is the only part of the book you've read. In all seriousness, I owe all that I am to you. I owe my love of reading to you. Thank you, Dad, for spending your weekends with me in Chapters while I hunted the aisles for Meg Cabot and V. C. Andrews books. Thank you for letting me hog the family desktop for hours as a kid, typing my short stories in Comic Sans font.

Lastly, thank you to my husband, John. I can't tell you how much I appreciate your unwavering support through this journey. You've allowed me to neglect you to spend hours feverishly hunched over my laptop writing before we even knew this "hobby" would lead anywhere. You've put up with my anxiety (summer 2020 when I was on submission, lest we forget), my endless toiling over plots, and even my obsession with the hot fictional men I've created. Thank you for always bringing me food while I write, and for dutifully peeling my clementines and removing all of the pith like Crystal does for Scott. You are my forever romance hero inspiration (along with Chris Evans, of course).

Keep reading for a sneak peek
at Amy Lea's next book

Exes and O's

E VERYTHING IS FINE. *EVERYTHING IS FINE.*

I mentally repeat that phrase as I haul myself up the stairwell to my new apartment. To my new life.

It's fine that I got mugged on the subway. It's fine that I'll need to cancel all my credit cards. It's fine that I'm moving into a new apartment, sight unseen. It's fine that it boasts a chronically broken elevator, even though I'm a staunch proponent of a sedentary lifestyle. IT'S ALL FINE.

When I reach the third flight, I take a momentary lean against the wobbly handrail, balancing my heart-shaped throw pillows. In between wheezes, I force my mouth into a smile, a trick I use to reset when I'm spiraling into a negativity vortex.

There's no reason to hate on my brand-new digs. It may not be the Ritz, but from what I've seen of the rundown orange-tiled entryway and probably-haunted cement stairwell, it's the nicest place I can afford on the direct subway line to the hospital that isn't a roach-infested basement apartment.

As I press onward and upward, I remind myself change is good. This move is more than just the apartment. It's a new chapter of my life. A chance to start anew, after ten months of wallowing, mourning the life I was supposed to have with my ex-fiancé, Seth.

This time last year, I was blissfully engaged, planning an elaborate Cinderella-inspired dream wedding from the comfort of our Beacon Hill condo. Then, six months before the wedding, Seth decided the season finale of *Survivor* was as good a time as any to pick a dramatic, *War of the Roses*-level fight, concluding he "couldn't tolerate me anymore."

The tribe had spoken.

Seth Reinhart would be the tenth man to break my heart.

Starting my life over was a trip, to say the least. But after months of therapy and starfishing on Crystal's floor, I've finally come into my own.

I've embraced a morsel of change, starting with a bold haircut (a blunt Khloé Kardashian bob). My bookstagram account—a niche corner of Instagram where literature-obsessed folks bond over pretty pictures of books—is thriving. I've secured my trusted inner social circle of exactly two—my sister and Mel—the respective Carrie and Samantha to my Charlotte (even though we're all probably Miranda).

Maybe this year I'll surprise everyone and take up a new hobby, like looming, archery, or mountain biking. Seth always resented my lack of hobbies, aside from reading. Maybe I'll purchase a succulent, or seven, and name them after the von Trapp children from *The Sound of Music*.

I'm reinvigorated with endless possibilities by the time I reach unit 404. So much so, I open the unlocked apartment door with triple the force than necessary, like a pro dancer taking center stage, making an impassioned entrance into my shiny new life.

The moment I enter, it's clear that this new chapter is no improvement from the last. In fact, it's worse.

Before me is a magnificently muscled, entirely naked tattooed man bending an auburn-haired woman over the kitchen island.

Welcome home, Tara.

• • •

THINGS GO TITS up from there. Literally.

I let out a bloodcurdling screech from the depths of my gut, tossing my throw pillows in the air. The auburn-haired woman yelps, endeavoring to cover at least half her enviably ample bosom. The tattooed man curses and dives for cover behind the butcher block island, like a World War I solider under siege in the muddy trenches.

But it's too late for me. I saw *it*.

The penis belonging to my new roommate, Trevor Metcalfe.

It's not like I expected to cross the threshold into a *Sex and the City*-worthy life of fabulous riches, cosmos, whirlwind romance, and girlfriends who are readily available to drop their lives at a moment's notice whenever disaster strikes. But I was not expecting *this*.

Normally, I wouldn't entertain the prospect of moving in with a stranger. But the rent was cheap, I have student debt, and anywhere was preferable to my parents' place, where I'd be forced to compete for attention with Hillary, Mom's ankle-biting, narcissistic chihuahua. Besides, Trevor is Scott's best friend and co-worker at the fire hall. I figured it was safe to trust my soon-to-be brother-in-law, but apparently you can't trust family.

"You'll never see each other with your shift work. It'll be the same as living alone," Scott had assured me.

The illusion of living alone seemed plausible, given that mine and Trevor's conflicting schedules prevented us from meeting prior to today. We've only exchanged a couple texts, which consisted of me requesting the dimensions of my new room for my bookshelf. No small talk.

The topless woman gapes at me, justifiably peeved I interrupted her big O. Aside from disappearing into the void, I do the next best, highly logical thing: mumble a vague yet sincere apology, cover my eyes, and sprint away in the only direction possible— down a short hallway.

"This is fine. It's all fine," I mutter, taking refuge through the first door on the right. I slam it shut, savoring the relative coolness of the door against my searing skin.

As a nurse, I see genitals aplenty, particularly during my stint in the ER before I transferred to the neonatal ward. But making eye contact with a live human (a mega-ripped human, to be precise) while in the throes of passion, a mere ten feet away, is a first.

When slowing my breath becomes a Herculean task, I try a technique my therapist taught me. *Take in your surroundings. Note everything logically, with no judgment.*

I'm in a tiny, outdated bathroom. It's white from floor to ceiling, save for the plush navy-blue towel hanging behind the door and the matching hand towel next to the sink probably belonging to a man with a nice, sizable— Nope. We're not going there. Focus, Tara.

Cracked yet clean ceramic subway tiles adorn the wall in the gleaming glass shower. For a bathroom formerly shared by Scott and Trevor, two thirty-something men, it's impossibly clean. I run my index finger along the rim of the smooth porcelain sink. It's spotless. Not a stray man hair or glob of dried toothpaste to be found.

Weak and weary, I park myself on the porcelain throne. I should probably commence a new search for another place to live, but the very prospect of probing the bowels of Craigslist prompts a heaving gag. Instead, I administer eye bleach in the form of Tik-Tok videos of baby farm animals until my feet lose all circulation.

There's movement outside the door. Footsteps. Hushed voices. Doom plagues my gut. I have to face the music at some point. Like a coward, I delay the inevitable by FaceTiming Mel.

She answers immediately, preening her ultra-lush lash extensions. She's a curvy influencer, like Crystal. Except instead of fitness, Mel's specialty is fashion and beauty, and all things aesthetically pleasing. Today, a shimmery purple shadow sweeps across her eyelids, accentuating her dark eyes. Her contour is also on point, showcasing her bone structure. She's so stunning, it's frankly offensive.

Based on the floor-to-ceiling window behind her, she's at home in her bougie apartment in the Theater District. "Where the hell are you?" she asks.

"I'm hiding in my new bathroom," I whisper.

"Why are we whispering?" She lowers her voice conspiratorially.

"Because. I just walked in on my new roommate. Naked."

She lets out a strangled gasp and slaps a hand over her violet-painted lips. "Naked? As in, ass out?"

"Penis out. Actually, he was more than naked. He was boning in the kitchen," I explain, taking it upon myself to snoop in the shower.

The moment I open the hefty glass door, I'm hit with a manly, far-too-sexy spiciness that's surely a biohazard. I sniff the body wash to confirm the origin of the scent and it immediately clears my airways. Cinnamon and cedarwood, according to the bottle. Next to the body wash is a basic, two-in-one shampoo and conditioner combo.

Poking around a virtual stranger's shower feels illicit, but technically this is *my* shower now. I've already seen this man's nether regions, so does it really matter if I know his preferred brand of toothpaste (Colgate Max White Expert Complete)?

"Jesus, take me." Mel clasps a hand over her chest and pretends to faint on her chaise. She quickly rights herself, fully alert and ready to sip the proverbial tea, which she likes piping hot. "Okay, tell me everything. On a scale of Danny DeVito to Henry Cavill, how attractive is he? Spare no detail."

"I wasn't looking at his face." His face was but a blur, on account of his naked body, which definitely leans in favor of the Cavill side of Mel's scale. The memory will live on forever, seared onto my retinas.

"I take it you're gonna hide in there until the end of time?"

"Yes. I think I'll just rot in here." I examine the glittery soap dispenser next to the sink that doesn't belong among the rest of the practical, low-maintenance products. It's labeled *Toasted Vanilla Chai*. This is a woman's touch if I ever saw one. Maybe it belongs to the big-breasted auburn-haired woman.

As Mel tells me about a time she accidentally walked in on her parents doing the dirty, I swiftly move on to the medicine cabinet. Before opening it, I catch my hopeful reflection in the mirror and cringe. What was previously a perky ponytail this morning has sagged. I try tightening it to add volume, inadvertently making it worse. There's zero volume to be had here. Each strand is dead slick to my scalp and severely pulled back, accentuating my shiny forehead. I really need to blot.

Giving up on myself entirely, I explore the cabinet. Inside is an opened packet of assorted colored toothbrushes, a shaving set, a single razor, a bottle of shaving cream, Listerine mouthwash (Cool Mint), and a jumbo bottle of Tylenol.

As I pluck the bottle from the shelf to examine the expiration date (expired in July 2021), a floorboard creaks in the hallway, right outside the door. Panicked, I fling the Tylenol back where I found it and side-shuffle away from the sink. A few beats of deafening silence tick by before there's a knock.

"Tara?" Trevor's voice is gravelly and baritone. Very audiobook-worthy.

"Mel, I gotta go," I whisper, frantically ending the call before she can respond.

"You okay in there?" he asks.

"Totally fine. More than fine. Why wouldn't I be?" Yikes. I sound like Minnie Mouse on uppers. I make it a point to lower my voice. "Was she your girlfriend?"

There's a beat of silence. "No. She's not my girlfriend. She just left, by the way."

"Oh," I say, mildly disappointed. It would have been nice to have another woman around, like an unofficial roommate of sorts, especially since the majority of Crystal's and Mel's time is devoted to their respective long-term, committed relationships and full-time thriving Instagram careers—both of which I lack. While I love bookstagram, it's a hobby, not a career.

There's another extended silence before Trevor says, "Listen, I'm sorry we had to meet like that. I didn't think you were moving in until later today. I feel like an asshole."

I sink to the floor behind the door, noodle legs pulled to my chest. "It's fine. I mean, it's your apartment technically."

"It's half yours now."

"Do you regularly have sex in communal living areas?"

"Well, not anymore." Based on his half chuckle, I picture a charming, tilted grin that could melt the panties off any given straight woman. "I swear I'll disinfect the whole kitchen. Thoroughly."

"Much appreciated," I say genuinely. It's nice knowing the surface I eat my Pop-Tarts over will be devoid of bodily fluids.

A few beats go by. "So, uh, are you ever gonna come out of the bathroom?"

"That depends. Are you still naked?"

"I'm fully decent, I swear."

I press my cheek closer to the door, craving the vibrations of his voice. "I might stay in here a little longer. It's comfortable." This tiny space is actually kind of soothing, reminiscent of a Scandinavian spa.

His footsteps disappear down the hall, only to return a few seconds later. "I have Cheetos. And don't worry, I washed my hands."

My mouth waters instantly at the tried-and-true sound of a crunching bag. Be still my heart. I reach to turn the knob, opening the door wide enough to make a grabby-hands motion through the crack. He's still not visible, with the exception of his hand as he passes me the bag like a dicey drug deal. There's a light dusting of ashy brown hair on his wrist and knuckles. His palm is massive, almost twice the size of mine. I catch the tail end of a detailed, dark gray tattoo in the area below his thumb, but before I can make out the design, his hand disappears behind the door.

Starved, I descend on the bag, ripping it open like an ape. In the span of under three minutes, I've demolished at least a quarter. Ashamed of my blatant gluttony, I slide it back through the crack. "Sorry, I've had a traumatic day."

The bag crunches. "Shit. Because of me?"

"No. My day was already a wash before you."

"Why?" he asks, passing the bag back.

"Today was supposed to mark a brand-new start. A turning point in my life. But I got mugged on the subway," I admit through a crunch, "by a guy with some serious soul mate potential. The meet-cute was going so well until he stole my purse."

"Wait, you got mugged? And what's a meet-cute?" He repeats *meet-cute* slowly, like it's a foreign concept. I watch his large hand reach through the crack for the Cheetos. There's a Roman numeral tattoo on his wrist, partially obscured by his sleeve. I take a mental photo so I can decipher it later.

"A meet-cute is when two love interests meet for the first time," I rattle off impatiently. "But yes. I got mugged. I was reading on the subway when this guy next to me started chatting me up. You should have seen this guy, Metcalfe. He was a snack. Definitely didn't look like a mugger. Not that muggers have a particular look, but you know what I mean . . ."

We pass the bag back and forth as I rehash the story of Nate, from that initial moment of eye contact to when he jacked my purse (and all my hopes and dreams).

"Well, that's shit luck either way," he says, sympathetic to my plight.

"Right? I'm starting to lose hope. Every time I meet a potential man, something goes horribly wrong. The last guy I met through a friend seemed normal, until he requested photos of my feet."

"Foot fetish?"

"Apparently. I don't want to fetish-shame, but I think I'm cursed. Today it's a mugging. Tomorrow, probably a kidnapping. Some guy will lure me to his car with candy. I'll go because I like free food. And he'll toss me in the trunk and set my body on fire." I grimace at the missed opportunity of flaunting my latest favorite number, a high-necked pink dress, in an open-casket funeral. I've already advised Crystal of my wish to be buried in it and she's assured she'll make it happen.

"Okay, that got dark real fast. This is why you should never trust strangers with candy," Trevor warns.

"Technically you're a stranger with Cheetos," I remind him, fishing a rogue Cheeto from the floor. I toss it in the trash can next to the sink.

"You're a stranger too. In my bathroom. Who knows what you've done to my toothbrush."

I have the sudden urge to change our stranger status. The hinges squeak as I pull the door open, poking my head out like a meerkat emerging from the protection of its sandy burrow.

Trevor is, indeed, fully clothed, his back resting against the wall, long legs extended in front of him.

His effortlessly tussled mop of dark hair juxtaposes the short, neatly trimmed sides. Even through his Boston Fire Department hoodie, his biceps are mature, unyielding tree trunks. In comparison, mine are flimsier than a rice noodle.

His Adam's apple bobs as he takes in my disheveled ponytail riddled with dry shampoo, scanning downward over my oversized maroon sweatshirt that reads *Nonfictional feelings for fictional men* in Times New Roman font.

Now that he isn't nude and his tattoos are adequately covered, I'm able to assess the color of his eyes. They're the color of honey, like an inferno of crackling firewood resisting merciless golden flames. They probably take on a mossy hue when the light hits them just right. Under the protective swoop of dense lashes, they're foreboding, guarded. And when his gaze meets mine, my stomach betrays me with an uncalled-for barrel roll.

In an effort to maintain an iota of normalcy, I squint to blur his face out of focus, distracting myself with a humongous Cheeto. "Should I trust you, deliriously handsome stranger?"

His mouth shapes into a crooked smile as he stands, towering over me on the bathroom floor. "Nah. Probably not."

Amy Lea is a Canadian bureaucrat by day and a contemporary romance author by night (and weekends). She writes laugh-out-loud romantic comedies featuring strong heroines, witty banter, mid-2000s pop culture references, and happily ever afters.

When Amy is not writing, she can be found fangirling over other romance books on Instagram (@AmyLeaBooks), eating potato chips with reckless abandon, and snuggling with her husband and goldendoodle.

Ready to find
your next great read?

Let us help.

Visit prh.com/nextread

Penguin
Random
House